M☾NSHADE

Vampire Conclave
Book 1

By

INTERNATIONAL
BESTSELLING AUTHOR

S.J. WEST

S.J. WEST

COPYRIGHTS

Cover Design by Paper and Sage Design, all rights reserved.
Interior Design and Formatting by Carolina Silva, all rights reserved.
Proof Read by Allisyn Ma.

Published by Watchers Publishing: December, 2016.
www.Sjwest.com

Writer. Storyteller. Daydreamer.

Books in the Watcher Series

Anna
Lucifer
Redemption

The Dominion Series

Awakening
Reckoning
Enduring

Other Books by S.J. West

<u>The Harvester of Light Trilogy</u>

Harvester

Hope

Dawn

<u>The Vankara Saga</u>

Vankara

Dragon Alliance

War of Atonement

<u>Vampire Conclave Series</u>

Moonshade

Sentinel

Conclave

TABLE OF CONTENTS

ACKNOWLEDGMENTS

I would like to express my gratitude to the many people who were with me throughout this creative process; to all those who provided support, talked things over, read, wrote, offered comments, allowed me to quote their remarks and assisted in the editing, proofreading and design.

I would like to thank Lisa Fejeran, Liana Arus, Karen Healy-Friday, Misti Monen, and Erica Croyle, my beta readers for helping me in the process with invaluable feedback.

Thanks to Allisyn Ma, my proofreader for helping me find typos, correct commas and tweak the little details that have help this book become my perfect vision. Thank you to Carolina Silva for creating the New Covers, the Interior Design of the books and formatting them.

Last and not least: I want to thank my family, who supported and encouraged me in this journey.

I apologize to all those who have been with me over the course of the years and whose names I have failed to mention.

CHAPTER 1.

It all started about two weeks ago. I woke up one morning, feeling anxious about something. It's just like the feeling I used to get when I was a kid on Christmas mornings. I would want to rush downstairs as soon as I woke up to see what Jolly Old Saint Nick had left me underneath the Christmas tree, but I knew I had to wait for my parents to wake up or Santa might not be as generous the next year. That's the exact same feeling I have right now. Like there's a present somewhere just waiting for me to discover it. The only obstacles are: one, I have no idea what it is and two, I have no clue where to start looking for it. My heart literally feels like it will shrivel up inside my chest if I don't discover the whereabouts of my secret gift, but my mind is a complete blank as to where I should begin my search.

I decide to tell my best friend, Kaylee, how I'm feeling. I always thought Kaylee and I could pass for sisters. We're the same age, and have the same oval face and high cheekbones. Her hair is a bright shade of red cut in a cute short, layered style; whereas mine is long and a dark auburn color. She has green eyes, and I have brown eyes. She's a cute, petite 5'4" and I'm almost 5'7". Well, on second thought, maybe we don't look that much alike, but we were raised as sisters, so that should count for something.

When I was ten years old, Kaylee and I had a sleepover at her house. The next morning I learned the home I shared with my parents caught on fire, destroying not only the house I grew up in but also my life. After the death of my parents, Kaylee's folks went through the legal hassle of adopting me. Since I have no living relatives, they saved me from being swallowed up by the foster care system and raised me in a loving home where I was truly a part of the family. The Hugheses weren't rich by any standards, but they always made sure Kaylee and I never wanted for anything important. We lived in a quaint neighborhood at the end of a cul-de-sac in a nice ranch-style home with the obligatory minivan parked in the driveway.

The first year after the loss of my parents was a tough one for me. If it hadn't been for the unconditional love the Hugheses supported me with, I'm not sure how my life would have turned out. It's quite possible I could have ended up living on the street if the state had tried to shuffle me around between different foster homes. I count my lucky stars every day that I was blessed with the perfect people to help me cope with my grief.

After Kaylee and I graduated from college with our degrees in education, she married her high school sweetheart. Ever since we were children, Kaylee has always written stories and dabbled in poetry. With her love of the English language, she decided to be a high school English teacher. I, on the other hand, was always drawn to science and the logic behind how things work, so I decided to be a biology teacher. We were lucky enough to both find jobs at the Pecan Acres Junior High School. Yesterday was our last day of the spring term, which ended up being perfect timing for me. I'm not sure I could have concentrated on my classes, considering my current state of mind.

Kaylee's gained a lot of weight in the past seven months, but I guess she has a good excuse. She *is* growing little Emma Louise after all. The only problem with trying to discuss things with a pregnant woman is that her responses seem completely driven by the raging hormones running rampant inside her body.

"Maybe this anxious feeling you're having means you're about to find the love of your life," she enthuses excitedly while we sit at her kitchen table. "You know, your horoscope for this month said you would meet new and interesting people."

"I don't believe in that mumbo jumbo. You know that," I tell her, absently playing with my half-empty cup of coffee on the table. Even though this is supposed to be a relaxing Saturday morning breakfast with my sister, I'm unable to shake the uneasy feeling that I'm supposed to be somewhere else more important.

"Sarah, you need a man in your life," she sighs.

Kaylee and I have had this discussion at least twice a month since she became the poster woman for marital bliss. She is determined to have me engaged by my twenty-fourth birthday. Luckily, that means I have precisely a year before she goes into super psycho matchmaker mode.

"I wish you could find someone like my Ben," she says with a dreamy look on her face.

Ben Whitaker is Kaylee's husband. We all went to high school and college together. Ben and I never really hit it off. We only tolerate one another because we have to share Kaylee, but I have to give him props. He does make my sister extremely happy, and that's all that matters in the long run.

"You got lucky," I tell her, feeling a small unwelcome pang of jealousy. "Not everyone can find the person they're meant to marry when they're sixteen."

Kaylee places a comforting hand over the one I have resting on the table beside my cup of coffee. "There's someone out there meant just for you. I know it."

"Ever the optimist." I try to smile, but my facial expression doesn't quite make it that far.

"One of us has to be where your love life is concerned."

I finish my coffee and make up an excuse about needing to restock my kitchen with groceries.

"Hey, would you mind telling me how Emma is feeling today before you leave?"

I can't help but smile at Kaylee's constant desire to be reassured her baby is emotionally well-adjusted. However, I guess if I had access to that kind of information about my own unborn child, I would want to know too.

Ever since I can remember, I've always been able to sense what other people are feeling. I'm sort of like Deanna Troi on Star Trek, an empath. Sometimes it's a real pain in the ass sensing the emotional states of strangers, but the certainty of knowing the people you love the most love you back just as fiercely is priceless. I've learned how to dampen my ability when I need to, if for no other reason than to just keep my sanity intact. There are some real weirdos out in the general population. The world is a much happier place when I don't know they're out there.

I put my hand on Kaylee's bulging belly. Normally, I don't have to touch someone to know what they're feeling, but since little Emma is still safely snuggled inside her mother's womb I need the extra closeness to distinguish Em's feelings from Kaylee's.

"She's happy," I report, cherishing the pure, innocent emotions emanating from my little niece. "And she loves her mommy very much."

Kaylee smiles and places her hand over the one I still have on her bump. "Thank you."

I bend over and kiss Kaylee on the cheek before turning back around to grab my purse off the table.

"Don't forget, we're taking you out for your birthday tonight. So don't eat a big lunch," Kaylee sternly orders.

I roll my eyes at her. "How could I forget? You've been reminding me every day for a month now about our big secret adventure. What *do* you have planned?"

"If I wanted you to know, I would have told you a month ago. Just make sure you wear that dress you wore to the faculty dinner."

"So we're going somewhere fancy?" I ask, doing my best to glean some tidbit of information about her plans.

"Stop trying to make me tell you anything, birthday girl. Just do what the pregnant woman says so you make her happy."

"As you wish, Princess Butterball." I bow in Kaylee's direction, and get hit in the head with a wadded-up paper towel.

"Ohhh, just you wait," Kaylee says like a portent of doom, narrowing her eyes and pointing her index finger at me. "When you're as big as a house with your first child, I'll remember you called me that."

I laugh and wink at her before heading down the hallway to the front door.

"And try to take a nap this afternoon!" she yells at my back. "We're going to be out late!"

I wave my hand over my head as I make my way out the door so she knows I heard her. After I get into my newly purchased silver Toyota Camry, I crank the engine and end up sitting in Kaylee's driveway for a good five minutes, trying to decide where it is I want to go. I don't really need groceries. I haven't been able to eat that much in the past two weeks. In fact, I haven't slept that much either. If I can just figure out why I have this feeling that I'm supposed to be somewhere specific, maybe I can get back on track and start living normally again.

I put my car into drive and take off down the road, having absolutely no idea where I'm going, which is so unlike me. I always plan things out before I do them. Kaylee often picks on me for my obsessive-compulsive disorder, but I know she appreciates my organizational skills, especially when it comes to planning parties and vacations. She doesn't have to think about anything when we're traveling together. All she has to do is enjoy all my hard work. But, it really isn't work to me. I feel happier when I know specifically what it is I need to do. I suppose that's why I feel so unhappy right now. I don't know what to do, and I don't know how to plan for something I can't figure out.

I decide to drive around town for a bit to take my mind off my problem. Pecan Acres is a small city in Louisiana, no more than eighteen-thousand people living within its limits. If we want to go to a big city, New Orleans is only an hour away. My town has the basics:

restaurants, a mall, a movie theater and, of course, every small town's staple of survival, a Super Wal-Mart.

I find myself driving down Bayou Road where the new and old moneyed families live. Some of the houses are old-style antebellum-era homes built in the Greek revival style, and some are newer, more up-to-date versions trying to imitate the historical homes but failing miserably. Personally, I prefer the older mansions. They have a sense of history locked into every nook and cranny, unlike the new construction, which just seem like expensive wannabe knock-offs to me.

I feel an unexplainable urge to pull off to the side of the road in front of one of the older homes. It's a custom-built red brick mansion with grand Georgian scroll molding over the front door and four large Greek Corinthian white columns lining the front porch. My anxious feeling seems to subside somewhat as I continue to study the manor. I'm not sure why, but I feel a violent urge to run up to the front door and barge inside. There's something in there pulling at me, compelling me to throw common sense out the window and simply follow my instincts. Before I completely lose my mind and do something I'll regret later, I shift my car back into drive and head to my apartment.

When I finally make it home that afternoon, I try to do what Kaylee suggested and take a nap. I end up tossing and turning in bed until it's time for me to get ready for my big night out with her and Ben. I pull out the dress she wants me to wear from my closet to see if it needs to be ironed. Luckily it doesn't. If there is one thing I hate doing in this world, it's ironing clothes. It's a little black knit dress with a twisted halter empire bodice and short skirt that comes to just above my knees. It's a simple outfit but formal enough to wear to a nice restaurant.

As usual, Kaylee and Ben are late picking me up. Ben knocks on my apartment door almost thirty minutes after the time Kaylee said they would be there.

When I open the door, I smile politely at Ben who is dressed in a nice baby blue button-down shirt and khaki slacks.

"Better late than never, right?" I joke.

"You know how she can get," Ben grins. "We can't leave the house if she has a hair out of place. Are you ready?"

I grab my small black purse from the coat tree and lock the front door before I step out. I follow Ben back to the new family vehicle he and Kaylee just purchased in expectation of Em's arrival, a silver Dodge Durango.

"I'm pregnant," Kaylee uses as an excuse for their tardiness as I slip into the back seat behind Ben's. "I move a lot slower now."

"You know that excuse isn't going to work after you have the baby," I tease her, buckling my seat belt.

"By then she'll have moved on to 'It's the baby's fault'." Ben chuckles as Kaylee playfully slaps him on the arm.

"You two need to be nicer to me." Kaylee sticks her bottom lip out to garner our sympathy. "I'm doing the best I can."

"We both love you more than anyone else in the world," I tell her. "So stop pouting."

Kaylee sticks her tongue out at me, but I know she isn't offended by our teasing. Plus, she likes being reminded how important she is to both Ben and me.

"So, can you tell me what my birthday surprise is now?" I ask.

Kaylee turns her head to look back at me. "We're going to New Orleans and eating at Arnaud's. Then we're takin' you dancing at a new club on Bourbon Street!"

"Seriously?" I must have heard her wrong, right? "You're actually taking me clubbing in your condition?"

"My doctor said it would be ok as long as I took it easy. So, don't worry, mother hen. Little Em and I will be just fine. Who knows, maybe you'll meet somebody while we're out and about."

I shake my head in exasperation but remain mute on the subject. I turn my head to watch the passing scenery outside the window. Unfortunately, there's not much to keep my eyes busy on the highway besides pine trees and the occasional swamp. I don't want to argue with Kaylee when she's trying to do something nice for me on my birthday. Although, I can already tell she's going to be in full matchmaker mode this evening. I just can't believe she's actually thinking about pawning me off on some random stranger at a bar! I hang my head and silently pray for divine intervention. I would like to be spared any embarrassment on my birthday, but the odds of that happening don't seem to be in my favor.

The food at the restaurant is probably wonderful. To be honest, I can't really tell. I haven't been able to taste food for two weeks. I almost feel guilty for not being able to enjoy my meal since I know the entrees are on the expensive side at this restaurant. I hate not being able to enjoy the filet mignon I ordered. I'm sure if things were normal it would have tasted like a little slice of heaven in my mouth. To be totally honest, I'm relieved when dinner is finally over.

By the time we leave the restaurant, it's already ten o'clock.

"Shouldn't we just head home?" I ask them as we stroll down a crowded Bourbon Street. Saturday night in New Orleans probably isn't the best time to come with a pregnant woman. I try to play defense and walk in front of Kaylee so people who aren't paying attention to where they're going, or are simply too drunk to care, run into me first.

"No, we're going dancing," Kaylee states in her 'don't you dare argue with me' voice.

We end up at a nightclub called the Cat's Coven. Kaylee knows I'm not much of a dancer. It's not that I can't dance. I just don't like to dance in public. From the way the people inside the club are acting, you would think it was everyone's birthday and not just mine. There's a raised wood dancefloor in the middle of the room. It's so full of gyrating bodies I don't see how Kaylee expects to survive within the crush of people. There's a DJ playing music on his own platform against a sidewall. A full bar made of mirrors is located at the back end of the room and is swarming with needy patrons trying to purchase beverages. Kaylee and I sit at one of the small, stool-high tables near the dance floor while Ben fights the crowd to get us some drinks.

I'm not much for imbibing in alcohol, but I do enjoy the occasional Crown and Coke. Ben brings one back for me, a Corona for himself, and a ginger ale for our Kaylee.

I'm about halfway through my drink when I feel the hairs on the back of my neck stand on end. Someone is staring at me. Usually when I'm in a crowd of people, I block my empathic ability so I'm not bombarded by a multitude of mixed emotions all at once. For some reason, I'm not able to block out the emotions of this particular person. Their feelings are a jumbled mess, but the one that stands out the most is hunger. It's not a sexual hunger, either. No, this is more primal than even that. It's almost as if this person wants to eat me alive, literally. What in the world is that supposed to mean?

Kaylee crooks her index finger at me, silently beckoning me to come closer to her. I lean forward so I can hear what she wants to say over the loud music reverberating against the walls of the nightclub.

"There is a gorgeous guy behind you who hasn't been able to take his eyes off you since we got here," she informs me, lifting her eyebrows suggestively as she attempts to play her role as Cupid.

I lean back on my stool and turn a little in my seat so I can take a sneak peek at the man Kaylee is eyeing as a potential suitor for me. Before I even locate him, I know without a shadow of a doubt that he will be the same person whose emotions I can't keep out of my mind.

The room is dark, only lit by the multi-colored lights flashing chaotically across the dance floor. The rhythm of the music seems to beat in time with the hammering of my heart as I slowly turn my head to look where I know he's standing.

I see him leaning against one of the concrete pillars in the room, his arms crossed loosely in front of him. He's wearing a dark grey button-down shirt and black jeans. If I were to say he's just handsome, I feel like it would be an insult to his beauty. The

19

confident way he holds himself gives him an air of royalty. He reminds me of an Eastern European prince with his dark, short-cropped hair and perfectly pale skin. He has a strong face with a full bow-shaped mouth and hauntingly dark deep-set eyes. His forehead is slightly wrinkled in a troubled frown as he continues to meet my steadfast gaze. The longer I stare at him the stronger his disapproval with me grows. I suddenly feel like a kid who has done something wrong. For some inexplicable reason, I don't like feeling as if I've disappointed him.

Most people will give you some sign to acknowledge your presence when you catch them staring at you, but this man doesn't even flinch or try to look away. He just continues to stare at me without any hint of apology or embarrassment. The longer we gaze at one another, the stronger his need to be closer to me becomes. His emotions are so raw and open they almost overwhelm me. There is something so familiar about him, yet strange and mysterious at the same time. The rapid beating of my heart causes a tightness to form inside my chest, making it difficult for me to take in a full breath. I'm the one who ends up looking away first, trembling slightly from the encounter.

Kaylee touches my arm, breaking the spell the stranger just cast by forcing me to look up at her.

"Are you ok?" she asks, obviously worried about my reaction to the man.

I nod my head and try to smile reassuringly. The doubt in her eyes tells me I'm not fooling her for one second.

"Well, try to pull yourself together because Mr. Gorgeous is heading this way."

I didn't think my heart could hammer against the wall of my chest any faster than it is, but somehow it finds a way to add an extra beat. I can physically feel him get closer to me. With every step he takes the connection between us becomes more solid, like there's an invisible string tethering us together, growing more taut the closer we come to one another. Oddly enough, I feel myself begin to relax. The anxious feeling I've been living with for the past two weeks slowly begins to dissipate.

I know the exact second he's standing behind me and can't stop myself from automatically turning around to face him.

He leans forward and whispers into my ear, "Come."

He holds out his hand to me, not worried in the least bit that I will refuse his order.

Normally, I would have just laughed in a guy's face if he had said such a thing to me. But with him, it's like I don't have a will of my own. I find myself placing my hand into his, eager to follow him wherever he wants to go. I can only imagine this is what it must feel like when people are hypnotized.

His skin is cold to the touch, like he's been standing inside a walk-in freezer for hours. Yet I don't flinch away from his frigid caress. In fact, I feel myself wanting to melt into him, providing him all the warmth my body has to offer.

Without saying another word to me, but keeping his dark brown eyes fixed on mine, he leads me onto the dancefloor where the music suddenly changes to a slow song. He wraps his arms around my waist and I drape mine over his shoulders, clasping my hands loosely around his neck. We sway to the music for a while, just staring in each other's eyes. There's a soft protectiveness in his gaze that makes me feel inexplicably safe. For some reason I can't fully understand, I know I can trust this man with my life.

He slowly pulls me in closer to him. His cold cheek brushes against mine as he whispers in my ear once again.

"You need me as much as I need you," he says with a husky yearning, making my body shiver with anticipation of his next words. His voice sounds so familiar and yet completely foreign to me. He has a slight European accent I can't quite place. It sounds like a mixture of various dialects. "I know you've been feeling like there's something you need to find. As if a piece of you is missing. I *am* that piece. I'm what you've been searching for these past two weeks. Don't try to fight it, Sarah," he murmurs before kissing the tender flesh just below my ear. He proceeds to kiss his way down the side of my neck, resting his lips on the pulsating artery just below the thin layer of skin. His breathing becomes labored as he opens his mouth and tightens his lips around my throat. The sharp edges of his teeth gently graze my skin, as if he's testing how tender the flesh is in that spot. I feel slightly drunk on the intoxicating aroma surrounding him, a mixture of chocolate and cinnamon. I want him to do something to me, but I'm not quite sure what that something is supposed to be.

Finally, he raises his head and looks in my eyes.

"Find me, Sarah…"

When he pulls away and leaves me standing on the dancefloor, I feel completely bereft by the suddenness of his departure. I feel light-headed from the encounter, almost like his touch was a drug. I don't want him to leave without me but am unable to make my feet move to follow him. Every cell in my body yearns to chase after him and demand to know who he is and why he means something to me. Maybe if I at least had his name I *could* find him again. What he said to me was the complete truth, not a boast.

I do need him.

I just don't know why.

CHAPTER 2.

I know the moment the stranger leaves the nightclub. The anxious feeling I've been trying to temper for the past two weeks somehow triples in intensity. I feel like someone who was given the cure to a debilitating disease only to have it snatched out of my grasp before I'm able to take it. Frustrated, I clench my hands into fists and notice that the palms of my hands have become cold and clammy. I feel light-headed and realize that's because my breathing has become extremely short and labored.

I'm not sure what just happened.

All I'm certain of is that my life has just been set on a course I'm completely helpless to control.

After a few seconds, I finally regain the use of my legs and walk off the dance- floor. Still feeling shaken by my encounter with the stranger, I sit down heavily on my stool at the table next to Kaylee. She immediately waves a hand at me, telling me with her gesture that I need to come closer. It's the only way for us to hear each other over the volume of the music playing.

"Holy cow, Sarah, I thought he was going to eat you alive!" she says excitedly. "What was that all about anyway? You never let guys touch you like that in public, not even when you're dating them."

I pull back slightly to look in Kaylee's concerned eyes. I can't even entertain the thought of telling her the truth about what just transpired, yet I don't want to lie to her either.

I shake my head a little before leaning back in to tell her, "I don't know what happened to me. It just felt right."

"Did you at least get his name?" Kaylee asks eagerly. "Or better yet his phone number?"

"No," I tell her despondently.

Kaylee sighs in clear disappointment. "Well, if it's meant to be, you'll see him again."

If I don't see him again, I'm afraid she'll end up having to visit me in the loony bin.

"Do you think we could leave?" I ask her, still feeling a bit jittery from the encounter. "I'm really not feeling well."

"Ok," she says with a small, sympathetic smile. "You're the birthday girl. We'll do whatever you want."

Now she says that…

Once we're on the road back home, Kaylee's pregnancy kicks in and she quickly falls asleep, sparing me from having to answer any more of her questions about my unusual experience in the club. The drive back gives me time to mull over what the stranger said and attempt to formulate a plan of action.

Why did he tell me I would know where to find him? I don't even know his name! How am I supposed to figure out where he lives? I spend a few frustrating minutes wracking my brain in a vain attempt to decipher his cryptic statement. Then it hits me. The mansion on Bayou Road that I was drawn to earlier that day. Could it be possible that he lives there? Maybe that's why I felt such a strong compulsion to go into the house that afternoon. It's as good a place as any to begin my search. For the first time in two weeks, I feel excited. I have a plan, and every cell in my body tells me I'm right.

When we get to my apartment, Kaylee is still asleep. I ask Ben to tell her that I'll call her the next day. Perhaps by then I'll have the answers I've been searching for these past two weeks. I pretend to unlock my front door until I'm certain Ben has driven away. As soon as I see the back lights of their Durango heading down the street, I get into my car and drive a little faster than the law would like to the house on Bayou Road.

The interior lights of the old mansion are all on. It's almost as if the house is anxiously anticipating my arrival. I park directly in front of the home and turn off my car's engine. I sit there in the dark, staring at the door, suddenly second-guessing my rash decision to come here at such a late hour. Should I go in? Is he even here? Am I completely delusional? Should I have brought a gun?

Unexpectedly, my mind is made up for me. The front door opens and out steps a classically-beautiful older woman. If I were to guess her age, I would say she's in her late sixties. Her snow-white hair is cut into a stylish bob that gives her a youthful appearance. She's dressed in a simple white silk blouse, dark blue slacks, and black heels.

"Well," she calls out to me from the open doorway, bending slightly at the waist in order to see me through the passenger window of my car. She has an expectant look on her face. "Are you going to sit there all night, dear, or are you actually going to come inside the house?" she asks with a cultured British accent.

I take in a deep breath to help steady my nerves and open my car door to step out onto the circular concrete driveway. I push the door closed behind me and slowly begin to make my way to the front porch, where the woman is patiently waiting for me.

"Hello, Sarah, my name is Helen." She holds her hand out to me as I step up to her. I shake it, wondering to myself how it is she already knows my name. Her hand is soft, warm, and silky-smooth. There's a faint scent of lavender surrounding her, which gradually calms my nerves. "It's nice to finally meet you. Well, now, let me look at you." She studies my face with a critical eye. I involuntarily straighten my shoulders as if she's a drill sergeant and I'm a cadet under her inspection. "You certainly take after your mother, thank goodness," she observes, nodding her head approvingly. "Same intelligent eyes and expressive face."

"You knew my mother?" I ask relaxing my shoulders. I've never met someone from my mother's past before now.

"Of course," she says, as if it should have been common knowledge to me. "I've known your family for generations. In fact, I helped raise most of them."

"Perhaps you shouldn't confuse her just yet, Helen."

I know that voice. How can I not? I haven't been able to get his words out of my head since we danced together. Danced…that word doesn't adequately describe what happened between us at the club.

I look past the front door's threshold and up to the top of the stairs leading to the second-floor landing. The stranger from the nightclub stands there looking just the same, but this time he isn't frowning at me, not exactly anyway. He's able to keep his facial features completely expressionless, but his eyes betray him when our gazes meet. Even more telling, to me at least, are the emotions he's feeling. Without him having to say or visually express it, I know he's happy to see me. If I'm being honest with myself, I'm happy to see him, too. I'm nervous because I don't understand what's going on between us, but happy all the same.

He walks down the stairs with a confidence I envy, like he owns the world and doesn't care what anyone else might think of him. The closer he gets to me the less anxious I feel. His presence acts as a balm on the anxiety I've been feeling lately, yet being near him again also causes an excited flutter in the pit of my stomach.

"Welcome, Sarah," he says with his unique accent, coming to stand in front of me and keeping my gaze trapped with his. I wasn't able to see his eyes clearly in the dim nightclub, but now I see that they're a warm hazel color. "I'm glad to see you trusted your instincts."

"I didn't have much of a choice," I reply, which is true. It was either come here or live in torment all night long, wanting to come here.

"Well," he says, obviously pleased with my honesty, "I guess you have a lot of questions for us. Why don't we all go into the living room where it's more comfortable?"

Helen leads the way into the house. She veers to the right in the foyer and passes underneath an archway, which leads to a well-appointed living room. It's decorated a bit too old-fashioned for my taste, with a floral settee in the center, flanked by two beige, wingback chairs over a Persian rug on the wood floor. There's a fireplace on the far wall with a white painted mantel and two in-wall bookcases framing it on either side. The walls in the room are painted a pale yellow, which imbues it with an air of springtime. Scattered around the room are crystal vases holding various flower arrangements composed of white daisies and coral roses. A white baby grand piano stands in front of a bank of encased windows. A set of French doors lead out onto a patio where I can see the faint glistening of moonlight in the water of a large pool just beyond the doors.

Helen sits on the settee and pats the empty spot beside her, silently inviting me to sit down. The stranger sits in one of the wingback chairs across from me. I suddenly realize I can't keep calling him 'the stranger'.

"What's your name?" I ask him bluntly, not seeing any sense in beating around the bush. I have questions, and he has the answers. "And how do you both already know mine?"

"My name is Julian Movila, and I knew what your name was going to be even before you were born."

What he says doesn't make a whole lot of sense to me. He isn't that much older than I am. How could he have known my name before I was born?

"What's happening to me? Why do I feel so connected to you? Have we ever met before?" I ask in a desperate rush of words, needing answers.

Julian looks at Helen like I've just confirmed some suspicion that they both shared about me. He is definitely feeling disappointed again, but this time I get the distinct impression it's not me he finds fault with.

"Your mother never told you about her family's history with me?" he asks, keeping his growing frustration simmering just beneath the surface.

"No, she never talked about her family, and I never really thought about it too much. At least not until she and my dad died, and I had no family to take me in."

"I see," he says, casting his eyes away from mine as he considers my words. His hands, which have been resting casually on the arms of his chair, involuntarily seem to clench into fists. Even without that physical tell, I would know he's angry with my mother. The feeling surrounds him like a barbed wire fence.

"Are we related?" I prod impatiently, because he isn't providing me with answers as quickly as I would like.

"No," he answers resoundingly. When he looks back at me, he doesn't bother to hide his frustration. "We are most definitely *not* related, but we are bound to one another by blood."

"Ok, you just lost me," I confess. "How can we be 'bound by blood' if we're not related to one another?"

"I thought Clarissa would have had the good sense to explain things to you when you were a child," he says, far too rudely for me to ignore.

"Don't talk about my mother in that tone of voice," I warn him tersely. "She was a wonderful woman who loved me more than anyone else in this world. If you can't speak civilly about her in my presence, I will leave here and never come back. Do we understand one another?"

Julian feels a moment of panic after hearing my threat, but it quickly changes to a feeling of acceptance. I know he won't be losing any sleep over my idle threat. Even if I wanted to, I'm not sure if I could do what I just said. My compulsion to be near him is too great, but that doesn't mean I wouldn't give it my best try.

"The situation would be easier for you to understand if she had told you about your heritage instead of having a stranger explain things to you," he replies, choosing his words more carefully.

"Just tell me what's going on," I implore. "I haven't been able to eat or sleep properly for two weeks. What's happening to me?"

"I hate to be the bearer of bad news, Sarah, but two weeks ago, your grandfather passed away in his sleep," Julian tells me.

"Grandfather?" I had a grandfather. Why didn't my mother at least tell me about *him*?

"His name was Nicolas Voss." Julian attempts to hide the impact my grandfather's death had on him, but I can sense how deeply the loss still affects him.

"I'm sorry to hear that he's gone," I say, trying to be sensitive about the situation, "but what does his death have to do with the way I've been feeling?"

"When he passed away, the bond he and I shared was transferred to his closest living relative. I assumed it would be your mother until I realized she had also passed away." I can tell he's genuinely sad about hearing of my mother's death. Even if I didn't have empathic abilities, I would have been able to tell that from the shadow of sadness in his eyes. "But it didn't take me long to discover the bond had been passed on to you instead."

"Bond?" I ask, thinking it an odd word to use. "What kind of bond are you talking about?"

Julian's expression becomes drawn with uncertainty. I sense he's worried how I'll react to his answer.

"Generations of your family have been bonded to me. We provide each other with what the other one needs."

"You're being a little too cryptic with your answers," I say, feeling slightly frustrated. "All you're doing is forcing me to ask more questions. Just tell me what's going on. I'm smart. I feel confident I'll be able to follow along."

A corner of Julian's mouth lifts in a half smile. Well, I'm glad my frustration is amusing him, *not*.

"All right, if that's the way you want it." He leans forward in his seat, hands clasped before him, looking me earnestly in the eyes. "I'm a vampire and your family has been bonded to me for the past four hundred years. Only your blood can satisfy my thirst and give me the strength I need to survive, and only I can satisfy the ache you feel inside."

I stare at him for a moment, attempting to work through what he just said. The first thing that comes to my mind is that he's a lunatic. The second possibility that crosses my mind is that I'm being punked. I let my gaze travel around the room, looking for a hidden camera. Both ideas seem ludicrous, but more plausible than believing he's a real vampire. I decide to try to make light of the situation. If he *is* crazy, it might prevent him from attacking me while he's living in his delusional world. If I'm being filmed, at least I'll come off as having a sense of humor about it.

"That last part sounded like a really bad come-on line," I try to joke. "You haven't just escaped from some insane asylum, have you?" I look at Helen. "Either of you?"

"No, dear, I'm afraid we're both perfectly sane and sober," Helen replies indulgently. "Julian is telling you the truth."

"So, you're a vampire?" I ask him skeptically.

He sits back in his seat. "Unfortunately, yes."

"Are you a vampire, too?" I ask Helen.

"No." She smiles as if I've amused her with my question. "I've just had an unnaturally long life."

She did say something about raising generations of my family when I first came through the door.

"So how old are you?" I know you aren't supposed to ask a woman her age, but I get the feeling Helen won't mind answering my question.

"Oh," she tilts her head to the right as her eyes drift off, looking at nothing in particular. I begin to wonder if she's doing the math in her head. "Almost three-hundred now, I think." She looks back at me and shrugs her shoulders slightly. "After the first hundred years I stopped counting."

"Yeah." I've had about enough of Crazyville for one night. I stand from my seat on the settee. "Well, I think I should be leaving now. I hope you two enjoy living in your little fantasy world together, but I'm afraid I'm not on the same level of crazy as the two of you seem to be. I have a real life I need to be getting back to."

Julian quickly stands from his chair and strolls over to the mantel above the fireplace to retrieve something. He turns back around and hands me a clear jewel case with a DVD inside it labeled *Clarissa.*

"Watch this," he urges me. "Your mother left it for your grandfather and me before she left us. Maybe it will help you understand that what's happening to you is real and prove to you that we aren't insane." He says the last word with a touch of amusement.

I take the case, if for no other reason than to find out if there really is a video of my mother on the DVD.

I rush out of the house as quickly as I can without making a fool out of myself by running hysterically back to my car. Thankfully, neither of them tries to follow me out. The drive back to my apartment seems to take forever. Once I reach the safety of my own home, I throw my purse down on the couch and kneel in front of the TV, fumbling in my haste to turn the DVD player on and insert the disk Julian gave me. Within seconds, my mother appears on the screen. She's younger than I remember and very pregnant.

"Are you ready yet?" she asks someone, presumably the person operating the camera.

"Yeah, go ahead," the off-camera voice says. I immediately recognize it as belonging to my father.

Seeing my mother look so young and full of life almost had me in tears, but hearing my father's voice makes me burst into sobs. All my feelings of loss and missed moments with them bubbles to the surface, making me relive their passing all over again.

"Dad, Julian," my mom says into the camera. "I know this is a cowardly way to do this, but there's no way I can say what I need to face to face. If I did, I wouldn't be able to leave." She almost cries saying the last word. I can see the glistening of unshed tears in her eyes as she attempts to hold her emotions in check. After she pulls herself together, she finishes what she started.

"I want you both to know that I love you dearly. You're two of the best people I know in this world, and I hope you'll be able to forgive me in time. I need to leave you both in order to give my little Sarah a normal life." She lovingly rests a protective hand on her protruding belly. "I want her to have a regular life for as long as she can without having to worry about vampires and everything else that's associated with our world. I hope you can understand my decision and not hate me for it," she pleads into the camera. "I promise to return when you die, Daddy. Please forgive me for leaving you like this, but you've had me by your side for the past twenty-five years of my life. I want to give Sarah all of me while I can, before I inherit the bond to Julian from you. Julian, I hope you can understand how important it is to me for Sarah to have an ordinary human existence while she can. I want her to experience life the way it's meant to be lived. I don't resent the fact that you and I will one day be bonded to one another, and I don't resent the fact that one day you and Sarah will be bonded. It's just…" My mother seems a little lost for words to adequately explain everything she's feeling.

"Anyway, Sarah's father and I will be moving somewhere I doubt either of you will ever think to look for us. Julian, you know as well as I do that once my father dies neither of us will be able to hide from the other. Hopefully, you'll live a long, long time, Daddy. At least long enough for Sarah and me to make a lifetime of memories before my life is no longer my own." She blows a kiss into the camera. "I love you both. Please forgive me for leaving you."

Seeing my mother again and hearing her voice is more than I can bear. I continue to cry, unable to make myself stop. The pain of losing her and my father feels like a fresh wound ripping through my heart. I can't prevent myself from replaying the DVD at least a hundred more times just so I can see my mother's face and listen to her words. Eventually, what she's saying sinks in between my sobs. What Julian told me is the truth. He wasn't joking, and he isn't crazy.

Eventually, I begin to make peace with what's expected of me.

I only wish the normal life my mother yearned for me to live could have lasted a little while longer.

CHAPTER 3.

I decide to take a shower and change my clothes before I go back over to the house on Bayou Road. Even though it's almost three in the morning, I'm sure Julian is awaiting my return. He has to know my desire to be with him again is far too strong for me to ignore. To be honest, I feel trapped. Whether I like it or not, he and I are permanently connected to one another by some sort of mystical 'bond'. The vow of *'til death do we part* seems to be literal for us from what my mother said in the video. But what does it all mean? What was my mother talking about when she said "everything else that's associated with our world"? What else is out there that I need to know about besides vampires?

I suppose the one question that keeps running through my mind is: why didn't she better prepare me for my future? Maybe she planned to tell me on my sixteenth birthday: "*Oh, and by the way, along with the car we got you, I should probably mention that you'll also have the honor of inheriting a gorgeous, albeit moody, vampire when I die.*"

I suppose my mother thought she had plenty of time to inform me about my inheritance. I *was* only ten when she and my father perished in the fire. It's obvious she never thought about dying at such an early age. Who does? From what she said in the video, she wanted me to have an ordinary life for as long as I could. Clearly, it was something she never had the chance to live. It might sound odd, but I feel like this experience has given me the opportunity to know my mother a little bit better.

My mom was one of those rare individuals who always viewed life through rose-colored glasses. I don't think I ever saw her sad, or mad for that matter. She never raised her voice to me or disciplined me too stringently. She made sure I grew up in a loving environment that fostered exploration and made me confident enough in my own skin to trust my decision-making skills. She wasn't just my mother. She was my friend and confidante. The more I think about her the larger the void she left in my life seems to grow. I push her memory to the back of my mind for now. I have problems in the here and now that need to be dealt with as quickly as possible.

By the time I park in front of Julian's house again, it's almost five o'clock in the morning. Will he have to go back into his coffin before the sun rises? Most of the vampires I've seen in movies and TV shows usually burn to a crisp in a blazing heat of glory if even one ray of sun touches their skin. Is he like that? Considering how pale he is, I can well imagine he hasn't seen the sun in the past four hundred years.

After a while, I realize sitting in my car isn't going to provide me with the answers I need, and I can't ignore the overpowering desire I feel to be with Julian again.

As I walk up to the front door, I know it's unnecessary to knock and announce my arrival to the man waiting inside. He already knows I'm here. When I reach the door, I simply open it as if I'm walking into my own home. Straightaway, I feel his presence in the direction of the living room, patiently waiting for me to return to him.

I find Julian sitting in the same wingback chair as before, his eyes closed and head tilted back on the headrest as if he's taking a nap. He looks even more handsome in such a relaxed pose, making it difficult for me to take my eyes off him. When he does finally open his eyes, he slowly turns his head to the side to look up at me.

"Are you ready to discuss things now?" he asks in a quiet voice, without a trace of impatience or condescension.

His face remains impassive, but I know he's pleased to see me again. Well, more than pleased; he's overjoyed that I came back to him so quickly. His feelings both overwhelm and comfort me. I get the impression he doesn't show his emotions readily to others. For one of the few times in my life, I'm thankful for my empathic abilities.

I retake my spot on the settee and direct my attention towards Julian. He watches me with a guarded expression. I think he fears I'll run out of the house again, but he should know I can't do that. Even if I wanted to turn my back on him, I don't believe I would physically be able to leave. Whether I like it or not, we're bound to one another for the rest of my life. All I want now is to know why.

"I'm sorry about what I said to you earlier," I begin. "But you can't blame me for thinking you and Helen were insane. I mean, you tell me that you're a vampire, and that Helen is three hundred years old. Did you actually expect me to believe all of that on just your word? What sane person wouldn't have some doubt?"

Julian sighs in resignation. "Like I said earlier, Sarah, I wish your mother had better prepared you for this while you were still young. As humans grow older, they become more closed-minded and resistant to the possibility that creatures such as myself exist in the real world around them."

"I understand why she didn't," I say, defending the choices my mother made for me. "She just wanted me to have a normal life while I could."

"But she knew your future," he reminds me gently. "She knew you would have to share the bond with me eventually."

"Tell me about this bond." I feel a need to get off the subject of my mother's failings in preparing me for my life. "Why are we connected? Why does being near you make me feel so much better?"

"Why we are connected the way we are is a mystery, even to me. I wish I could give you a complete answer to that question but I can't. All I can do is tell you what I've been able to piece together through the years."

I know he isn't eager to fill in all the blanks for me, yet he feels obligated to tell me as much of his story as possible.

"Have you ever heard of Erzsebet, or Elizabeth, Bathory?" he asks.

I immediately shake my head. "No, I haven't. Should I have?"

"Not necessarily. She was born in 1560, and I believe her death is the reason descendants from your family line and I are bonded to one another."

"Did she make you into a vampire? Was she a vampire?"

"Patience," Julian says with a wry grin, but I know that he's secretly pleased by my curiosity. "I promise to answer all of your questions, but it will take some time, Sarah. My world, the world your mother tried to protect you from all these years, is very complicated. You won't be able to learn everything there is to know in a single day. I've lived four hundred years and still don't know everything about it."

"I'm sorry if I sound pushy," I apologize. "It's just that all of this is like some sort of fairytale."

"It's far from a fairytale," he says in a grave voice. There's a warning in his eyes, cautioning me not to be so enthusiastic. "Parts of it are more like a nightmare."

"Please," I say, sitting back on the settee and trying to rein in my natural inquisitiveness, "continue. I'll try not to interrupt you again."

Julian doesn't resume telling me his story right away. He simply looks at me as if he's trying to decide something. I can feel him warring with himself, but then a peaceful aura surrounds him once he's made a decision. Finally, he stands from his chair and walks over to me, taking the empty spot beside me. A sense of calm surrounds me like a pool of bliss, washing away my anxiousness.

"Thank you," I tell him, and I know I don't have to go into an awkward explanation about why I'm thanking him. I find comfort in the fact that he needed to be nearer to me as much as I needed him close.

"And thank you for coming back to me so quickly," he replies with an almost- smile. "I was worried you might try to run away. As you said, all of this is a bit insane, and you seem like a very logical person. Quite frankly I'm surprised you're sitting here, willing to listen to what I have to say."

"You should thank my mother for leaving you that video," I tell him. "If I hadn't heard her confirm the existence of this bond, I wouldn't have come back. I would have just lived with this ache I feel."

"Then we would have both perished."

Julian's statement was made so matter-of-factly that it takes my brain a moment to accept what he said.

"Are you telling me," I say, "that if I don't give in to everything that goes with this bond between us that we could die?"

"In a way," he says simply, without elaboration.

"I think you need to start explaining things to me," I tell him.

Julian takes a deep breath before he begins.

"In 1575, Elizabeth married Count Ferencz Nadasady and earned the title of countess. Since her family was more prestigious than Ferencz's, he accepted her surname of Bathory. They were extremely wealthy back then. I believe they had up to ten castles at one time, but lived in Cachtice Castle in northern Slovakia for most of their marriage. Neither of them were good people. Ferencz was infamous for being a sadist and gaining joy from torturing others. Elizabeth was only fifteen when they married, and she eagerly went along with the things her husband showed her. After a while she began enjoying the torture just as much as he did, even more so I think. The Bathory family was an inbred lot. Back then, they had no understanding of genetics, or how inbreeding can actually decrease the mental capacity of progeny. If you consider that fact and the way her husband behaved, it's no wonder she turned into a serial killer."

"How many people did she kill?" I have to ask, finding myself morbidly fascinated by the story.

"During the trial, the reported number went well above six hundred, but that was an exaggerated estimate. The real number was a little over a hundred within a thirty-year timeframe."

"Still," I say, unable to comprehend how someone could purposely kill so many people, "quite a lot for one person to murder."

"She didn't do it all alone," he tells me with a small shake of his head. "She had the help of a few trusted friends within her inner circle. And…" Julian stops. I see his Adam's apple bob up and down as he swallows hard. I know what he needs to say next is hard for him to admit. He breaks eye contact with me, and I can feel him start to withdraw into himself.

I reach out, resting a light hand on his arm closest to me. "Don't pull away," I beg him, knowing that if I don't stop him from retreating emotionally from me now I'll never be able to get this close to him again. "Nothing you can tell me will make me leave you."

I feel his body relax underneath my touch, yet his emotions are still in turmoil as he considers his options.

"I helped her," he confesses with a troubled frown.

Automatically I pull my hand away from him, feeling as if I shouldn't have just made my declaration that I would never leave him.

"You tortured people?" I ask, suddenly finding it hard to breathe.

Julian shakes his head. "No, but I might as well have."

I sigh in relief, but hold myself back from feeling that emotion fully until after I hear the rest of his explanation.

"Then how did you help her?" I ask in a whisper, needing to know the answer yet frightened to hear what he might confess to next.

"I was one of her servants," Julian says. "In 1609, my sister and I went to work in her household when we were in our mid-twenties. During that year, I did things that I didn't completely understand the consequences of until it was too late."

"What did you do that you feel so guilty about?"

"The countess said I had a trusting face," Julian says derisively with a shake of his head. "During that year, she invited twenty-five impoverished noblewomen to stay with her at the castle. Before that time, we had all heard rumors about a torture room Frenecz had built for her in the castle, but I never truly believed it existed. It wasn't until she asked me to bring her one of the noblewomen that I learned it was real. Back in those days, torturing a servant was a fairly common practice among the elite."

"Really?" I ask aghast. "That's horrible."

"We weren't seen as more than livestock to the nobles. In their eyes, we weren't human. We were just creatures who served them in any way they needed to be served. Anyway, it wasn't until then that I learned how truly sadistic she was." Julian glances over at me. "There were tales about Elizabeth. People said she bathed in the blood of virgins to maintain her youthful appearance."

"Did you see her do that?" I have to ask.

"Not exactly. I did see her covered in blood when she came out of the room, but I think it was just because it splattered onto her. No, I saw her do something I thought was much worse at the time."

When Julian remains silent, I prod, "Which was?"

"I saw her drink their blood like it was wine," he says, like it's his sin he's confessing.

"She drank the blood of the girls she killed but she wasn't a vampire? To me, it sounds like she *was* a vampire."

"She didn't need the blood to survive. She drank it because she got off on it."

"Got off on it," I ponder. "Are you saying it satisfied her sexually?"

"That and mutilating the girls' bodies seemed to do the trick for her. She was insane with bloodlust. We all knew she was crazy, but it's only recently that I've figured out what was wrong with her. If she had lived in this time-period, I believe she would have been diagnosed with schizophrenia."

I want to make a joke and ask him if he's sure he's not crazy, too, but I decide to refrain from acting on my natural snarky instincts. Julian is being sincere in his explanation about his past, and I don't want him to stop. I know he holds vital information that I need to be made aware of concerning his world. It might even save my life one day.

"If the countess hadn't started killing noblewomen, her sins probably would have gone unnoticed, but people started to pay attention when the daughters of influential families began disappearing."

"Did they catch her?" I ask.

"Yes. One night, the authorities came to the castle and discovered the dead bodies of a few girls. Three of Elizabeth's cronies were arrested and subsequently executed for their crimes."

"And what happened to the countess herself?"

"Since she was of noble birth, they simply walled her up inside a room within a tower of her castle. They left small slits in the wall to feed her and provide her fresh air to breathe, which was a kindness she didn't deserve, if you ask me. She spent three years in that room before she finally died."

"So, when did you become a vampire?" I ask. "How did that happen?"

"It happened on the night of Elizabeth's death," Julian tells me. I can feel his uncertainty as he says, "To be honest, I'm not sure what happened. I can't remember much about that night... none of us can."

"So, there are more of you? More vampires?"

"Yes, there were ten of us in the beginning."

"So, in the whole wide world, there are only ten vampires in existence?"

"No. There are only eight pure-blooded vampires left."

"What happened to the other two?"

"They died."

"And how do you kill a vampire?"

Julian raises an eyebrow at me. "You should be aware that if I die, my companion at the time dies along with me."

I hold my hands up to him, palms forward. "I didn't want to know so I could kill you myself," I profess. "I was just curious if you can die the same ways vampires do in the movies."

"Sunlight has no effect on me. Garlic is scrumptious in my book, even if my sister hates it, and a wooden stake through my heart only stings a little. There are only two ways I can die." He pauses as he considers me. I get the distinct feeling that he's judging my trustworthiness. Finally, he says, "I can only die if my companion dies or if I lose almost all of my blood."

"I assume you figured this out when the ninth and tenth vampires died."

"Yes," he confirms, looking and feeling uncomfortable talking about the subject. "One of them fed on his companion for too long and drained her of blood. She died in his arms, and he followed her into death."

"And the other one?"

"He had an accident that made him bleed out faster than his body could heal him. He ended up dying from his injuries, and his companion passed away at the same exact moment."

"So, the rest of you have always had a companion to feed off of?"

"Yes. We've all been fortunate in that respect. You've all been very fertile."

I have to snicker at that one.

"You still haven't explained how this happened to you and my family. Why are we bound to one another?"

"My apologies," he says with a tilt of his head. "I was getting to that before we got sidetracked. Like I was saying, we don't know the specifics of what happened to us, but we do know magic was involved."

"Magic? Like Merlin kind of magic?" I don't know why I'm surprised by his casual use of the word. Of course magic was involved! How else do you explain the unexplainable?

"Yes," he answers, "in a way. I'm sure you've come into contact with a witch or two during your life, you just didn't know it. There's at least one in every city in the world, no matter how small."

"Are you telling me this bond we have is caused by a spell?"

He nods. "A very powerful one at that."

"Who cast it?"

Julian shrugs. "I wish I could tell you, but I don't know. All any of us remembers is waking up in the dungeon of Cachtice Castle with our heads resting on the point of a pentagram. We don't remember how we got there or who cut our throats."

"Someone cut your throats?" I say, imagining in my mind's eye such a gruesome scene. "Was it part of the spell?"

"It had to have been. I think they wanted to drain our blood for some reason, and that, plus whatever else they did, left us thirsting for it when we woke up. We were all practically dead by the time we made it out of the castle. The only thing that kept us going was an incredible urge to return to the one person we each loved most in the world. I went back to my wife and..." Julia stops. He looks away from me and closes his eyes. I'm not sure if his reaction is because he's reliving that night in his mind or if he's having trouble finding the words to describe what he did once he made it back home. I hear him sigh and he finally looks back at me to continue his tale. "I went back to my wife and attacked her. I was so thirsty for her blood that I couldn't stop myself from gorging on it. Luckily, I regained my senses before I completely drained her. By biting her, I unwittingly made her my first companion that night."

"Wait. Are you telling me that your wife was one of my great-grandmothers?" I ask in disbelief.

"Yes," Julian says, "she was."

"Well, doesn't that make you my great-grandfather?"

Julian shakes his head. "No. I couldn't remain married to her because I needed her to have a child to carry on her bloodline for me, and she wouldn't do that unless she could remarry."

"I didn't realize people got divorced back then."

"We didn't. She and I simply moved to a new town and told everyone there that we were brother and sister. My wife was very beautiful. It didn't take her long to find a suitable husband."

"And you were ok with that?" I ask in disbelief. "Didn't you just say you loved her?"

"I loved her more than anyone else in the world," Julian defends. "And that's what doomed her and your family to this fate. We believe that the spell that was cast made us return to the one we loved the most and feed on them to replenish our own blood supply. What we didn't realize at first was that only the blood from that person and their children would be enough to keep us alive."

"What happens if you feed on someone else's blood?" I ask. "Or can you?"

"Two of us have befallen that fate," Julian says. "I would rather be dead than live like they do."

"Why? What happened to them?"

"They went insane," he says, looking distraught. "It's ironic in a way. They didn't want to keep feeding on their loved ones, so they tried to get what they needed to survive by ingesting the blood of others. They ended up losing what little humanity they had left and turned rabid, for lack of a better word."

"And they're both still alive?"

"Yes. They still have their companions' family lines going, but it's only so they can live. They don't feed on them anymore. Apparently, once you've tasted the flesh of others, you don't want your companion's blood any longer."

"Are you able to turn someone into a vampire?"

"Not precisely. We can't give another person immortality, but we can curse them with the same ravenous need for blood that we have. The humans who are turned actually end up with a shortened lifespan. Knowing that the window of their life is closing faster than it should makes them seek retribution for what was done to them."

"That's horrible."

"That's my world."

I can see now why my mother wanted me to have a normal life for as long as I could. Knowing that there are actual monsters lurking in the shadows makes everything seem so much more real now. There's no way for me to turn back the clock and escape all of this. Julian may be describing his world, but he's also explaining what I'll have to contend with for the rest of my life.

"So why are the descendants of your wife the ones who are bound to you? Why only her blood?"

"That was a great mystery to us for a very long time. It was only until modern science discovered how to unravel the mysteries of DNA that we were able to understand what caused the bond."

"So it's not just some magical mumbo jumbo?" I ask in relief.

"Not all of it," Julian says cautiously, picking up on my skepticism. "Part of it is magic, and part of it is science. Though, I seriously doubt whoever did this to us understood what they were doing on a molecular level. Magic has a way of using nature to accomplish what the caster desires to happen."

"What's the science behind it all, then? I can understand that better than blaming it purely on some obtuse mystical force floating around in the universe."

Julian smiles faintly. "You are so much like your mother. She was always the logical one in the family."

"I think most people can cope with changes in their lives if they're explainable."

"Well, from what I understand, my companions and I share a symbiotic relationship with one another. When I first drank the blood of my wife, portions of her genes were spliced into my own. My body in turn produces what is essentially a virus specifically designed to interact with your genetic code. This virus is transmitted from me through my saliva every time I bite you. It attaches to your cells and injects my altered genetic material directly into them. Your cells transcribe my DNA, which in turn provides you with traits like increased speed, agility, strength, and stamina."

"Ok, so in a way it's sort of like gene therapy," I say, thankful I can at least understand that part. "But why do I feel this undeniable urge to be close to you, and why did I only start to feel it when my grandfather died?"

"I'm afraid that's where magic comes into play. I can't explain that part any other way. I know you want a logical answer, but that's the best I can give you right now."

I won't lie and say that I'm not disappointed. I was hoping there would be a sensible explanation behind my attraction to Julian. Having it lumped in with 'it's magic' really doesn't make me feel any better about the situation. If there was a logical reason, I might be able to find a way around it. No such luck, I guess.

"So, what is Helen? How has she been able to live for so long?"

"Our bite can shorten a human's life, but our blood can extend their life well beyond a normal mortal existence."

"So, you gave Helen some of your blood three hundred years ago? Why?"

"For the most selfish reason of all, loneliness. I wanted someone who would stay by my side and live for longer than seventy or eighty years. I needed someone I could rely on."

"How much longer do you think Helen will live?"

"It's hard to say, but she was only sixteen when I changed her. I would put her age at about sixty-five now. So, I suppose she could live another 150 to 200 years," he shrugs. "I simply don't know."

"When you drink my blood," I say hesitantly, "will it hurt?"

"Not much," he reassures.

I freely admit that I'm not looking forward to being bitten by Julian, but I'm mostly concerned about how the virus in his saliva will change me.

"After I drink from you the first time," he says, "you'll end up falling into a deep sleep."

"For how long?"

"I can't say for sure. For some it takes only a day and for others it's taken as long as a week to reawaken."

I shake my head. "I can't be gone that long. Kaylee would start to worry about me."

"Is that the pregnant woman you were with last night?"

"Yes."

"And the man. Was he her husband or your lover?"

"Most definitely her husband," I'm quick to reply. "I don't have a boyfriend at the moment."

"Why not?" he asks, as if what I said is completely unacceptable.

I shrug my shoulders. "I don't date much. Never have."

"That's going to need to change, Sarah, and as soon as possible."

I'm about to make a pithy retort about how he can keep his opinions to himself and his nose out of my love life, but then I remember why he just said what he did.

"You need me to have a child you can bond with after I die."

Julian nods his head. "It's just the way things have been done for a very long time now. Maybe it would be easier if you simply thought of it as a family tradition."

"And if I don't have a child, will you end up dying when I do?"

"Yes."

I sense the thought of his own death doesn't bother him too much.

"Why is staying alive so important to you?" I ask. "I get the feeling you would welcome death."

Julian studies me for a moment like I'm a curiosity. "Why does it seem like you know precisely what I'm feeling all the time?

During this whole conversation, you've been able to judge my moods and tell just how far to take your questions. How is that possible?"

I stare at him for a while, trying to judge whether I should entrust him with my deepest, darkest secret. The only other person in the world who knows about my ability is Kaylee. We never told her parents, and she never told Ben. I always thought we would carry my secret to our graves. Julian continues to watch me, waiting for an answer to his question. I decide to tell him my secret. If I do end up having a child to continue my family's tradition it's possible my progeny will inherit my ability, and Julian will need to understand it might be a part of every descendant after me.

"I'm an empath," I confess. "I can tell what people are feeling."

His eyes widen a bit in surprise, but he quickly recovers. "I've heard of people like you, but I can't say I've ever met one before. You're very rare, Sarah."

"I guess rare is nicer than saying I'm a freak of nature," I half-laugh, not feeling comfortable discussing my peculiar gift. "At the beginning of this conversation, you said Elizabeth Bathory was responsible for what happened to you. How can that be true if she was already dead when you were changed?"

"She was a student of the occult and had dealings with witches who drew on the dark arts for their power. The ten of us who awoke in that room were the ones who gave the most damning testimony at the trial. We believe the witches who befriended her cursed us as punishment for betraying Bathory's trust."

It's hard for me to imagine living four hundred years without any end in sight. Would I be happy with eternal life? It was a hard question to answer. Very few people want to die, but would living forever really bring any of us more joy?

"Besides the side-effects you mentioned," I say, "will I change in any other ways?"

"You'll become completely immune to any other vampire's coercion."

"Coercion?" I ask, not liking the sound of that word.

"At the nightclub, did you feel odd when you were with me?"

I slowly nod my head. "Yeah, I felt like I didn't have control of myself."

"We have the ability to put humans into a type of trance so that they do what we ask without fighting us. I apologize for using that on you, but we needed to talk. It simply wasn't the right place or time to have the conversation we're having now. I needed you to find me and come here of your own free will."

"I smelled cinnamon and chocolate while we danced," I tell him, remembering the strange encounter clearly.

"When people are under our spell, they tend to smell what brings them comfort. I suppose cinnamon and chocolate are smells that put you at ease. It makes it easier for one of my kind to relax people and make them submissive to our will."

"You said my blood will give you the strength you need. What did you mean by that?"

"Without regularly ingesting your blood, my body becomes weak. I've already started to lose some of my abilities, since I haven't fed in the last two weeks."

"What kind of abilities do you have?"

"Well, I'm strong and agile. I can see in the dark and hear conversations at a great distance. You know about the coercion. Oh, and I can fly."

He said it so nonchalantly I thought I might have misunderstood him.

"Did you say you can fly? Like, Superman fly?"

"Yes." He doesn't show it outwardly, but he's secretly pleased he was able to surprise me with his answer, just as he had intended.

"What's your kryptonite, then? Every superhero has a weakness."

He isn't prepared for my question and is immediately suspicious of my motives for asking it.

"As I said earlier, only your death, without having an heir to take your place, and the loss of a great deal of blood can kill me."

"Will I be able to fly, too, after we complete the bonding ritual?" I can't help but feel excited by the prospect.

"No, I'm afraid you won't be getting that particular ability."

"No night vision and super hearing either?" I ask, preparing myself for disappointment.

"I'm afraid not. I believe you only receive the gifts that will help you defend yourself."

"What exactly do I have to defend myself against?" I ask with open suspicion.

"There are forces in this world the existence of which you have no idea. Your abilities will eventually come in handy against them. Plus, it gives you more protection from the other vampires."

"Why would they want to kill me?"

"It's only the rabid ones I mentioned that we have to worry about," he says. "They believe those of us who abstain from drinking the blood of others are unnatural. They think that our refusal to become like them means that we should die."

"Have you and the others like you thought about killing them before they have a chance to kill you?"

"The subject was brought up during our last conclave, but none of us have acted on it."

We fall into an uneasy silence for a few seconds. Finally, I decide it's pointless to postpone the inevitable.

"Will you have to drink my blood every night?" I ask, unsure I actually want to know the answer to my question.

"We can start out with it being every other night until you get used to it, but eventually we'll need to get into a nightly routine. Are you ok with that?"

"Do I have much of a choice?"

Julian slowly shakes his head. "Not really. I'm sorry about that, Sarah. But if it's any consolation, you'll also gain the ability to heal faster. You don't have to worry about your friend asking why you have my bite marks on your neck all the time. The wound should heal within an hour of being bitten."

"I'm not sure that's very comforting, but it's good to know."

I try to think of something else to ask, but draw a complete blank. I know what Julian wants to do. I can feel how hungry he is. I'm just not sure how ready I am to go through with it.

"Is there anything else I should know before we do this?" I ask, trying unsuccessfully to avoid the inevitable.

"Yes." I sense he isn't too sure about how I will react to his next statement. "You'll need to move in with me."

"*Why?*"

"It would make it a lot easier for the both of us. The further away we are from one another after the bonding ceremony, the worse the need to be together will grow."

"I can't just move in here," I say heatedly. "Kaylee would think I'd lost my mind!"

"Maybe if you told your friend that we've fallen madly in love with one another she will be more apt to accept our new living situation."

"She would know something was up. She's not that stupid. I'm not someone who falls in love quickly."

"What if you keep your apartment for appearance's sake? I have no problem splitting my time between your place and this house. We can pretend we're dating if you think that would help explain things to your friend."

"She'd be over the moon if she thought I was actually dating someone seriously. Maybe it would finally make her stop trying to fix me up all the time with random men."

"Then she may be useful to us in the future."

Oh, yeah, I need to provide him with an heir so he'll have someone to bond with after I die. Well, we would cross that bridge when the time came.

"I hate to rush you," he says, standing to his feet. "But I'm afraid I won't be able to control myself for much longer. I was proud that I was able to back away from you while we were dancing earlier. I can't tell you how much self-control that took."

I stand from the settee, feeling extremely nervous about what will happen next.

"So, umm, how do you want to do this?" I ask, feeling out of my element in this situation.

Julian holds out his hand to me. I tentatively place mine into his.

"I think it will be easier for you if you're lying down. That way you'll be more comfortable when you fall asleep."

"I completely forgot about that part. Wait here one second." I quickly run out to my car and retrieve my purse from the passenger seat. I rummage through the contents and find my cell phone. I type out a text message for Kaylee, saying that I've gone out of town and don't know when I'll be back. At least that way she won't worry as much about me being gone.

When I walk back into the house, I find Julian waiting for me at the foot of the staircase leading to the second floor.

"I left Kaylee a text message so she doesn't worry about me," I tell him, sliding my phone back into my purse.

"That's a good idea," he praises, holding his hand out to me again. His skin is still cold to the touch, but somehow it seems so natural.

As I head up the stairs with my vampire, I wonder how my life became so monumentally screwed up in such a short amount of time.

CHAPTER 4.

When we reach the second floor, Julian leads me down a dimly-lit hallway and opens a door to a tastefully-furnished bedroom. It has a cherry wood four-poster bed with matching furnishings such as nightstands and chest of drawers. The walls of the room are covered with an embossed floral wallpaper in creamy beige and coral tones. The bed covers are pure white, which strikes me as strange considering what's about to happen on them. It's just my nature to worry that they'll be stained by my blood. It's a silly thought, considering the fact that I'm about to exchange bodily fluids with a vampire I barely know, but I guess the human in me is still thinking about the mundane practicality of everyday life.

With Julian's gentle guidance, he leads me to the bed at an unhurried pace, even though I can feel how anxious he is to feed.

"Don't be scared," he tells me in a calm, even voice. I faintly wonder if he's using his power of coercion on me, but soon realize that he isn't. He's simply trying to calm my nerves the old-fashioned way, with words and a gentle touch. "The initial pain from my bite will be fleeting. After that, all you should feel is a small bit of pressure as I drink."

"This will probably sound stupid to you," I begin, already feeling foolish for having to ask the question, "but do you have fangs?"

"No," he tells me, looking amused by my query. "I don't. I simply bite you with enough force to pierce your skin and draw out your blood. I'm not sure that brings you any comfort, though. Are you still all right with what I'm about to do?"

"Yes," I say, meaning the word. I know I should be scared, frightened out of my mind, actually, but I only feel a slight twinge of trepidation. For some completely unexplainable reason, I want him to do it. I want this to happen. Nevertheless, there's a small part of my psyche that's screaming: *Have you completely lost your mind? Run, fool!*

Maybe I have lost my mind. Maybe this is all a dream and I'm actually safely snuggled up in my bed, having finally succumbed to exhaustion after suffering through two solid weeks of sleepless nights. What I'm about to do is totally insane, but I've never felt more confident in a decision than I do this one.

"Lie down on the bed," Julian instructs as he begins to unbutton the front of his grey dress shirt.

"What are you doing?" I ask, not remembering him saying we had to have sex first. That isn't part of the deal, is it?

Julian looks at me in confusion for a moment, but I quickly see realization dawn on his features.

"I just don't want to get my shirt bloody is all," he promises.

Well, at least he's a practical-thinking vampire. I can actually appreciate that trait.

"What about the bed covers?" I ask, turning my gaze in the bed's direction. Since he's already brought up the subject of being neat, it doesn't seem like bad manners to voice my own concern. "Won't we get blood on them?"

Julian walks up to the bed's nightstand on the right-hand side and opens the top drawer. He pulls out a small black blanket similar in style to one I gave Kaylee at her baby shower. It has a quilted piece of fabric on one side and washable plastic lining on the other. Julian lays it across the pillow closest to him on the bed, quilted side up.

"There. Now we're ready," he tells me, continuing to take his shirt off as he walks around the bed to the other side and hangs it on the bedpost there.

Julian doesn't have huge muscles like a body builder, but he does possess a well- cut physique that's quite pleasing to the eye. In fact, I become a little uncomfortable as I watch him move around the room. I'm certain our relationship isn't supposed to have a sexual component to it. I am, after all, expected to have a child with someone else so my bloodline can continue to feed Julian. The thought makes me feel like a prized mare who is expected to mate with the stallion of her choice. I try to shrug off the feeling of being his property, but I know it will always linger like an unreachable itch in the back of my mind.

I sit down on the bed and slip off my tennis shoes before lying down on the bed. I try to make sure my neck is lined up with the middle of the mat beneath me. My heart is pumping a mile a minute, but I suppose that might be a good thing. It should help get the blood out faster for him. As I stare up at the white-painted ceiling, I begin to feel nervous. I have no idea what the proper protocol is when being bitten for the first time.

Julian lies down next to me, making the bed dip and creak with his added weight. I can feel the heat of his stare on me, but I can't seem to make myself look at him or say anything. I feel helpless and totally at his mercy. If he wanted to, I'm sure Julian could simply force me to give him my blood. I suppose I should be grateful he's being so patient. Otherwise, this scenario could quickly turn into a true nightmare for me.

"Sarah, look at me," he says in a voice that's both commanding and imploring.

I take a deep breath and slowly turn my head to meet his gaze. He's propped up on one bent arm, looking at me questioningly.

"What are you thinking?" he inquires softly as he seems to study every feature of my face intently, searching for something intangible.

"That I don't know what to do," I confess in a small voice. "Now that I'm laying here, I'm beginning to feel a little frightened."

He continues to study me thoughtfully, even though I can feel his hunger is about to tear him in two. He raises his free hand and brushes the hair lying across my neck off to the side.

"You don't have to do anything," he murmurs. "Just lie still. I'll do all the work. Would it help you at all if I used my coercion on you again, to ease your tension this first time?"

"No," I say determinedly. "No, if I'm doing this, I want it to be of my own free will. Not because you bewitched me into it."

He smiles faintly, and I know he's pleased with my answer.

"Very well." He leans in closer and touches the throbbing spot at the base of my throat with the tips of his fingers, the same exact place his lips had lingered just a few hours before in New Orleans.

He leans in closer to me, his head barely an inch away from mine. I can feel his cool breath chill my skin, and I involuntarily shiver. Just as he's about to bite me, I notice a shadow against the wall behind him. I turn my head toward the set of windows to the left of me and see the first light of day shine through the glass.

"It's almost daylight," I tell him, knowing I'm simply looking for any excuse at this point to delay the inevitable. "I guess it's a good thing sunlight doesn't bother you."

"Sarah, look at me."

I do as he bade and turn my head back to look up at him again. If I thought my heart was hammering inside my chest before, now I think it might be doing double flips. In the warm light of dawn, Julian looks devastatingly handsome. His lips are slightly parted and he seems to be breathing as haltingly as I am. The hunger he feels is mirrored in his eyes now, and he isn't trying to hide it from me anymore. For some reason, it makes him look even more handsome and primal. Suddenly, the thought of being bonded to him for the rest of my life seems a bit more thrilling of a prospect.

He reaches down and picks up my right hand, placing it against his smooth, hairless chest directly over his heart. I didn't think vampires had heartbeats, but there it is, pounding sluggishly against the palm of my hand. It's slow like a metronome adjusted to its lowest setting.

"Why is your heart beating so slowly?" I ask in a whisper.

"Because it's been so long since I fed."

"What would happen if you didn't feed for longer than two weeks?"

"If I went another couple of weeks without feeding, my body would start to shut down, and I would enter a coma-like state. Your blood literally keeps my heart beating, Sarah."

It wasn't said in the most romantic of situations, but it was probably the most romantic thing a man has ever said to me.

"I'm sorry, but I'm afraid I can't wait any longer. If you're not ready, I need to leave now before I lose control of myself." I can see his hunger pangs quite clearly on his face. He's been trying to hide it, afraid it would scare me away. Now, being so close to what he desires the most, he's having trouble restraining his baser instincts.

"I'm ready," I tell him. As he leans in closer to my neck, I keep my hand over his heart. I need the physical contact to remind me why I'm doing this.

The sharp edges of his teeth clamp down on the flesh at the base of my neck. Involuntarily, my body tenses as Julian bites me. Just as he promised, the pain is fleeting and all I feel is a bit of pressure as he begins to suck. I close my eyes as he continues to feed. The sound of him swallowing my blood is strange to my ears, and when he involuntarily moans in pleasure I feel my body react of its own accord. I've never been one to associate pain with pleasure, but with Julian, in that moment, that's what happens to me. Deep down, I think the idea of being the only one in the world who can satisfy his needs makes me feel powerful. Without me, he's left vulnerable to the world and even to his own body. He *needs* me, and having that type of control over someone else can be intoxicating.

As he continues to feed, I know that he feels happy and sad all at the same time. I think his sadness stems from regret for having to do this to me in the first place. I find a small bit of comfort in that fact. At least he understands what I'm giving up. This is the moment my mother's dream of me having a normal life dies. There's no turning back now even if I wanted to.

I keep my hand on his chest and feel the beats of his heart increase in speed and strength. For some reason I thought I would fall asleep almost immediately, but it takes a while before I feel that moment of pleasurable exhaustion you sometimes experience when you finally get the chance to lie down after a hard, busy day.

When Julian finally forces himself to pull away from my neck, I'm still awake, but I feel so tired I can't seem to open my eyes. I hear and feel him get off the bed and move around the room.

I muster up enough strength to curl up onto my side. Just before I fall asleep, I feel him lay a blanket on top of me. I smile at his thoughtfulness and soon find succor in a world of my own imaginings.

My dreams have never been filled with cute little puppies, fuzzy kittens, and magical rainbows. For some reason, they've always leaned more toward the macabre. While I sleep after our bonding ritual, I dream a plethora of things, but they all have one common element: Julian. The dreams have a surreal look and feel to them, like a Salvador Dali painting come to life in my mind.

The most vivid one includes Julian in a starring role. He and I are dancing across a sparkling ocean of liquid sand. We're dressed much like people do in New Orleans when they attend fancy Mardi Gras parties. Julian is wearing a mask that keeps changing shape between a cat and a bird. I'm wearing a traditional white mask of a normal human face, but it has tears of blood painted down both cheeks. I'm wearing a white silk dress with a crumpled skirt and matching rosettes scattered within the folds. It reminds me of a gown I saw while shopping for Kaylee's wedding dress. Julian is in a simple black tuxedo and bow tie. No music plays as we twirl like marionettes being guided by an unseen hand. The only sound is the ticking of a clock. As we dance aimlessly around on the sand, a trail of gaping black holes appears where our feet touch. This is the last dream I have before I wake. When I open my eyes, the image of us dancing in each other's arms is fresh in my mind.

I find myself lying in the same position I was in when I fell asleep. I'm still on my side, facing toward the windows in the room. Julian is sitting in a chair next to the bed, watching me with a thoughtful expression on his face.

"How do you feel?" he asks, his voice practically reverberating in the quiet of the room.

It takes a moment for my mind to register what he asked me. I'm not sure why, but I don't feel like myself. Something is definitely different, but I can't quite put my finger on what has changed.

As I continue to stare into his beautiful hazel eyes, I realize I don't know what he's feeling. His emotional state is completely cut off from me. Julian is like a blank page in a book without any words. Have I lost my empathic ability by bonding with him? Is it even possible for me to lose something that has been a part of me since birth?

I decide not to say anything just yet. What I'm experiencing could simply be temporary. Surely I haven't lost my gift. That's not possible, right?

"Rested," I finally answer. It's the truth. It's just not the complete truth. "How long did I sleep?"

"Only two days." He leans forward in his chair. "Did you have nice dreams?"

"I hardly ever have nice dreams," I confess. "They've always been a bit strange. But I did dream a lot about you."

"Interesting." He says the word like my small confession means something more to him.

"Did the other people you shared a bond with dream about you a lot?"

"Not that they ever told me."

Well, now I feel embarrassed. I just assumed it was because of our bond that I had dreamt so much about him. Feeling kind of stupid for admitting such a thing, I roll onto my back and look up at the ceiling, trying my best to figure out why I don't know what Julian is feeling.

"What's bothering you?" he asks.

I know he's concerned by the tone in his voice, but I can't feel his concern. It's rather disconcerting. I never realized before now how much I relied on my ability to sense what the people around me feel. The sensation of being disconnected from someone's emotions is making me feel panicky.

I look back over at him.

"I can't sense what you're feeling anymore," I tell him, deciding I need to share my worry with someone who might understand. "It's like my empathic ability is gone."

"Are you positive?" he asks, sounding doubtful that it's actually disappeared.

"Yes," I say with certainty. "I have absolutely no idea what you're feeling right now, and I should." I try unsuccessfully to prevent panic from saturating my voice.

Julian's gaze shifts to the floor for a second before he meets my eyes again. I may not be an empath anymore, but years of being one have taught me what certain expressions on people's faces indicate. I can tell he's struggling internally as to whether he should tell me something important.

"Perhaps it's just me you can't read," he finally says. "Let's go down to the kitchen and see if you can feel Helen's emotions. She's been cooking ever since I told her you would be waking up today."

"How did you know I would be?" I ask, slowly getting out of bed. I still feel a bit drowsy and stiff from my long slumber.

"I can usually feel when the person I'm bound to will awaken after the ceremony," he tells me as we leave the room together. We walk side by side along the hallway and down the grand staircase to the first floor.

The kitchen is located at the end of the hallway of the foyer at the back of the house. It's a bright, airy space with white painted cabinets, pale pink marble countertops, and stainless steel appliances.

There is a large kitchen island with a built-in sink and two wrought-iron chandeliers hanging above it. One of the doors of the refrigerator-freezer has an inset TV with a local morning news program playing on it.

Helen, dressed sharply in tan slacks and a blue and white button-down shirt, is pulling out a cookie sheet from the double wall oven when we walk into the room. The aromas of chocolate and cinnamon fill the air, bringing me a sense of calm.

"You're not using your spell on me, are you?" I whisper to Julian.

"No," he says aghast, looking slightly offended that I would even ask the question. "Besides, you're immune to that now, from me or any other vampire."

Well, that was good to know. I understood that I would be immune to others of his kind but I didn't realize it included him, too.

"Oh good, you're awake," Helen says, closing the door to the oven and turning around to place the freshly-baked cookies on a cooling rack on the kitchen island. "I made you some chocolate chip and cinnamon cookies. I hope you like them. I'm sure you're starving, you poor thing."

I sigh in relief as I look at Helen. I can feel how happy she is to see me. I haven't lost my empathic ability after all. Julian seems to be the one I'm cut off from for some reason. That idea seems odd to me. Considering the bond connecting us to one another, you'd think I would be able to read him more clearly, but perhaps since the bonding made me immune to his coercion spell it made him immune to my empathic ability. It seemed like a sound theory.

Julian looks at me and arches one eyebrow, silently asking me if I can sense what Helen is feeling. I smile in relief and nod my head, letting him know I can.

"You shouldn't have gone to so much trouble," I tell Helen, taking one of the cooled cookies off a rack. There must be at least two dozen already cooling on racks besides the ones she just pulled out of the oven. The dark-chocolate-cinnamon cookies contain mini-chocolate chips and chopped walnuts. I take a bite and gobble the cookie down in two seconds. I soon discover that I *am* starving. I quickly grab more cookies and eat them all in quick succession.

"See," Helen says triumphantly, pointing the spatula she holds in her hand at me while glancing in Julian's direction. "I knew she would be hungry. They always are."

I realize I feel as though I haven't eaten in a month of Sundays. I finish off all the cookies in about five minutes flat. Luckily for me, Helen is prepared for my ravenous feeding frenzy. She has an egg and sausage strata, a casserole dish full of chicken enchiladas, and a large crystal bowl filled to the brim with fruit salad ready for my consumption. I eat them all in one sitting. By the time I start eating the basket full of yeast rolls sitting on the kitchen table, I notice Helen and Julian standing off to the side, watching me like I'm a freak show at a circus. I can well imagine what the carney would be saying in the background: *"Come see the amazing Sarah Marcel as she devours anything and everything made of food! Don't get in her way though or she might just eat you too!"*

I finish eating the roll in my hand and slowly push what's left in the basket away.

"Sorry," I say sheepishly, feeling like a sinner for my gluttony.

"Well," Helen crosses her arms in front of her, "I don't think I've ever seen any of the others do that before."

"I promise you," I say, my cheeks growing hot from embarrassment. "I have never eaten like this before in my life. I don't know why I'm so hungry."

"Well it's obvious you don't eat much, dear. You can't weigh much over eight and a half stones."

I wasn't sure how much a stone represented in actual weight, but I did know I weighed 120 pounds on my skinny days.

"It's normal for people to be hungry when they first wake up after the bonding is complete," Julian reassures me. I can tell he's slightly amused by my show of appetite. He's almost smiling. "We've just never seen any of the others eat so much in such a short amount of time."

I hate to admit it to them, but I'm still hungry. The basket of yeast rolls is practically begging me to finish them. I also can't prevent my eyes from wandering over to a triple chocolate cake resting delectably on a glass pedestal on the kitchen island.

Julian comes over to the table and practically pushes the basket of rolls underneath my nose.

"Eat," he orders. "If you're still hungry, then you need to eat."

I don't need any more of an invitation than that. I have the rest of the rolls devoured before Helen brings me a pitcher of tea to help wash everything down. By the time I drink the pitcher dry, I finally feel somewhat satiated. I could have still eaten the chocolate cake, but I decide I should let what I've already eaten settle first. Plus, I don't want Helen to think she needs to cook me more food just yet. Hopefully, my hunger will wane as the day goes by.

"I feel full," I say, leaning back in my chair, patting the bulge of my stomach. It almost resembles a baby bump.

"Well, I need to go grocery shopping," Helen says with certainty. "Do either of you need something from the store?"

"No, I'm fine," Julian tells her. He's facing me with his back leaned against the kitchen island counter. I can't help but feel a bit shy under his steady gaze.

"I'm fine, too," I answer, not feeling like I should tell Helen I could really go for a few pounds of boiled shrimp and crawdads.

"Are you sure there isn't something in particular you would like for supper?" Julian prods, as if he can sense I'm not being truthful.

"Well…" I should just tell them what I want. If they haven't felt offended by my recent display of hunger, then they probably won't care if I ask for what I'm craving. "I wouldn't mind some steamed shrimp and crawdads, if they have any on sale."

"Crawdads?" Helen asks, as if it's a foreign word to her.

"The people at the store will know what they are," Julian assures her, glancing in Helen's direction before returning his full attention to me.

My inability to tell what he's thinking is disconcerting. He is certainly adept at masking his emotions from others behind an expressionless façade. Why, out of all the people in the world, does *he* have to be the one I can't read? I just hope he's the only one.

"All right then, I'll be back in a jiffy." Helen walks out of the kitchen towards the front of the house. I hear the rattle of keys and the opening and closing of the front door as she exits the house, leaving me alone with Julian.

I suddenly hear my cell phone ring. When Kaylee first became pregnant, I set her ringtone on my phone to the song "Baby Got Back". She professed to hate the ringtone, but it did make her laugh the first time she heard it. I distinctly remember leaving my phone in my purse, which was supposed to be up in the bedroom I had slept in, yet the sound is nearby.

I see Julian pull my cell phone out of one of his front pockets and press the silence button.

"Why do you have my phone?" I ask, feeling as if he's just invaded my personal bubble of privacy.

"Your friend Kaylee has called at least twenty times since yesterday," he reports a bit agitatedly, handing me my phone. "I got tired of hearing that ringtone, so I kept it on me to silence it when it rang."

"Why didn't you just turn the ringer off?" I ask, taking the phone from him.

"I was worried she might be in distress. I read the text messages and listened to the voicemails she left you to make sure she wasn't. I knew you would want to go to her after you woke up if she needed you."

I quickly look at all my missed calls. He's right. Kaylee has called me twenty times in the past couple of days, and left twice as many text messages. My heart sinks at the thought of lying to Kaylee about the new direction my life has taken. What am I going to tell her?

"Maybe now would be a good time to come up with a believable story about you and me," Julian suggests, coming to sit with me at the table.

"Oh, the lie I'm supposed to tell everyone about us dating?" I don't like to lie. I only do it to spare someone else's feelings. I think everyone has told one of their friends that they don't look like they've gained an extra ten pounds when they have or that their butt doesn't look big in a new pair of jeans. Of course they come and ask *you* those questions. They want to be reassured that they don't look fat. They're asking you because they already know how you'll respond.

"It's the easiest way to introduce me into your life," Julian says, being aggravatingly pragmatic about the situation. "Besides, from what you told me, it should make your friend Kaylee happy to know you've found someone to spend your time with."

I sigh. He's right. It is the easiest way to make him a part of my life that Kaylee will readily accept.

"Do you have any suggestions on how to explain where I've been the last two days?" I ask, being new to the lying game. I assume Julian has probably mastered it by now after four hundred years of existence.

"What if you told her we met each other later that evening by accident, started talking, and one thing led to another?"

"I'm not sure that'll work. If 'one thing leading to another' is code for sex, then Kaylee already knows I wouldn't jump into bed with a man I barely know. I definitely wouldn't just ignore her calls for a stranger either."

"Then what do you suggest?" Julian frowns. I'm not sure if he's disappointed in hearing that I don't sleep around, or that his brilliant idea has been rejected so readily by me. I know he needs me to become impregnated at some point during my fertile years, but surely he can't be disappointed to find out that I'm not promiscuous.

I sit there for a few minutes more, trying to think of a plausible reason that I would be completely out of contact. Then the solution presents itself to me.

"Besides you, did I inherit anything else from my grandfather?" I ask.

Julian's eyes narrow on me as if my query makes him suspicious of my motives for asking the question in the first place.

"You own all of my assets," he reveals almost reluctantly.

"What do you mean? How much is there?"

"After I accumulated a large amount of wealth, we made provisions to have each of my companions inherit all of my properties and money. It simply made it easier to do it that way instead of having to explain why the name on the accounts never changed generation after generation. So, yes, you've inherited quite a fortune, Sarah."

That's interesting and good to know.

"Ok, then. I'll tell Kaylee that my grandfather, who I never knew existed, died and left me his estate. I'll just say I had to go to New Orleans to take care of the paperwork. That explanation is a lot more plausible than saying I spent the last two days in your bed."

"Not nearly as exciting, though," he says. I could have sworn his statement was meant as a joke, but his delivery was so deadpan I can't be sure.

"Wait," Julian says. "What if she asks why your grandfather didn't contact you while he was still alive?"

"Hmm, good point," I reply. "Any suggestions?"

"You could tell her the truth," Julian says. "We never did give up searching for you and your mother, but she hid her tracks so well we couldn't find either of you. It's odd, but your last name is my first wife's maiden name. I never would have thought to look for a Clarissa Marcel. I guess your mother chose it because of that fact. I suggest you tell Kaylee that your grandfather had private detectives actively searching for you, and that one of them happened to find you right after his death. It's only a partial lie."

"Ok. That at least sounds plausible. I'd better call her before she gets the police involved." I flip through my short contact list to find her number.

While I smooth the ruffled feathers of my best friend, Julian leaves the table and walks over to the kitchen island. I hear him fiddling around, but don't pay him any attention as I talk to Kaylee. I let my sister berate me for not answering her calls, and explain that I've been in a lawyer's office most of that time and didn't have my phone on. After I tell her about discovering I have a grandfather and losing him in the same day, she immediately forgets to be mad at me and starts asking me about him. I don't know the answers to her questions, but I try to tell her as much as I can. I feign exhaustion from the events of the past two days and promise to come by her house the following morning. She orders me not to eat breakfast before coming over because she plans to make me my favorite breakfast in the world: Belgian waffles topped with Nutella and fruit.

"Make a lot," I warn her. "I have a feeling I'll be hungry."

When I get off the phone, I feel somewhat better about the situation with Kaylee. I didn't lie to her, but I didn't tell her the whole truth either. I fear my life will end up becoming a series of half-truths from now on. I don't like it, but I don't see any way around it either.

Julian walks back to the table, holding a glass platter with a quarter of the chocolate cake I eyed earlier lying in the middle of it and a large glass of milk.

"I thought you might like dessert," he says with a hint of a grin.

He thought right. However, this time I don't gobble my food down like a sow at a feeding trough. I take my time and try to eat like any normal human being.

As I eat the cake, I can't make myself stop staring at Julian. There's something different about him, but I can't quite put my finger on what it is.

"Have I grown a second nose or a third eye I don't know about?" he finally asks, obviously becoming annoyed with my gawking of his person.

"There's something different about you," I reply, still trying to figure out how he's changed. Then I see it. "Your skin isn't pale anymore." I put one of my hands on top of the hand he has resting on the table. "And you're not cold anymore either."

"No," he says, sliding his hand out from underneath mine as if he doesn't like to be touched. Or maybe it's just me he doesn't want touching him. Either way, I can take a hint.

"Why aren't you pale and cold anymore?" I ask, continuing to eat my cake and trying not to be offended by his reaction to my caress.

"As long as I feed on a regular basis, I look this way. It's only when my heart slows and isn't circulating my blood that I start to look pale and become cold to the touch."

"I guess that makes sense," I say.

I run my fork along the icing on top of the cake, making tiny troughs. I have some more questions I want to ask, but I'm not sure whether I should bother him with them now. I just can't tell if he's in the mood to answer them or not.

"I assume you want to ask me some questions," he finally says after the silence between us has become noticeable. "Feel free to ask me anything you want, Sarah. I'll try to answer what I can."

"Well, now that you mention it. I am curious about a few things." I'm thankful he opened the question door and is allowing me to step over the threshold for some answers about my family's past. "What did my grandfather die of?"

"Old age, like most of the ones who are bound to me do."

"Why is that?"

"I think it's because the virus I give you fights off most diseases which increases their immunity. It's very rare, but every once in a while one dies in an accident."

Like my mother did, I think to myself. If she hadn't died in the fire, she would be the one sitting where I am now.

"Did you just move into this house? I've never seen you around Pecan Acres before." And I would have most definitely remembered seeing him shopping at the local Wal-Mart. Julian would have been the talk of the town.

"Yes, we moved here a few days ago. When your mother said she and your father were moving somewhere neither your grandfather nor I would think to look for them, she was right. I didn't even know this town existed until I started to search for you."

"How did you know where to find me?"

"The same way you knew I was in this house. We're connected. We will always know where the other is."

I'm not sure I like that idea. Have I completely lost my privacy now? Will I ever have time to just be by myself?

"Where were you living before you had to come here?"

"A little town called Geneva in New York State. Your grandfather liked running the vineyard we owned up there."

"What was he like?"

"He was a good man. Honest to the core." Julian smiles as he fondly remembers my grandfather. It's the first real sign of emotion I've seen him openly display since waking up. It's obvious he cared for my grandfather very much. "You would have liked him. Most people did."

"I wish I had known he existed. I don't know why my mother kept me from knowing him." I can't prevent myself from sounding resentful, because that's how I feel. It would have been nice to know I had at least one living relative after losing my parents.

"If you had known him," Julian says, you would have had to know me, too. I don't think that was the plan your mother had in mind when she left. I've never agreed with what your mother did, but I understood the reasoning behind her actions."

"Did you resent her for leaving?"

"At first I did," Julian admits. "But after a while, I came to understand her desire for you to have a normal life. I never realized how hard it could be to live in my world. None of your ancestors seemed to mind. At least they never said anything to me about disliking it."

Julian's gaze drifts to the top of the table. It seems to be his habit to avert his eyes when he doesn't want anyone to know what he's thinking.

I can't help but sigh. He looks back up at me.

"What's wrong?" he asks.

"You're driving me crazy," I admit. "Since I can't read your emotions, you're really going to have to start expressing them more on your face. Or at least give me a hand gesture or something."

Julian grins. "I'm not one to show a lot of emotion. If you had been raised around me like the others, you would be used to the way I am."

"But I wasn't," I point out. "If I could still read you, it wouldn't be such a big problem, but I can't. So you're going to have to work with me here and learn how to be more expressive. If you don't, I'm going to go insane. It's already hard enough to be around you without my empathic abilities telling me how you feel. I can't imagine a whole lifetime of living this way with you."

"All right," he concedes. "I'll try to be more expressive, but only if you do something for me in return."

"What?" I ask hesitantly.

"Tell your friend Kaylee about me tomorrow."

"What's the rush?"

"The sooner you assimilate me into your life, the sooner we can break up and say we've decided to just be good friends. By then, we will have established our connection to one another, and you'll be free to find someone else."

"Oh, yeah, you need me to get knocked up so you can have an heir." I know I sound hostile, like a petulant teenager even, but I can't help it. I don't like the fact he expects me to find someone to fall in love with just so I can satisfy his heir quota.

"There's no reason to make it sound so dirty, Sarah." He frowns at me in disappointment. Well, at least it was an expression I could read. "It's simply the way things have been done over the years. Don't you want to find a man to fall in love with?"

"Who doesn't want to fall in love? I just didn't realize the time table for finding true love would be shortened for me."

"I have no intention of rushing you," he says, sounding offended by my statement. "But women your age generally already have a man in mind for marriage. You seem unconcerned that you don't."

"I have my reasons," I mumble, finishing the last morsel of chocolate cake on my plate.

Julian studies me for a moment before gently asking, "Would you like to talk about it?"

I look up at him and see sincere concern in his eyes for me.

I shake my head. "Not really."

"If you ever need someone to talk to, I'm always here for you, Sarah. We are a permanent part of each other's lives now."

I know his words are true and that I can trust Julian with my life and my secrets. I'm just not sure if he'll understand how much starting a family of my own scares me.

CHAPTER 5.

After I finish eating the slice of cake, I begin to feel sleepy again. Julian reassures me that it's normal for a newly-made companion to require a lot of sleep and escorts me back to the bedroom I slept in before.

"You should think of this room as yours," he tells me, leaning against the doorway as I make my way over to the bed. "In fact, you should think of this house as your home while we're here."

I was pulling back the covers on the bed, but his statement quickly brings me upright again. "What do you mean by 'while we're here'?"

"Eventually, we'll need to move away from this city. People will begin to wonder why Helen and I aren't aging if we stay here for more than ten years."

"I don't want to leave. This town is my home."

"We have no choice, Sarah. It's something we have to do to keep people from asking too many questions."

I know he's right, and that I'm probably being unreasonable, but did he really expect me to be happy about leaving everything I know and the people I love?

"I can come back for visits, though, right?" *At least give me that*, I pray.

"I'm sure we can arrange something for you." Even though he seems hesitant to concede even that much leeway, I'm glad he does. Otherwise, we might have ended up in a very heated argument.

I'm not about to leave my family behind just because he needs to suck my blood!

"Sleep well, Sarah," he says, pushing himself off the doorframe. "I'll see you when you wake up."

After he shuts the door, I crawl underneath the covers and try to get comfortable. I can still feel Julian's closeness. He hasn't gone very far. In fact, I'm pretty sure I heard him walk into the room right beside mine.

I snuggle up underneath the white comforter and fall asleep before Julian's bombshell can bother me anymore.

Sometime later, I'm awoken by the sound of a person humming close by. Before I even open my eyes, I know someone else is in the bed with me and that it isn't Julian.

When I open my eyes, I find a man lying on the other side of the mattress, raised up on one of his elbows and staring at me. He's handsome with olive-colored skin, lavender eyes, and short chestnut-brown hair that's slightly long on top and moussed to male model perfection. His face is triangular, with sharp predatory features. Facial hair covers the bottom half of his face, showing he hasn't shaved in at least a couple of days. It's long enough to be attractive, but not so long that it resembles a true beard and mustache. He's dressed in a black short-sleeve knit shirt and white jeans. If I were to make an educated guess, I would put his age at around thirty.

"Hello," he says with a rakish grin and a mischievous twinkle in his eyes.

I sit straight up in bed, holding the covers to my chest like a shield as if they'll protect me from the man.

"Who are you?" I ask, taking a quick reading of his feelings. He's having fun. I get the distinct impression he's gaining pleasure by surprising me with his unexpected appearance. There isn't any malice in his action, just a sort of adolescent enjoyment in being able to startle me.

He stands up from the bed and bows to me, one arm sweeping the air before him in a flourish.

"I am Adrian Costel. And you must be Sarah Marcel." He stands straight again and casually leans one shoulder up against the bedpost at the foot of the bed, crossing his arms loosely in front of him. He has a similar accent to Julian's but it's more pronounced, like he hasn't spent as much time in the States as my vampire companion.

"That only tells me your name," I say, feeling irritated. "It doesn't really tell me who you are."

Adrian smiles. "True."

"So, who are you?" I ask again.

"He's someone who shouldn't be in here."

We both look to the now-open doorway of the room and see Julian standing there, a murderous look on his face.

Adrian pushes himself off the bedpost and shrugs at Julian.

"I simply wanted to meet the newest addition to our happy little troupe. She's not like the others you've had, even if they all come from the same bloodline."

"You need to leave, Adrian." The forceful way Julian says his words makes them sound more like a threat than a request.

Adrian looks back at me and winks. "I'll be seeing you, Sarah."

He walks out of the room, feeling pleased with himself. I get the feeling he accomplished what he set out to do: annoy Julian.

Julian strolls to the foot of the bed, maintaining the scowl on his face. I know he isn't upset with me even without my empathic abilities telling me how he's feeling.

"Who is Adrian?" I ask, hoping Julian will be more cooperative than the subject of my question was.

"He is one of the pure-blooded vampires I told you about."

"Why is he here?"

"Visiting." Julian spits out the word in total disgust. "He's on his way to see my sister in New Orleans, but he chose to stop here when he felt my presence. Basically, he decided to stick his nose into my personal affairs."

"Felt your presence? You can feel where the other vampires are?"

"Yes, if we're in close enough proximity to one another. Generally, we have to be within a fifty-mile radius for it to work."

"You never mentioned that your sister lives in New Orleans."

"She's lived there for a few years now."

"Are the two of you close?"

"We used to be, in the beginning. When you've lived as long as we have, staying in touch becomes less important. We haven't seen each other for almost a hundred years, not since the last conclave."

"That's the second time you've mentioned a conclave," I say. "What sort of meeting is that?"

"Once every hundred years or so, we vampires come together to see who is still left alive and to discuss anything noteworthy."

"Where do you meet?"

"It varies. My sister is normally in charge of inviting everyone. She either invites us to the town she's living in at the time or another neutral location somewhere in the world."

"If it's been that long since you last saw your sister, you must be having another conclave soon?"

"Yes, very soon."

"I suppose I'll need to go to it." It isn't a question. I know I will need to go with Julian. If he's going to be in a meeting with others of his kind, he'll need to be as strong as he can be.

"Wherever I go, you must go," he says. His statement isn't an order, just the reality of our situation.

"I have a job," I tell him. "We're on summer break right now, so it's not a big deal to travel, but I think you need to know I intend to keep working. If you want to make travel plans, you'll need to arrange them around my schedule from now on."

"What do you do?"

"I'm the biology teacher at the local junior high school."

"I see." The corners of Julian's mouth twitch like I've said something that amuses him. Why can't he smile more often? He looks so handsome when he lets himself relax.

"Something funny about me working?" I ask.

"No, it's admirable," he replies. "How old are you? Twenty-three?"

"Yes, my birthday was the night you found me at the nightclub. We were out celebrating it."

"I see." He seems pleased because he lets himself grin. "So you don't make it a habit of drinking and dancing at clubs with total strangers?"

"No, that was all Kaylee's idea. I think she hoped I would meet someone there. It's her mission in life to have me at least engaged, if not married, before my next birthday."

Julian's smile falters a bit. He puts on his emotionless mask again, like he's trying to hide something from me. Or, does he do that even when he's hiding his own emotions from himself?

"Helen thought you might want to shower and change your clothes," he tells me, effectively shifting the subject of our conversation to something else as he nods to the chair by the window.

Lying across the back of it is a plain white T-shirt on top of a pair of blue jeans.

"She put some toiletries and undergarments in the bathroom for you also. After you get ready, come down to the kitchen. I'm sure you're hungry again."

As he leaves the room, he shuts the door behind him before I can give a proper salute. Sometimes he sounds just like a drill sergeant: *do this, do that.* I can only assume he's used to telling the people around him what to do. Something will definitely have to be done about that.

Helen seems to have thought of everything I need. She bought me items for my shower (shampoo, soap, razor, shaving cream) and girly essentials I normally use to get ready with (makeup, hair dryer, curling iron, hairspray, mousse, and deodorant). Apparently, she even made a trip to Victoria's Secret to buy me some panties and bras. I definitely owe her one.

After having slept in the same clothes for two and a half days, my body is in desperate need of a good cleaning and grooming. A little over a half hour later I walk downstairs, smelling a lot fresher than when I woke up. I find Julian and Helen in the kitchen. Julian is looking out the windows by the French doors that lead out onto the patio at the back of the house. Glancing outside I see Adrian, now dressed in a pair of white swimming trunks, lying on a lounge chair, soaking up the summer sun by the pool. There is also another man outside I haven't met yet. He's lean and of average height, with shaggy light-brown hair. He isn't as handsome as either Julian or Adrian, but he's cute in an athletic, soccer player kind of way.

"Well, I'm glad everything fits," Helen says approvingly as she eyes me in my new outfit. She's standing behind the kitchen island, stirring up a bowl of what looks like freshly made potato salad.

Julian ends his pensive ruminations and turns away from the window to look at me. I can feel his eyes traveling over me from head to toe and have to wonder what he's thinking. Feeling uncomfortable under his scrutiny, I start to fidget with my hair self-consciously.

"Thank you for buying me all that stuff," I tell Helen, forcing my eyes to look in hers and not at the bowl in her hands. I know if I look at it, I'll probably start salivating like a rabid dog.

How can I still be hungry? I ate more that morning than I usually do in a whole week! At this rate, I'm going to weigh a ton by the end of the month.

"If you ever need anything, just ask," she says with a wink and small smile of satisfaction. She sticks the spoon she was using to mix the potato salad with in the middle of it and slides the bowl over to me across the counter of the island.

"Go on," she says grinning wider. "I made it for you. There's no need to be shy about eating around here. You're going to need your strength."

I can't help myself. I pick the bowl up and hold it in front of me with one arm wrapped around it and the other hand eagerly lifting the spoon to my mouth. Thank goodness Helen is a good cook.

I walk over to where Julian is standing and can feel how tense his body is as he returns his attention to the two men outside.

"You don't like him very much, do you?" I ask, looking out the window at Adrian.

"He's not my favorite person in the world," Julian admits, staring pointedly at the cause of his tension.

"Why? Is he one of the bad ones you mentioned?" I remembered Julian speaking about the vampires who chose to feed on humans rather than their chosen companions.

Julian sighs. "No. He hasn't gone that far yet," he concedes. "But I feel like it's only a matter of time with him."

"Is that the person he's bonded to?" I ask, nodding to the man I haven't been introduced to yet. We both watch him walk to the edge of the pool and dive into the clear blue water with his arms stretched over his head.

"Yes. Hhis name is Daniel Bartran."

"So why is Adrian going to see your sister? Are they friends?"

The corner of Julian's mouth twitches up, like I've said something amusing.

"I suppose you could call them that. They're occasional lovers."

"Oh." I slowly turn my back to the window and walk over to the kitchen table. I set my bowl down and pull out a chair to sit in. I do my best not to show how embarrassed I feel for inadvertently asking such a personal question about people I don't really know. I guess I didn't turn away fast enough for Julian not to notice.

"There's nothing to be embarrassed about, Sarah. Having sex is a normal, physically gratifying thing for two people to engage in, human or vampire." He says the word 'sex' so casually, like it's no big deal. It's a big deal to me. I don't view it as a recreational tool like some people seem to. I actually need to love the person I share my body with.

"That's certainly true," Helen chimes in, leaning her hip against the kitchen island as she looks over at me. "I can remember when Julian and I first started having sex. It was glorious for those first ten years, but after that it became a bit stale."

I nearly choke on the potato salad in my mouth. I quickly swallow before I spew it halfway across the kitchen table.

"Ok," I say, trying to catch my breath, "that's way too much information for me. Can we please change the subject?"

"Oh come, dear," Helen says with a wave of her hand in my direction. "There's nothing wrong with talking about sex with family. Like Julian said, it's a natural thing to happen between two people, especially when they've been together for as long as he and I have."

I try my best to wipe the image of Julian and Helen in a compromising position out of my mind to no avail. I know she's probably talking about events that happened when she was younger, but picturing them as they are now, doing the deed together, is like a bad porn movie running inside my mind. I hunch my shoulders and hang my head over the half-eaten bowl of potato salad in a vain attempt to rid my thoughts of unwanted visions.

Then the strangest thing happens. Julian actually laughs. He's standing in the same spot by the windows when I look up at him. This time it's my turn to scowl. I know he's laughing at my reaction to the image of him and Helen *in flagrante*. I try to ignore him as I look back down at my bowl and continue to eat. At least it gives me time to think of something to change the direction of the conversation. Julian's laughter soon subsides into soft chuckles, giving me an opportunity to ask a question.

"Am I going to get fat?" I ask. It's a real worry. I hate shopping for clothes, but if I keep eating at this rate, that's what I'll end up having to do.

"No. You shouldn't gain any weight. In fact, you may lose some if you don't eat enough," Julian answers, still wearing an amused grin on his face when I look back at him. He knows what I'm doing. At least he isn't trying to embarrass me by calling me out on my quick change of conversation.

"Why am I so hungry?" I finally ask. It's a question I meant to ask that morning, but just couldn't stop myself from eating long enough to ask it.

"Your body is changing, becoming stronger," Julian answers. "Plus, your body knows it needs to store up more energy to make more blood for me to drink each day."

"How does it know to do that?"

He shrugs. "I haven't got a clue, Sarah. It's just the way things work. I didn't come up with the rules."

I make a mental note to try out this super strength and agility Julian mentioned I would gain from bonding with him. I don't feel particularly strong or agile, but I haven't put it to a test yet either. As soon as I have time, I'll find a private spot and experiment.

"Ah, Sarah, glad to see you up and about."

Adrian walks in through the French doors with Daniel close behind him. Daniel is using a white towel draped around his neck to quickly dry the shaggy brown mop on top of his head.

"Sarah Marcel," Adrian says as the two come to stand in front of me on the other side of the table. Good manners force me to ignore the last two spoons full of potato salad in the bowl and give them my full attention. "I would like you to meet my companion, Daniel Bartran."

Daniel holds his hand out to me. I stand to shake it.

"Nice to meet you," he says with an easy grin. "I'm sorry for the loss of your grandfather. It must have been a shock for you to find out about your connection to our world the way you did."

"I'm still in shock," I confess. "But I'll get used to it." Like I had any choice.

"It'll get better," Daniel says with a wink and a wider smile.

It's one of the first times I actually do feel like things will eventually get back to normal, at least as normal as my new life will allow. I immediately like Daniel. I have a feeling he and I will become friends given enough time. Plus, he has the added benefit of being one of the few people my empathic ability doesn't have to work overtime deciphering. A lot of people go through myriad emotions in a very short timeframe because their thoughts jump from one subject to the next so quickly. Daniel is one of the few people, like Kaylee, who seem to be in a perpetually good mood. I never asked, but I figured Kaylee was someone who actually did dream about cute little puppies and magical rainbows. That's the feeling I get from Daniel. He's a happy person most of the time, never one to be sad for long if he can help it.

"I've just had a brilliant idea!" Adrian says excitedly as he looks over at Julian. "Why don't we mate Daniel and Sarah?"

I'm not sure whose cheeks turn redder, mine or Daniel's. Poor Helen ends up dropping the cookie sheet in her hand, making an awful metallic clatter against the tile floor in the ensuing silence of the kitchen. Thankfully, it wasn't filled with cookies. That would have been a waste of good cooking.

"*Excuse me?*" I say to Adrian, unable to hide the incredulity I feel. "You do realize we're both standing right here in front of you, don't you?"

Adrian shrugs nonchalantly. "It's not like it hasn't ever been done before. Besides, Julian said you don't have a boyfriend, and Daniel hasn't been able to produce an heir for me yet," he sighs, clearly disappointed in his human companion's failings. "Why not have the two of you get together? It would solve all our problems. Besides, females who have been newly bonded are extremely fertile. I'm sure you could have two children within a two-year time period if you really put your minds and bodies into it."

Julian comes to stand by my side. "They're not cattle, Adrian. I won't have you making suggestions like that about Sarah. She isn't yours."

Ok, suddenly I feel like a piece of meat. The way Julian said his last statement made it sound like he considers me his property, not his companion. I decide not to berate him for his choice of words in front of Adrian and Daniel, though. It just doesn't seem like the right time to have that particular conversation.

"It was just a suggestion." Adrian shrugs again, like it isn't a big deal to him either way. "I'm sure Daniel wouldn't mind doing it for me. Sarah's quite attractive." Adrian looks me up and down, making me feel cheap. Well, at least I met with his approval as a mating partner for his pet human.

"Stop it, Adrian," Daniel whispers, turning his head toward his vampire, imploring him with his eyes to end the subject. "I think you've embarrassed us both enough for one day."

"Fine, I'll drop it. But I'll leave the offer open if you change your mind, Sarah."

I sense Julian's body tense up like a compressed spring. It feels as though he's getting ready to pounce on Adrian and beat him to death for making his lewd suggestion. A defusing of the situation seems to be in order.

"Thank you for offering Daniel up to me like a sacrificial lamb," I tell Adrian snidely. "But I think he and I can make up our own minds when it comes to how far we might want our relationship to go. You certainly don't have to pimp him out to me."

Adrian laughs and Daniel smiles at me. I feel Julian calm down a smidge, but I don't even have to look at him to know he's still scowling at Adrian.

"I get the hint," Adrian says, still chuckling. "I'm sorry if I sounded crude. It wasn't my intention. I just thought it would be a solution that would satisfy everyone." Adrian looks over to Helen. "Daniel said he was hungry. When will supper be ready?"

"Give me half an hour," Helen replies tersely, picking her cookie sheet up off the floor.

"Then we'll see you both a little later." Adrian bows in my direction before he heads down the hallway and up the stairs. I assume he's going to his room.

"I should go take a bath," Daniel says to me. "See you in a few, Sarah." He grins at me shyly before following the same path as Adrian.

I turn to look at Julian. Sure enough, there's a scowl on his face. He's staring at the empty doorway that Adrian and Daniel just departed through.

I'm not sure what cosmic intuition comes over me next, but I suddenly realize exactly what I need to do. I raise my hand to his temple and run my thumb across the wrinkles of frustration on his forehead, trying to erase them. Julian quickly looks down at me like he isn't used to being touched so casually.

"You shouldn't let him bother you," I whisper, lowering my hand to cradle his cheek against the warmth of my palm.

"I know," he murmurs, not pulling away from my caress like I feared he would. "I didn't appreciate him making you sound like a breeding animal."

I can't help but smile. Maybe he's starting to care about me a small bit. I let my hand drop back to my side.

"I can handle Adrian," I say confidently.

"I'm beginning to think you can handle anything." Julian almost smiles but it doesn't quite make it. He looks in my eyes with an intensity I've never seen in anyone else before. I can't tell what he's thinking or feeling, but it seems like we've crossed an imaginary barrier that was separating us. I know I can count on Julian to protect me, and I think he realizes now that I will always be loyal to him no matter what happens. Perhaps it was the final stage of the bonding between us. I'm not sure. All I do know is that we are a part of each other now, for as long as I live.

CHAPTER 6.

I stay in the kitchen to help Helen prepare supper. It seems only right to lend a hand since she's doing so much work to keep me fed. Julian excuses himself from our company and leaves the house without telling us where he's going or when he'll be back. Strangely enough, I know the moment that he leaves. His absence makes my chest feel like it's being ripped open, creating a void that only his presence can fill. How in the world will I ever be able to function normally again if I have to suffer through this excruciating emptiness every time we're apart? I can't prevent a heavy sigh from escaping my lips as I long for his swift return.

"He feels it, too," Helen says, obviously having heard my reaction to Julian's departure. She's stirring a pot full of some sort of oyster stew to go with the shrimp and crawdads she brought home for our supper. "He won't be gone long," she reassures me.

I try to busy myself by cutting up a tomato for a garden salad. Even with the distraction, I find it nearly impossible to concentrate on my task. For some odd reason, I can't get the thought of Helen and Julian being lovers out of my mind.

"So how does it work?" I finally ask her. "How does Julian's blood enable you to live for so long? He let you drink it and *Voilà*, you were granted the ability to live an extra five hundred years?"

"It wasn't quite that simple," she says, putting the cover back on the stockpot and turning her full attention to me. "I was almost dead when he found me. Some men attacked me on my way home one evening and left me for dead in a back alley after they each had their way with me. I'm sure I would have died if Julian had been one second later."

"Oh my gosh, Helen," I say in shock. "I'm so sorry that happened to you."

"Well," she says, continuing to stir the stew, "sometimes the worst thing that can happen to you leads to something wonderfully unexpected."

"Julian told me you were the only human he's ever changed. Why do you think that is?"

"I don't believe he views living forever as a blessing. The heartache of losing your loved ones can be unbearable at times." Helen tilts her head slightly as she looks over at me. "Although, I've noticed a change in him since the two of you bonded."

"A good or bad change?" I ask apprehensively, looking up at her from the cutting board.

Helen smiles. "Good. I can't tell you how long it's been since I heard him laugh, a couple of centuries at least. I have no doubt whatsoever that the two of you will be good for one another."

I silently debate with myself whether I should ask Helen what I really want to know. It's none of my business, of course, but if I'm going to be living in the same house as them, it seems like a reasonable question to ask.

"So, are you and Julian a couple?"

Helen burst out laughing as if I've said the funniest thing ever. After she catches her breath, she replies, "I'm sorry. I shouldn't have laughed so hard at an honest and sincere question. It's just that we haven't had that type of relationship in hundreds of years. The first ten years we spent together were wonderful, I'll admit, but I finally realized Julian didn't love me. He never had. To be honest, I'm not even sure any of the vampires have the capacity to truly give their heart to someone anymore. It seems like being turned into what they are meant they had to lose that part of themselves. I left him when I realized he would never be able to care for me the same way I did him." As Helen reminisces about the past, I can feel how sad she is reliving those memories. "I remember hoping I was wrong about Julian's feelings for me and praying he would track me down and beg for my return to his side, but he never did. I eventually found a man who truly could love me with all his heart. We married, but weren't able to conceive children. Now I know that what Julian did to save my life also caused me to be unable to bring new life into the world. That's why they never give their companions their blood to drink. It would irrevocably end the bloodline and doom them to a limited time on Earth. Anyway, John and I were together until his last dying breath, and I haven't loved anyone else since. I doubt I ever will. I think a love like ours only comes once in a person's life."

I feel a selfish relief from hearing Helen's words. For some reason, I don't want her and Julian to be lovers or have any kind of romantic involvement with one another.

"When and why did you return to Julian?" I ask, curious to know how she ended up being his housekeeper.

"After John died, I didn't have anyone else. It can be a terribly lonely existence living for so long by yourself. I eventually found Julian again and decided to stay with him until I die and can be reunited with my John in the afterlife. Since I returned, I've helped each generation of your family raise the heir who would eventually bond with Julian, except for you of course."

"Are you sorry Julian gave you his blood?" I ask.

Helen gives her shoulders a little shrug. "Things are the way they are. I can't change them. I'm not even sure I would if given the opportunity. Without Julian doing what he did for me, I never would have met John or experienced the best years of my life. Sometimes things happen for reasons we can't fully comprehend when they occur. All we can do is live and see where the future takes us."

After hearing her words, I know that's what I'll have to do. Wait and see where my future with Julian will go.

Helen and I prepare the dining room table for supper that evening. I get the feeling we're eating our meal in there because of the presence of our guests. For the most part, I bet we'll normally eat together in the kitchen when it's just us.

Helen informs me that she bought some more clothes for me if I want to change for supper. I take her suggestion as a subtle hint that my T-shirt and jeans ensemble aren't suitable attire for the evening meal. She tells me the clothes are hanging in the wardrobe inside my room.

I go up to my bedroom and search through the clothes Helen purchased. I have to admit Helen has excellent fashion sense. She even bought me matching shoes for most of the outfits. I can only assume she bought them during the last couple of days while I was sleeping. I choose a simple black-and-white-print cotton dress with solid black shoulder straps and banded hem with inverted pleats around the waist. A pair of simple black heels helps complete the look.

I curl my hair and put on a little extra makeup to enhance my features. For some reason, I want Julian to be proud to call me his companion in front of the others. When Julian returns to the house, the tear in my heart immediately stitches itself back together. I hear him walk into the room beside mine, making me almost giddy with happiness that he's back home. I find it odd how just his presence can make me feel content, and wonder if this is how people who are in love react when they're around one another. I know I'm not in love with Julian. Nevertheless, I think the analogy is a sound one.

When I step out of my room to go downstairs, Julian walks out of his room at the same exact moment. I turn to face him and feel my heart skip a beat when I see how handsome he looks. He's dressed in a pair of well-tailored black slacks and a long sleeve white button-down shirt unbuttoned at the collar.

He turns his head to look in my direction and allows his eyes to travel the length of me in a non-critical way.

"You look nice this evening, Sarah," he says, walking up to me and holding out his arm for me to take. "Shall we go down to entertain our guests?"

I slide my arm through his and follow him down the stairs and into the dining room.

Adrian and Daniel are already present. They're standing beside one of the windows in the room, having a hushed conversation. They stop talking as soon as they see us. I can tell Daniel is feeling embarrassed, and Adrian is feeling smug. I can only wonder what that's all about.

Daniel smiles at me, genuinely pleased to see me again so soon. He strolls up to Julian and me as we walk further into the room.

"You look beautiful, Sarah," he says, taking my free hand with his and bowing to kiss it.

"Thank you." I can't help the small blush that appears on my cheeks. I'm not used to being complimented. Generally, I stay away from people in social situations. It's made me a bit of an introvert, but I don't think there's anything wrong with that. For the most part, people don't appear that bad on the outside, but having a direct line to their emotions has always given me a fuller picture of their true nature. A lot of men judge you on the basis of whether they want to have sex with you, and most women compare you to themselves in a vain attempt to judge which of you is smarter or more attractive. Being judged is an uncomfortable feeling, which is why I make it a general rule not to socialize much.

I feel Julian drop his arm to his side. At first I think he's simply letting me go so I can take my seat, but then I feel him grab my hand with his and twine our fingers together, showing a certain intimacy between us that doesn't actually exist with the gesture. I look up at him and notice that he's staring at Daniel with an almost hostile expression. Surely he isn't still mad about earlier. Besides, that wasn't Daniel's fault. It was Adrian who made the vulgar suggestion that Daniel and I should have children together to satisfy both of their heir needs.

Daniel must notice Julian's expression as well. He immediately lets go of my hand and turns to walk to the other side of the table to take his place on the right of Adrian. Julian pulls out my chair for me at the table. Reluctantly, he lets go of my hand to help me push it back up. Both vampires sit at the ends of the table with Daniel and me sitting to their right. Helen soon appears with a cart filled with eight large bowls of food. She places four of them directly in front of Daniel and the remaining four in front of me. One bowl is full of shrimp and crawdads. One is filled to the brim with the oyster stew she prepared earlier, and one has the garden salad I helped her make. The last bowl is filled with Helen's signature, and delectable, yeast rolls.

"I picked these up for you, too," she says, handing plastic bibs to Daniel and me. "The lady at the counter said those crawdads might make a mess, and I didn't think you would want to ruin your clothes."

We thank Helen for her thoughtfulness before she leaves the room. Neither of us is shy when it comes to eating, and we immediately begin to dig into our meal with gusto. I can't believe I'm already hungry again. Absently, I notice that Helen didn't leave anything for Julian and Adrian to eat. I assume that means they don't eat real food, just the blood of their human companion.

"What's in the soup?" Adrian asks, sniffing the air and raising his head a notch to peer into Daniel's bowl.

"Oysters mostly," Daniel replies, taking a spoonful into his mouth.

"Ahh, oysters," Adrian nods his head as if he heartily approves of the ingredient. "I've often heard they make a powerful aphrodisiac." Adrian smiles down the table at me.

Ok…hint taken…

I smile back at him. "I think you're supposed to eat them raw, not cooked, in order to raise the libido."

"Really?" Adrian replies, leaning forward slightly in his chair. "Do you know a lot about aphrodisiacs, dear Sarah?"

"Not really, I'm just full of useless information. I watched too much TV as a child."

Adrian chuckles and Daniel smiles, continuing to eat his harmless oyster stew.

I chance a glance in Julian's direction as I bring my next spoonful of soup to my mouth. The only expression I see on his face is a slight narrowing of his eyes in Adrian's direction.

Adrian starts up a conversation with Julian in what I can only assume is Hungarian. I don't understand a word of it and decide to concentrate on eating my meal. I have the soup eaten in no time at all and notice Daniel switch bowls just as I do. We both choose the salad next. Almost at the same time, we bring our bread bowl and shrimp and crawdad bowl in front of us. I can't help but smile. I look over at Daniel.

"I bet I can finish mine before you do," I challenge.

He smiles back. "You're on, little lady."

It's the first time I notice the change in my agility. I'm able to manipulate the shells off the shrimp and heads and tails off the crawdads so quickly my eyes are having a hard time keeping up with what my hands are doing. Unfortunately, I don't win. Daniel finishes literally two seconds before I do.

"I win!" he says, raising his hands in victory as if he just completed the Tour de France in record time.

"Only because you've had more practice with this super agility thing," I tell him, begrudgingly admitting defeat.

"Don't be a sore loser," Daniel says with a quick wink in my direction as he picks up the napkin from his lap to wipe the juices and seasoning off his hands.

"I'm not," I answer back. "In fact, since you won, I'll take you to the kitchen and make you a banana split. I'm pretty sure I saw everything we need for those in there earlier."

"Well, I can't pass that up." Daniel immediately scoots his chair out from the table and stands.

I guess it isn't until then that I notice how quiet our vampire companions have become. I look over at Julian and see him watching me with a guarded expression.

"Enjoy your dessert," is all he says to me.

"We will," I reply. I feel as though I've done something wrong in his eyes, but I don't have a clue what it is.

As I wait for Daniel to come to my side of the table so we can walk to the kitchen together, I glance at Adrian and see his mouth stretch into a gloating grin. He's happy to see a blossoming friendship develop between Daniel and me. I'm sure he hopes we'll become even more than that to one another.

I lead Daniel down the hallway to the kitchen. Helen is wiping the counters down as her last task to make the kitchen spotlessly clean.

"Done already?" she asks flabbergasted, looking at the clock on the microwave oven to check the time. "Did I not prepare enough?"

"There was plenty," I assure her, opening the freezer compartment and finding the box of Neapolitan ice cream I spied earlier while I was helping to prepare the salads. "We just thought it was time for dessert."

I grab a couple of bananas from the fruit bowl by the refrigerator.

"Well, I guess I had better go get your dirty dishes. Then I'll be through for the evening."

"Let me help you with that," Daniel offers.

It's just as well. By the time I have our banana splits ready, Daniel and Helen have the dirty dishes back and in the dishwasher.

Our desserts turn out much larger than I had originally planned. I end up using three bananas each. I split the carton of Neapolitan right down the middle and decorate my creations with chocolate syrup, caramel syrup, maraschino cherries, nuts, and whipped cream. They almost look like one of those desserts at roadside cafés where they dare you to eat it all in one sitting for a free meal.

We decide to eat our sinfully delicious banana splits out on the patio at the table by the pool.

Daniel holds my chair out for me just like Julian did at supper. After he sits down and takes his first bite of the ice cream, he moans in pleasure.

"There's nothing better than eating things so chock full of calories that they would make regular people scream and run away in disgust."

"So, they weren't just pulling my leg?" I ask. "I won't gain any weight from eating all this food?"

"Nope, not an ounce; isn't it wonderful?" He smiles like a kid who was given the keys to a candy store before shoving another spoonful of ice cream into his mouth.

I can't help but laugh at him. We both become distracted with wanting to finish our ice cream as soon as we can. I think it only takes us about five minutes to clean our bowls. Daniel sits back in his seat and rubs his slightly bulging belly gratifyingly.

"That was just what I needed. Thank you, Sarah."

"You're most welcome, Daniel." I sit back in my chair and tilt my head back far enough to look up at the stars in the sky. It's a brilliantly clear summer night. The stars twinkle above us like diamonds encrusting a tapestry.

I feel Daniel's eyes on me so I continue to stare up at the sky, curious to see where his emotions go. I know he's happy. But I assume that's just from the feeling of being satisfied by all the food we just ate. He also seems curious. I can only guess he wants to know more about me and how I'm coping with a world he was probably raised in. If I'm being honest, I'm curious about Daniel, too.

Then his feelings betray him. Like a lot of men, he has a moment of lust. I'm flattered, but I don't want him to get any misleading ideas about me. With all the talk Adrian did earlier about mating the two of us, it's no wonder Daniel's thoughts turn to sex. I reason that it's only a natural response to the events of the day. He probably isn't genuinely interested in me that way, but the idea of us becoming lovers has been planted in his mind. The power of suggestion can be a hard one to resist.

I sit up straighter in my chair and look over at Daniel.

"So where do you and Adrian live?" I ask, attempting to get his mind to switch gears.

"We've lived a lot of places. At the moment, we have a home in New York City. It's easier to keep a low profile in cities as large as that one. There are so many people there hardly anyone pays much attention to you unless you want them to."

Unexpectedly, I feel Julian leave the house again. I close my eyes against the pain that forms inside my chest and let out a heavy sigh in disappointment. How often does he intend to leave me like this?

"I hate it when he does that," I say, unconsciously touching my chest, feeling as though a piece of it has just been unceremoniously ripped out again.

"Julian left?" Daniel asks in surprise, already having surmised the cause for my distress.

I open my eyes and nod. "Do you feel empty inside when you're away from Adrian?"

"We all get that feeling. I think it's meant to keep us close to one another."

"Well, it's certainly effective." I tried to keep the frustration I'm feeling out of my voice, but I know I failed miserably.

"You'll get used to it after a while," Daniel tries to reassure me. "It's always more painful right after the bonding ceremony."

If Julian knows how his leaving can affect me, why does he keep doing it? Maybe he doesn't care about me at all. If he did, he wouldn't intentionally hurt me this way. I hope what Daniel said is right because I really do want to keep my teaching position. But if being away from Julian continues to feel this torturous, I'm not sure that'll be possible.

"Mind if I ask you a personal question?" Daniel asks, looking at me shyly.

"Ask away," I reply, considering myself an open book. There isn't much in my life that I try to hide from people. Although, with the introduction of Julian into my life, that will inevitably have to change. Now, I do have something that I have to keep secret, even from the ones I love.

"Would you want to go out on a date with me sometime?"

Uh-oh.

"Is this you asking or Adrian asking?"

Daniel grins. "I'm the one asking. I already told Adrian to get those ideas out of his head. But I can't help it if he's put some into mine."

"I don't know, Daniel..." Right away, I realize I have the perfect out of this awkward situation. "Julian and I are planning to tell all my friends that we're dating. That way we can introduce him into my life naturally. I don't think it would be a good idea to date two guys at once. It would just be too out of character for me. I'm pretty sure my friends would get suspicious."

Daniel hangs his head. "And she lets me down easy with the ol' 'my vampire is my boyfriend' excuse."

I know he's sincerely disappointed but he chooses to blow it off as a joke, which is fine with me. I don't want this conversation to get too serious. I want to keep Daniel at arm's length and just as a friend for now, nothing more. All I need in my life are more complications.

"I'm flattered that you asked," I tell him, which is the truth. I don't get asked out much, which is probably my own fault. I just don't socialize enough to get asked out. Daniel is someone I would have tried dating if the circumstances were different.

I feel Julian return home and know he's close by. I glance in the direction of the pool house and see him standing in the shadows beside it, watching Daniel and me. Normally, I would have felt creeped out by someone hiding in the dark, watching me. But I feel oddly protected by Julian's voyeurism. Plus, he has to realize I know he's there. Why is he hiding?

"Thank you for letting me down easy," Daniel says. "Can we hang out together occasionally? I have a feeling Adrian plans to stay in New Orleans for a while. It would be nice to have a friend to do things with from time to time."

"I would like that. Besides, you never know where friendship can lead."

At least that gets a big smile out of my new friend.

"Very true," he agrees.

I feel Julian leave again. I can only assume he flew away because of the suddenness of his departure and the distance he's able to cross in such a short amount of time. I'm not sure why, but I get the feeling Julian doesn't like me spending time with Daniel. I know he probably heard us with his 'super hearing'. Why my making a new friend would upset him, I have no idea.

"Daniel!" we hear Adrian call from the direction of the house. "I'm hungry!"

Daniel looks over at me and rolls his eyes. "Nothing like being treated like a traveling blood bag," he quips but stands from his chair. He picks up his empty bowl. "I guess I'll see you tomorrow, Sarah. I normally just end up falling asleep after he takes what he wants from me."

"Sweet dreams, Daniel," I say, feeling sorry for my new friend and the tense relationship he seems to have with his vampire companion.

Daniel walks back to the house, but I stay put. I don't particularly want to have to exchange pleasantries with Adrian. I would much rather just ignore his existence.

I remain outside for well over half an hour, hoping to feel Julian's return. When he doesn't come back to the house, I pick up my empty bowl and walk back into the kitchen. I find Helen sitting at the table with a cup of tea in one hand and the local newspaper in the other. She looks up at me and smiles, but I just don't have the will to lie about how I truly feel.

"Why isn't he here?" I ask her as I stand stock-still, on the verge of tears over Julian's absence.

"Oh dear," she says, standing from her seat and coming over to take the empty bowl out of my hand. "Why don't you sit down? I'll make you a cup of tea."

Like a zombie, I do as she asks because I honestly don't have a better idea of how to spend my time.

After Helen brings me a cup of the same tea she's drinking, she sits back down in her chair.

"Doesn't he know how much I need him right now?" I ask her as unwelcome tears begin to blur my vision. I hate crying, but I find that I can't stop myself from doing it in this situation.

"I don't know what's going through his mind right now," Helen admits with a shake of her head in disappointment. "He's never left a newly-made companion before."

"Is there something wrong with me?" I sob, unable to control what are essentially irrepressible feelings. I've never felt this vulnerable before in my life. It's all strange to me, and I know the one person who should care that I'm hurting this much doesn't seem to care at all. Julian's indifference to my suffering is what hurts me the most. He obviously isn't concerned about the pain he's causing me, but I don't know how to fix that. I don't even know if it can be fixed.

"Selfish git," I hear Helen mumble under her breath as she stands from her chair and walks over to give me a hug. "Don't you worry, my dear, I'm going to give him an earful when he finally does show his ungrateful face around here again. He knows how much you're giving up to become his companion. He should be showing you more respect than this, that's for sure!"

I allow myself to cry while Helen does her best to comfort me. I'm grateful to hear her take up for my feelings, and wonder what my life would have been like if she had helped raise me. I can well imagine us being good friends.

Once I pull myself together, I tell her that I'm exhausted and just need to get some sleep. It's mostly true, but I also just want to work through my feelings in solitude. I feel like I'm acting irrationally. I've never been one to cry at the drop of a hat, but there doesn't seem to be anything I can do about it.

"Some rest will do you good," she agrees. "And don't fret about Julian. He'll come home soon. I know he will."

I walk up to my room and find a pair of pajamas already laid out for me on my bed. I silently thank Helen for her thoughtfulness. I'm certain Julian didn't do it. To him, I'm just an afterthought.

After I change clothes and slip into bed, the emptiness of not having Julian close by overwhelms me again. I feel betrayed. I feel unloved and uncared for by him. The one person in the world who is supposed to care for and protect me has chosen not to be there when I need him the most. The ache inside my chest grows to unbearable proportions, like a heavy weight of despair has completely replaced my heart. I can't prevent the sobs that wrack my body and pierce my soul.

I'm not sure how long I cry: minutes, hours? Finally, I feel his body press against my back as he wraps his arms around me, enveloping me in his warmth. Involuntarily, I turn into him, resting my head on his naked chest but still sobbing.

"I'm sorry, Sarah," he murmurs, running one hand up and down my back in a comforting motion. "I should have come back sooner."

Damn right you should have, I want to scream at him. You shouldn't have left me in the first place, is what I want to say but I can't seem to stop crying long enough to get the words out of my mouth. I'm mad at and happy with him all at the same time. Mad that he left me when I needed him and happy he returned and is holding me in his arms now.

Unexpectedly, he begins to sing to me. I'm not sure what he's saying. It sounds like the language he was speaking in with Adrian. The song has the lilting cadence of a lullaby. Julian isn't the greatest singer in the world, but it doesn't bother me. At least he's showing that he cares, even if it's only a little bit. Could it be that he isn't the heartless wretch I thought he was?

I decide to let go of my anger and cuddle up to him as close as I can get. I begin to hiccup slightly from crying for so long and hard. After a while, I'm finally able to catch my breath. The warmth of Julian's body so close to mine and the way his hand continues to trail along the curve of my back makes me feel more than just comforted. Such close contact begins to arouse certain needs my body has. I immediately try to clear my mind of such thoughts. Julian is my vampire, to take care of for as long as I live. I'm expected to give him an heir to carry on my family's bloodline. I can't just throw all that responsibility out the window because I'm horny.

Yet, what am I supposed to do to curb my desire? What can I do to resolve the situation to my satisfaction?

"Julian," I say in a soft voice as I raise my head from his chest to look in his eyes, "drink from me."

I see a frown form on his face. "I told you we could take that slow, Sarah. I can wait until tomorrow night."

"But I can't," I reply, pulling away from him to lie flat on my back. I pull my long hair away from my neck. "Please," I beg, "drink."

Julian raises himself up on an elbow as he looks at me and considers my request. I fear he's going to refuse my offer, refuse me, but I suppose that was a silly notion. I doubt there are many of his kind who will reject an offer from their companion to feed when they're being begged to do it.

He leans over and gently kisses the base of my neck, tasting the flesh right above my throbbing artery. The warmth of his mouth and the soft, teasing motion of his lips against my skin causes my breathing to become shallow. I lift my hands and cradle his head.

"Drink, Julian," I beg again. This time he doesn't hesitate with gentle foreplay.

The sharpness of his bite causes me to groan in pain, but as I feel him take what he needs from my body I begin to feel a sense of euphoria. The more he drinks the more I want him to drink. As I continue to hold his head to me, I suddenly realize I have all the power in this relationship. He needs me a lot more than I need him, and that knowledge comforts me more than anything else.

"Stop," I order him, feeling his mouth immediately leave my flesh as he lifts his head to look down at me.

In the dim light of the room, I can see the glistening of my blood covering his lips. I begin to wonder what it must taste like to him, and decide there's only one way to find out.

I sit up slightly and lean over until our faces are so close we can each feel the other's breath against our skin. Julian watches me, but gives nothing of his feelings away. In that moment, I don't care what he's feeling. All I want to do is quench my curiosity.

I move my face closer to his and watch his mouth open slightly of its own accord. With one quick flick of my tongue against his lips, I instantly taste my blood. I find it slightly metallic, yet bordering on sweet.

"Do I taste good to you?" I ask him.

He doesn't answer right away. I see him swallow hard before saying, "Yes."

"Have all of your companions tasted like me?"

Again, he doesn't speak for a few seconds before replying, "No. Your blood is sweeter for some reason. I don't know why."

"Hmm, interesting," I reply before lying back down on my pillow.

Julian watches me with a guarded expression. It's the first time I've seen him look uncertain when dealing with me, and I can't help but feel a sense of satisfaction in having confused him.

"Lie down with me until I go to sleep," I order, testing the new dynamic of our relationship.

Without protest Julian does as I say, taking me back into his arms and allowing me to cuddle up against him once more.

"Would you mind singing to me again?" I ask, curious to know how far he's willing to go to keep me happy.

Julian clears his throat and does indeed begin to sing again.

I smile. The warmth of his body and the smooth cadence of his song soon lull me into a dreamless and restful sleep.

CHAPTER 7.

When I wake up the next morning Julian is gone, but only from my bed. I can still feel his presence in the room beside mine. He isn't the only one I can feel or hear for that matter. I would have thought the walls would be thicker in a house as old as this one, but the wall between my room and Julian's must be paper-thin because I can hear the conversation between Helen and him quite clearly.

"What were you thinking, Julian? Do you know what that poor girl went through last night while you were out gallivanting around who knows where? You knew she would need you! Why weren't you here for her?"

"I find it difficult to be around her," Julian answers simply, without an ounce of emotion.

"Difficult?" Helen's voice raises an octave. "Why? You should feel more comfortable around her now than you do me, for God's sake!"

"I can't explain it," Julian says, letting his frustration show in his voice. "It's hard for me to be near her. I don't like being around her."

He couldn't have said anything worse if he tried. I feel my chest and throat tighten, like someone is strangling me. How can he say such things about me and mean them? Isn't he supposed to feel as bad as I do when we're apart? How can he not want to be near me? What's wrong with me in his eyes?

After my breakthrough last night about our relationship, I thought Julian truly cared about me, but hearing his words to Helen completely obliterates whatever it was we were building between us.

"You're not making any sense," Helen says contemptuously. "Whatever your problem is, you had better get over it. That child needs you, and I won't have you hurting her any more than you already have! She is giving up everything she knows and everything she ever dreamed of being to help you! Act like the man I know you can be for her, Julian, not this creature who runs away whenever he wants just because he finds something difficult to handle."

Julian says something so low all I can hear is a mumble.

"Well, too late!" Helen tells him before she storms out of his room, slamming the door in the wake of her righteous fury.

I can't make my body move so I lie in bed for a few minutes more, trying to let go of the pain Julian's words have caused me. How could he have been so loving and kind when he held me in his arms and sang to me the night before, and then say such cruel things to Helen this morning concerning how he truly feels about me? It doesn't make any sense at all, but maybe you have to be a logical person to understand that fundamental fact.

I hope Daniel and Adrian haven't heard the conversation between Julian and Helen, but I'm sure Adrian probably did. If I could hear it, he would surely be able to with his vampire hearing. Now, on top of knowing I'm not wanted by Julian, I'll have to deal with the embarrassment of Adrian being privy to how my vampire truly feels about me, too. I place my hands over my face and moan my aggravation. This day isn't starting out very well.

At least I already have a good excuse to be away from the house this morning. I promised Kaylee I would come to her home for breakfast, and I plan to keep that promise. I force myself out of bed and take a quick shower. I don't even bother putting on much makeup. I rarely wear that much anyway. A little powder, mascara, and lip-gloss are all I need not to feel completely naked to the world. I blow my hair dry and put it up in a ponytail. From the clothes

Helen bought me, I choose a simple white peasant blouse and blue jeans. I pick out a pair of gold thong sandals with a sling-back strap to finish my casual look.

I grab my purse and cautiously open the door to see if anyone is in the hallway. Thankfully, it's empty. I know Julian is still in his room so I slip out as quickly as I can and practically hop down the stairs two at a time. Just as I reach the front door, I hear someone clear his throat behind me. Involuntarily, I turn around and find Adrian leaning against the doorway to the living room, grinning at me.

"Going somewhere?" he asks.

"I told my sister I would have breakfast with her this morning," I explain, even though I don't really owe him any sort of explanation.

"Your leaving wouldn't have anything to do with Julian's little conversation with Helen this morning, now would it?"

He's happy about what he heard Julian say. Why? I'm not sure. Maybe he's just a sadistic pig who likes seeing people miserable.

"I don't know what you're talking about," I lie, trying to pretend I didn't hear the same conversation he did. "Besides, I made my promise to my sister yesterday morning. I really need to go. She's expecting me."

"Have fun." His smile is deceptively sweet. "I'm sure Daniel will be eagerly awaiting your return."

"When are you planning to leave?" I ask. The sooner he's out of the house, the better I'll feel. I get the distinct feeling Adrian is someone who likes to stir up trouble wherever he goes. The sooner he's gone the better. Though, I will hate losing Daniel so soon. I enjoy his company, and it's nice having another vampire companion to compare notes with.

"Tomorrow," Adrian replies, keeping his fake smile plastered on his face even though he doesn't really feel like he owes me an answer. "Will you miss us?"

"I'll miss Daniel." I don't see any reason to lie. Adrian has to know I can't stand him. I don't think I've tried very hard to hide how I feel.

Adrian chuckles. "Well then, I'll have to make sure he visits you regularly while we're in New Orleans."

"I'd appreciate that. Listen, I really need to be heading out. I'm running late as it is."

"Of course, Sarah. I'm sorry I delayed you."

Before I turn back around to the door, I catch a glimpse of Julian standing at the top of the stairs. I'm not sure how long he's been there, but it doesn't really matter.

"I'm going to Kaylee's house," I tell him, feeling like I should say something and not totally ignore his presence.

"See you when you get back," he replies with a curt nod.

I step out the door as quickly as I can without making it look like I'm trying to make a great escape, which is exactly what I'm doing.

My car isn't parked in front of the house where I left it, so I walk around the side of the house where I know the garage is located. I find my car, but I also find a few more vehicles that practically have me drooling with envy. There's a blood red Aston Martin Vanquish parked on the left side of my car and a yellow Ferrari Enzo on the right. My poor little Toyota Camry looks like the redheaded stepchild of the bunch. Sort of the way I feel when I'm around Julian and Adrian. I notice a motorcycle parked near the far wall of the garage. It looks like a custom build, not one you would be able to buy right off the showroom floor. It's black and chrome and looks expensive. That's about all I know.

I hop into my Toyota and cautiously back it out of the garage, petrified I might make a wrong move and inadvertently scratch one of the vehicles beside me. Thankfully, I make it out of the garage safely. Once I'm on the road to Kaylee's house, I sigh in relief. I feel the pain of distancing myself from Julian, but I try to push it to the back of my mind. If he doesn't like being around me, then I won't burden him with my presence any more than necessary. In fact, I intend to spend the whole day with Kaylee and stay at my apartment this evening. Julian said we could skip a day of feeding, and that's what I intend to do. I refuse to stay somewhere I'm not wanted if I don't have to.

I realize I'm probably acting like a rebellious child but he hurt my feelings with his careless words, and I don't feel like I owe him more than what's absolutely necessary.

I see the Hughes Mobile parked in Kaylee's driveway. It's an older model Honda Odyssey that desperately needs to be replaced. I think Kaylee's parents keep it as a reminder of days gone by when they used it to shuttle us girls to soccer practices, school plays, and the occasional trip to Disney World when they could afford it.

My spirits feel lifted just thinking about seeing my adoptive parents. At least I'll be surrounded by people who truly love me and want to be around me, unlike one person in particular, who shall not be named.

I walk up the sidewalk, trying my best to ignore the persistent yearning I feel to jump back into my car and drive recklessly fast, back to Julian. I hope Daniel is right and that eventually I'll cease to feel this unbearable pain inside my chest when I'm out of Julian's presence.

Kaylee's mom, Susan, stands waiting for me at the open front door with a big smile on her face.

"I feel like it's been forever since I saw you last." She immediately pulls me into her arms as soon as I'm within her reach. To feel truly loved by someone is a blessing. I always feel that way when I'm around Kaylee and her parents.

I never did feel comfortable calling them Mom and Dad. I felt like it would be disrespectful to the memory of my own parents. Kaylee's parents weren't offended and told me to at least call them Susan and Pete, not Mr. and Mrs. Hughes.

"It's only been a week," I remind her, hugging Susan back as hard as she's hugging me.

Kaylee's mom pulls back but places her hands on my forearms, searching my face with a critical eye.

"You seem different," she says, trying to puzzle out what it is she senses. Leave it to mothers. They always know when something has changed in the lives of their children. "Kaylee told us about your grandfather. Are you all right?"

"I'm fine. I didn't know him." I shrug. "I didn't even know he existed until a couple of days ago. Now that all the paperwork is done, I just want to forget about it."

I don't like lying to her, but how can I possibly tell her the whole truth? Would she even believe me? I would like to think she would, but how can I expect her to accept something so out there only crazy people would believe it's true?

"You know you can tell me anything," she reminds me.

"I know."

She isn't convinced that everything is fine and dandy in my world, but I know she won't push the matter either. It just isn't her way.

"Well, come on in. Pete and Kaylee are making the waffles. I hope you're hungry, because I think they made enough to feed an army."

In fact, I'm ravenous. Even though Susan thinks they may have made too much food, I have a nagging suspicion that they haven't made enough to satisfy my newly-acquired appetite.

When we step into Kaylee's kitchen, the aroma of freshly-baked waffles and sizzling bacon hits me like a ton of bricks. I didn't realize I was so hungry until I smelled food.

"Ah, there she is," Pete says, walking around the island where Kaylee is keeping a watchful eye on the waffle maker. He gives me a big bear hug before letting me go and asking, "How are you doing, sweetie? We heard about your grandfather."

"She's fine, Pete," Susan says. "We've already talked about it."

Pete nods his head, getting the hint to drop the subject.

"Kaylee told us we needed to make you a big breakfast because you were going to be extra hungry."

"Yep," I say, nonchalantly taking a waffle from the platter on the counter. "I'm starving."

"Well, sit down," Kaylee practically orders. "Everything's almost ready."

I surreptitiously eye the platter of waffles and know there won't be enough to satisfy my hunger, especially if I have to share them with three other people.

Kaylee and her dad bring the waffles, a plate full of bacon, and a bowl full of fruit salad to the table. There's freshly-squeezed orange juice and milk to drink. I take a glass of each.

"Don't forget the Nutella," I casually remind them, remembering quiet clearly that I was promised the deliciously delectable hazelnut spread.

I do my best not to look like a complete pig while I eat but my family still watches me with morbid fascination, like I'm a participant at a competitive eating competition.

"I don't think I've ever seen you eat so much so fast without spilling something on yourself," Kaylee says in true amazement.

I stick my tongue out at her. "I warned you I would be hungry."

"Yeah, but since when do you eat ten waffles in one sitting?"

Since I bonded with a vampire, I think to myself. I decide Kaylee doesn't need to know that I'm still hungry even after ten waffles, ten strips of bacon, half a jar of Nutella, and most of the fruit salad. She would most likely take me to the hospital and make them check me for a tapeworm.

"You're not pregnant, are you?" Susan asks, openly eyeing my waistline for any sign of a baby bump.

"No," I reply a bit too emphatically out of nervousness, "just hungry."

"She'd have to have a boyfriend to become pregnant," Kaylee tells her mom, not trying to hide her disappointment in my perpetual single status.

Was now the right time to bring up Julian? It's as good a time as any, I supposed.

Even if he doesn't really want to be near me, we are still going to have to explain his constant presence in my life somehow. We're stuck with each other whether we want to be or not.

"I've actually started seeing someone."

Kaylee looks surprised. Susan looks pleased. And Pete looks suspicious.

"Who?" Kaylee asks eagerly. "And when did *this* happen?"

"The guy from the club you took me to. The one I danced with."

Kaylee's eyes grow so large they practically bulge out of their sockets at my news.

"He actually lives here in town," I inform them as I push my empty plate away and lean back in my chair. "In fact, he just bought a house on Bayou Road."

"What does he do for a living?" Pete asks. Typical father question.

"I think his family has money," I answer, not sure what else to say. "I don't think he has a job, per se."

"Hmm…" I can tell Pete isn't pleased with my answer. He's a firm believer that men should work, whether they're independently wealthy or not. Julian will have to prove his worth to Pete Hughes if he ever wants his respect.

"How did you end up meeting him again?" Kaylee asks.

"We were getting gas at the same time at the Stop and Go here in town," I answer quickly, surprised the lie just fell out of my mouth so easily without giving it a second thought. I should have known Kaylee would want all the details. If I had been thinking straight this morning, I would have concocted a better story before I came over here. "I had supper with him last night, and we're supposed to go out again tonight."

Kaylee sits back in her chair, unconsciously rubbing her belly as she looks at me thoughtfully. "What's his name?"

"Julian Movila."

"What's he look like?" Susan asks.

"Gorgeous," I have to admit. At least that isn't a lie. "He has soft brown hair that's silky to the touch, and hazel eyes so deep you could get lost if you stared into them for too long."

"Uh-oh," I hear Kaylee say knowingly as she continues to stare at me. "I think I know that look."

"What look?" I ask, convinced Kaylee has misread my expression.

"Could it be that our girl has finally found someone she can fall in love with?" Susan asks, looking at Kaylee in a conspiratorial way.

I get the distinct impression that the two of them are planning something. Whatever it is, it probably doesn't bode well for me.

"I think we should meet this man," Pete says unexpectedly. "Why don't the two of you come to our house for supper tonight?"

My heart literally leaps into my throat. This isn't what I had planned.

"He's already made a reservation for us at the Dancing Rabbit for tonight. You know how hard it is to get reservations there," I say, hastily coming up with something plausible that will get me out of bringing Julian face to face with my family so soon. "Plus, we've only gone out once. Things might not even work out between us. I don't think you guys need to meet him just yet."

Pete's eyes narrow on me. I fear he might know I'm lying because I'm a notoriously bad liar. It's one reason I hardly ever do it.

"Why don't we let Sarah decide when she wants us to meet her new man?" Susan suggests to her husband, trying her best to hint that maybe he's pushing things a little too fast for me.

"If he's someone you might get serious with," Pete says, "I want to meet him eventually."

"I promise you'll get the opportunity to meet him one day. Just let us get used to one another first before you put the blindfold on and make him stand in front of the Hughes firing line of questions."

Pete smiles because he knows I'm right.

About an hour later, Kaylee's parents leave to do some grocery shopping at the local Super Wal-Mart. I help Kaylee clean up the breakfast dishes.

"Where's Ben this morning?" I had meant to ask that earlier but food and talk about Julian got in the way.

"He had to go over to his dad's house to fix his computer. Something about a virus I think. You know that old man is addicted to downloading free porn. It's a wonder he doesn't get more viruses on his computer than he does."

I laugh. It's either that or get sick to my stomach at the indecent picture that forms inside my mind starring Pete's dad.

"So, do you have any plans for today?" I ask her.

"Nope, Em and I are as free as birds. Want to do something?"

Kaylee and I end up going shopping for baby clothes. She has a ton already, but we both reason that a girl, even if she's a newborn, can't have too many clothes and shoes. We spend most of the day at the mall until I become so hungry I have to stop and eat. Luckily, the local Mexican restaurant is having a lunch deal, two meals for the price of one. Kaylee laughs at me when I make my order and mirrors her mother's question about me being pregnant.

"I *am* pregnant and I don't eat that much," she says while I'm eating my second dessert.

"I know. I'm just really hungry for some reason."

"You know," Kaylee says with a knowing grin. "I almost always get hungry when Ben and I are having great sex."

"TMI," I exclaim between spoonfuls of chocolate lava cake. What was with everyone telling me about their sex lives lately? First Julian and Helen, and now Kaylee.

"Well spill," she says, leaning forward as far as her belly will allow. "Did you and Mr. Gorgeous have sex last night?"

I almost choke on the cake in my mouth. "Have you lost your mind? You know I wouldn't do that with someone I barely know."

"I know, but I was hoping." Kaylee sits back and sighs. "I worry about you being so celibate. It just isn't healthy."

"Neither is hopping into bed with a total stranger. Just let me go at this at my own pace, ok? Who knows," I shrug, "maybe Julian is the one."

"Do you really think so?" Kaylee asks, her face filled with newfound hope for me.

"You never know," I say, detesting myself for giving her false expectations.

It's almost three o'clock by the time Kaylee and I make it back to her house. After we unload everything, I tell her I need to go get ready for my fictional date with Julian. What I really end up doing is dropping by the grocery store and loading up a cart with food. I end up spending three hundred dollars on groceries. At this rate, I'm sure I'll need to dip into my savings account just to keep myself fed.

After I put away all the groceries, I grab a bag of Oreos and a gallon of milk before planting myself on the couch in front of the TV. There isn't much on so I pop in a DVD, *World War Z* with the handsome Brad Pitt. I don't know why but zombie movies relax me. Maybe I should have taken that as a hint that the undead were my thing.

I'm munching on two Oreos in my mouth when my cell phone rings. I don't recognize the number so I hit 'silent' to stop the ringing. A few seconds later it beeps, indicating that I have a new voicemail. I hit the button to listen to it.

"Sarah," it's Helen's voice, "I was just calling to see when you will be returning home. I have supper ready. And…" she seems to hesitate before saying anything else. In an urgent whisper, she says, "Julian has been a complete bear since you left this morning. Please, for the sake of my sanity, can you come back home as soon as possible? I'm not sure I can take much more of him and his insufferable attitude."

I let out a heavy sigh. I don't want Helen to have to contend with the consequences of my little tantrum. Refusing to give in to my need to be with Julian is only meant to hurt him. I hadn't even thought about how it would affect those I left behind to contend with his wrath.

I quickly grab my purse and keys and head back to the mansion.

As soon as I step over the threshold, the hole in my heart heals itself. I silently curse under my breath, wishing Julian didn't have this type of hold over me.

"Oh, thank heavens!" Helen says, walking up the hallway to greet me. She immediately hugs me as soon as she can. "Thank you for coming back so soon. I don't think I could have taken another minute of his abhorrent behavior."

"I got your message," I reply, returning her hug. "I'm sorry he made your day miserable."

"Think nothing of it, dear," she replies, taking a step back from me. "He deserved it."

She looks at me and raises an eyebrow. "I assume your absence was because you heard our conversation this morning in his room?"

I don't see any point in lying to her. She has obviously already figured things out, and I need at least one ally with whom I can be completely honest.

I nod my head. I don't need to say or do anything else for her to understand.

Helen sighs. "I can't say I understand what's going on in that addled brain of his when it comes to you. I've never seen him act this way before with someone he's bonded to."

"Is there something wrong with my blood?" It's a question I kept asking myself that day. Is there something I'm feeding him that makes him act so out of character? He did say the night before that my blood tasted sweeter to him than anyone else's before me. Maybe there *is* something wrong with me…

"I don't think so, dear," Helen says, taking my question quite seriously. "I've never known anyone to have something wrong with their blood."

I was out of ideas then. It's the only explanation that makes any sense to me.

"Come on." She puts one of her arms around my shoulders. "I made you and Daniel some supper. He said he wanted to eat in the kitchen tonight since Adrian is out."

"Out where?" I ask as we walk towards the back of the house.

"I think he went to Biloxi. I didn't ask too many questions. The longer he's out of this house the better, is my opinion."

I totally agree.

As I walk into the kitchen beside Helen, I already know who will be waiting for me there.

Julian is sitting at the table with Daniel, who has already started to eat his supper. When Julian looks up at me, I feel a jolt of electricity course through my body. Damn it, why does he have to affect me the way he does?

"I'm glad to see you were able to find your way back home," he quips irritably, not even attempting to keep his aggravation with me out of his voice. "I thought you might have forgotten where we lived."

"No, I have a pretty good memory," I inform him curtly, feeling my temper flare with his open animosity. "I just wasn't sure when I should come back. I didn't want to force my presence on anyone."

"You're always wanted here," Julian replies, taking offense at my retort. "You belong with me. Don't forget that."

"I don't think there's any chance of me forgetting that." I try to rein in my ire, but he's making it almost impossible. I usually don't let my temper show, but I'm not about to just stand and take his open rudeness. "I'm quite aware that we're stuck with each other whether we want to be or not."

Julian's chair makes a horrible scraping sound against the tile floor as he quickly stands from it. "Well, I won't burden you with my presence any longer, Sarah. Enjoy your meal."

He storms past me and out of the kitchen. I hear him stomp up the stairs and slam his bedroom door. Secretly, I'm relieved he didn't leave the house again. After a whole day of being apart I need to feel his presence, and I hope he needs to feel mine, too.

CHAPTER 8.

I sit down at the table with Daniel, who is staring at me with a concerned expression on his face after witnessing the verbal altercation between Julian and me.

"Are you all right?" he asks.

"I'll be fine," I reply, even though I'm not actually sure I will be. How am I supposed to feel when I know how much Julian detests being around me? All I want right now is an explanation about why he dislikes being around me so much.

"Here, dear," Helen places a casserole dish filled with some sort of taco casserole on the table in front of me. "Maybe a good supper will perk your spirits back up."

One good thing about staying at Julian's house is the fact that he can foot the bill for my increased appetite. Plus, Helen is a great cook; everything she's cooked for me so far has tasted wonderful.

I notice Daniel has the same casserole to eat in front of him but is already half- way through with his.

"Would you like to go out for ice cream later?" Daniel asks. "It might make you feel a little better."

"I would, but I told my family Julian and I are going out on a date tonight. I can't take the chance they might see me and you together," I tell him regrettably.

"Ahh, yes, the ruse to introduce him into your life more easily. You don't seem like someone who enjoys lying to people."

"I don't." I take a spoonful of the casserole into my mouth before I can finish my thought. It keeps tempting me with its delicious aroma while it sits in front of me untouched. After I swallow, I continue, "I told them we were going out to eat at the Dancing Rabbit."

"Dancing Rabbit?" Daniel questions with an amused laugh. "That's an odd name for a restaurant."

"Yeah, I have no idea why it's called that but it's been here forever. It's a little upscale. I haven't actually been there before."

It only takes Daniel a few minutes more to finish off his casserole. Just as I'm about to take the last bite of mine, Julian comes downstairs dressed in a pair of grey slacks, a plum dress shirt, and a jade green tie. Even though I'm still mad at him, I can't prevent the small leap my heart does at how nice he looks. There's no arguing that Julian is a devastatingly handsome man.

"What are you all dressed up for?" Helen asks as she wipes the counters down with a wet washcloth.

Julian looks at me. "I heard you say you told your family we are supposed to go on a date. I thought it might be a good idea if we actually did it."

"You have to make reservations in advance to get a table at the Dancing Rabbit," I inform him.

It's the truth. Pecan Acres might be a small town, but that doesn't mean people here don't like to go out and eat at fancy restaurants.

"I already called them. They had someone cancel a reservation this evening. If you can be ready within the next half hour we can make it there on time."

I should have thought about Julian being able to hear my conversation with Daniel. And if he heard that, he probably heard Helen and me talk when I first got back home. It's obvious he's aware I know how he really feels about me. I suppose it's just as well. Secrets are always hard to keep. More times than not, they get found out.

"Besides," he continues, "if you've never been to the restaurant, how are you going to answer questions Kaylee will undoubtedly ask you about our date?"

He makes an excellent point. I did inadvertently back myself into a corner by picking a restaurant I've never actually been to myself. Kaylee and Ben went there to celebrate her pregnancy. If I can't answer her questions about the place, she'll instantly know I lied to her.

I finish the last bite of my casserole before I stand up from my chair.

"I guess I'll see you when we get back," I say to Daniel.

"I'll be waiting," he replies.

I brush by Julian in the kitchen entryway as I walk out of the room. I suddenly get a whiff of his cologne and make a note to myself to ask him what brand it is. Once I'm inside my room, I already know what I'm going to wear. I saw the dress hanging in the wardrobe the night before, but it seemed a little too fancy to wear to a supper in your own home. It's made of a papaya-colored stretch-satin with a halter top, sweetheart neckline, and tucked side seams for a fitted silhouette. I pick a pair of simple thin-strapped silver sandals to go with it.

Half an hour isn't a lot of time to get ready for a fancy night out on the town. I don't even have time to shower. Thank God I thought to shave my legs that morning. I put on a little bit more makeup and curl the ends of my hair quickly with a large-barrel curling iron. Having my hair up all day in a ponytail has given my strands some extra volume. Within twenty minutes, I'm ready for my fake date with Julian.

When I go back downstairs I accidentally collide with Daniel, who was coming around the corner from the living room. He steadies me with his hands on my shoulders.

"Sorry, Sarah." His eyes quickly sweep me from head to toe. He lets out a slow, appreciative whistle. "Wow, you look amazing in that dress."

"Thanks." I feel my face grow warm under his continued perusal of me in my new outfit.

"Are you ready to go?" I hear Julian ask curtly.

I look beside us and find him standing there with a slight scowl on his face. I'm not sure what I've done this time to earn such a look from him. Maybe he doesn't like the dress I'm wearing, or maybe his features are cemented into a permanent glower whenever I'm around now.

Daniel lets go of my shoulders and takes a step back.

"You two have fun," he tells us, even though he looks doubtful I'll gain much enjoyment from the evening ahead of me.

"Thank you," Julian says as he waves a hand in front of him, indicating he wants me to precede him out the front door.

We walk to the garage in silence. The yellow Enzo is gone. I assume it must have belonged to Adrian. Julian walks up to the red Aston Martin and opens the passenger door for me. I slip into the black leather bucket seat and rest my arm on the large console separating the driver and passenger sides.

Julian strolls around the front of the car and gets into the driver's seat. The ride to the Dancing Rabbit is made in uncomfortable silence. It's like the old expression of there being an elephant in the room that no one wants to discuss.

Eventually, we'll have to talk about why he doesn't like being around me. But it seems like a conversation he should initiate. Although, I'm not sure how long I'll be able to keep myself from asking him for an explanation. I desperately want to know what's causing him to dislike me so much, and he's the only one who can answer that question.

It takes us ten minutes to drive to the restaurant. The parking lot is packed with cars when we arrive, but Julian gets lucky and finds someone near the entrance backing out to leave. I've always found it a little silly for women to wait on men to come open their car doors for them. So, as soon as Julian shuts the car off, I open my own door and get out. He doesn't seem to mind my independent move and casually takes my hand when we meet at the front of the car.

As soon as we step through the double glass doors of the restaurant, we're only a couple of steps away from the maître d' podium. We walk up to it, and Julian tells the man standing behind it his name.

The man grabs a couple of menus and quickly leads us to a table in the middle of the room. I would have preferred a table off to the side where we wouldn't be the center of attention, but our location does ensure that everyone present will see us together. Besides, isn't that the point of this whole charade? To have people believe we're a couple?

Julian pulls out my chair in a gallant maneuver before taking his own seat. He immediately reaches for my hand across the small table. I have no other option but to place my hand in his since everyone in the room seems to be watching us. I had put up my wall to block out the emotions of those around us, but I slowly let it down to see what people were feeling.

Most of the women are feeling envy and lust. I can't say that I blame them one bit. Julian is playing his role of the besotted lover to the hilt. He almost has me fooled into believing he truly cares, considering the way he's looking at me with his smoldering hazel eyes. The emotions of the men in the room come as no surprise to me either. I remember hearing about a study that says men think about sex at least 34 times a day. I quickly put my wall back up, not wanting to know what the people around us are feeling anymore. I begin to feel a little conspicuous. Maybe I should have rethought the tight- fitting dress I'm wearing.

"You look lovely this evening, Sarah," Julian says, bringing my hand up to his mouth and brushing his warm lips against the back of it.

"Thank you," I whisper back, feeling a bit shy and completely out of my element. For the most part, the guys I've dated in the past never took me out on fancy dates like this. The most extravagant we got was the Olive Garden or Red Lobster.

"Is something wrong?" Julian asks. "Your cheeks have that red hue they get when you're feeling embarrassed about something."

"Do they?" I put my free hand up to my face and notice that my cheeks are indeed warm to the touch. I lean forward slightly and whisper, "I'm a little uncomfortable with the feelings of the men in the room. I'm thinking I shouldn't have worn this dress."

Julian smiles. "Well, of course they want you, Sarah. You're beautiful. I'm a very lucky man."

If only he meant the words he just said. But I know the truth of his feelings for me. I'm sure having to be so intimate with me is annoying him a great deal. He's a good actor, though. I have to give him props for being so convincing. He almost has me believing he means what he's saying.

Our waitress comes over and takes our orders. I request the steak and lobster platter. Julian does the same.

"Can you eat real food?" I whisper, trying my best not to be overheard by those around us.

"I could but I won't be. Just wait and see. We'll both be leaving here with empty plates."

I'm curious as to how he plans to pull that one off.

"Sarah?"

I look up at the calling of my name, and see Janine from work standing beside our table. She's the vice-principal at Pecan Acres Junior High School.

"Hey, Janine, how are you doing?"

"Oh, just fine." I see her look over at Julian as if she's waiting for a formal introduction.

"Janine, this is Julian Movila. He just moved into town."

Julian stands up and bows slightly to Janine before shaking her hand. "It's a pleasure to meet you."

I fear Janine is going to swoon on the spot after she hears Julian speak. I can't deny his accent is attractive.

"It's a pleasure to meet you, too," she breathes out, completely taken with my date. "So, how long have the two of you been dating?"

"Only recently," Julian answers smoothly. "Sarah has become the reason my heart beats so quickly nowadays, though."

I can't keep from smirking at that remark. It's certainly true but not for the reason Janine is surely thinking.

"Well you're a very lucky woman, Sarah." Janine eyes Julian up and down, right and left, every which way she can. Her open ogling of my companion begins to annoy me.

"I guess I'll be seeing you at work in a couple of months," I say to her, hoping she'll take the hint and skedaddle.

"You betcha." She turns to Julian and smiles coyly. "Hope you like it here in Pecan Acres. We could defiantly use more men like you in our town."

"I'm flattered you think so," Julian says, bowing slightly to her again. Now *he's* irritating me. Can't he see what kind of woman she is?

"Y'all enjoy your meal. I hope I see you later."

Finally, Janine walks past our table to return to her own in the corner of the room where her date is impatiently awaiting her return.

"Everyone in town will know about us now," I say confidently. "Janine will make sure of that."

"Good; the sooner the better."

I don't appreciate the subtle reminder that we need to have a relationship and breakup as quickly as possible so I can find a suitable sperm donor for the next heir. That's all Julian really wants from me, right? I attempt to let go of my anger before it has a chance to take root. We're supposed to be acting like two people falling in love. I don't think having an argument during a romantic supper will do much to foster that illusion.

When our meals arrive I quickly dig into mine, being mindful not to eat too fast. I don't need to start any more rumors about me in town. Plus, I don't want to get my new dress dirty by splashing lobster juice all over it. Julian slowly cuts his steak up into cubes and goes through the motions of cracking open his lobster. Halfway through my meal, he does something so fast I'm not even sure if he actually did it or if my plate magically refilled itself. Somehow, he switches our plates.

I look up at him and see my half-eaten plate on his side of the table now.

"How did you do that?" I ask, astounded by his trick.

"Super agility, remember?" he says, grinning at me as he enjoys the fact he was able to surprise me.

When I'm almost done with his plate, he switches them back again so I can finish my original meal.

Our waitress takes our empty plates and brings around the dessert cart. I spy a chocolate croissant bread pudding with vanilla ice cream and bourbon sauce begging me to devour it. Julian passes on dessert but he takes my bowl and spoon away from me as soon as the waitress leaves our table.

"What are you doing?" I whisper, not understanding his motives. He certainly doesn't want to eat it, and I most definitely do.

He scoots his chair closer to mine and uses the spoon to scoop up some of the bread, sauce, and ice cream before bringing it up to my mouth. I look in his eyes and feel my blood course through my veins a little bit faster. When his gaze drops to my throat, I wonder if he senses the increased beating of my heart.

I allow Julian to feed me the dessert and wish for a second time that evening that the moment could have been real. I find myself wishing he really cared for me as much as he's pretending to.

Wait. What is *wrong* with me? Am I actually falling for my obstinate vampire companion? No. Absolutely not! I refuse to. He is a heartless cad who doesn't care about anything but getting his daily meal out of me and an heir to carry on my family's tradition. I positively, unequivocally, refuse to allow myself to fall in love with someone like Julian. Sure, he's gorgeous, but he knows it. When he makes an effort he can also be completely charming. But he isn't suitable boyfriend material. Besides, that type of thinking can only lead to heartache on my part. He's only around me because he has to be, not because he wants to be. I know that for a fact now. I heard him say it just that morning.

"You're very good at this," I tell him between spoon feedings.

Julian looks up from the bowl he's scooping from and asks, "Good at what exactly?"

The way his eyes sparkle in the dim light of the room makes me completely forget what I was going to say. It takes me a few seconds before I can think coherently again.

"At pretending," I finally answer.

"Hmm," is all the response I get back from him before he feeds me the last of the bread pudding.

Ok, what in the Sam hill was that supposed to mean? It was a totally unsatisfactory response.

After I eat dessert, our waitress brings us the check and we leave the restaurant. I see Janine wave bye to us and, only because it's the polite thing to do, I wave back.

We get into Julian's car and head home. We're almost there when Julian glances in my direction and asks, "Would you like to do something with me?"

My guard immediately goes up. "Like what?"

He gives me one of his rare genuine smiles. "It's a surprise, but I think you'll enjoy it."

I admit that I feel shocked he wants to spend time with me outside of our little act to convince the general population of Pecan Acres that we're dating one another. My curiosity gets the better of me, and I have to find out what he's up to.

"Ok," I answer, silently wondering what I've just agreed to do.

When we get back to the house and out of the car, Julian takes my hand and heads directly towards the backyard. I quickly take my shoes off, not wanting to ruin them by walking through the dewy grass. Once we reach the middle of the yard, Julian takes my shoes from my hands and gently lays them on the ground beside him.

"I want to show you something that not many people get the chance to see," he tells me as he begins to take his tie off.

I stand there in silence wondering if he's about to do a striptease for me. He tosses his tie to the ground and then proceeds to unbutton his shirt.

"Just how naked do you intend to get?" I ask, feeling a bit uncomfortable with the situation.

"I'm just taking my shirt off so it doesn't get ripped open in the back," he assures me with an amused smile. "Don't worry, Sarah Marcel. I promise to keep my pants on… this time."

I feel my eyes widen in shock after his little add-on, which causes Julian to chuckle. I'm glad I can amuse him so much with my uncomfortableness, *not*.

"You're going to hear and see some things that might cause you alarm," he warns me. "I don't want you to worry, though. It doesn't hurt me as much as you might think from all the blood."

"Ok," I say, becoming frightened as I take a couple of steps backward, "what the hell is about to happen? You're starting to freak me out, Julian."

"I want to show you how I can fly," he says, looking truly worried over my reaction. "I don't want there to be any secrets between us, and this is something that I've only shared with a select few."

I begin to feel bad. I can tell whatever Julian is about to do is important to him, and sharing it with me is his way of letting me know how much he trusts me with his secrets. Cautiously, I inch back two steps.

"Ok," I tell him, bracing myself for whatever it is I'm about to see, "how do you fly? To be honest, I just thought you flew around like Superman."

Julian smiles. "Close, but not quite. Are you ready?"

I take in a large gulp of air and nod my head. "Go ahead."

It happens so fast it takes my mind a moment to catch up with what my eyes just witnessed. In less than a second, a pair of wings appear to sprout out of Julian's back. I know I heard a ripping sound just before I saw them, and that there was a splatter of blood that sprayed out onto the ground behind him. As I study his new wings, I realize they remind me of the way artists draw dragon wings. Julian spreads them out and I notice that they're semi-transparent. While I watch, they begin to turn red in color from the top down, almost like…

"Are they filling up with blood?" I ask in amazement and, I'll admit, slight disgust.

"Yes," he tells me, watching my reaction closely. He doesn't say as much, but I can see how important it is to Julian for me to accept this part of him.

I study the wings for a moment more before I ask, "Can I touch them?"

Julian seems to breathe out a sigh of relief, but it's so imperceptible it would probably go unnoticed to anyone who wasn't paying close attention.

"Yes," he says in a soft voice. "You're free to touch me anywhere you want, Sarah."

His statement causes me to drag my eyes away from his wings and look at his face.

He looks amused. Typical.

I just shake my head at him in exasperation and take a few steps closer.

Tentatively, I stretch my right arm out and run the tips of my fingers along the membrane of his wing to discover what it's made of.

"It feels like skin," I say, "but it's baby soft."

"It is skin," he confirms. "My skin."

"And why does it feel so soft?"

"I can heal incredibly fast," he begins to explain. "When the bones erupt from my back to form the wings, the newly-formed skin that my back regenerates is pulled by the bones and stretched out to make the wings."

"That's kind of cool, actually," I say, unable to stop myself from rubbing my full hand down the length of his wing. Out of the corner of my eye, I notice Julian shudder slightly. I immediately drop my hand back to my side.

"Am I hurting you?" I ask, worried he allowed me to touch his wing even though he knew it would cause him pain.

"No," he tells me, staring into my eyes without a hint of humor. "It wasn't pain that I felt when you touched me."

If it wasn't pain he felt, then did he feel pleasure? I decide the best course of action is not to delve too deeply into the subject.

"Would you like to fly with me?" Julian asks unexpectedly.

"Are you kidding?" I ask excitedly. "I would love to! What do I need to do?"

"Just stand still," he instructs, coming to stand behind me. He wraps one of his arms snuggly around my waist. "I need to place one hand on your chest. Is that all right with you?"

"I…guess," I say hesitantly, unsure if Julian is taking advantage of the situation just to feel me up. I quickly decide that isn't his motive. Julian has too much class to stoop to such a low level. Besides, I doubt he's ever needed to make up such a lame excuse to feel a woman's breasts.

I'm not sure if I'm relieved or disappointed when Julian places his right hand directly on my breastbone.

"Are you sure you'll be able to hold onto me?" I ask. "You know how much I've been eating lately."

When he chuckles, I can feel his chest move against my back. It's a nice feeling and promptly puts me at ease.

"Don't worry," he tells me "I'm pretty strong." He tightens his hold on me and warns, "Here we go."

At first, I only feel a slight breeze as his wings begin to flap and he propels us into the air with his legs. I can't help the giggle that escapes from between my lips as we become airborne. It's a lot like when you're on a trampoline with a friend and can't stop giggling as you jump up and down together. As we fly higher and higher into the air, I notice a change in the temperature and feel thankful for the coolness.

The city looks so different from this altitude: all lights and no sound. I can see the high school I work at in the distance, all lit up. Particular landmarks, such as the mall and Super Wal-Mart, aren't difficult to find either. I look for Kaylee's house but can't quite make it out, but I do see the street she lives on.

There's a brisk breeze at our elevation, but it feels wonderful compared to the stale humidity hovering near ground-level.

"Do you like it?" Julian whispers into my ear as the wind whistles around us.

I turn my head slightly to look at him behind me. He has an expectant look on his face as he watches my reaction to flying with him.

"It's beautiful up here," I say, not even trying to hide the awe I feel. "How do you not spend all of your time just flying around like this?"

He smiles. "I do it a lot at night. You'll be asleep most of the time so you won't miss me."

"Don't you sleep?"

"Yes, but I only need an hour or two each day."

"Do you dream?"

"Sometimes." He stares at me for a moment before saying, "I've been having a lot of dreams about you lately."

"Really?" I ask, shocked by this revelation. I'm not only surprised that he dreams about me, but I'm also surprised he's admitting it. "Are they nice dreams?"

His smile turns into a sly grin. "Some are nicer than others."

I'm not quite sure what to say, so I decide it's better not to say anything at all. I don't want to ruin the moment.

"We should probably be getting back," he tells me, tightening his hold on my body. I'm not sure if he does it because we're making our descent and he's concerned about losing his grip on me when we land, or if he simply wants to hold me closer. I would like to think it's the latter.

I feel a slight jolt when we land. I slowly start to take a step forward when I feel Julian's arms tighten around me, holding me in place. I wait to see what he'll do next.

"I'm sorry you heard what Helen and I were discussing this morning. I didn't even think about you being able to hear our conversation until it was too late."

I don't say anything because I get the distinct impression that he's not through telling me what's on his mind.

"I won't lie to you, Sarah. I do find it hard to be around you."

"Why?" I have to ask before it drives me crazy.

"You make me... *feel* too much."

"And that's a bad thing?"

"Sometimes it's unbearable, but it's nothing you can control. I just need some more time to learn how to deal with it. I don't want you to feel like you have to stay away from me, though, like you did today. I tried to run from you last night, but it only caused us both a lot of pain. I won't do that again. All I ask is that you be patient with me for a little while longer. I promise that I'll try to be a better man for you."

I look back at Julian to see an earnest expression on his face. Even though I can't tap into his feelings, I know he'll do his best to keep the promise he just made.

Julian reaches down to the grass and retrieves my shoes. Before I can react, he sweeps me off my feet and begins to carry me back to the house. I don't make a protest. In fact, I don't say a single word.

I lay my head against his shoulder, allowing myself to forget I am an independent woman of the modern age as I let the man I'm with take care of me.

CHAPTER 9.

When we walk through the French doors of the kitchen, Julian sets me back onto my feet. I can see Daniel bent over as he looks through the refrigerator. I assume he's searching for something to snack on.

Julian hands me back my shoes, and I tell him, "Thank you."

Daniel stands straight when he hears me speak and turns around to face us. I notice he's holding a large Tupperware container with what looks like some sort of yellow cake, strawberries, and whipped cream concoction inside it.

"How was the Dancing Rabbit?" he asks, closing the fridge and walking over to a drawer in the island where the silverware is kept.

"The food was excellent. We had a good time," I answer, feeling shy all of a sudden. It isn't as if it was a real date. I shouldn't feel like a teenager who has just gone out with the most gorgeous guy in school, but that's the emotion I'm experiencing. I feel flush with hope and excitement, wondering where my relationship with Julian might go after tonight. I try to quell my romantic notions and stop them from running rampant through my mind like the bulls in Pamplona, unstoppable and erratic.

"I should leave the two of you alone," Julian says. "I have something I need to take care of before I come to your room tonight, Sarah. I won't be gone long," he promises.

"I'll be waiting," I reply, deciding not to ask him where he's going. It's none of my business anyway.

Julian looks over at Daniel and says rather pleasantly, "Enjoy the rest of your evening."

He walks back outside and closes the door behind him.

"Well that was interesting," Daniel says, continuing to stare out the door as Julian walks away.

"What was interesting?" I ask.

"They rarely let people see them with their wings out," he informs me.

"He let me watch how they're formed," I reveal.

Daniel whistles, clearly impressed. "That's really special, Sarah. I'm not sure Adrian has ever let someone watch him do that. Julian must really trust you."

I don't say anything, but I hope Daniel is right. I want Julian to trust me more than he's ever trusted anyone in his life.

"Are you too full to help me eat this?" Daniel holds up the Tupperware bowl in his hand.

"I don't think I'll ever feel full again," I confess, wondering how true my statement really is.

Daniel grabs two spoons from the silverware drawer.

"Come on then," he tilts his head toward the living room. "They're playing a *Doctor Who* marathon on TV. I just came in here to get a snack in between shows."

"A fellow Whovian I see." I take the spoon Daniel offers me while we walk down the hallway to the living room. "I knew you and I were kindred spirits."

Daniel and I sit in front of the 4K TV hanging above the mantel in the living room. We begin to watch David Tennant and Billie Piper run through a corridor of a space ship being chased by a dalek. It seems like the Doctor and his companions are always running away from something. Halfway through the episode, I begin to wish I had thought to change clothes before getting caught up in the show. I catch Daniel glancing over at my breasts more than once. After the tenth time, I grab the throw blanket lying across one of the wingback chairs and cover myself with it, pretending I feel cold. I soon learn that was an even bigger mistake.

Being the gentleman that he is, Daniel scoots closer to me and gingerly places his arm across my shoulders, saying he has plenty of body heat to share. Unfortunately, his feelings betray him. He wants to do something, but he isn't sure if he should. I feel his hand start to rub the ball of my shoulder, as if he's testing the waters to see how I'll react.

He seems to be working up the courage to do something. I can feel it. I know I need to stop any romantic notions he might be having before he acts on them and ends up embarrassing us both. But how can I do that without seeming too obvious? I definitely don't want to hurt his feelings. He's such a sweet guy. He just made the unwise decision of picking me to start a relationship with.

"Sarah…" Julian calls to me from the entryway of the living room, taking in the scene of Daniel and me sitting so close together on the couch. I thought he would be mad at the intimate picture we present, but he looks amused by my predicament. "Are you ready?"

I feel a wave of relief wash over me and quickly stand up. I toss the throw blanket I was using to aid my modesty back onto the chair I originally plucked it from.

"I guess I'll see you in the morning before we leave," Daniel says, clearly disappointed by my sudden departure.

"Ok, see you in the morning." I probably sound a little rude, but I don't really care. I just want to get out of the room and away from Daniel's romantic intentions as fast as I can.

Julian turns away from Daniel to follow me up the stairs at a short distance.

"I hope I didn't interrupt anything," he says in a low voice so Daniel can't hear. "The two of you looked awfully cozy together."

I can almost swear Julian is mocking me. I glance at him over my shoulder and see that he's smiling like he's holding in a laugh.

"No, you didn't interrupt anything," I say, continuing to make my way up the stairs. "Though your timing couldn't have been more perfect," I mumble under my breath but, of course, he still hears me and chuckles softly.

When I reach the door to my bedroom, Julian says, "Let me know when you're ready. I'll be waiting out here."

I nod, letting him know I understand and appreciate the privacy. I go into my bedroom and find a white nightgown on my bed. I stare at it for a moment in complete bewilderment, wondering why Helen would set out something that's so sexy for me to wear. Did she believe I would be inviting Daniel to share my bed that evening? Surely not. Then why would she leave me something with a neckline that practically plunges to my waist, and material so thin I'm sure you can see straight through it? It's a beautiful garment, but I simply can't wear it in front of Julian.

I pick the nightgown up and hang it in the wardrobe. I don a T-shirt and a pair of shorts to wear before opening my bedroom door to invite Julian inside.

"I'm ready," I tell him.

He strolls into the room, looking at my ensemble with raised eyebrows.

"Didn't you like the nightgown?" he asks me.

I close the door behind him before answering, "I wasn't about to wear that in front of you. I don't know what Helen was thinking by leaving it out for me."

"She didn't leave it out," Julian tells me. "I did."

Well, that certainly puts a new twist on things.

"Did you set out my pajamas last night, too?" I have to ask.

"No, that was all Helen," he replies, sounding disappointed in her choice of evening wear for me. "I thought you might like something more feminine than a T-shirt and flannel bottoms." He eyes me up and down. "Apparently, she was right and I was wrong."

I clear my throat and walk over to the bed. For once, I'm completely speechless. Anything I say could be taken the wrong way, and I don't want to run the risk of ruining the dynamic between

Julian and me right now. Our relationship is fragile, and I don't want to erase the progress we've made tonight.

When I pull back the covers on the bed, I notice that the sheets have been changed because they're no longer spotted with blood. I feel bad that Helen had to go through all the trouble of putting new sheets on because of my impromptu feeding of Julian the night before.

"Do you have another one of those mats?" I ask him. "Like the one we used the first time?"

Julian walks over to the nightstand I'm standing in front of and pulls out the top drawer.

"Helen will always keep a clean one in here for us," he states, pulling out a black quilted mat. He lays it on the pillow in front of me and walks around to the other side of the bed before slipping his shirt off.

"Mind if I ask where your wings went?"

"The bones collapse and go back inside my body," he tells me. "When that happens, the skin is sloughed off. I didn't think you would want to see that."

I don't openly admit it, but he's dead right about that.

Julian tosses his shirt onto the chair beside the window and looks over at me expectantly.

"Would you like me to turn the lights off?" he inquires.

"Yes, please," I say.

As Julian walks over to flip the light switch by the door, I lie down on the bed and await his return. My mind drifts back to the previous night when I practically begged him to drink from me. I'm not sure how I found the nerve to act so brazen. I wish I could channel that side of myself whenever I wanted because I begin to feel nervous.

Julian's hand is on the light switch, but he doesn't turn the overhead light off. Instead, he turns around to face me.

"Would you like for me to read to you before we do this?" he asks. "It might calm your nerves a little."

"That would be great," I say in relief. I didn't realize my anxiousness was showing that much.

"I'll be right back," he tells me, opening the door.

I listen as he walks down the hallway and enters his room. It only takes him a couple of minutes before he's back in my bedroom and closing the door behind him. He walks over to the nightstand on his side of the bed and turns on the lamp there. Then he walks over to the light switch to turn off the overhead light before climbing into bed with me. I lay on my side to face him as he opens the book to the first page.

"What are you going to read?" I ask, not seeing a title on the front of the hardcover book he's holding.

"Bram Stoker's *Dracula*," he answers.

I look up at his face and see him grinning as he finds the first page of the story.

"You think you're funny, don't ya?" I ask him, unable to stop a grin of my own from appearing on my face.

"I've been known to be amusing on occasion," he admits. "But don't get used to it. I am a vampire after all, and we're notoriously moody creatures."

"I'm a woman. I understand mood swings all too well."

Julian clears his throat and begins to read to me.

Honestly, I could listen to Julian read the phonebook and find it interesting. His accent is so unique that I'm still having a hard time placing it. It sounds mostly British, but I know Julian is originally from Hungary.

While he turns a page, I interrupt his reading by asking, "What kind of accent do you have? I can't quite tell what nationality it is."

Julian looks over at me and says, "Well, I was raised in Hungary, but I've also lived in England and France for most of my life. It seems difficult to live anywhere and not pick up certain inflections of each culture's dialect. Why? Does it bother you?"

"Oh no," I'm quick to say. "I like it. I've just never heard one like yours before. Please, keep reading. I love the sound of your voice."

Julian grins and does exactly what I tell him to do.

After a while, I become drowsy and end up falling asleep before Julian is able to feed. Sometime during the night, I wake up. I'm still lying on my side. When I open my eyes, I see that Julian remained in bed with me. He's on his side, too, facing me with his eyes closed. I assume he's taking his required two hours of nightly rest. The room is dark now, with only the light from the streetlamps outside illuminating his face. I lie still and just watch him.

How can a man be so beautiful? I mean, I've found men attractive before, but not like Julian. Did he always look like this or did becoming a vampire transform him in some way? Even Adrian is gorgeous, though it irks me to no end to admit that about him. The problem with Adrian is the fact that he knows he's good-looking and tries to use it to his advantage. That sort of narcissism instantly makes him unattractive to me.

Without really thinking about it, I reach out and begin to trace the side of Julian's face with the tips of my fingers. I start at his temple and slowly work my way down across his high cheekbone to the tip of his chin. I begin to pull my hand away, but I only get as far as lifting it from his face before he grabs my hand. With his eyes still closed and without saying a word, he gently places my hand back on his face. I don't need him to say what he wants. His gesture said it for him.

I begin to caress his face again, but this time when I reach his chin I let my fingers venture up to his plump lips, allowing myself the pleasure of tracing their fullness. My heart begins to race as I imagine myself leaning over and pressing my own lips against his. Would he pull away or welcome the intimacy? I'm not sure. I get the impression there's an unwritten rule when it comes to what the relationship between a vampire and his companion should be. I don't think we're supposed to fall in love, but a part of my heart is yearning to make that leap of faith with Julian. Yet, I'm positive there's no way I can tell him how I'm feeling. If he knew, I feel sure he would place a wall between us that no amount of time would be able to tear down.

When I pull my hand away a second time, Julian doesn't try to stop me. Instead, he opens his eyes to look in mine, and we simply stare at one another for a long while. I wish I could tell what he's feeling as he looks at me, but his face remains as impassive as ever and holds no clue to his true thoughts.

Finally, I whisper, "Are you hungry?"

Julian's gaze slowly sweeps the length of me. I begin to wonder what precisely he might be hungry for. When he meets my gaze again, he simply says, "Yes."

I roll over onto my back and expose my neck, breathlessly waiting for him to come closer. He slides over to me underneath the covers and leans his head down towards my neck. I feel the first tentative touch of his lips against my flesh and close my eyes, expecting to feel his bite next. Instead of feeling his teeth pierce my skin, I feel his lips make a slow trail of small, delightful kisses around the base of my neck, causing me to lose my breath and tingle from head to toe from the pleasurable feel. I part my lips just enough to drawn in a quick and much-needed breath. I'm not completely sure what Julian's intentions are, but in that moment, I really don't care. All I know is that the warm, wet feel of his mouth as it travels across my skin is intoxicating, and I don't want him to stop.

Once Julian kisses his way to the other side of my neck, I feel him dip a little lower and kiss his way back across my chest, just above my breasts. Now I wish I had worn the nightgown he laid out for me because it would have given him easy access to other parts of my body that are screaming to be touched by him. Perhaps that was his intention all along and I royally botched it up by being modest.

Julian slides his mouth back up to the base of my neck again to his usual spot, and bites me quickly in order to draw out the blood he needs to survive. The thought that I'm able to keep him strong makes me feel proud to be his companion and, given more time with one another, maybe we can become even more.

I end up falling back to sleep while Julian feeds. It's unintentional, but tiredness overtakes me and I drift off before I can stop myself.

The next morning, I wake up early so I don't miss Daniel's departure. When I make it downstairs to the kitchen, Helen is busy scrambling some eggs while Daniel keeps a watchful eye on the bacon frying in the cast iron skillet.

"Good morning," I say to them, coming to stand closer to the pair and breathing in the intoxicating aromas of eggs and bacon cooking.

"Did you sleep well?" Daniel asks me as he scoops up the bacon with his spatula and places the crispy strips on a plate with paper towels to soak up the excess grease.

"Yes, did you?"

"Not really," Daniel admits. "Adrian didn't come back here last night."

"Is he all right?"

"Yes, he's fine. He's on his way back now. He said he would be here within the hour."

"Sarah, would you be a dear and pull the biscuits out of the oven for me, please?" Helen asks.

I grab the red silicone oven mitt on the counter by the stove and pull out the large tray of biscuits from the oven, depositing them into a breadbasket on the kitchen table.

Once the eggs and bacon are also brought to the table, Daniel and I make a game out of seeing who can finish eating breakfast first. He wins again, of course.

"So, what is my prize for winning this time?" he asks as we help Helen clean the dishes.

I shrug. "I don't know. What is it that you want?"

"Hmm, can I have a raincheck? I don't believe it's the right time to ask for what I really want."

I notice one of Helen's eyebrows arch after hearing Daniel's mysterious choice of words.

"Sure," I say, not seeing any harm in a raincheck, "just let me know when you decide."

I don't think Daniel could have smiled any bigger. "Great."

Daniel excuses himself from our company, telling us that Adrian is close by and that he needs to pack up his belongings. Just as Daniel walks back downstairs with his suitcase, Adrian strolls through the front door.

"Ah, good, Daniel, you're ready to leave," Adrian says, closing the door behind him. "I trust they treated you well while I was away?"

"Of course they did. You know you don't even have to ask that," Daniel tells him, clearly irritated by Adrian's insinuation.

Julian appears at the top of the stairs and walks down to join us. It's the first time I've seen him all morning. He's wearing a white Henley with grey piping at the neck and sleeves and a pair of dark-wash denim jeans.

Adrian looks up at Julian and smirks for some reason.

"I suppose I'll be seeing you again tonight?" Adrian asks him.

"Do I have a choice?" Julian responds, sounding irritated by Adrian's question.

"I suppose not, unless you purposely want to make your sister unhappy with you. And for goodness' sakes' and my sanity on this visit, don't piss her off any more than you have to, Julian."

"We'll be there," Julian pledges, clearly wanting to drop the subject.

I can only assume Julian is including me in this 'we', even though I don't have a clue what the two of them are talking about.

Adrian looks at me and bows at the waist.

"I will see you this evening, dear Sarah. Try to ensure Julian makes it on time. He's notorious for being late to our little soirées."

"I'll do my best," I reply, even though I still don't have a clue what either of them is referring to, but I'm not about to let Adrian know that little fact.

Daniel leans in toward me and gives me a quick peck on the cheek. "See you tonight, Sarah."

"See ya."

Once Adrian and Daniel walk out the door, I motion to Julian for him to follow me into the kitchen.

Once there, I ask, "Is Adrian out of earshot?"

Julian tilts his head like he's listening to something.

"He is now," he tells me a few seconds later.

"What's all this about your sister? Are we going to go see her?"

"She called this morning to tell me she's throwing a party to welcome Adrian to New Orleans. Apparently she tried to contact me yesterday, but I wasn't in the mood to talk to anyone, much less her."

Well, that was partly my fault. My refusal to come back here had put Julian in such a bad temper he didn't even want to talk to his only living relative.

"It's all right," I tell him. I can't very well place all the blame for the surprise on his shoulders. "So, what kind of party is it? And that's woman-speak for how nice do I need to dress."

Julian grins. "Don't worry about your outfit. I have that one covered."

"You mean you already have something for me to wear?"

"Yes."

When he doesn't elaborate on what it is I'm supposed to be dressed in for the party, I immediately become suspicious.

"Can you at least show me what I'm expected to put on before we go to your sister's place?"

"Yes," he hesitates before continuing. "You should probably know that if there are any other female companions in attendance, they will be wearing the same dress as you, just in a different color."

"Exactly the same?" I ask, finding such a notion strange.

Julian nods. "It's simply tradition. It lets everyone present know that you belong to me."

Well, that just made me feel special all over.

"Would you like to see it?" he asks.

"Yes," I reply apprehensively, "I would."

Julian holds his hand out to me and we walk up to the second floor together. In the hallway near my room, there is a pull-down latch hanging from the ceiling that I never noticed before now. Julian pulls on it and a flight of stairs descends to our level, leading up to the attic. He flips a switch on the wall beside us that turns on a light in the space above. He then motions for me to precede him up the steps.

The attic is large and almost completely full of cardboard boxes in various sizes. It's so big someone could convert it into another floor for the house, if they wanted to spend the time and money to finish it out.

"Walk straight ahead," he instructs.

I walk down the narrow corridor that has been left between the boxes and come to a tall one marked *Companion*. Julian comes up behind me and lifts the top off, which allows the front piece of cardboard to drop down in front of me. Hanging inside the box are several sizes of the same dress.

I reach in and lift one of the dresses by its hanger, pulling it out for a closer inspection.

"Umm," I say, looking at it in its entirety and not seeing much there, "are you sure this is a dress and not a table cloth?"

Because that's exactly what it reminds me of. The dress is of a sheer purple fabric with lacy white floral appliqués strategically placed to hide all my girly parts. I silently pray there's a shawl or something else that's supposed to go over it.

"I know it doesn't look like much," Julian admits, "but you'll look beautiful in it, if that's any consolation."

"It really isn't," I complain, placing the dress back inside the box and quickly searching for one in my size. Once I have the right one, Julian closes the box back up.

"Why do you have a stock of this dress in different sizes?" I ask.

"My sister sent them over. We originally thought it would be your mother who would need one, and we didn't know what size she would be. It was just simpler to buy one in every size so she would have a dress that fit."

When we go back down the attic stairs, I go directly to my room so I can try the dress on.

After I have it on and look at myself in the full-length mirror, I see that the dress isn't quite as revealing as I first feared. In fact, it's rather elegant and sexy.

There's a soft knock on the door and I hear Helen ask, "Can I come in, Sarah?"

"Please, come in."

Helen walks into the room and smiles when she sees me.

"You look gorgeous," she praises, closing the door behind her. "But I knew you would."

"I feel conspicuous," I confess.

"Nonsense," Helen admonishes, coming to stand in front of me. "You'll be the most beautiful companion there. I dare say Mira will be green with envy when she sees you."

"Who's Mira and why would she be envious of me?"

"Mira is Julian's sister, and she'll be envious of you because she always wants to be the most beautiful woman at her parties. I'm afraid she'll have to settle for second best this time."

"You're being too kind, Helen," I say, brushing off her compliment. "If she looks anything like Julian, I'm sure she's gorgeous beyond all reason."

"You don't give yourself enough credit, Sarah," Helen says exasperatedly. "I see I have a lot of work ahead of me to build up that self-esteem of yours."

I don't say anything. I'm not going to argue with someone who's just trying to pay me a compliment. I know I'm pretty, but so are a lot of other people in the world. If Helen wants to think I'm beautiful, even though she's biased since I'm practically family in her eyes, then I won't even attempt to argue with her. There's nothing wrong with having at least one person in the world think so highly of me.

Helen helps me take the dress off and says she'll press it to make it look more polished. She tells me Julian wants to leave right after lunch, and that I should pack whatever I might require for an overnight stay.

"Mira's parties usually last until the sun comes up," Helen warns me, draping the dress over her arm. "So pack whatever you think you might need. I'll let you borrow one of my bags since that was something I forgot to buy for you the other day. If you forget something, don't worry about it. I'm sure we can buy whatever you leave behind in New Orleans."

After Helen goes to her own room to pack, I start to gather up the items I think I will need for our little trip. Picking out something to wear on the car ride down ends up being harder than I thought. I'm not sure if I should go casual (T-shirt and jeans) or wear a dress. I decide to wear a simple peach-colored maxi dress to travel in and pack the T-shirt and jeans for the ride home tomorrow.

I'm packed and ready to go by the time Helen calls me down for lunch.

I know Julian is still near the house, but I can sense he isn't inside it.

"Where is Julian?" I ask Helen, as she brings me a plate with the largest steak I have ever seen. It's as big as a roast. I begin to wonder how big the cow it came from must have been.

"He's tuning up his bike. He plans to ride it to New Orleans."

"Oh, I thought he would be riding with us."

"No, dear, only you and I will be taking the car. It does have a backseat, but it's barely big enough for a child to fit in much less an adult."

I'm slightly disappointed Julian won't be with us during the drive. I was looking forward to us spending more time together. I decide not to voice my disappointment to Helen, though. Julian did admit to me last night that he was having a hard time being around me because of how I make him feel. I suppose he needs some adjustment time to get used to having me as his companion. All I can do is respect what he needs right now and give him some distance.

After I eat, Helen and I walk to the garage to put our luggage in the Aston Martin. Julian is just walking out of the building, wiping grease off his hands with a blue shop towel.

"Is the bike ready to go?" Helen asks him.

"Should be now," he answers, not bothering to stop as he walks past us to go back into the house. "Just give me a few minutes to change clothes, and I'll drive behind you to New Orleans."

When we enter the garage, we quickly deposit our bags in the trunk of the Aston Martin, and await Julian's return.

He comes back out dressed like a true biker in a black leather jacket, chaps, and boots. He looks great and a bit rebellious in a James Dean-Mad Max sort of way.

"I'll follow behind you," he tells Helen as he puts on his shiny black helmet and pulls the visor down over his face.

When he turns around to mount his bike, I can't help but smile. Julian's chaps don't cover his perfectly formed derrière, which is quite visible in the pair of tight fitting jeans he's wearing. Helen has to clear her throat to refocus my attention and shame me into getting inside the car so we can leave.

The trip isn't as painful as I feared it might be. Julian stays true to his word and rides behind us the whole way down. Once we get close to New Orleans, Helen seems to know exactly where she's going. Mira's house is on the outskirts of the city, in Metairie. There are quite a few nice homes in her neighborhood, so when Helen pulls into Mira's driveway I'm not too surprised by how large it is.

Mira's three-story home isn't just a house. It's a castle made of blue sandstone with an orange tiled roof. I can only guess that the home is somewhere in the neighborhood of 14,000-square-feet. I've always had a good eye for real estate since Susan and Pete Hughes are real estate agents. They taught me a few things about sizing up square footage of a home in a single glance and estimating its value just by looking at it from the street. If I were to guess, I would say Mira's home is worth at least $8 million, considering its size and location.

We park in front of the mammoth mansion and are greeted by two women and a man dressed in typical black and white servant outfits.

Julian parks his bike behind the Vanquish while the butler introduces himself to us.

"My name is Fredrick," he tells Helen and me as Julian walks over to stand beside us, taking his helmet off. "I am Ms. Movila's butler." He turns to Julian. "I presume you are Mr. Movila?"

"Yes. This is Helen and Sarah," Julian says nodding to us. "If you wouldn't mind, the ladies need to freshen up and change before the party this evening. I'm sure Mira has their rooms ready."

"Julian!"

I predicted Julian's sister would be gorgeous and I quickly find out I was right. She's at least 5'10", shaped like a Barbie doll, with straight long brown hair and bangs framing an oval face. She has the same striking hazel eyes Julian does. She throws herself into her brother's arms, looking deliriously happy to see him.

"Hello, Mira." Julian returns his sister's hug and even gives her one of his genuine smiles.

Mira steps back from him and immediately finds me with her eyes.

"You must be Sarah," she says, holding out her hand to me. Her expression is friendly enough, and if I wasn't able to tell what she was truly feeling I might have been fooled by the happy expression on her face. There is an undertone of hostility I don't quite understand in her feelings and a smidge of jealousy that has me baffled as well.

"Hi," I reply, plastering a congenial smile onto my face. "It's nice to meet you."

Mira looks at Helen and just nods her head in greeting. Helen does the same, which strikes me as odd. Surely the two of them have known each other for a long time. Isn't a verbal greeting in order?

Mira takes Julian by the arm. "Come inside. You have to see the house. It's absolutely *gorgeous.*"

"I should make sure Sarah is settled in first," Julian tries to argue, for which I'm grateful.

Mira waves a hand at her butler. "Fredrick, dear, would you please see that the ladies get settled in their rooms while I show my brother around?"

"Of course, Ms. Movila." Fredrick bows his head in his mistress's direction.

"They'll be fine," Mira assures Julian, tugging on his arms so he'll follow her into her castle.

Julian turns to me. "Do you need me to be with you?"

I would have felt more comfortable with him near, but that seems like admitting I'm scared to be on my own in Mira's domain. I'm not about to give her an upper hand like that.

"Go ahead," I tell him, doing my best to look unconcerned about his absence. "Helen and I will be fine."

Julian hesitates, like he knows I'm lying, but he continues to follow Mira into her house anyway as she jabbers on about the Richardsonian Romanesque Revival mansion.

Fredrick keeps true to his word and personally escorts Helen and me to our rooms. I'm not sure why but Helen is placed in a room on the third floor while mine is located on the second.

"Why can't I have a room beside Sarah?" Helen asks Fredrick as we're putting my things in my room.

"Servant quarters are located on the third floor, madam, and guests on the second," he curtly informs her.

I worry Helen's head will explode at any second as her face turns the color of a ripe tomato she's so indignant.

Even I know Helen isn't a real servant. She's a trusted friend and confidante who happens to take care of things around Julian's home. She is nothing like Fredrick and the maid drones who follow his every dictate.

I feel even worse for Helen when I see the room they expect her to spend the night in. While my room is furnished with a bed so large I'm not even sure I'll be able to climb into it on my own, Helen's room looks like it was made for a dwarf child. She ends up having to crouch just to reach the twin bed in the room because the ceiling is the slanting part of the roof. Fredrick shows her the community bathroom that all the servants are expected to share at the end of the floor's hallway.

"This room is just ridiculous, Helen. Why don't you stay with me in my room?" I beseech her, not wanting to think of her having to spend the night in such cramped quarters. I have to stand by the doorway because the room won't fit two people. It barely fits one.

"Not on your life," she states stubbornly, crouching down to get to the bed with her suitcase, almost having to get on her knees.

I stifle my laughter at the scene she makes trying to reach her bed. It isn't funny, but the picture of Helen trying to act like everything is normal is just too much for me.

"I will not let that woman think she has insulted me!" Helen tosses her suitcase onto the bed and yanks it open.

"I thought the two of you would be friends after all these years, not mortal enemies," I admit.

"She and I have never seen eye to eye, especially where Julian is concerned."

Finding this curious, I ask, "Why is that?"

Helen sits on the bed, having to lean forward slightly so she doesn't hit her head against the ceiling.

"Mira is a selfish creature," Helen answers, not bothering to hide the hostility she feels towards Julian's sister. "If it hadn't been for her, Julian would have never been made a vampire. You would think that sort of thing would humble a person, but Mira has never seen her affliction as a curse. She loves the way she is because she will always be beautiful and young. She has no desire to be anything else."

"What is it that the two of you disagree on concerning Julian?"

Helen hesitates. I know she's withholding vital information from me. She feels conflicted about wanting to tell me what's going on and her unwavering loyalty to Julian. Her loyalty wins out.

"Julian will tell you in his own time," she answers. "I would rather not say anything about his private affairs. When he wants you to know, he'll tell you I'm sure."

I silently pray that I don't have to wait too long.

CHAPTER 10.

I head back down to the second floor, still feeling awkward about Helen's room assignment. It's clearly an insult on Mira's part and one that irks me to no end. In my eyes, Helen does not deserve to be so blatantly disrespected, and it speaks volumes about Mira's true character.

Just as I'm about to open the door to my bedroom, I hear a friendly voice joyfully call out my name. When I turn to look down the hallway, I watch as a smiling Daniel walks up to me. It's nice to see a familiar face within Mira's citadel of intimidation.

"Glad to see you made it," Daniel says, casually leaning in and lightly kissing me on the cheek in greeting. "This sure is a big house, isn't it?"

"Gargantuan," I agree. "Are you all settled in for your stay here?"

"Yeah." He tilts his head to the left. "My room is right across the hall from yours, so if you need anything just let me know."

"Thanks. I will." I am somewhat relieved Daniel will be so close. At least I know I have one ally nearby.

"Ahh, Sarah," I hear Adrian croon.

Daniel and I look towards the head of the stairs and see him ascend the last step. "I see Daniel has found you. He was concerned you might arrive late and miss the festivities all together."

"We left right after lunch so we would get here early. I think Julian wanted to give me some extra time to get ready for the party."

"No doubt you will look stunning in your companion outfit." Adrian walks to the door of the room on the right-hand side of mine. "Well, well, well, I see we're practically roommates." He grins at me somewhat lasciviously, and I can tell he's pleased with the sleeping arrangements.

"I should probably start getting ready," I tell the men. It's still early, but I need a good excuse to get away from Adrian's creepy gaze. I wish Julian was with me. I seriously doubt Adrian would be so open with his blatant leering of my person if he was around. "See you both at the party."

Before either of them has a chance to say anything else I quickly step into my room, thankful for the sanctuary it provides.

The large bathroom connected to my room has a claw-foot bathtub that I decide to take advantage of. After a long, warm soak, the tension I feel about attending the party begins to ebb away. As I'm drying off with a towel, Helen comes into my room to help me get ready for the evening. She's definitely more adept at handling my hair than I am, so I let her style it for me. She has it curled into cascades of soft wispy waves before I know it. I do my own makeup, but I take her advice about making it a bit more dramatic than how I normally wear it. I apply a bit more eye shadow, mascara, and lipstick.

When Helen lays my dress out on the bed, I realize I'm missing one crucial element to my glamorous ensemble.

"I don't have any shoes!"

Helen slaps the palm of her right hand against her forehead as if she's suddenly developed an excruciating headache.

"Good Lord, I completely forgot about shoes," she moans despondently. "I must be getting forgetful in my old age."

While we're discussing whether Helen has time to run into town to buy me some shoes, there's a knock on my door.

"It's Julian," I tell Helen. I can feel his presence out in the hallway.

"You didn't happen to bring any shoes, did you?" Helen inquires as she opens the door for Julian.

"Uh, no," Julian says looking confused. "Sarah doesn't have any shoes?"

When Julian walks in, I feel like all the oxygen in the room suddenly disappears. I can't seem to remember how to breathe as I contemplate how dashing he looks in his outfit.

Is it proper to call a man stunning? That's the only word that my befuddled brain can come up with as I stare at him.

He's dressed in what looks like a black tuxedo but the jacket has a satin mandarin collar and button-less front, which is edged in black satin. His shirt is made of dark red silk with a white collar and cuffs peeking out of the sleeves. He's wearing a matching red vest and no tie. The shirt is folded where a tie should have been with a single black button holding the folds together mimicking a tie.

Julian stares at me, too, with his infuriatingly expressionless face.

"We forgot shoes," is all I can think to say to him.

Julian narrows his eyes at me for a moment as if he suspects there's something wrong with me. I probably look like a besotted schoolgirl, completely overwhelmed by the situation she finds herself in, which is precisely how I feel.

"I'll go see if Mira has some you can wear," he tells me before I can ask him not to. I'm sure Mira will get a kick out of hearing the country bumpkin doesn't have any shoes to wear to her grand gala.

A few minutes later, Julian returns with a shoebox in his hands.

"These should fit you," he says before kneeling in front of me on one knee and taking the lid off the box. Inside is a pair of Jimmy Choo shoes. I'm sure they cost as much as my monthly rent. They're nude in color with 3-inch high heels and a bejeweled bow on the side. They will certainly go with my dress, but does he honestly think I'll be able to dance in shoes that tall without breaking an arm or a leg? Possibly both...

"I can't wear those," I tell him as he takes one out, acting like he's going to put them on me himself.

"Of course you can," he professes. "They're your size."

"That isn't what I mean," I say irritably, because he's talking to me like I'm a child. "I'll break my neck trying to wear those things. I tried to wear high heels to my senior prom and almost broke my neck just trying to walk down the stairs."

"Sarah," Julian says indulgently, looking up from his kneeling position, "with your added agility, you can probably walk a tightrope twenty feet in the air in these shoes and never take one misstep. You need to trust me. You'll be fine."

Oh, yeah. I had forgotten about that. I still haven't put my new super powers to the test. Well, not really. I don't think eating contests with Daniel count as a proper trial of my superhuman agility; definitely not super-strength.

I lift one foot off the floor and let Julian slip the shoes onto my feet.

Once the shoes are on, I walk back and forth in front of him to test my balance. I find that he's right. I don't feel awkward in the shoes at all. In fact, the added height makes me feel more confident.

"I guess I'm ready," I say, turning around to look at Julian.

"You'll be the belle of the ball tonight," Helen says, beaming with pride. "I just wish I could witness Mira's reaction when she sees you."

"You won't be there at all?" I ask. I just assumed she would be coming with us.

"No, dear. The help isn't allowed to attend the big event."

"I talked to Mira about that." Julian's annoyance with his sister is obvious in his tone. I'm glad to hear it. "She won't make that mistake again, Helen. I apologize for her rudeness to you."

"It's just as well. I've always wanted to visit Canal Street and Jackson Square to see what all the fuss is about. You two have a wonderful time tonight. Don't worry about me; just watch each other's backs."

What was that supposed to mean? I don't have a chance to ask because Helen leaves the room.

Julian looks back at me and allows himself a moment to study how I look in my companion outfit.

"I think Helen is right," he tells me, lifting his gaze to meet my eyes again. "Mira is going to be jealous when she sees you in that dress, considering how beautiful you look in it."

"Thank you," I say, averting my gaze from his because I don't want him to see how his words are affecting me.

I'm a complete idiot. I know I can't have a future with Julian, but that's what my heart is starting to yearn for. I don't even know if he would want the same thing. Sure, we've sort of had a couple of make-out sessions, but neither of us has brought them up in the light of day. I'm not sure why that is, either. It's almost like those moments are separate from our normal lives. Yet what about my life has remained normal since meeting Julian?

"Shall we go?" Julian holds his arm out to me expectantly. I slip my arm through his and take a deep, steadying breath.

"Don't worry," he says, patting my hand for added reassurance. "Everything will be fine."

As we walk down the stairs to the first floor, I can hear the soothing strings of an orchestra playing outside.

Julian walks me to the back of the house to a pair of doors leading out onto a veranda. It appears that most of the guests have already arrived and are enjoying themselves immensely as they talk and laugh with one another. Mira's backyard is like a miniature version of the garden at the Palace of Versailles. My arm involuntarily tightens around Julian's, betraying my nervousness.

"It's all right," he whispers in a calm voice. "None of them are going to bite you, Sarah. Only I get to have that pleasure."

I can't help but laugh a little at his joke. When I look over at him, he winks at me.

"Come on, I want to introduce you to Petru. He's a very old and dear friend of mine."

As we walk through the throng of people, it feels like everyone's eyes are on us. I'm sure I'm just allowing my imagination to run away with me. We walk up to a young man, who doesn't appear to be older than eighteen, with a face so beautiful and perfectly proportioned he almost looks feminine. He has short black hair that's stylishly messy and is wearing a simple black tuxedo with a bow tie.

"Petru," Julian says to the young man, "I would like to introduce you to my new companion, Sarah."

Petru doesn't bother with shaking my hand. Instead, he kisses me straight on the lips. It's a chaste kiss, but a kiss nonetheless. Julian doesn't seem to mind, so I don't let it bother me either. There was no sexual intent behind the peck anyway. It was more like a kiss an old friend would bestow upon you after being separated for a great length of time.

"It's an honor to meet you, Sarah." Petru's accent isn't as smooth as Julian's, but not quite as harsh as Adrian's.

"I'm pleased to meet you, too, Petru."

"I think you've caught the attention of everyone here," he whispers to me in a conspiratorial manner as his gaze travels around the throng of partygoers present.

So I wasn't just imagining things. Everyone *is* looking at us.

"And why wouldn't they?" He smiles at me with a boyish charm that helps put me at ease. "You are exquisite."

I try my best not to blush, but I'm pretty sure I fail miserably since Petru begins to laugh.

"Don't worry, dear Sarah. I'm sure Julian will protect you from anyone who's foolish enough to attempt bedding you this evening."

I can't think of a witty retort to his statement. What would have been a decent response?

"Enough, Petru," Julian admonishes, not taking his friend's comments as being disrespectful. "I think you've embarrassed Sarah enough for one night."

"Well, I'm just telling her the truth, old friend. If my predilections steered toward the fairer sex, I would certainly be considering a romp in one of your sister's bedrooms with your companion."

"*Enough.*" Julian says more forcefully, as if he's warning Petru that he needs to temper his words. "Sarah has no idea what types of creatures are around her. She needs our protection more than she needs you teasing her."

Petru smiles. "Quite right." He snaps his heels together as if he's a soldier, and bows to me. "Forgive me, Sarah. I forgot you're new to our world. I will do my best to ensure your safety this evening."

Am I in actual danger here? That hadn't even occurred to me. What could be dangerous at a party, besides the possibility of choking on a pig-in-the-blanket or tripping over my own two feet? The latter of those two concerns has been a constant worry for me ever since we stepped out of my room.

I assume Petru is a vampire since Julian referred to him as an 'old friend'. As far as the rest of the people at the party are concerned, I don't have a clue who or what they are. I decide, for my own safety, I'll need to bring down the wall protecting me from the feelings of those surrounding us so I can better gauge who might be a threat and who isn't. I don't want to do it. I never do it in such a large crowd. If I have to guess, there are probably close to a hundred people present. But if Julian and I are in danger, I need to use all of the resources available in my small arsenal of gifts to protect us.

I slowly test the people around us first. Most are just curious about me. I presume that's because I'm the newest addition to the vampire community. I let my guard down a little further to include more in my circle, and come into contact with someone who has rather volatile and hostile emotions towards almost everyone present. I glance over my shoulder to find the person of interest. He isn't hard to pick out of the crowd.

Standing by the water fountain, holding the stem of a champagne glass loosely between his beefy fingers, is a man who reminds me of Dwayne "The Rock" Johnson when he was in his prime wrestling form. He's staring at us with a gaze that can only be described as hard and contemptuous. I'm not sure how long I stare back at him, expecting him to turn away or acknowledge the fact that I'm looking at him. Julian has to touch me on the shoulder to regain my attention. I turn my head back around, but I can still feel the stranger's eyes on me.

"Who is he?" I ask Julian.

"What is he would be a more appropriate question," Julian answers, quickly glancing in the stranger's direction. "He's a werewolf named Damien. I would suggest you stay away from him."

"Why? Is he dangerous?"

"He doesn't like vampires; most werewolves don't."

"Then why is he at a party thrown by a vampire?"

"Good question," Petru remarks dryly, staring over my shoulder at the werewolf. "I've never understood what it is your sister sees in those mangy mongrels, or what they see in her for that matter, if I'm being honest."

Julian shrugs. "You would have to ask her those questions. I can't say for sure. She *has* always liked dogs for pets, though."

Petru guffaws so loudly the people around us start to openly gawk at him. He doesn't seem to mind their attention, and I know then that I will like Petru very much. He's a free spirit who doesn't care what other people think about him. How I wish I could be that comfortable in my own skin. Maybe it takes living four hundred years to build up that sort of self-esteem.

"What other types of people are here?" I use the term 'people' loosely because I don't know what else to call them.

Petru looks to the right of us and nods his head. "Over there you have the alfar."

"What's an alfar?" I have to ask, never having heard the term used before.

"The word you would use to refer to them is elves," Julian explains, "but they hate being called that. They're definitely not the cute little elves Santa has working in his workshop. These would more than likely burn the North Pole down to the ground."

"That's their queen in the middle of them, wearing the large crown," Petru points out. "Her name is Shael."

When I look over to where Petru indicates, I expect to see a group of light- skinned, pointy-eared people. I'm surprised to find that they look disappointingly normal. Some are pale, but for the most part they all have varying shades of skin tones ranging from white to black. I try to see if their ears are pointy, like Tolkien described them, but unfortunately their ears look pretty normal, too.

The queen is the only one who even comes close to what I expect an elf to look like. She is the palest person I have ever seen, and her skin is as perfect as porcelain. She's wearing a brown silk dress with a feathered bodice. Her hair is long and blonde. A tall wispy crown made of platinum and diamonds adorns the top of her head. Her eyes are as green as emeralds and her lips shine ruby red. When she laughs, it's almost like light emanates from her. It's obvious she's a person content with her life and happy with those around her. A small movement catches my eye near her feet, and it's only then that I notice the cat sitting next to her.

It's a white cat, but unlike any normal house cat I've ever seen. If anything, this cat looks more elvish than most of the elves, or alfar, surrounding it. It has a long svelte body with short, shiny white hair. Two pointy ears jut out from the top of its upside down triangular face and two prominent blue eyes are watching those around the queen with immense caution. I've never been able to sense the feelings of animals, but this cat is different. I'm getting a definite vibe of restlessness from it. While I stare at it, the cat turns its small head and looks directly at me. Its eyes form narrows slits as if it's sizing me up. Then it turns to the queen and meows. She quickly bends down to pick up the feline and cradles it in her arms as though it's a cherished friend, not just a pet.

"What kind of cat is that?" I ask my companions.

"We've been told it's an Oriental Blue Point Siamese cat," Julian tells me, also looking at the queen. "Though, I've had my suspicions he's more than just a feline."

So do I. He is definitely not ordinary.

"What else are here?" I ask Petru, since he seems to be in the mood to introduce me to the gathering of creatures surrounding us and increasing my knowledge of the supernatural.

He looks at the group of people directly behind him and turns back around to me.

"Back there are the witches and warlocks. Nasty bunch for the most part. I wouldn't bother messing with any of them, if I were you. They're very temperamental, and jealous of us for having eternal life."

I take a quick look behind Petru and make a mental note not to involve myself with them. From the wave of discontent and jealousy I sense from the group, I understand Petru's warning all too clearly. Although, there *is* one bright light in the midst of their darkness. He's standing slightly away from the others, talking with a witch who is obviously enamored with him. He's handsome and of average height and weight, with light brown hair parted to the side. I sense he doesn't want to be at the party, but he is curious about something he hopes to see here.

The small orchestra draws my attention by playing something very loud in order to ensure everyone turns toward them. Fredrick, Mira's butler, walks out onto the balcony with a spotlight shining down on him.

"Ladies and gentleman, I would like to present your hostess for the evening and the guest of honor: Mira Movila and Adrian Costel!"

The crowd gives polite, yet controlled, applause as the two make their dramatic entrance into the party. I end up hearing a few snickers around me when the couple appears before us on the veranda. I have to admit I would have snickered, too, if Julian hadn't been standing right next to me. Since Mira is his sister, I can't disrespect him in such a way.

The pair comes out onto the balcony dressed like a king and queen. Mira is in a beautiful white satin ball gown with gold embroidered fleur-de-lis scattered around the skirt. Adrian is dressed in a black velvet jacket with a white ruffled shirt underneath and gold pantaloons with white stockings and black gold buckled shoes.

What makes some people snicker, almost including myself, are the obnoxiously large feather contraptions each is wearing across their shoulders. They have to be at least three feet tall and just as wide covered in white feathers, gold ribbon, and crystals. I can only assume they're only able to balance them on their shoulders because of their strength as vampires.

They walk hand in hand to the edge of the balcony.

"Welcome dear friends," Mira shouts, smiling to her captive audience. "Thank you all for coming to my little get-together to welcome Adrian to our fair city. Make sure you say hello to him when you get a chance, but above all else have a good time!"

Everyone claps and cheers politely as the king and queen of the ball make their way down to us lowly commoners. When they reach the foot of the steps, a group of servants is there, waiting to take the feathered ornamentations off their shoulders. Mira and Adrian make their way through the guests and eventually end up in our little circle of three.

"Enjoying the party?" Mira asks us, gracefully grabbing two glasses of champagne from a passing waiter's silver tray. She hands one of the glasses to Adrian. It's odd to see him be so submissive. He is definitely a different creature around Mira.

"You've chosen some interesting guests, Mira," Petru says. "Aren't you worried that a fight might break out?"

Mira's lilting laughter fills the air. "Oh, Petru, you simply don't understand the politics of living in New Orleans. If I didn't invite everyone, there would be hurt feelings, and fights definitely would occur. This way no one feels slighted, and I get to keep the peace in my city."

Mira doesn't say 'my city' like most people would, meaning it was the city they live in. No, she actually means the words literally. This is her city. She actually views herself as the Queen of New Orleans.

Mira's eyes glance in my direction, like I'm not worthy of her looking at me for long. But in those few short seconds, I could feel her jealousy before her enormous ego kicked back in. Once she reminds herself that she's the fairest maiden in all the land, she looks back at me.

"So, Sarah, have the men told you what types of creatures are here this evening?"

"Yes. I've learned a lot tonight."

She smiles politely and takes a sip of her champagne before continuing. "This is just the beginning of your education, I'm afraid, but I'm sure Julian will be able to bring you up to speed in no time at all on what else is involved in our little section of the universe."

I have no idea what she's talking about, but I'm not about to let her think I'm scared of what I don't know.

"I'm sure he will," I answer. "I look forward to learning more about everyone."

Mira's smile falters. She feels a moment of fear but quickly hides it underneath a layer of contempt. I can't tell what she's afraid of, but I know the contempt is for me.

"Enjoy the rest of the party," she tells us, taking hold of a strangely silent Adrian's arm. It's almost like being around Mira has castrated him. "We need to go greet our other guests."

Petru looks at me and winks. "Now that's what I like to see."

"What?" I ask, not having a clue about what he's referring to.

"Someone who doesn't bow down to Mira's overgrown sense of self-importance. She needs to be reminded every once in a while that she isn't the queen of all she surveys."

"She's just trying to find her way like the rest of us," Julian says in defense of his sister's behavior. "She doesn't mean any harm."

"Mira may not mean harm, but she's caused it in this city."

"What do you mean?" I ask.

"Before Mira came, all of the supernatural creatures pretty much kept to themselves and didn't bother one another unless it was absolutely necessary. When she arrived here ten years ago, she put together a Council of Elders. Each faction has one seat on the council, and they control what happens in New Orleans now."

"What do you mean? What are they controlling?"

"Most everything," Petru shrugs. "They control where certain creatures can live and work. Sometimes they act as high judge and executioner when someone transgresses against them. I can wholeheartedly say I will never live in this city."

"How did you happen to be here for the party?"

"Oh, I had some business to take care of and my companion wanted to have a look around the city. That's where he is right now."

"Excuse me, I'm so sorry to interrupt."

We all turn to see the alfar queen standing beside us. She's still cradling her strange white cat in her arms. The cat stares at me with its penetrating blue eyes. I can feel that he's extremely excited about something. The feeling I get from the queen herself is odd, to say the least. She feels a sense of love for me, which seems strange since we've never met before this moment. Although, I must admit that I also feel an unexpected connection to her that I can't explain.

I'm unsure what to do in the presence of royalty from another race until Petru and Julian bow at the waist. I quickly follow their lead and curtsey.

"Good evening, Queen Shael," Julian says with the utmost respect. "Are you enjoying the party?"

"Well, I was having a perfectly fine time until Viktor decided it was time he left me."

"Your cat decided?" Petru questions, seeking clarification of her words.

The queen nods, looking sad. "Yes, he says the time has come for him to experience other adventures." Queen Shael looks at me. "Can I ask what your name is, sweet child?"

"Sarah," I answer. "Sarah Jane Marcel."

"Sarah, you have been granted a great gift this evening. I hope you appreciate it as much as I have." With those words, she proceeds to hand me her cat.

"I don't understand," I say, cradling the feline against my waist. Why did she just hand me her cat? What am I supposed to do with it?

"Viktor has chosen you to be his next guardian. Take care of him, Sarah, and he will take care of you."

The queen is sad about losing her pet, but she also feels a sense of gratitude towards him.

"He has seen me through the darkest days of my life and brought me through to the other side of them sane. I can only hope he helps you with whatever is about to happen in your life. Keep him close," she says, almost like a warning. "While others around you may let you down, he will never disappoint you. And he will love you like no other ever will."

Ok, that's a weird thing to say about a cat.

Is now a good time to tell her I'm allergic to cats? It doesn't seem like it. For the Queen of the Alfar, giving Viktor up is harder than anything she has ever had to do in her life thus far. I can feel how it's tearing her heart in two to give him to me.

She leans toward me and whispers in my ear. "If you ever need my help, Sarah Marcel, simply ask Viktor to contact me. He can always find me wherever I am."

"Yes, ma'am." I don't know what else to say to her. Apparently, my new cat has a direct line to the alfar queen. How many cats can you say that about?

Shael kisses Viktor between his ears and on his perky pink nose.

"Thank you for all that you have done for me," she tells him lovingly. "I will never forget you, and you will always be my friend, no matter where you are."

She stands straight and curtsies to us before turning around and making her way back to her brethren.

Julian and Petru watch the queen walk away before turning their attention back to the skinny white cat in my arms.

"What just happened?" I ask them, still feeling confused by Queen Shael's actions. "How can a cat choose its next owner?"

Viktor gives an indignant meow and lifts his head chin first into the air, like I've just insulted him by calling him a mere cat.

"Like we said earlier," Julian replies, petting the cat on the head to which Viktor gives a contented purr. "We don't believe he's a regular cat. It's a great honor to be chosen by him, Sarah. As far as I know, he's only ever belonged to alfar royalty. I've never heard of him choosing a commoner."

Well, that made me feel special all over. How was I, a lowly commoner, supposed to take care of some alfar royal heirloom? I didn't even like cats. I didn't care for dogs either. I just wasn't a pet person!

I can feel at least two hundred eyes staring straight at me, but one of them is filled with almost pure hatred. I cautiously peer over Petru's shoulder and see Mira staring directly at me. On the outside she is a picture of calm, but on the inside, a place only I can sense, she is a boiling cauldron of jealousy and hate. There are a few others scattered around the party who are feeling jealous of me, but none of them match the ferocity of Mira's emotions. She covets what I have been given, even though I don't understand what the big deal is. He's just a cat, right?

CHAPTER 11.

I'm unsure what to do with the cat, but I guess I should have known that the decision wouldn't be mine to make. Not long after choosing to be with me, Viktor jumps out of my arms and prances his way up the incline of the stone rail that leads up to the veranda. Once there he sits down like a prince, surveying the comings and goings of his subjects. I always thought cats had a natural superiority complex, but Viktor takes it to a completely new level. I don't get the feeling that he left my arms because he's upset with me, though. He simply seems to want to view the party from a better vantage point.

The orchestra seated directly underneath Viktor's position starts to play a song that seems to signal the beginning of the dancing portion of the evening. Mira and Adrian are the first to take the dancefloor while everyone else watches them twirl around in time with the music. Not long after they start dancing Mira waves her hand in the air, inviting the rest of the party to join them.

"May I have the first dance?"

I turn to look behind me and find the warlock I saw earlier standing there now. His blue-grey eyes twinkle with expectation as he awaits my answer.

"Shouldn't you keep to your own kind, *warlock*?" Petru asks gruffly, coming to stand slightly in front of me in a protective manner, almost completely blocking the stranger from my view.

I feel Julian's hand join with mine, entwining our fingers in an intimate gesture as if he's branding me as his.

"I have the pleasure of the first dance," Julian informs him. "Perhaps another time."

"I see," the warlock says in disappointment. Although, I get the feeling it isn't because he won't be able to dance with me. I think he's disappointed by the way my vampire friends are treating him.

"Perhaps later you will be free to choose your own partner for a dance," he says, bowing his head to me respectfully before turning around and walking away.

Julian maintains his hold on my hand as he leads me to the dance floor. I'm not sure if I can dance the way everyone else is, twirling about like the Cinderella in a jewelry box I once owned as a child. I take a deep breath and pray that my newly enhanced agility will come into play here, saving me from making a complete fool out of myself.

"Just follow my lead," Julian instructs, placing one hand on my waist and raising the hand he still holds into the air. "Everything will be fine."

I do what he says and discover how easy it is to mimic his steps a millisecond after him. I doubt anyone at the party can tell I'm only mirroring my partner's movements. I do feel a bit like a puppet being led around on a string, but that doesn't matter. As long as I don't humiliate myself or Julian, I'm ok with being a marionette. I end up making it through the entire dance without a single misstep.

"You did wonderfully," Julian praises, bowing before me as he kisses the back of my hand.

The warm feel of his lips against my skin sends a pleasurable tingle from my fingernails to the tips of my toes. I hope he can't sense how his touch affects me, but I suspect he does from the way his mouth forms a knowing grin.

"Now it's my turn," Petru announces, unceremoniously plucking my hand out of Julian's and into his own.

"Just be careful with her." Julian's eyes narrow on his friend in warning. "And keep your steps well-defined so she can follow them easily. She's never danced like this before."

"Overprotective much?" Petru pulls me closer to his body, clamping a firm hand on my waist. "I promise to get her back to you in one piece. For goodness' sake, Julian, it's just a dance."

Before Julian can make a reply, the orchestra begins to play a new song.

"Whatever have you done to my best friend?" Petru asks exasperatedly as he twirls me around the dance floor.

"What do you mean?"

"I've never seen him act so possessively over a companion before. I mean, look at him. He's practically jumping at the chance to cut in if he catches me making a mistake."

As we pass Julian, who is standing on the outside of the dancing circle, I notice what Petru means. My vampire companion is keeping a watchful eye on me, but as we pass by everyone else I notice he isn't the only one. I look up to the top of the veranda, where Viktor is lounging comfortably, and see that the cat is keeping a keen eye on me as well.

"It's probably because I'm new to everything," I try to reason. "He still needs for me to have a child for him, too. I'm sure he's just worried something might happen to me before I can ensure his continued immortality."

"You don't know Julian like I do," Petru says, a sense of melancholia filling his words as an equally sad smile touches his lips. "He isn't worried about dying. Sometimes I think he would welcome it."

"Why do you say that?"

"He sees the spell linking your family to him as a burden to whomever he's bound to. If he could kill himself and not doom the next person in line to the bond to sure death, I think he would do it. But there's no way of telling if it would work. I know he considered it before he became bound to you."

"He was going to kill himself?" The mere thought of Julian killing himself makes me tremble. I miss a step in the dance and inadvertently tread on Petru's toes.

"Sorry," I apologize, completely chagrined by the return of my clumsiness.

"No worries, Sarah." Petru smiles down at me in understanding. "It was my fault. I probably shouldn't be telling you these things anyway. I'm sure Julian will be upset with me for divulging his deepest, darkest secret to you."

"I won't say anything to him," I promise.

"He already knows. Super-hearing, remember?" Petru reminds me.

I briefly glance in Julian's direction as we pass him again, and notice the scowl on his face as he stares daggers at Petru.

Once the music stops, signaling the end of the dance, Julian is by my side in a matter of seconds, roughly taking my arm with one hand. I look up at him and see that he's still scowling as he stares at Petru.

Petru bows to me. "Thank you for the dance, Sarah. I hope we can do it again some other time."

I'm not even given a moment to make a reply before Julian practically drags me off the dancefloor.

"What's wrong with you?" I ask him curtly, trying to keep up with his quick, long strides.

"Petru should have never said what he did to you," Julian replies angrily.

"He's your friend," I defend. "I think all he wants is for you to find a way to be happy with the way you are. It's been four hundred years since you were turned, Julian. Don't you think it's time you accepted your fate?"

"No," he says tersely. "The day I accept that I can't break the curse is the day I give in to being a monster." Julian brings me to the foot of the steps to the veranda and turns around to face me. I can see the turmoil of emotion in his eyes. Even though I can't read his feelings, I can still see that being a vampire is slowly consuming his soul.

"Break the curse?" I ask. "How?"

Julian's eyes remain steadfast on mine, but I can tell he's still aware of his surroundings.

"Nothing," he says, even though I get the feeling he simply doesn't want to discuss the true meaning behind his words while we're among those surrounding us. "It's just a fool's wish. Perhaps one day I can find a way to live with what I am, but today is not that day."

Julian's gaze lifts from mine as something captures his attention from somewhere behind me.

"Another would-be suitor approaches," he grouses, letting go of my arm and taking a step back.

If Julian had been anyone else, I would have said he sounded jealous.

I turn to find out who he's looking at and see Daniel approaching us. Daniel's dressed in a conspicuously white suit, white shirt, and blood-red tie. I can only assume this is what male companions are forced to wear, and that red is the color signifying that Daniel belongs to Adrian.

"Are you just now joining the party?" I ask as he comes to stand with us.

"Adrian wanted his meal before the dance, and I always get extra hungry when he feeds early. Have you been to the kitchen here?" There is a sense of awe in Daniel's voice about the place.

"Not yet." The reminder of food, however, immediately makes me eager to find it. I guess that's to be expected. I haven't eaten a bite since lunch that afternoon. My nervousness about the party made food take second place to my own paranoia.

"You have *got* to see it," Daniel declares. "Anything you might be hungry for is in there."

"I'll probably go there later." Actually, there is no probably about it. I will head to the kitchen as soon as I can politely disengage myself from the festivities.

"Mira always treats her companions well and provides them with anything they might want," Julian adds, "especially when they're pregnant."

"I believe the baby is due in a couple of weeks," Daniel says. "From what I understand, Mira's companion has been restricted to bedrest by her doctor until the birth. That's the only reason she isn't here this evening."

"Excuse me."

The warlock who had asked me to dance earlier now stands two steps behind Daniel.

"I was wondering if you might be free for a dance now," he says, looking directly into my eyes, purposely ignoring the two men on either side of me.

I must admit that I'm impressed with his tenacity. It takes a lot of guts to come back so soon after being rebuffed by a vampire.

I look over at Julian, waiting for him to do or say something to prevent me from dancing with the stranger, but my companion remains stone-cold silent and simply stares at the warlock with an impassive expression.

It seems rude to turn someone down twice. Although, I didn't say no to him the first time. It was said for me.

"Only if you tell me your name," I tell him, thinking this a reasonable request.

"Gage Morgan, Ms. Marcel," he answers with a polite bow.

"You already know mine?" I ask, finding it curious.

He smiles as if I've said something amusing. "I believe everyone here this evening knows who you are...may I call you Sarah?"

I nod, feeling even more self-conscious than I already did. I don't know why it should come as a shock to me that most of the people at the party already know my name. I should have expected it. I guess it's because I've always tried to stay in the shadows during social events, not purposely allowing myself to be cast in the limelight.

Since Julian hasn't made a vocal objection to my accepting Gage's offer, I walk away from my companion's side and accept the arm Gage politely holds out for me to take.

"Be careful, Sarah," Julian cautions just before we start to walk away.

I turn around and look at him, nodding my head to let him know that I heard his request.

"Thank you for agreeing to dance with me," Gage says as we near the dancefloor.

"Why were you so persistent about it?" I ask.

"Because I wanted to dance with the most beautiful woman here," he answers smoothly. "Isn't that reason enough?"

I know he's telling the truth… as he sees it anyway.

Gage takes hold of my hand and places his other hand on my back at the waist. We stand together on the dancefloor, waiting for the orchestra to begin its next song which starts only a few seconds later.

"So, is the story true?" he asks me. "Did your mother really raise you without any knowledge of our world?"

I don't see any harm in answering his question. It seems like almost everyone here knows about my past anyway.

"Yes, she did."

"And what do you think of us?"

"What do you mean?"

"Are you frightened to find out that what you thought was just fantasy is actually real?"

"Yes and no. I admit there are some people here who make me uncomfortable."

"I don't make you uncomfortable, do I?" he asks with an affable grin.

"No," I answer. "I don't believe you're a danger to me."

"Hmm, then I guess I'm not being mysterious enough. Don't most women like a little darkness in their men?"

"Not always," I assure him. "Most of the time we just want someone who cares enough about us to listen to what we have to say."

"I would say that sentiment goes both ways."

We're silent for a moment as we continue to dance. I want to ask something but I'm not sure what his reaction will be to my question. I decide it doesn't matter. He'll either answer it or he won't. Either way, this might be the last time I ever see Gage.

"Why do you distance yourself from the other warlocks and witches?" I ask.

"Noticed that, did you?" He's flattered to find out I paid that much attention to his behavior at the party. "I get tired of hearing the same old arguments and jealousies vented whenever we get together. They're a selfish bunch, for the most part."

"Why did you come to the party if you don't like to be around them?"

"I came to see you," he admits freely. "It's rare we have an outsider enter our midst. Fresh blood as it were," he jokes.

"Why are you all so curious about me?"

"You're new and a little mysterious. Plus, most of us have never seen Julian. It's the first time he's ever visited his sister here in New Orleans. I must admit I was as curious to see him as I was you. He's something of a legend."

A legend? Well, this I have to know more about.

"What do you mean by that?" I ask.

"He doesn't socialize much, so hardly anyone knows anything about him. Do you like being bonded with him?"

Even though it seems like Gage is asking a sincerely curious question, I still get the feeling he's digging for information he doesn't need to know. Julian's warning of 'be careful' makes me hesitant to answer Gage's seemingly harmless inquiry. Ultimately, I decide that my relationship with Julian isn't anyone else's business.

"I'm content with my life, if that's what you're asking. I don't resent being bound to him."

The song we have been dancing to comes to an end. While everyone is clapping, I curtsey to my partner.

"Thank you for the dance. I should be getting back to my friends."

Gage bows at the waist. "And thank you for trusting me enough to leave your companion's side for a short while."

There is a meow at my feet. I look down to find Viktor pawing at my shoe as if he's trying to garner my attention. I bend down to pick him up, and cradle him in my arms before I turn away from Gage and walk back to Julian and Daniel.

"Did he behave himself?" Julian asks me as I come to stand in front of him. His tone of voice reminds me of the way Kaylee's dad questioned me after my first date when I was sixteen.

"Yes, he was a perfect gentleman." Absently, I begin to pet Viktor between the ears but, strangely enough, this doesn't earn me a purr from my new feline friend. Viktor's body feels as tense as a piano wire in my arms. His ears are pointing straight up as if he's on high alert. I watch as he turns his head to where the alfar queen is standing.

Queen Shael looks our way and her eyes grow wide in alarm. She says something to the tall black man standing beside her, and that's the last I see of the queen before all hell breaks loose.

I know we're in trouble when an orange bloom of fire shoots straight up into the air like a firework. There's a lot of angry yelling, which seems to cause a small number of people to run towards the veranda to escape what's about to happen. Many of the partygoers emanate extreme excitement for the fight they all feel is about to take place.

"Get in the house!" Julian shouts to Daniel, who doesn't need to be told twice. He sprints towards the house just as Julian grabs me around the waist. I see his wings burst from his back just before he flies us straight into the air and far away from the ensuing melee. Viktor lets out a startled yelp of surprise for being so rudely yanked from the ground towards the heavens.

Julian flies through the sky at a much faster pace than the first time he took me flying. After a few minutes he lands, setting me down a few yards away from the front of the Saint Louis Cathedral. The few tourists standing around us stare in awe, but I don't have time to deal with them just yet.

"What's going on?" I ask Julian as he slides a hand into his front pocket and pulls out his cell phone.

"I'm not sure," he answers hurriedly. "It looked like one of the warlocks cast a warning spell at one of the werewolves."

He quickly finds a number on his phone and presses dial before placing it up to his ear.

"Helen, are you near Jackson Square?" he asks quickly before saying, "Come to Saint Louis Cathedral. Sarah will be waiting for you."

He ends the call and hands me the phone.

"She's on her way. Walk over to the front of the cathedral and stay there until she finds you."

He turns from me and starts to flutter his wings back and forth in preparation of flight. Just before he takes off, I clamp a hand around his forearm and bring him back down with a strength I didn't know I possessed until that moment. Viktor jumps from the arm I was cradling him in and walks a few steps away.

"Where are you going?" I demand of Julian. "You're not going back there, are you?"

"I have to, Sarah," he says, hastily disengaging my hand from his arm with a strength that's far greater than mine. "Mira will need my help getting things back under control."

"I don't want you going back there!" I say in a scared voice. I'm frightened of what I don't understand, and completely terrified that something bad will happen to Julian. "There's so much hatred there, so many of those people were just waiting for something like this to happen. You might get hurt!"

"I'll be all right," he promises. "I won't let anything happen to me. I treasure your life too much."

I hadn't even thought about that aspect of our bond. If he dies, I die too. At least I wouldn't have to live through the heartache of losing him.

"I need to go back now, Sarah," he says more urgently. "I have to help."

On impulse, I grab the front of Julian's shirt and bring his lips down to mine. If we end up dying tonight, I don't want to regret never having given him a true kiss. There's no way he can be absolutely sure nothing will happen to him; accidents happen all the time. I don't want to die with any regrets, and I want him to know how much I care about him.

My heart beats as fast as a freight train as I move my lips against his, kissing him with an urgency and desperate need to let him know how much I want him to return to me. I feel an empty ache begin to fill my heart when I realize something important.

Julian isn't kissing me back.

I pull away from him, lifting my hand to my lips as I silently wish I could reverse time. What have I done? Did I make my move too fast? Will he bring a stop to what's been building between us because I foolishly rushed things? As he stands there, staring at me without an ounce of expression on his face, I wish I could disappear into the ground for all eternity.

"I'm sorry," I whisper to Julian, not knowing what else to say because I'm simply too embarrassed. "I'm so sorry," I repeat before turning my back to him and walking away to put as much distance as I can between us.

I'm only able to take two steps before I feel Julian grab my left hand and whirl me back around to face him. He places one arm around my back, crushing my body against his, and cradles the nape of my neck with his other hand. When he brings his lips down to mine, I want to cry from joy. His lips move across mine with a hunger similar to the first time he drank my blood. Only this time, he doesn't seem interested in taking something from me; he wants to share himself with me. I get the distinct feeling he desperately wants me to know how much he cares. Does he love me? I have no idea. But if this kiss is any indication of his true feelings for me, he definitely likes me… a lot.

When he finally pulls his lips away from mine, there's a fire in his eyes that wasn't there before.

"I'll be back," he promises in a hoarse whisper, before flapping his wings and ascending into the air. I watch him fly across the sky for as long as I can, but he fades from my view only a few short seconds later.

"Are you guys making a movie?" a little blonde girl asks me.

I look over at her and see that she's standing in front of her parents, who are staring at me in utter shock. When I look around the area, I can see about twenty people wearing the same exact expression.

"Yes," I lie, smiling as I say it because people always tend to believe a person who looks friendly. "We're making a vampire romance movie."

"Are you famous?" she asks as her eyes light up in childlike wonder.

"Not yet," I tell her, "but maybe this movie will make me famous one day."

"Come on, Mary Jane," the girl's mother says. Unfortunately, the mother looks doubtful I'm speaking the truth. "We should let the lady work and get back to the hotel."

"Bye!" Mary Jane says as her mother takes her hand, and they all walk away from me rather hurriedly. The other people seem to accept my lie and return to what they were doing before Julian deposited me here. So many movies and TV shows are made in New Orleans nowadays, my lie was completely plausible to the crowd.

"Meow!"

I look over towards the church and see Viktor watching me from his place on the sidewalk step in front of the cathedral. If I didn't know any better, I would swear the cat is smirking at me.

"What?" I ask him as I walk closer to his position. "Haven't you ever seen someone happy before?"

Viktor makes something that sounds like a snort before he proceeds to preen himself. I sit down with him and close my eyes, trying to etch Julian's kiss into my memory. What if he only kissed me because he thought I was embarrassed by his lack of responsiveness to my kiss? Was it a pity kiss? It didn't feel like one, but it did seem like something Julian would do.

How would the two kisses change our relationship? Most importantly, how do I feel about him? Do I love him? Having never been truly in love before it's hard to say, but I do know he's able to make my heart ache in ways I didn't even know it could.

"What happened?" A harried Helen rushes towards me down the sidewalk, rounding the gate of the church as she clutches four large shopping bags in her hands.

"Someone started a fight at the party," I tell her, standing up. "Julian went back to help stop it."

Poor Helen. From the way she's struggling for air, I can only assume she ran most of the way to the church.

"He should have told you it wasn't an emergency," I say to her as she takes a seat on the steps beside me, doing her best to catch her breath.

"Don't fret about me," she says, waving a hand in the air. "I'm just getting old, is all. There was a day, not so long ago, that I could have run a marathon through this city and won!" She laughs. "Not anymore, though. I'm afraid those days are far behind me."

"I see you did a little shopping," I comment, eyeing the bags in front of her.

"You can't come to New Orleans and not shop," she replies, as if the mere thought of not buying something while visiting the city is a sin.

Viktor walks between us and sticks his head into one of the bags, as if searching for something in particular.

Helen stares at the cat for a moment before looking over at me.

"That's not the alfar queen's cat, is it?" she asks in amazement.

I pick my nosey cat up and lay him across my lap. He seems to like it there because he rolls onto his back like a dog would, meowing to me as if demanding that I rub his belly.

"Silly cat," I laugh. Since the kiss with Julian has placed me in such a good mood, I relent to his pushy demand and begin to stroke the soft skin on his stomach.

"She gave him to me tonight," I tell Helen. "I have no idea why. She just said he decided it was time to move on."

"Well, that beats anything I have ever seen," Helen declares, clearly impressed. "As far as I know, he's only belonged to alfar royalty."

"That's what Julian told me." I can't help the smile that spreads across my face as his name passes over my lips.

"What else happened this evening?" Helen asks. When I look up, from the cat sprawled across my lap to her questioning gaze, I can't keep the smile on my face from spreading my lips even wider.

Should I tell her what happened? Maybe she would have a deeper insight into what it all means.

So I tell her everything that happened that night, ending with Julian kissing me before he left.

"Well, that's definitely interesting," she says, becoming silent in thought for a few scant seconds. "He's had lovers in the past, including me, but he always made sure they knew there could never be anything more than friendship between them. You, my dear, are a special case since he literally needs you in order to survive. I'm surprised he's openly showing you affection, but it gives me hope that he's finally allowing himself to feel love again."

Out of nowhere, I suddenly feel a sharp pain deep within my chest. It's so close to my heart I fear it's about to burst out of my body. Involuntary, I cry out in pain. I press my hand against my breastbone, desperately trying to take a breath.

"Sarah! What's wrong?" Helen quickly kneels in front of me, shooing the cat off my lap.

"I don't know," I tell her, feeling the pain ease a little into an aching throb. "Something's wrong, though. We need to find Julian."

"All right, dear, wait here. I'll need to go back to the parking garage and get the car. It's going to take me a little while, but I'll be back as soon as I can."

I nod, letting her know that I understand. Helen leaves her bags with me and sprints off to get the car. Viktor mewls beside me. I pick him up and cradle him in my arms, gaining comfort from his presence.

"Something's wrong, Viktor," I say in a breathless whisper. "Something's wrong with Julian."

Viktor licks my face with his warm little pink tongue. I don't stop him. I take solace in his small act of kindness.

As I sit on the steps in front of Saint Louis Cathedral, the only thing that I'm certain of is that Julian is in trouble and needs my help.

CHAPTER 12.

It probably only takes Helen ten minutes to get the car and come back for us, but it feels like hours. The pain in my chest has subsided somewhat by the time I get into the car and we're on our way back to Mira's house. My gut tells me that time is of the essence, and I urge Helen to go as fast as the Vanquish will allow her. The engine growls to life as she pushes it to its limits and races down the streets of New Orleans. For an elderly woman, Helen has great reflexes as she maneuvers through what little traffic is left on the road at this late hour. The trip back to Mira's takes less than five minutes. Quite impressive for a ride that should have taken a little over twice that much time.

I immediately jump out of the car, and run pell-mell into the house even before the vehicle comes to a complete stop. It's the first time I put my bond with Julian to the test and allow it to guide me through Mira's mansion to find him. I run up the stairs, pass my own room, and open the door to one that is two doors down from Daniel's.

Petru, Mira, Adrian, and Daniel are all standing inside, having a hushed conversation in the far corner of the room. Julian is lying unconscious on the bed, with what looks like a small tree limb sticking out of his chest. I run to stand by his side.

"Why haven't you taken that thing out of him yet?" I yell at them furiously.

"We were debating whether he would bleed to death before his body could heal itself," Petru tells me with an irritating sense of calm. "And I think you can help him, Sarah."

"What do you need me to do?"

"That just might work," Mira says, eyeing me up and down like she's trying to determine whether I'm capable of the task they have in mind. "With a fresh dose of her blood, he should be able to heal fast enough. Plus, she can replace whatever he loses, but we still need to find a way to wake him up so he can feed."

I climb onto the bed, being careful not to jar Julian with my movements. All I need is to make the situation even worse. I brace my hands on either side of his head and lean down to whisper into his ear.

"Julian, please, don't leave me," I beg. "I need you."

When I look back at his face, I see his eyelids slowly flutter open. The grimace of pain etched on his too-pale skin almost makes me wish I hadn't awoken him.

I lean down and press my neck against his mouth so he can feel the throbbing vein there between his lips.

"Drink, Julian," I beg.

"Sarah…" he whispers weakly in protest.

"Drink," I order more forcefully, because I'm not about to lose him to some dumb tree limb.

I feel his teeth clamp down and bite. At first he only suckles on my blood, too weak to do much else. After a minute or so, he regains enough strength to swallow in a steady, rhythmic pattern.

Petru comes to stand beside us.

"This is going to hurt, my friend," he warns Julian as he wraps his hands around the wood. "I'm sorry."

Petru yanks the limb out of Julian's chest in one quick movement.

I feel Julian wince. His groan of pain vibrates against my neck, and I feel his jaw clamp down even harder on my throat, sucking out my blood so fast I can actually feel it flow out of the holes in my neck as he drinks.

I start to become woozy and know that I'm going to lose consciousness soon. He's taking too much of my blood too fast, but I don't know if I should tell him to stop. I assume he'll know when he's taken enough for him to survive. Everything around me begins to spin out of control, and I start to see floating dark circles. I feel so tired my bones begin to ache, and all I want to do is lie down. I can't seem to keep my eyes open as I slump down on top of Julian, my life force draining away.

"Julian," I hear Petru say anxiously. "You have to stop! You're killing her!"

I immediately feel Julian's teeth release their hold on my throat.

"I'll take her to her room," I hear Daniel offer.

"No!" Julian cradles me to his chest protectively. "Leave us! I will take care of her."

Julian's protest is so adamant I don't hear anyone try to object. The only sound I hear is the shuffling of feet and the click of the door being closed.

I want to open my eyes and tell Julian I'm all right, but I have absolutely no energy left to do something so simple. I know I'm on the verge of death. I feel eager to let the darkness envelop my soul and finally reunite me with my parents.

"Sarah," the sadness in Julian's voice forces me to refocus my thoughts on him and turn my back on the sweet succor death is so kindly offering. "Sarah, I need you too. Please, don't leave me now. Not after it's taken me this long to find someone like you."

"I'm not leaving," I tell him drowsily. "Just let me sleep, Julian. Just let me sleep."

If I can just take a little nap, maybe it will be enough to help me regain my energy. I hope that when I wake up, I can find out what the kiss Julian and I shared earlier in the evening really meant to him.

I'm not sure how much time passes before I awaken from a dreamless sleep. I immediately feel the silky warmth of someone holding me close. When I muster up the strength to open my eyes, I find myself staring directly at Julian's bare, but healed, chest. His arms are holding me protectively close to him.

"It worked," I say, lifting a hand to touch the spot on his chest from where the tree limb had been protruding the night before. I tilt my head up so I can look at his face.

He doesn't try to hide what he feels for me in this moment like he normally does. I can clearly see his relief on his face now that I'm finally awake.

"I almost killed you last night," he says, as if the bed we're in is a confessional.

"But you didn't," I'm quick to remind him. "I'm alive. I'm perfectly fine." That isn't the complete truth. My neck hurts a bit, which seems strange. My throat feels sore and stiff, like it's been bruised.

"You're a horrible liar." He gently glides the tips of his fingers along the curve of my throat until he reaches the spot where he bit me.

I wince involuntarily.

Julian sighs.

"I'm sorry," he says, his voice full of remorse. "My bite went too deep. It will take you longer to recover from it this time. I should have had better self-control. I promise you that won't happen again."

I look back down at his chest and run my hand over where the limb had been. There isn't even a scar.

"What happened last night?" I ask. "How did you end up with a limb in your chest?"

"It was complete chaos when I got back here." Julian's tone tells me he didn't expect to come back and find things so out of control. "The alfar guard had to help us separate the witches and warlocks from the werewolves. One of the wolves snatched the limb off the ground and threw it straight at Mira's back."

I should have known he was injured doing something heroic.

"So you stepped in the way to save her from being impaled by it?"

"Yes. I've always been her protector. It was just instinct to do what I did. Luckily it missed my heart, but just barely. I'm sorry I put your life in danger like that, Sarah. If I had bled out…"

"It's all right, Julian. You did what you had to do to protect your sister. I understand that."

"No, it isn't all right. I should have been more careful. If anything ever happened to you because of me…"

I can see the fear he feels from his brash act of chivalry quite clearly on his face. I take his hand and place it over my heart. He looks down, staring at our joined hands.

"I didn't die," I remind him, letting him feel the beating of my heart. "I'm perfectly fine."

He keeps his hand over my heart even after I drop mine away. I feel its warmth slide down my chest, grazing the side of one breast through my bra as it comes to rest against my waist.

I can't tell what he's thinking in that moment. Is he remembering the kiss we shared the night before? Does he intend to kiss me like that again now? I desperately want him to. I want to see if it will help me sort out what my feelings truly are for him.

"Did you undress me?" I ask him.

He nods, looking in my eyes. "I thought you would be more comfortable. Besides, the top of it was soaked with blood. I also had to change out the bedding."

"Too bad you stopped at only the dress," I tease, watching for his reaction.

Julian grins. My heart aches with happiness when I see it.

"I would have taken the rest off, but I didn't think you would appreciate waking up naked in my arms."

I laugh nervously. "True. I suppose I should feel grateful to you for protecting my modesty."

We fall silent for a moment. I feel like he wants to say something else to me, but he either isn't sure how to say it or isn't sure what my reaction will be, perhaps both.

"Sarah," he begins hesitantly, "are you hungry?"

I know it isn't the question he was deliberating about, but the mention of food refocuses my mind and makes it a top priority.

"I'm starving. Can you take me down to the kitchen to get something to eat?"

"No," he says, getting out of bed. "I'll bring you something to eat. You need to rest, especially since you haven't eaten since yesterday. With the amount of blood I took from you last night, I'm surprised you're not feeling the after-effects of it this morning."

"I feel ok," I tell him, rising to a sitting position. Julian puts two pillows against the headboard for me to lean back on and brings the comforter up to my waist. I still feel a bit too exposed, though.

"Can you go to my room and get me a shirt?" I ask him.

Instead, Julian looks in his overnight bag and pulls out a long-sleeve white button-down shirt. He walks back over to the bed and hands it to me.

"Will this do for now?" he asks.

I nod, slipping the shirt on and buttoning it up.

Julian leans down and kisses me on the cheek. "I'll be back as soon as I can."

"Ok."

I watch him walk out the door and can't help but sigh at the loss of his presence. So, we've gone from a passionate, toe-curling kiss to a brotherly one on the cheek in less than a few hours. Great.

"Meow."

I look over at the chair by the window and see Viktor curled up there, watching me with his curiously observant blue eyes.

"I don't understand him at all," I say to the cat, needing someone to talk to about Julian. "Do you?"

"Meow." Viktor leaps from the chair to the bed in one smooth arc of feline agility. He saunters up to me and lies down on my lap, facing me.

I rub his side, finding comfort in his closeness.

"Maybe I should figure out how I feel about him first, what do you think?" I ask him. I suddenly wish I could call Kaylee, but I left my cell phone at Julian's house. Helen would understand, but I have no clue where she is right now. Attempting to use a cat as a surrogate for my friends seems stupid, but what else can I do?

"You were there when he kissed me last night," I tell Viktor. "I've never been kissed by a friend like that. So it has to mean he might actually have feelings for me, right?"

"Meow."

I take that as a yes.

"I just wish he would give me some sign that he remembers kissing me. Why didn't he say anything about it?" The more I ponder that question, the more aggravated I become.

By the time Julian returns to the room with a tray full of food, I'm ready to pounce on him like Viktor might a mouse and demand to know what the kiss we shared the previous night really meant to him. As fate would have it, I'm not given the opportunity because Helen and Daniel follow him into the room.

"You gave us such a fright last night," Helen says, coming to stand at the foot of the bed, with Daniel by her side.

"I thought you were a goner for sure," Daniel admits, looking relieved to see me alive.

"I'm fine," I assure them both. "Just hungry."

On the tray is a platter with five omelets, a bowl of link sausages, another plate filled with beignets sprinkled with powdered sugar, and a pitcher of freshly squeezed orange juice. Viktor relinquishes his position on my lap so Julian can stand the tray across my thighs. I start eating the beignets immediately.

"Do you need anything else?" Julian asks me.

I shake my head since my mouth is full.

"I'll be back up in a little while. I need to take care of something." He turns to Helen and Daniel. "Don't leave her alone until she's finished eating her breakfast. She should regain her strength afterwards, but until then I would rather one or both of you stay with her."

"I won't leave," Daniel is quick to reply as he walks over to sit on the opposite side of the bed from me, indicating he's taking a watchful post.

Julian raises a critical eyebrow at him but doesn't say anything before he leaves the room. However, he does push the door to the bedroom wide open behind him.

After Julian is gone, Daniel fills Helen and me in on what really started the fight at Mira's party.

"Apparently one of the witches had been flirting with Damien all night. Do you know the pack leader of the New Orleans werewolves?"

"Not personally," I say through a mouthful of sausage, "but I saw him there last night."

"Well, she had been leading him on all night. When she started to brush him off like he was a mangy mutt, he got upset and grabbed her by the arms, calling her a whore and all sorts of other crude names. That's when the witch's brother sent up the warning spell, but once you get a werewolf riled there's really nothing you can do to make them back off. Once Damien attacked the witch's brother, the other witches and warlocks got involved. When that happened, Damien's pack attacked to defend their leader."

"Julian mentioned that the alfar guard helped get things under control," I say.

"Yeah, you don't want to mess with an alfar if you don't have to. They're taught from an early age how to fight with all types of weapons, including their bare hands. I don't know if that's why Mira always invites them to her parties or not, but they certainly came in handy at this one. Between them and the four vampires that were there, it still took a long time before they had things under control. I don't think Mira will be having any more parties anytime soon. And Damien is definitely on the outs with her since someone from his own pack tried to kill her with that tree limb."

"But why did he try to kill her?"

"From what I understand, Mira and Damien have been lovers for quite a while now. It could be that Damien got jealous of Adrian being here, and ordered his pack to kill Mira if they were given an opportunity to do so. Wolves are like that. They would rather kill their mate than share."

"Lovely," I quip sarcastically.

"Well, enough talk about jealous werewolves," Helen says with a wave of her hand. "I'll go to your room and find you something suitable to wear," she tells me. "Won't be but a moment, dear."

Helen leaves the room and shuts the door behind her. I wish she had left it open like Julian did. It doesn't feel proper to be in a room alone with Daniel, especially since I'm half-naked. I concentrate on cutting up one of the omelets, doing my best to ignore the fact that Daniel has scooted further across the bed, making the distance between us disappear.

"Where did Julian take you when the fight broke out?" he asks me.

"Saint Louis Cathedral."

"Ahh, that makes sense."

"Why do you say that?" I ask, shoving a large piece of egg into my mouth, trying to look as unattractive as I possibly can.

"Vamps can't stand on hallowed ground, and a werewolf will never kill you in a holy place. They think it's bad luck."

"What happens to a vampire when they try to stand on holy ground?"

"They get thrown off it."

I swallow the food in my mouth quickly. "Are you serious? By what?"

Daniel shrugs. "Who knows? The hand of God maybe?"

I think of myself as a Christian, not a devout one who attends church every Sunday but one who believes in God in my own way. The thought of Him refusing to let Julian walk across holy ground seems ludicrous. He can't help what he was made into.

"Sarah…" I hear Daniel say in a hesitant voice, filled with portent.

Uh-oh. Here it comes. I brace myself for whatever it is Daniel is about to ask me.

"I was wondering if you would like to go see the Louisiana Philharmonic with me. They're having a performance in a couple of weeks."

If Daniel only saw me as a friend and not a potential girlfriend, I would have said yes right away. But I know what he wants, and I have no desire to lead him on. He's a good person, and I don't want to give him the wrong impression.

I set my fork down on my plate.

"Daniel, I'm really flattered by your offer but I can't do that right now. I need to figure some things out first. If we had met a week ago, I probably could have given you the answer you want, but now…"

"Sarah… he can't love you."

I stare at him, wondering if he's been hiding the fact that he can read minds from me all this time. "What do you mean?"

"If you think Julian can return the feelings you have for him, you're wrong. Vampires can't love anyone."

"How do you know that?" I ask defensively.

"Adrian told me once. He said ever since they were changed, and bonded with the one person in the world they loved the most, none of them has been able to feel real love for anyone. Julian will never love you the same way you love him. You'd be wasting yourself on him, Sarah. At least think about my offer before you dismiss it because you think you're in love with Julian."

I remember Helen telling me that Julian seemed incapable of returning the love she felt for him when they were together. Is it possible that what Daniel says is true, and none of them can fall in love? Is it part of their curse?

Helen walks back into the room with the T-shirt and jeans I had packed for our trip home.

Daniel stands from his seat on the bed. "I'll go so you can get dressed. Don't leave without saying goodbye."

Once Daniel is out of the room, I work on finishing my breakfast. Viktor saunters across the bed to sit by my side, and we both watch Helen arrange my clothes on the chair by the window.

"Do you really believe what you told me a few days ago? That vampires are incapable of loving anyone?"

Helen looks over at me. "Yes, I think it might be true," she replies. "And I also think that it's quite possible for miracles to happen. My most fervent hope is that you can help Julian find a way to love again. Perhaps you're the person he's been waiting for. I don't know. I wish I could tell you. All I do know is that he cares for you deeply, more than I've ever seen him care about anyone else since I've known him. But I'm not the person who can tell you if Julian loves you or not, Sarah. Only he can answer that question."

It's an honest answer, and I can't ask for more than that from her.

Once I finish my breakfast, Helen offers to take my tray back down to the kitchen. I thank her and get out of bed after she's gone. Viktor lies at the foot of the mattress and watches me as I change clothes. I don't know why, but having him keep an eye on me so intently begins to make me feel uncomfortable. I turn my back to him and begin to change into my clothes. I have my jeans on and am just reaching for my T-shirt when Julian walks into the room unannounced. I quickly turn my back to him and slip my shirt over my head.

When I turn back around to face him he's still standing only a couple of steps inside the room, staring at me.

"Did you need something?" I ask him when he remains silent.

He clears his throat and says, "I was wondering if you would like to go on a small adventure with me on my bike before we go home."

"Yes!" I'm so excited by the prospect that I forget to be embarrassed about him catching me getting dressed.

I've always wanted to ride on a motorcycle but never knew anyone who had one. The thought of riding behind Julian on some grand adventure makes my pulse quicken. Is his offer just a way to lift my spirits after saving his life? Or does he simply want to spend time with me all alone? It's impossible to tell without my empathic abilities, because he's a master when it comes to hiding his emotions from me. Either way, it doesn't matter. He wants to spend time with me, and that's all I need to know for now.

CHAPTER 13.

Julian returns to my room with a black leather vest, chaps, boots, and helmet. He then asks me to put them on.

"I know it's a little warm to wear these, but I would feel better knowing you were protected as much as possible," he tells me.

I don't mind wearing the extra clothing. I like the fact he wants to keep me safe.

"Where did you get all this stuff on such short notice?" I ask, studying all the leather pieces.

"Mira's companion likes to ride bikes, too. She told me to take them when I asked if she had anything you could borrow for our little excursion. She seems to believe it will take her a while to regain her figure after the baby is born, and by then she'll want something new anyway."

After I get dressed in my new biker chick wear, Julian takes our bags down to the Vanquish, where Helen is waiting to leave. When I hand Viktor over to her, he gives a meow in protest.

I rub the top of his head lovingly.

"I won't be gone long," I reassure him. "And you'll be perfectly safe with Helen."

He lifts his pink nose in the air and turns his head from me in a display of indignation. It's obvious he's offended with being handed off like some ordinary pet.

I lean down and kiss him on his pert nose. "You'll be fine. When I get home, I promise to give you a special treat."

This seems to mollify him somewhat. He looks back at me and meows.

"You two be careful," Helen says, settling Viktor in the passenger seat.

"We'll see you back at the house in a few hours," Julian tells her, straddling his motorcycle and putting on his helmet.

"Sarah!"

I turn to see Daniel jogging down the steps from the house towards me. I completely forgot about finding him to say goodbye before we left. Julian told me earlier that he had already made our goodbyes to Mira and Adrian, for which I was thankful. I didn't particularly want to see either of them before we left. When I asked him about saying goodbye to Petru, Julian was a little cryptic and just said I would get a chance to make my farewells to him later.

"I'm so sorry," I tell Daniel, holding my helmet loosely down by my side. "I meant to find you earlier."

Daniel gives me a quick hug and peck on the cheek.

"No worries, Sarah. I just wanted to wish you a safe trip home." He glances at the bike and Julian, taking in the situation. "Make sure you hold on tight."

"I will," I promise. In fact, I'm looking forward to having a good excuse to snuggle up with Julian.

"Listen," Daniel says in a hushed tone, "my offer still stands if you change your mind. I'll be going to the concert either way. Just let me know if you want to give it a try."

Give 'us' a try is what he clearly means, but doesn't say in front of mixed company.

"See you later," I tell him, not wanting to rehash something I've already given my answer to. "You take care of yourself while you're in this house."

"Yeah, I will. Talk to you later." He gives me a half-smile and turns away to go back towards the mansion.

I put my helmet on and climb onto the small seat right behind Julian that's meant to carry a passenger. It doesn't look big enough to carry a baby, much less a full-grown woman. I brace my feet on the shoe pegs Julian points out, and wrap my arms around his waist as tightly as I can without making it seem like I'm a complete chicken.

The thrill of riding with Julian through the streets of New Orleans is just what I need this morning. I feel free and curiously safe, considering we're traveling 70 mph on the open interstate without the added safety of airbags and a metal cage to cushion the blow of the asphalt rushing beneath our feet.

Julian pulls off I-59 and merges onto I-10. It isn't the normal way home, but maybe he just wants to take the scenic route. He did say that we were going on a little adventure, after all.

Eventually, he turns off I-10 and onto US Highway 90. We pass a green road sign indicating the mileage left before we arrive in Waveland, Mississippi. I want to ask why we're going there, but it's physically impossible. Instead, I just hold onto Julian and try to enjoy the feel of his body against mine while the bike hums beneath us.

Before I know it, we're on a road called Beach Boulevard, which is true to its name since it runs along the white sandy beaches of Waveland. Julian pulls off into a parking lot next to the beach and comes to a stop between two blue public porta-potties. I actually do need to go to the bathroom, but porta-potties are definitely not my thing. I would rather wait until after we get home than sit on one of those toilets.

Reluctantly, I release my hold on Julian's waist and sit up straight to stretch my back. He takes his helmet off so I do the same, tossing my hair a little to untangle the strands from my head.

It's still early in the morning, probably only nine o'clock. Most people are already at work. There is only one other car in the parking lot, a shiny black Mercedes S550.

"What are we doing here?" I ask Julian.

He looks at me over his shoulder. "Meeting Petru."

"Why this place?"

"I didn't want any prying ears to hear what we need to discuss. Mira's home just has too many curious people milling about."

Julian gets off the bike and holds out his hand to help me stand from it. We set our helmets on the seat of the bike. After straddling it for well over an hour, my legs have lost some of their feeling. It takes me a minute to stop walking bow-legged as the blood begins to circulate back into my lower extremities.

There is a 50-foot concrete jetty leading from the beach area out into the water. Large grey rocks are piled on either side of it down to the water line. I see Petru and a boy no older than eighteen standing at the end of the concrete pier, looking out at the Gulf of Mexico.

When we approach, they both turn to face us. Petru is feeling extremely excited about something and the young boy is anxious. I assume the boy is Petru's companion. I didn't get to meet him the previous night at the party because he wanted to explore New Orleans while it was going on. For some reason, I never pictured him to be so young.

"A pleasure to see you up and about, Sarah," Petru says, kissing me on the lips just like he did the night before. Apparently, it's just his way. "I would like to introduce you to Nathaniel, my companion."

Nathaniel holds his hand out and I shake it.

"It's a pleasure to meet you," he says. As his eyes quickly look me up and down, I feel a sudden surge of lust from him.

I can't blame the boy. I think I look pretty hot in my biker chick outfit, too, which isn't how I view myself very often. Besides, he's only eighteen, or close enough to it. What teenage boy doesn't have trouble controlling his hormones around the fairer sex?

Nathaniel reminds me of a young Jared Leto, but with dirty blonde hair and brown eyes. He attempts to act as mature as his counterpart, but I can still sense his pent- up insecurities. He's shy by nature and unsure of himself in ways Petru probably hasn't been in hundreds of years. He has a good heart and loves Petru like a father, which appears to be the role Petru sees himself filling in Nathaniel's life.

"So, have you learned anything since the last time we spoke?" Julian asks Petru.

Petru smiles. "I desperately wanted to tell you last night, but there were just too many people around. I found someone who might have the answer we've been looking for all these years."

"Who is it? Where are they?" Julian's excitement at Petru's news startles me for a moment. I've never seen him this enthusiastic about anything before.

"She's a descendant of Dorka's. I've only spoken with her on the phone briefly, but she said she had information that might be able to help us. The only problem is that she's out of town at the moment, and doesn't plan to return home for a few days yet."

"Who's Dorka?" I ask, thinking it an odd name and wondering if it's Hungarian.

"She was a witch in Bathory's household," Julian tells me. "She was executed for helping Elizabeth torture and murder all those girls. Our theory has always been that either some of her family, or perhaps even members of her old coven, are the ones who cursed us. We've been searching for them for centuries, but it's only because of modern technology that we've been able to track down anyone associated with Dorka's family." Julian turns his attention back to Petru. "What makes you think she can help us?"

"She says she has one of Dorka's old diaries. It might hold a clue to help explain the spell that was used on us. I know it's a long shot, but it's the first tangible lead we've had in years. If she did write the spell down in the book, perhaps she also wrote down how to reverse its effects."

I can't stay quiet any longer. What they're talking about seems to tie into something Julian alluded to the night before at the party.

"Excuse me," I say, "I hope I'm not out of line here, but are you saying you may have found a way to not be vampires anymore?"

Julian looks at me. "Petru and I have been searching a long time to find a way to remove our curse. We've had a few dead-end leads, but this is the first time we've been able to find someone directly linked to Dorka." He looks back at Petru. "When is she supposed to be back, and where does she live?"

"She doesn't live that far away from here, actually," Petru says excitedly. "She has a home in Destin, Florida, on the beach. She should be returning to it within a few days."

"Contact me as soon as you find out something. I want to come with you when you go to meet her."

"I will, brother." Petru gives Julian a guy hug, brief and not too close. "As soon as I hear from her, you'll be the first one I contact."

Petru and Nathaniel walk back down the concrete jetty to the parking lot, presumably to the Mercedes parked there.

"So you've been trying to find a cure all this time?" I ask Julian, finding the possibility fascinating.

He nods, turning away from the departing backs of Petru and Nathaniel to look out at the ocean. The gulf breeze is cool at this time of day and the sound of seagulls fills the air around us. The ebb and flow of the ocean water against the rocks of the jetty is soothing in its natural rhythm.

"Petru and I aren't like the others," he continues, staring at nothing but the horizon, lost in his own ruminations. "They enjoy living as immortals. We don't." He finally turns to look at me beside him. "All we have ever wanted is to live the lives we were born to, nothing more. Plus, if we can break the curse on ourselves, it stands to reason we can break the bond and set you and Nathaniel free."

To be honest, I'm not sure how I feel about that. Losing my bond to Julian seems wrong for some reason. Perhaps it's because I'm genetically predisposed to desire the bond, or it could be because I'm falling for my vampire companion. I'm not sure which reason is the truth. It's possible they both are.

"You could go back to your life and live normally, just like your mother wanted you to," Julian says in a detached voice. "You wouldn't have to stay with me any longer, Sarah."

But I want to stay with him, doesn't he understand that? Why is he so ready to leave me when the mere thought of being separated from him causes me pain?

"I like being bonded to you," I hear myself admit.

Julian takes my hand. "I would never abandon you, Sarah. If we find a way to break the curse, I hope we can still be friends."

Friends. Great. The one thing people hate to hear from someone they really like or even possibly love: '*Hey, let's be friends*'. I can't help but sigh in disappointment.

"Is there anything wrong with us remaining friends?" he asks me, apparently sensing my mood.

I get the distinct feeling he's teasing me. When I look up at his face, the twinkle of amusement in his eyes and lopsided grin make me certain of his deliberate teasing. What game is he playing? Does he want me to say how I feel about him? It's almost like he's egging me on so I'll reveal my hand before he does. If I knew that he cared for me romantically, I wouldn't mind telling him how I feel, or how I think I might be feeling about him. But one kiss, even though it was incredible, doesn't mean he loves me, and I'm not about to give him the upper hand.

"No, there wouldn't be anything wrong with us being friends," I finally reply.

"Good." He smiles and raises the hand he still holds up to his warm, red-stained lips. His mouth lingers against my skin a few seconds longer than if it was just a friendly kiss.

The coastal wind blows through his hair, making him look even more wild and handsome. Seriously, does he have to be so gorgeous? It just doesn't seem fair. How am I supposed to remain friends with someone who makes my heart do flips inside my chest whenever he looks at me or touches me?

"We should probably go back home," he says, still holding my hand. "I wouldn't want Helen to worry about us unnecessarily."

We walk back down the jetty, holding hands as if we're two lovers who just stopped to take in the ocean view. I wish that small illusion was true. It's then that I realize I already know what my true feelings are for Julian. I realize I don't need to talk to Kaylee to know that I've fallen in love with him.

CHAPTER 14.

The ride home takes a little over an hour. During that time, I weigh the pros and cons of falling in love with Julian. One good thing is the bond we already share. It ensures that we'll never be away from each other very often, but it's also something I have to place in the con column. If Julian's feelings never mirror my own, I'll end up being in a relationship that's one-sided for the rest of my life. That possibility doesn't paint a very pretty picture for my future happiness, but I'm not sure there's anything I can do now to stop how I feel about him. Will I end up carrying a torch for someone who can never love me back? Who knows? Only time will be able to answer that question.

The next item I put in the con column is the dilemma of having an heir for him to bond with after I die. It hasn't been said directly, but I assume Julian is unable to father children. If that's the case, how can I conceive a child for him to bond with if we're in a relationship together? Considering the times we live in, I suppose I can just go down to the local sperm bank and buy someone's donated little soldiers to solve that problem. I can't say it's the picture-perfect scenario to start a family, but it would work in a pinch.

I guess I always pictured myself in Kaylee's position when I found my Mr. Right, rather than the one I find myself in with Julian. I assumed I would marry the man I loved, live in a nice house, and start a family the traditional way. I suppose, like everyone else in the world, I always saw my life following the natural order of things.

My next obstacle will be finding a way to gauge how Julian really feels about me. Unless he just flat-out tells me he loves me, how am I supposed to figure out what his true feelings are? I groan inwardly at the irony of it all. Having been an empath all my life, there were times I prayed God would take away my ability so I didn't have to know what people were feeling all the time. Now, when I need my gift the most, it doesn't work on the one person I desperately need it to. The word 'unfair' keeps popping up in my mind. After years of being plagued by my ability, you would think it would have the decency to work in my favor just this once.

When we pull into Julian's circular driveway, I immediately notice Kaylee's silver Durango parked in front of the house. Julian parks his motorcycle directly behind it. As we're getting off the bike, Kaylee toddles out the front door with a glass of sweet tea in one hand while she rubs her belly with the other. If I didn't know any better, I would swear her stomach is even larger than it was only two days before when I last saw her.

Julian sets both of our helmets on the bike's seat while I walk up the steps to greet Kaylee.

"What are you doing here?" I ask, giving her a brief hug and kiss on the cheek.

"Well, when you didn't return my calls, I got worried. Mom and Dad know the real estate agent who sold your new boyfriend this place, so I decided to come by to see if you were here. I was worried about you, Sarah."

"I'm sorry," I say, completely chagrined for not letting Kaylee know where I was going and how long I would be gone. "I forgot to take my cell phone with us to New Orleans. I promise I'll keep it close by from now on. You don't need to be worrying about me in your condition."

I feel Julian come stand behind me and see Kaylee's eyes dart in his direction. It seems that fate has decided it's time introductions between the two of them were made.

I turn sideways so Julian and Kaylee can meet face to face.

"Kaylee, this is Julian. Julian, my sister, Kaylee," I say, watching both of their reactions to each other.

Kaylee holds out her hand to Julian. He immediately shakes it.

"It's nice to finally meet you," Kaylee says with a smile.

"Sarah has spoken of you often," Julian replies. "I'm sorry if we made you worry. The trip to New Orleans was a spur of the moment decision."

"That's what your housekeeper said."

"Have you been here long?" I'm not sure what Helen has already told Kaylee about the reason for our sudden trip and don't want to unintentionally contradict anything she's already been told.

"About twenty minutes." Kaylee looks away from me and back to Julian. "You have a lovely home. Helen showed me around a bit."

"Thank you," Julian says with a small smile. "You're welcome to come here any time you wish to visit."

"Why don't we go inside?" I suggest. No pregnant woman should be out in the heat of a Louisiana summer if she doesn't have to be.

"No, I need to get back to the house and help Ben. That was the main reason I was trying to get in touch with you. We're having our annual summer block party tonight, and I wanted to invite you and Julian to come."

I quickly recognize this is Kaylee's none too subtle way of arranging a meeting between Julian and her parents. Before I can make up an excuse to get us out of having to go, Julian ends up answering for the both of us.

"We would love to come," he tells her.

"Great!" Kaylee says excitedly. "Why don't the two of you come over around six?"

"Should we bring something?" I ask.

"Just yourselves. Ben's cooking enough to feed the whole neighborhood I think," she giggles.

I instantly doubt he'll even make enough to just feed me. I will definitely have to eat before we go there. All I need to do is make a pig out of myself in front of the people in Kaylee's neighborhood. There are some busybodies there that I know for a fact will be watching every move Julian and I make with their super snoopy eyes.

Kaylee hands me her half-finished glass of tea and leans in toward me to whisper in my ear. "He's gorgeous! I want hot juicy details about this trip to New Orleans later."

She kisses me on the cheek and says her goodbyes to Julian before leaving. We watch her walk away and witness her struggles as she attempts to pull her pregnant self up into the Durango's driver's seat.

Being the gentleman that he is, Julian hurries down and helps her get settled behind the wheel. This chivalrous act definitely earns him some brownie points with my sister.

As Kaylee pulls away, she smiles at me and waves with a wink. Yep, she likes Julian. Although, that might not be saying much. Kaylee likes just about everyone she meets.

"She's a sincerely nice person," Julian says as he comes to stand in front of me. "I can see why she's your best friend."

"Everyone likes Kaylee," I reply a bit wistfully.

"You're a nice person, too, Sarah."

I look at Julian. He doesn't seem to understand why I envy Kaylee so much.

"I can never be like Kaylee," I tell him. "I know how people really feel, and I have a hard time putting blinders on to who they truly are. I'll never see people through the rose-colored glasses Kaylee was born with. It's impossible for me to like everyone."

"You have a slightly cynical view of the world," he says, looking as though he's worried about me for some reason.

"It's my reality," I reply. "Not all people are good and not all people are bad. I can't pretend to like someone I have no respect for. I just wasn't made that way."

"How do you see me?"

Of course he had to ask me that question. I feel my face flush and have to wonder just how red it looks. Julian begins to smile, so I figure it's as red as an apple.

"I can't read you anymore, remember?" I pray that's a good enough answer, and that he'll drop the subject.

"But you must have your own opinion of me without relying on your empathic abilities," he prods. "I want to know what you think of me."

"If you tell me what you think of me," I try to bargain, "I'll tell you what I think of you."

"Hmm," he carefully mulls over my offer for a few seconds. "Maybe this discussion would be better left for another time."

He starts to walk towards the front door, but I put a hand on his arm to stop him. He turns back around to look at me.

"Is it that bad?" I ask, not sure I actually want to hear his answer.

"No," he says, studying something in the pools of my eyes. "I would just rather have this discussion later. It's not the right time, Sarah."

I let go of his arm. Julian hesitates as he continues to look at me before he finally turns around and walks into the house. He leaves the door open, expecting me to follow him inside, but I don't go in right away.

Is there something wrong with me? Is that why he refused to tell me what he really thinks?

"Meow."

I look down at my feet and see Viktor looking up at me expectantly. I pick him up and cradle him in my arms. He must have known I needed comforting because he leans his head back, and proceeds to wash my neck with his tongue as I walk into the house and head to the back where the kitchen is located. Julian is telling Helen we've been invited to the neighborhood block party.

"She invited me, too," Helen says.

Thank God for Helen and her cooking skills. She's standing by the stove, frying up some sausage in a frying pan, and I can smell biscuits already baking in the oven.

"You should come," I tell her, standing beside Julian on the other side of the kitchen island from Helen.

"I think I would prefer a quiet night at home after all the drama at Mira's," she says with a tired sigh. "But you two go have fun. I'm sure this will provide you with the perfect opportunity to show everyone that you're a couple."

I, for one, am looking forward to the night ahead. I know Julian will be an attentive suitor, even if it's just for the benefit of those we'll be around.

While I eat the lunch Helen prepared for me, Julian excuses himself and goes up to his room. When he comes back down he's dressed in only a pair of dark blue swimming trunks with a white beach towel draped around his neck.

"Have a nice swim," I tell him, forcing myself not to openly gape at his body as he saunters half-naked through the kitchen.

He smiles. "Thanks."

I try my best to pay attention to my food but soon find myself standing by the window, watching Julian dive into the blue water of the pool while I stuff my face with Polk's sausage and buttermilk biscuits.

Helen comes to stand beside me and we watch Julian swim.

"I think you should tell Julian how you feel about him, Sarah," she advises me.

"Helen," I whisper in an admonishing tone, "he can hear you. Super-hearing, remember?"

"He can't hear me when he's underwater like that," she replies. "The water distorts our voices."

"Do you think I'm nuts?" I have to ask her. "I haven't known him for that long. How can I be in love with someone I barely know?"

"The moment I saw my John I knew that I would love him for the rest of my life," Helen tells me. "Sometimes, when the person and moment is right, time becomes irrelevant."

"I can't tell him," I say shaking my head. "I'm not ready to do that yet. I need to know what he feels for me first. It would just be too embarrassing to bare my soul to him and then find out that he doesn't feel the same way."

Helen sighs. "I just want the two of you to find happiness. It's been so long since he was happy. I think all he needs is a little push in the right direction."

"I'm scared of rejection," I confess as I watch Julian rise out of the water like some Greek god described by Homer. "I'll do it eventually," I promise her. "I just need a little more time."

"Don't wait too long," she cautions, placing a comforting hand on my back. "Jump in and take a chance, my dear. I don't think you'll regret it."

When Julian comes in from his swim, I'm watching Viktor lick the bowl of cold milk I gave him dry.

"I need to go to my apartment," I inform Julian. "I haven't been there in a while, and I want to make sure everything is all right. While I'm there, I'm going to go ahead and pack some clothes to bring over here."

"All the new clothes Helen bought you are yours," he tells me, looking as if he's wondering why I need to bring my own clothing over.

"I know, but Kaylee will get suspicious if I keep wearing new clothes. She might think I'm using you as a sugar daddy or something. I would just feel better wearing some of my own stuff, especially to the block party. It's not a designer-dress-wearing kind of event. More a shorts and tank top type of thing."

"Mind if I go with you to your place? I would like to see it."

I quickly run the state of my apartment through my mind. Do I have any dirty clothes strewn across the floor? Is my bed made? Are the kitchen and bathroom clean? Since I couldn't sleep well the two weeks prior to Julian finding me, I had used the extra time to clean my apartment until it practically shined. If there was ever a good time for Julian to see my place, it's now.

"Sure. I would enjoy the company."

"Let me change," he says, continuing to walk through the kitchen. "I won't be but a minute."

I decide to follow him up to the second floor so I can take off all the black leather I'm wearing. I quickly exchange the heavy boots for my tennis shoes.

Viktor follows me back down to the front door and paws at my leg.

"Do you want to come, too, little fella?"

He leaps into my arms, effectively giving me his answer.

Julian walks down the stairs, dressed in a black polo shirt, jeans, and black loafers.

"Will this do to wear to the gathering?" he asks.

"Yes, that'll do." I know he'll end up having every female at the party drooling into their sodas. "Just don't smile too much while you're there."

Julian looks at me like I've said something extremely odd. "And the reason for that is?"

"You're already going to have all the single and most of the married women there panting after you like dogs in heat. If you smile, you might give some of the older ladies actual heart attacks."

He chuckles. "You worry about the oddest things."

I shrug before opening the front door for us. "Just calling it like I see it."

We take my car to my apartment. Viktor rides in the back seat, looking out the window as we drive through town. He acts like he's a sightseer. After we park in the parking lot of my complex, he jumps out as soon as I open his door and walks straight up to the door of my apartment as if he already knew where he was going.

When I open the door to my apartment, I do a cursory survey of the interior to make sure I haven't forgotten some mislaid piece of underwear on the couch or something equally embarrassing. Luckily, the inside is as clean as I remembered.

Julian walks in behind me and does a quick once-over of my place with his eyes.

"Seems small," he comments worriedly.

"I don't need much space since it's just me," I defend.

"Hmm…"

While I leave Julian in the living room, Viktor and I go to my bedroom to retrieve some of my clothing and other items I might need while I'm staying at the house on Bayou Road. I catch sight of Julian as he leans against the doorway to my bedroom, watching me pack.

"May I come in?" he asks.

"Sure."

My bedroom doesn't have a lot in it: a queen-size bed, chest of drawers, small desk where I keep my laptop and school supplies, and a series of black and white pictures of my family hanging along one wall.

Julian walks over to the pictures and begins to look at them. He comes to a standstill when he notices one of my mom and dad hanging directly above my desk. It's one in which they're laughing into the camera. It's a picture I took of them on our last trip to Disney World together.

"Sarah," Julian says, sounding somewhat dumbfounded by something he sees in the candid photo. "Is that your father?"

"Uh, yeah," I say, wondering why a picture of my dad comes as any shock to him. "That's my dad. Why? Does he look so different that you don't recognize him?"

Julian reaches out and snatches the 11x14 picture from the wall, staring at it with a critical eye.

"It all makes sense now," I hear him mumble, more to himself than for my benefit.

"What's wrong? Why do you look so surprised?" I ask.

"I never knew who Clarissa married," he reveals, a note of awe in his voice as he continues to stare at the picture. "Your grandfather and I just assumed it was some boy she fell in love with from school." Julian turns around, still holding the framed photo, and looks at me. "Did they ever tell you much about your father's family?"

"No," I reply with a small shake of my head. "All they ever said was that they were all dead, just like my mom's. Why?"

Julian frowns. "His family isn't dead. In fact, you met his sister last night."

Now it's my turn to be confused. "His sister was at Mira's party?"

"Shael, the alfar queen."

I feel like a wall just hit me in the face. I have to sit down before I collapse from the shock of it all. Viktor saunters over and leaps up onto my lap. Absently I begin to pet him, feeling the deep purr of his pleasure at my touch reverberating deep within his chest.

I can't stop staring at the light blue carpet in front of me. I feel dazed and confused by Julian's revelation about my dad's heritage. How could my parents not tell me I was part of another race? Couldn't they have at least left me a note explaining things? Why had they left me so unprepared for a life they knew I would eventually have to deal with?

Julian places the picture of my parents back on the wall and kneels in front of me, forcing me to break the trance I'm in to look at him.

"You're not just part alfar, Sarah. You are heir to the alfar throne. As far as I know, Shael is unable to have children. That makes you the sole heir as far as Moonshade bloodlines goes."

"Moonshade?" I ask. "Is that my dad's real last name?"

Julian nods. "There are five alfar houses. The one your father was a part of is called House Moonshade. I believe they chose that name to honor the magical power of a solar eclipse, which is also part of your house's crest."

"So what does that make me?" I ask, still trying to wrap my mind around the implications of being part alfar. "Am I some kind of princess to them?"

"Yes," he answers simply.

"But I don't want to be someone that important," I state rather forcefully. "I just want to be me and stay with you until I die."

Julian smiles at me wanly. "I'm afraid you're far too important to the alfar, Sarah. They won't simply let you slip into the background." Julian looks down at Viktor. "And he knows that. It must be why he chose to leave the queen and be with you."

"No," I say adamantly, shaking my head. "They don't have to know. Only you and I know the truth. We'll just keep it that way. We can do what my mom and dad did. Just run off somewhere so no one can find us."

"Meow!" Viktor's very vocal protestation almost sounds like he's accusing me of speaking heresy.

"I think the queen knew who you were last night," Julian tells me. "She just didn't say anything openly to you about it. I can't say I blame her, considering who was at the party." Julian sounds far too calm and reasonable about all of this. Why isn't he freaking out about it like I am?

"What if they make me leave you?" I question, steadily becoming more upset. "I mean, can they do that? *Will* they do that?"

"No, of course they wouldn't do that." He's saying the words I want to hear, but I can tell he's not completely sure what the alfar might expect from me.

"If they try to give the throne to me, I can abdicate it, right?" I ask, trying my best to think of a scenario where I can at least hope to retain my life as my own.

"I've never heard of that being done," he replies. "But Shael isn't that old. She'll remain queen for a long time to come. This isn't something that you need to worry about right now, Sarah. It's just something you need to be aware of. I'm sure when the time is right, the queen will contact you and let you know what's expected."

My meeting with the queen all makes sense now. The love she felt for me had been real. The connection I felt with her hadn't just been some sort of alfar thing. It was a family thing, blood speaking to blood.

"So I should just let her contact me first?" I ask Julian, feeling somewhat relieved that I don't have to do anything yet.

"I think that's the best course of action," he says. "But she *will* contact you eventually. You're the only living relative she has left."

I don't want to be heir to the alfar throne. For one, I don't know what the hell that means. And two, anything that might separate me from Julian is completely unacceptable.

We sit there in mutual silence for a moment. All I can think about is what it means to be part of the alfar royal family, and Julian, well, I have no idea what he's thinking about. He just stares at me like he wants to say something, but can't quite make the words come out of his mouth.

"Is there something else you want to tell me?" I ask, hoping he might want to say something about his feelings for me.

"Maybe later," is his reply.

I stop myself from sighing in disappointment. He probably isn't thinking about love anyway. Not after finding out I am what I am. Wait a minute…

"Do you think that's why it's hard for you to be around me? Because I'm part alfar?"

The expression on Julian's face doesn't change. "I'm not sure."

"Do you have a natural aversion to the alfar? Is that why my mother kept her relationship with my dad a secret from you?"

"No, I get along with them just fine, but some have powers similar to the witches and warlocks. You could have inherited your empathic ability from your father's side of the family."

What a non-answer. "But what does that have to do with the way I make you feel? Is there something else about me that bothers you? Something alfar-*ish* that I don't know about?"

"Let me worry about that, Sarah. I told you I would figure out a way to handle it."

"Handle *what?*" I ask in frustration. "You haven't told me what it is about me that bothers you so much. Maybe I can help you."

"It isn't bothering me as much anymore," he says with a hint of a smile. "I'm getting used to it."

Used to what? I want to scream. He can be so aggravating sometimes. I love him but I really want to strangle the answer out of him right now.

Julian stands. "Why don't you finish packing up what you want to take with you? I saw an ice cream shop on the way here. I'm sure you could use a snack right about now."

Why does the mention of food make me put everything else I'm thinking about on the back burner? A loaded banana split is the only thing I can concentrate on now.

I pack as quickly as I can. The ride over to the ice cream shop is just what I need to get my mind off learning about my father's family. I just wish I could have brought Viktor inside the store with us. I have to leave him outside in the summer heat, but he doesn't seem to mind sitting out on the sidewalk. I make a mental note to take him to a veterinarian for shots and tags. While I eat my ice cream, I talk Julian into making a short detour to Pet Smart for some cat supplies.

By the time we check out, I end up spending three hundred dollars on things for Viktor. I couldn't help myself, though. Every time he seemed interested in a toy, I had to get it for him. I would have bought him a tree apartment but I couldn't. It simply wouldn't have fit in my car. But I did get him a plush fur-lined cat bed, an automatic cat food and water feeder, a white leather collar encrusted with rhinestones, a retractable leash, a self-cleaning litter box, a box of Fancy Feast variety pack gourmet cat food, toys, and grooming items. Everything a self-respecting cat of an alfar princess needs.

It makes me wish I had asked the queen about his personal effects. Well, I guess she was my aunt really. Aunt Shael, the alfar queen. Honestly, it sounds like a bad title for a B-movie.

By the time we get back to Julian's house, my home away from the apartment, it's five o'clock. We'll need to leave by 5:50pm to get to the block party on time. Julian helps me get all my stuff into the house and set up in my room. Once we're done, Viktor yawns and immediately curls up in his new bed for a nap. I hop in the shower to rinse off. After the motorcycle ride earlier, I feel like I have grit in places that need to be washed.

By the time I'm ready, we need to leave for the block party. I don't have the luxury of eating anything before we go, and all I can do is hope I won't completely embarrass myself by overeating at the cookout.

CHAPTER 15.

The block party is already in full swing by the time we arrive. We have to park Julian's Aston Martin on the side of the street because they've already set up table barricades to block thru-traffic. The center of the party starts at Kaylee and Ben's house and stretches out a block on either side of them. It looks like everyone is here, at least fifty people in all. Some are already in their lounge chairs, sitting in groups of three or four talking and enjoying each other's company on this balmy summer evening.

The requisite mosquito-repelling lamps are out in full force on every table surrounding the partygoers in a force field of DEET. The smell of barbecue is definitely in the air, making my mouth water at the mere thought of grilled hamburgers, sausage, and chicken. I pray everyone brought too much food to eat so there will be enough to assuage my insatiable appetite. As Daniel said, it's nice to be able to eat anything you want and not gain any weight, but it's also a curse to be almost constantly hungry.

I spy Kaylee resting in a foldout chair as she nurses a frosty glass of ice water with Susan, Pete, and Ben sitting beside her in front of her house. A gaggle of neighborhood children stand huddled around her, taking turns putting their hands on her belly to feel the baby kick. The smaller kids giggle with glee at feeling the tiny life of Little Miss Em inside Kaylee's womb. When we approach, they scatter like leaves in the wind, allowing me to finally introduce Julian to my adopted parents.

Pete and Ben stand from their lawn chairs, like most men usually do when being introduced to another man. I guess it's some sort of genetically-engineered response. If they remained in their seats, it would probably be taken as a sign of weakness.

I give Kaylee's dad a hug. "Pete, I would like to introduce you to Julian."

Julian holds out his hand. "A pleasure to meet you, Mr. Hughes."

"Glad to meet you, too, son."

I make the same quick introduction to Ben and notice Pete sizing Julian up. He seems pleased by what he sees, but remains wary. I assume his guarded attitude is for my benefit. He wants to make sure Julian is good enough for me, like all fathers do when their daughter brings home a young man, even though Julian isn't that young. He's actually older than the neighborhood we're standing in.

I introduce Julian to Susan while Ben unfolds two chairs he had lying on the sidewalk beside his seat for us to sit in. He positions them directly in front of their chairs. As I had suspected, it's the Hughes firing line. I'm curious to see what sorts of questions they will ask Julian.

It's definitely shaping up to be an interesting evening.

"So tell us a little about yourself," Pete says to Julian as he sits back down in his chair and twines his fingers together over his belly. "What kind of accent is that?"

"Partially Hungarian, partially British and French. I moved around a lot when I was younger," Julian answers. I get the distinct feeling he expected to be questioned by my family. He doesn't seem to mind. He's completely relaxed, and seems to welcome any inquiries they have for him.

"What brings you here to Pecan Acres, if you don't mind me asking?" Susan leans forward slightly in her chair, her full attention focused on Julian.

"I have a sister who lives in New Orleans. I wanted to be closer to her and this seemed like a nice quiet town to settle down in."

"Why not just live in New Orleans?" Kaylee asks.

"I didn't want to live in such a large, busy city. I don't like a lot of heavy traffic."

"What do you do for a living?" Pete asks.

I knew this would be one of the questions most important to him.

"I own a few businesses, but they're mostly taken care of by people I've hired to oversee them."

"What kind of businesses?"

"Hotels mostly. We cater to traveling business people and other special guests. I usually try to visit each one twice a year to make sure they're running smoothly."

"What do you do with all your free time?"

"I have a lot of hobbies that keep me busy, but I have to admit working on my motorcycle is a favorite one of mine."

That is pretty much all Julian had to say to get Pete to forget about the interrogation and switch the conversation to talk about motorcycles. Pete has wanted one for as long as I can remember, but he hasn't been able to talk Susan into letting him have a bike. She argues that they're too dangerous and that he's too old to be riding one. While Julian tells Pete about his custom motorcycle, Ben gets up to tend to his barbeque. Susan and Kaylee ask me to help them bring out the food they have in the house.

As soon as we step inside, Susan takes me by the arm.

"Kaylee told me Julian was gorgeous, but I had no idea!" Susan says, giddily excited for me. She truly hopes I've found someone to love in the man I brought to meet my family.

"So, spill," Kaylee says, opening the refrigerator door to pull out a bowl of potato salad. "What happened in New Orleans? What did the two of you do there, or do I even have to ask?"

She sets the bowl on the counter and looks at me, waiting impatiently for some sign of my true feelings for Julian and probably some juicy details about our trip.

"We had a good time. Julian's sister had a party. That's why we went."

"That's what Helen told me," Kaylee says, completely unsatisfied with my answer. "I want to know about the intimate details. What did the two of you *do*?"

I just rolled my eyes at her. "We didn't *do* what you're thinking we did. We just started dating, Kaylee."

I can feel Kaylee's frustration with me, but she simply sighs her disappointment.

"Well, I don't see how you're keeping your hands off him." Susan grabs a couple of bags of potato chips off the kitchen table and the bowl of potato salad from the counter in front of Kaylee. "If I was dating him, I'd make him stay in bed with me for at least a week."

"*Mom!*" Kaylee shivers at the thought of her mother being a sexual creature. "Unless you want your granddaughter to be born prematurely, don't paint pictures like that inside my head."

Susan sticks her tongue out at her daughter. "I'm just trying to give Sarah something to think about. I'd better get back out there and make sure Julian doesn't talk your father into buying a motorcycle. That's all I need."

Susan walks out of the kitchen, leaving Kaylee and me alone.

"Sarah." I always know Kaylee is going to talk seriously when she says my name like that. "Don't cut yourself off from him like you normally do when you start to have feelings for someone. Ever since you lost your parents, you've been standoffish with people. I know you say it's because of your abilities, but you and I both know it goes deeper than that. You're just scared of caring for someone and then losing them. Don't do that this time. I really like Julian. I think he would fit in with us."

"You barely know him, Kaylee," I point out.

"I know enough," she says confidently with a slight lift of her head. "I may not be an empath like you, but I can read people in a different way. Judging from the way he looks at you, I think he cares for you a great deal. Just promise me you'll let your heart lead you in the right direction this time. Don't overthink things like you usually do when things start to get serious with a guy."

"Ok."

"Promise?"

I nod. "I promise."

I'm not sure I have a choice in the matter anyway. My heart has already decided I'm in love with Julian, even though my head keeps warning me that it's probably a horrible mistake.

Susan comes back in and helps us take out the rest of the food, which includes a delicious-looking strawberry shortcake. It taunts me with its delectable sweetness, begging to be devoured on the spot.

Julian is still talking with Pete, but the conversation has apparently moved on to cars since Pete is sitting in the driver's seat of Julian's Vanquish. Julian stands on the sidewalk, talking to Pete through the open door of the car. He must feel me staring at him because he looks up and gives me a wink and a smile.

Didn't I tell him not to smile too much while we were here? I wasn't just worried about the older ladies at the block party. I was hoping to keep my heart rate at a normal pace for most of the night, but if he keeps winking and smiling at me I'm not sure how I'm going to manage that feat.

"That sure is a good-looking man you've got there, Sarah. How did you manage to land him?"

Standing beside me is Martha Rite. She's lived next to the Hughes family all my life. Martha is the quintessential nosey neighbor. I was told she had been quite a beauty in her younger years. I could only assume she was trying her best to hold onto her youth by keeping her hair dyed black and slathering on so much makeup I'm sure she has to use a Dremel to sand it all off at night. She's one of those people who smile and say kind words to your face, but as soon as your back is turned she'll spread wild rumors about you, even if there isn't a kernel of truth to them just to stir things up. I hate being around her and always try to find a way to stay out of her gossip-mongering reach. I'm surprised she hasn't come up with some asinine story about me, because I'm pretty sure she knows I can't stand her.

"Just got lucky, Ms. Martha." If you keep your answers short and simple with her, there's less ammunition she can use against you later.

"That's certainly true. Lucky, lucky girl," she says, eyeing Julian with ravenous eyes. Feeling a woman in her early seventies become sexually aroused is not a pleasant experience.

When I look back at Julian, he has a slight frown on his face. He says something to Pete and leaves my second father sitting in his car to play with the controls. Julian walks over to me like he's on some important mission.

"Hello," he says to Martha, stopping to stand beside me.

"Julian, this is Martha Rite." I feel compelled by common courtesy to make the introduction. I would rather have spared him from having to endure her presence, but there's nothing to be done about it now. He is officially in her clutches.

"A pleasure to meet you, Julian."

The way Ms. Martha is undressing Julian with her eyes suddenly makes me lose my appetite, and that is quite an accomplishment in my book.

"If you don't mind, Ms. Martha, I would like to have a private moment with Sarah."

"Of course." Martha seems a little taken aback by being dismissed so quickly after just meeting Julian. "I need to go talk with Mimi anyway. You know she and Grady are getting a divorce."

I hate hearing that news. I've always liked the couple who lived across the street from the Hugheses. I hope it's just one of Martha's overexaggerations.

"You two have fun." She smiles her fake smile and walks away from us, swishing her hips a little too much for my liking.

I look at Julian. "Is something wrong?"

"No. It just seemed as though you were uncomfortable talking to that woman. I thought I would provide you with an excuse to get away from her."

He certainly is perceptive. "Thanks. That's precisely how I was feeling."

Julian takes a step closer to me, closing the distance between us to only an inch. He places his fingers underneath my chin, tilting my face up until our eyes meet. He smiles at me and lowers his lips to mine in a kiss that doesn't last very long, but is long enough to not be misconstrued by those watching as just a friendly peck.

When he pulls his lips away from mine, I feel him place his arms around me loosely. He stares down at me, searching my face with his eyes.

"Have I ever told you how naturally beautiful I think you are?"

I have to swallow before I can answer. "I don't think so."

"You're one of the most beautiful women I've ever seen," he tells me. "And I'm not just saying that. I mean it."

I understand what he's implying. He's telling me he isn't just saying it because we're surrounded by people who are supposed to think we're dating and on the precipice of falling in love with one another.

"Thank you." I don't know how else to respond. I feel extremely shy all of a sudden.

"Why does it embarrass you to get compliments?" he asks, still holding me close like we're lovers.

"I'm just not used to it," I confess, "especially not from someone like you."

"What does that mean, *someone like me*?"

"Someone gorgeous and completely out of my league. In the real world, guys like you don't go out with girls like me."

"That's ridiculous, Sarah." He sounds offended by my statement. "Any man would be thankful to have someone like you on his arm. Just look at the way Daniel practically falls all over himself whenever you're around him." I note a bit of jealousy in Julian's tone. "Plus, that warlock was irritatingly persistent at Mira's party, too."

"It was just a dance he wanted, not me."

"Don't be naïve. He wanted you. A lot of men at that party wanted you."

I wasn't comfortable talking about this subject with Julian. I only want one man to desire me and he's holding me in his arms, acting like a jealous lover about would-be suitors who are miles away from us. All of them are merely footnotes in my mind.

Was Kaylee right earlier? Does Julian care about me the same way I care about him? How am I going to know the real answer to that question unless I ask?

"Do you care about me, Julian?" I hear the words come out of my mouth but am completely dumbfounded I found the courage to ask the question. My desire to know the depth of his feelings for me seems to have overridden my better judgment.

"I do care, Sarah," he answers in a hoarse whisper. "Probably a lot more than I should."

"Why would you say it like that?" My question comes out sounding like a desperate plea.

"Because you make me feel things I haven't felt in a very long time. I'm finding it hard to keep our relationship the way it should be."

"And how is it supposed to be?"

"You have to understand something. Your family has been my family for centuries. In a way, I've always felt like a second father to most of the ones I'm bonded to. But since your mother took you away before you were born, I don't feel that sort of connection with you. Yet, I still feel loyal to your mother and grandfather. I'm not sure they would approve of me wanting you the way I do."

This just keeps getting better and better. "What do you see happening between us, Julian?"

"I'm not completely sure," he confesses, cupping the side of my face with one of his large, warm hands. "But I do know I haven't felt this way about anyone in a long, long time."

I'm about to pluck up my courage to ask him if he loves me, but the same group of kids who were standing by Kaylee when we first arrived start to recite the K-I-S-S-I-N-G song to us, ending the verse about me and a baby carriage. I feel slightly embarrassed and warn them that the first one I catch will be the recipient of a good tickling.

There's always one slowpoke in a group of kids and this one ends up being little three-year-old Sue Anne Bridget. I catch her underneath the arms and lift her high in the air. The other kids end up tackling me, and we all fall into a heap of arms and legs on Martha Rite's lush green lawn. If there is something Martha loves just as much as herself, it's her front yard and its immaculate landscaping. She rushes over to shoo us all off her grass, telling me I'm old enough to know better. I completely agree with her to keep the peace and half-heartedly admonish the children for causing damage to Ms. Martha's turf.

I wink at them all before I turn to leave so they know I'm not mad at them.

When I walk back over to Julian, he has a frown on his face.

"What's wrong?" I ask him, slightly out of breath from the exertion. We were having such a good discussion before being interrupted. I hope he isn't going to hide his feelings from me now, when I'm so close to figuring out what they are.

"You're good with kids," is all he says, not looking at me but at the group of children still running around chasing one another in a spirited game of tag.

"I'm a teacher. I think it's just in my genes."

I can feel him pulling away from me emotionally but I don't understand why.

"We should probably get back to your family," he tells me.

He takes hold of my hand, but I can already feel the distance between us becoming as deep and wide as the Grand Canyon. Did I do something wrong? I can't honestly think of anything that would cause him to start acting so strangely.

The rest of the evening goes by pleasantly enough. Julian plays the role of the besotted suitor for our audience, but I can tell his heart isn't in it anymore. What could have made him change his attitude so quickly? Right when I thought he was on the verge of professing his true feelings for me, something changed his mind.

Before we leave the party, Kaylee pulls me aside and reminds me of my promise to her.

"I think I already love him," I confide to her in a whisper, not wanting to hide my true feelings from my best friend any longer.

"I already knew that," she whispers back. "I know you better than you know yourself sometimes. I could see it on your face this afternoon at his house. Why don't you tell him?"

I shake my head. "It's complicated. Plus, it's probably too soon to be declaring that I love him. It might scare him off."

"Nonsense," she says in an agitated huff. "You just march yourself over there and tell him how you feel, Sarah Marcel. Besides, he's probably waiting for you to make the first move before he says how he feels about you. Men are like that. They don't want to be the first one to unleash the L-word."

"I'll think about it." It's the most I can promise. I'm not someone who wears her feelings on her sleeve for everyone to see. If Julian ends up rejecting me, I'm not sure it's something I can recover from easily.

The tension between Julian and me on the ride home is palpable. I want to ask him what's wrong, but the determined scowl on his face keeps me from doing it. He seems almost angry about something. Is he mad at me? If so, why? What the hell did I do?

When we get home, we walk to the house side by side in silence. He opens the front door for me and then proceeds to walk up to the second floor without saying a word. I follow him up, thinking it's time for him to feed, but he walks into his room and closes the door behind him without even looking back at me.

Ok. Enough is enough. I walk up to his door and lift my hand to knock but suddenly lose my nerve.

"Come in, Sarah," I hear him say from inside the room.

Of course he knew I was there. We always know when the other is close.

I place my hand on the cold brass knob and turn it to walk into Julian's private sanctuary.

His room is much like my own, except he has a dark brown comforter on his bed with tan and white accent pillows scattered against the headboard. He's standing in front of the solitary window in the room, staring out at the front lawn. The faint scent of his cologne permeates the air, helping to ease my anxiousness but only by a little bit.

As I push the door shut behind me, my nervousness acts like a vacuum in my mind, sucking out all the questions I intended to ask him.

"What do you want?" he asks me gruffly, getting to the crux of the matter even if it was in a cruel voice. He may have invited me in, but he seems to want to make it clear that he sees my intrusion as an invasion of his privacy.

His rudeness is just what I needed to spur my mind back into motion.

"Did I do something wrong?" I ask. "Why are you so mad at me?"

"You didn't do anything, Sarah. I just remembered my place is all."

"Your place?" I ask, feeling even more confused by his answer. "What are you talking about?"

"I shouldn't have told you the things I did at the party. My role in your life isn't meant to be as your lover."

"Why not?" I question heatedly.

He finally turns his head away from the darkness outside to look at me. "You deserve a better life than the one you would have with me. You should have a life like Kaylee does. That's who you are. I realized that when you were playing with the children. I can't give you a family, not the one you deserve anyway."

"Do you love me, Julian?" I blurt out. I'm proud I had the courage to ask, but I'm not sure I have the courage to hear his answer.

He turns his attention back to the window.

"Don't, Sarah," he whispers wearily.

I walk up to him and stand by his side until he finally looks at me.

"Don't what?" I ask softly.

"Stop making me feel the love you have for me. It's addictive and unbearable all at the same time," he says in a hoarse, almost pained voice.

"You're not making any sense," I tell him, shaking my head in bewilderment.

He turns to face me fully, like he wants to make sure I hear what he's about to say next.

"I can feel your emotions, all of them. I know you love me."

I feel my heart lurch inside my chest, and I suddenly feel as though I'm standing naked in front of Julian.

"What do you mean you can feel my emotions?" Then everything finally clicks into place in my mind. That's why he finds it hard to be around me. "Do you mean you're an empath, too?"

"Only with you. I can only feel what you feel."

"But how?"

"It happened right after we bonded. I can only assume you passed something on to me through your blood. Whatever it is, it causes me to be more in tune with your feelings. It's the only explanation I can come up with. Now that we know your father was an alfar, it could be some sort of magic that was passed down from him."

"So I lost the ability to feel *you*, but you gained the ability to know how *I* feel?"

"It seems that way."

Well, I didn't have anything to lose then.

"I do love you," I tell him, taking a step closer to him. He looks down at the carpet under our feet, either unable or unwilling to look me in the eyes. "I won't apologize for that, because I've never felt it this strongly for a man before."

"Sarah." He closes his eyes and says my name in a strained voice. "You shouldn't love me. I'm not good enough for you."

"Shouldn't I be the one who decides that? Can you honestly stand there and tell me you don't feel the way I feel? If you can, I'll walk out of this room and we'll never discuss this again. But if you can't..."

I don't get a chance to finish what I was about to say. Julian rushes me, enveloping me in a bone-crushing embrace. He kisses me like a man who desperately wants me to know how he truly feels. He's no longer trying to hide behind a mask of indifference, and is willing to show me just how much he wants me. He picks me up in his arms easily and lays us both down on his bed. His lips never leave mine, and I find it increasingly more difficult to breathe, like my lungs are starving for oxygen. But I refuse to let him go. I thread my fingers through his hair and roll him over onto his back, spreading my thighs to straddle his hips. I feel his arousal for me and can't help but smile on the inside, knowing I can have that sort of effect on him so quickly.

For one of the first times in my life, I feel completely connected with the man I'm about to make love with. And he isn't just any man; he's someone I can see myself building and sharing the rest of my life with. Just when I think I have everything I could ever want, it all comes crashing down in an instant.

Julian lifts me off him and quickly stands from the bed, leaving me in a panting heap.

"What's wrong?" I ask, completely confused by his sudden withdrawal.

"This is wrong," he says, shaking his head at me adamantly. "I can't let this happen between us."

"It's not wrong," I argue, sitting up on his bed. I hold out a hand to him palm up, desperately wanting him to come back to me. "Please, Julian, don't do this. I love you. I want to be with you."

"You're just a child. You have no idea what's best for you!" The vehemence of his outburst catches me off guard, but I quickly recover.

"I'm a grown woman. I'm perfectly capable of making decisions for myself and I've decided I want you! You can't stand there and tell me you don't want me, too, because I already know you do."

"It doesn't make this right. Nothing can."

He turns away from me and storms out of his room, leaving the door wide open as an open invitation for me to leave, too. I follow him but he's too fast for me. By the time I run down the stairs and follow his path out the open front door, he's already gone. I search the night sky but only see stars. My heart feels the distance he's placing in between us as he flies away. It aches inside my chest, and I'm left to wonder why he's being so stubborn. The bond of blood we share makes our separation even worse with the added physical distance.

Unable to bear the ache of his absence and rejection, I run up to my room and crawl into bed. I cry quietly until exhaustion overtakes me and I fall into a troubled sleep.

CHAPTER 16.

I wake up sometime during the night and have to flip my pillow over to find a dry spot to rest my head. I feel the soft, quiet landing of Viktor's paws on the other side of the bed. He walks over and lies down on the extra pillow beside me. I turn over onto my side, hoping to find a little bit of comfort from the cat's presence. My heart stops beating for a millisecond when I see a naked man lying where my cat should have been.

"Meow," he says with a rakish grin on his face.

I jump out of bed like a frog that has unexpectedly landed on a hot sidewalk. I stare at the man, trying to judge with my empathic ability if he's a threat to me. It's obvious he doesn't mean me any harm, but that doesn't stop me from taking a mental inventory of the items in the room and whether they can be used as a weapon, just in case.

"Who the hell are you?" I demand.

The blonde-haired, blue-eyed man stretches his lithe, muscular body out on the bed and casually laces his fingers behind his head, completely at ease with his nakedness. If I had to guess, I would put his age somewhere around twenty-eight. He's smiling at me, enjoying my surprise at his unexpected appearance.

"I'm Viktor, Sarah. I thought it might be a good time to introduce myself to you properly." He has a distinct British-sounding accent, cultured in a Daniel Craig, James Bond sort of way. In fact, he kind of looks like Paul Bettany.

I know he's telling me the truth, but I can't stop myself from looking around the room for Viktor the cat, my white feline friend.

I look back at the man as realization sets in. "What are you?"

"A friend," he assures me with an affable grin. "I don't take this form often, but I thought you might need someone to talk to."

"That doesn't answer my question," I say, slightly irritated. "*What* are you?"

He sits up on the bed and leans his back against the headboard.

"If you had been raised the way you were supposed to be, you would already know the answer to that question." He sounds just like Julian did when he learned my mother hadn't prepared me for my life as his companion.

"Listen, the last thing I need right now is a lecture on how poorly my parents prepared me for my life. If you're supposed to be a friend, then you shouldn't have a problem explaining what you are to me."

He nods. "You're quite right. I'm sorry for being so rude. You see, a long long long time ago, I was a cat, just as you have seen me. It wasn't until one of your great- grandfathers worked his magic on me that I became a creature who can change from a cat to a human at will. He wanted someone who would always remain loyal to the alfar royal family and serve in whatever capacity his future children and grandchildren might need. To some, I've merely been someone to confide their troubles to; to others I've been a father or a brother, even a lover when the opportunity presented itself. I can take whatever role you need me to. But for you," he squints his eyes at me, "I can't quite tell if it's a brother or a lover you need the most."

"Why don't we stick with friend," I suggest.

"Friend it is then," he says, standing from the bed and walking over to me.

I try my best to keep my eyes focused on his face, but the appendage swinging between his legs is very distracting.

He holds his hand out to me for a formal handshake. It seems an odd thing to do considering the fact he's already licked me all over my face, and I've rubbed his belly numerous times. But I shake his hand anyway. It seems impolite not to.

I'm not sure why, but I do feel extremely comfortable around him. I know it isn't logical to feel like he's an old friend, but I have no way to explain my reaction to him except that it might be a genetic trait. Perhaps my ancestor did something to make Viktor's duality seem normal to his progeny.

"If we're going to be friends, I am definitely going to have to get you some clothes," I insist.

"Must I?" he whines. "They're so restricting. I really don't like them at all."

"For my peace of mind, I would appreciate you wearing them." I walk over to my wardrobe and pull out a bed sheet from the extra set stored there. "Here," I say, handing him the sheet. "Put this on for now. I'll try to get you some proper clothes soon."

Viktor takes the sheet and drapes it around his body, toga-style.

"Well, this isn't too bad," he concedes, looking down at his ensemble. "I never had to wear clothes around Shael."

I choose to ignore the implications of his statement. All I need is to hear tales of the sexual exploits between my cat and the Queen of the Alfar.

"So how does this work? Are you able to transform into a human any time you want?" I ask. "Or are there rules?"

"I can take this form when I want, but I usually don't unless I think my services are required. To be honest, I prefer being a cat. Human thoughts can be so complicated and cumbersome. Cats are quite simple. We eat, sleep, and play. Everything else is taken care of by our owners."

I can understand preferring the simple life of a cat. It would certainly be easier than dealing with the daily dramas of being human.

"How many people know you can change forms? Obviously Julian doesn't know, or he would have warned me."

"As a general rule I only transform in front of the immediate members of the royal family. Although there have been occasions when I've revealed myself to others, but those instances have been very rare. Like I said, you would know what I was if you had been raised the way you should have been. We would already be friends by now, Sarah. But since your father decided to abandon us to be with your mother, you weren't given a proper education. That's one reason I decided to come to you now, to help prepare you for your reign as queen."

I feel a headache coming on. I have way too many things going on in my life all at once. How am I supposed to think about being the Queen of the Alfar when all I can concentrate on are my feelings for Julian?

"Can we not talk about that tonight?" I ask him.

He walks up to me and places his hands on my shoulders. When I look in his eyes, I can see his concern for my well-being.

"Do you need to talk about him?"

"I don't understand why he left me." It feels good to have someone I can openly talk to about Julian. I'm sure Helen is fast asleep, and Kaylee doesn't have all the facts about the circumstances of my new life. Viktor is just what I need right now. It suddenly dawns on me that my ancestor was very wise in making him. Sometimes you need a friend who can keep a secret and always take your side in an argument.

"I think he loves me, Viktor, and he knows I love him."

"Yes, I heard what went on in his room," Viktor reveals. "Thin walls and big ears make for some interesting eavesdropping."

"Good," I say in relief, "at least I don't have to tell you about everything that happened. If I had to say the words out loud, I might start to cry again."

Viktor draws me into his arms and hugs me close. "Don't waste your tears on someone who obviously just needs time to figure out how to deal with his own feelings for you. Vampires are solitary creatures by nature. They generally only develop a caring relationship with the one they're bonded to. If Julian has really fallen in love with you, then you have accomplished something no one has ever been able to do."

I hold onto Viktor, soaking in his warm and caring nature as a way to mend the void in my heart from Julian's rejection and distance. It's bad enough I feel the ache of his refusal to admit his love for me, but the added pain of being physically separated from him is almost too much to bear. I try to keep in mind what Daniel said about the pain of separation becoming duller as time goes by, but from the way I feel right now I highly doubt the agony will ever diminish.

"Come, you need to get some rest. Let the vampire throw his little tantrum. He'll be home by the time you awaken. From what I understand, he feels the same pain you do when you're separated. He won't be able to stay away from you for very much longer."

I let Viktor lead me back to bed and tuck me in underneath the covers. He lies down beside me and holds me in his arms. I lay my head against his chest and let myself relax enough to find sleep.

The next morning Viktor, in his cat form, is lying across the top of my pillow over my head like a hat. I raise myself up on an elbow and look at him softly snoozing in his sleep. Last night was certainly a trip. Finding out Viktor can shift between a human form and his natural cat one was a development I didn't see coming.

I know Julian is nearby. I can feel his presence, but it's also apparent that he isn't inside the house.

I put on a pair of shorts and a T-shirt I brought from my own wardrobe before walking down to the kitchen. Helen is there, busily preparing my breakfast for me.

"Good morning, Sarah," she practically chirps. "Did you have a good night's rest?"

"Honestly? It ended up being ok." With Viktor's revelation, the night hadn't been a complete disaster. *At least I know I have one person who understands everything about me and is on my side.*

"Well, why don't you sit down at the table, and I'll bring you your food."

While I'm eating the breakfast of scrambled eggs, bacon, and croissants Helen prepared for me, I ask her, "Where is Julian this morning?"

"Out in the garage," she answers, standing by the sink as she washes the skillet she used to make the eggs. "He said something about tuning up the Aston Martin."

Avoiding me is what he's really doing out there, I think but don't say out loud. Well, two can play at that game.

"I think I'll go out today and do some shopping. Would you like to come with me?"

Helen looks thrilled by my offer. "That would be fun! Thank you, Sarah. It's been ages since I went shopping with another woman. I think the last time I had such an excursion was with your mother before she decided to leave us."

"Well, let's make a day of it then," I say, becoming more excited. "I'll call the salon I go to and see if we can get the full treatment this morning, my treat. Then we'll hit the mall and see what kind of damage we can do to my credit card."

"Sounds like a plan. Oh," Helen snaps her fingers, remembering something. "I'll need to be back here by at least three, though. Julian said he invited someone for supper this evening. He asked me to tell you to dress nicely for his guest."

I can't say I appreciate being ordered around, but that wasn't Helen's fault.

"Who's coming?" I ask out of curiosity.

"He didn't say. All I got out of him was that it was an acquaintance he made at Mira's party."

I have no idea who it could be and don't waste time dwelling on the matter. I have plans of my own for the day.

I make a call to the salon I usually go to and book us for the works: hair, makeup, pedicures, and manicures. I tell Viktor what we're going to do, but he doesn't seem very interested. Apparently, he's more concerned about getting a nap in while I'm away because he curls up on his fluffy cat bed and promptly closes his eyes.

While I change clothes, I feel Julian come into the house and hear him walk into his room. I hate to admit that I feel somewhat relieved by his closeness. At least I won't have to pretend nothing is wrong between us when Helen and I go down to the garage to get into my car.

Helen is a pure joy to be around for the rest of the day. Having a girls' day out has definitely lifted her spirits. It's the least I can do for her, considering all the work she has to do just to keep me fed on a daily basis.

After we're through being pampered at the salon, we go out to eat at a local restaurant called the Gilded Crown. It's an Italian restaurant that serves a never-ending soup and salad lunch. I'm sure the waiter thinks I'll eat them out of business, but I limit myself to six bowls of soup and six plates of salad. We then head to the mall and shop until we have to leave in order to make it back home in time for Helen to prepare supper.

Since Julian suggested I dress nicely for our guest, I bought a new dress to wear that evening. It isn't a dress I see myself wearing often, but I feel the need to look my best. Maybe if I look irresistible, Julian will stop being so stubborn and admit he cares for me more than just as his companion. Yeah, I know the thought is a fanciful one and not very realistic, but I don't know what else to do to make him wake up and realize he can't hide from his feelings for me forever.

Since my hair and makeup are already done, all I'll need to do to prepare for the evening is put my dress and shoes on. With all the extra time I have before I need to do that, I decide to help Helen in the kitchen. I'm cutting up some vegetables for a salad when Julian walks into the kitchen.

My heart starts beating double time, making my blood pound through my veins. It feels like my stomach is filled with a thousand monarch butterflies all straining to find a way to escape.

"Did the two of you have a nice day out?" he asks us, not looking at me but at Helen.

"Yes, we did," Helen says with a big smile on her face. "I haven't had that much fun in a long time. It's nice to have another woman in the house again."

"Hmm…" Julian doesn't sound so sure.

I keep my eyes on the cucumber I'm slicing, attempting to make sure I don't cut off a finger in the process. I feel Julian's eyes fall on me briefly before he leaves the room. Thankfully, Helen doesn't comment on Julian's odd behavior. I really don't want to talk about it anyway.

Helen finally shoos me out of the kitchen, forcing me to leave and get ready for our mystery guest. The dress I bought for the occasion is a short-skirted, one-shoulder, black stretch charmeuse sheath dress with pleats under the bust line and a close-fitted bodice with ruched side seams. It zips up the side, leaving the front and back seamless. I decide to keep my hair down like the salon styled it. I finish the outfit with a pair of simple black high heels.

"Stunning. Absolutely stunning."

I turn from the full-length mirror in the corner of my room to see Viktor lounging on his side of my bed, naked again of course. I walk over to the TV in the room and turn it on to provide interference from prying vampire ears.

"Please put the sheet on," I beg him as I stare at the TV screen for my own modesty's sake.

I hear him get up from the bed and walk behind me to the chair by the window where I draped the sheet earlier. Once I know he's covered up, I turn to face him.

"Am I right in assuming this dress is meant to catch the eye of a certain stubborn vampire we both know?"

"You assume right," I tell him. I run my hands down the sides of the dress self-consciously. "You don't think it's too much, do you?"

"Personally, I don't think you need it to get his attention. You already have that. But men sometimes need to be reminded of what they are missing out on." Viktor eyes me from top to bottom. "And I can assure you he'll be second-guessing his decision in leaving you last night even more when he sees you this evening."

I want to believe Viktor, but I still have my doubts about Julian's reaction to me. Will he think I'm trying too hard? He did tell Helen to make sure I dressed up for our dinner guest. If he says anything derogatory to me about the way I'm dressed, I'll simply remind him I'm only following his orders.

"Well, wish me luck," I tell Viktor as I head out the door.

When I don't get a reply, I turn to see that Viktor has already transformed back into his preferred cat form, untangling himself from the sheet crumpled on the floor to go back to his comfy bed. When I reach the downstairs, I see Julian sitting in the living room, flipping through the channels on the TV. His back is to me, but I know he senses my presence because he falters in his channel surfing. He's sitting in his favorite wingback chair, so I have to walk around the back of it in order to stand in front of him.

His eyes travel the length of me before they meet my gaze.

"You look nice this evening," he says without showing an ounce of emotion. He returns his attention back to the TV and continues to flip through the channels, effectively ignoring me.

That was it? I look *nice*?

"Ditto," I say tersely, even though just the sight of him is making my heart do flips inside my chest again, which I hate. If he can feel my emotions, then he knows exactly how I'm feeling: completely devastated just by his presence. He's dressed in a pair of dark grey slacks and a white long-sleeve button-down shirt opened at the collar.

I'm not sure what else to do, so I ask a question.

"Who did you invite for dinner?"

"Gage Morgan."

"The warlock from Mira's party?" I can't help but be surprised by this development. I thought Julian didn't care for the persistent warlock.

"Yes."

"Why did you invite him to come here?"

"I wanted to thank him for his help in controlling the other warlocks and witches during the brawl. Without him, it's possible we could have lost some lives."

He didn't tell me about Gage's involvement in the fight. I'm happy to know I was right about the warlock's nature.

The doorbell rings, saving me from having to think of anymore small talk.

"I'll get it," I tell him, feeling the need to put a little distance between us, even if it isn't a lot.

Gage stands on the front porch, holding a colorful bouquet of Gerbera daisies. I have to admit, he is quite handsome with his high cheekbones, slender nose, and easy grin. He reminds me of a young Brad Pitt but rougher around the edges, not quite so angelic-looking.

"Hello, Sarah." His eyes quickly take in my dress. "Wow. You look stunning this evening."

"Thank you." I step out of the doorway to give him room to come into the house.

He walks in and hands me the flowers. "These are for you. I hope you like them."

"I love Gerbera daisies," I admit. "They're one of my favorite flowers."

"Gage." Julian walks out of the living room and holds his hand out to our guest. "I'm glad you could make it. Sorry about the short notice."

"No problem. I was just happy to get the invitation." Gage looks at me as if I'm the one who invited him, not Julian. I immediately become suspicious.

"Sarah," Julian looks at me. "Why don't you take Gage to the back patio? That's where everything is set up."

"Follow me," I tell Gage. About halfway down the hallway, I notice Julian isn't following us. I come to a complete stop and turn back to look at him. "Aren't you coming?"

"No, I have some things to take care of this evening." I can tell he's lying. "You two enjoy your meal. Helen outdid herself." He walks out the front door, leaving me to entertain the guest he invited.

"I'm sorry about that," I say to Gage, continuing to walk down the hallway through the kitchen. I notice Helen is nowhere to be seen. I lay the flowers on the kitchen island and show Gage to the back patio.

The scene outside looks like something you would see in a sappy romance movie. The table has been set for two, with a white tablecloth and a small arrangement of red roses and candles. Scattered around in the pool are those floating candles shaped like a water lily, illuminating the glassy surface with a warm glow. The fine bone china and baccarat crystal we used for Adrian's dinner is set in place, along with a large assortment of finger foods. I invite Gage to sit down.

While he's putting his napkin in his lap, Gage glances over at me and says, "You didn't invite me here, did you?"

"No," I'm quick to answer. It ends up coming out sounding unintentionally rude, but it's the truth. "I thought Julian invited you."

"He did, but he made it sound like you wanted to see me again."

"When did he invite you?"

"Late last night. He came by my house and asked me if I wanted to come here this evening."

"I see." Well, I guess that answers my question about where he went last night. "Where do you live, if you don't mind me asking?"

"Gulfport, on the beach."

So Julian went all the way to Gulfport just to find me a date. How sweet of him. I can feel my temper begin to flare white-hot.

"Is something wrong?" Gage asks, looking concerned.

Apparently, I'm not hiding my irritation with Julian from him very well. I have to remind myself it isn't Gage's fault that he's here. He was simply given misleading information. I'll have to wait to have my discussion with Julian later, in private...without witnesses.

"I'm sorry if he misled you into thinking I was the one asking you to come over. I promise it won't happen again."

Gage grins. "I don't mind as long as you don't. I don't want to force my company on you, though. I can leave if that would make you feel better."

I shake my head. "No, stay. As long as you're here we might as well get to know one another. You're the first warlock I've ever met. I would love to know more about your life."

I reach for a platter of mini-quiches, offering him first pick. Gage accepts my universal offering of goodwill in the form of food.

"What do you know about us?" he asks.

"I know you can cast spells," I say, feeling ignorant admitting I know virtually nothing in front of an expert on the subject. "I'm afraid that's the extent of my knowledge."

"Well, the first thing you should understand is that not all warlocks and witches are made equal. There are different levels."

"Do you go to warlock and witch school to gain levels? Please tell me Hogwarts is real," I jokingly beg.

"No, I'm afraid Hogwarts isn't real," Gage chuckles softly. I can tell he wants to let out a louder laugh but is too polite to do such a thing. "The levels range from one to ten, and you're pretty much stuck with whatever level you're born with. The only thing that can be taught is how to use the correct spells for the right occasion, but basically, we're home-schooled when it comes to magic. Other than that, we lead normal human lives."

"What level are you?"

Gage smiles. "I'm a ten."

Of course he is.

"So I'm assuming the higher the level you are the more powerful your magic is."

"Correct."

"So, what types of powers do you have?"

"Each of us is able to use one of the four basic elements: fire, water, earth, or air. There are a few of us who have what's called spirit magic, but it's very rare. Our major powers all depend on which element we can control."

"Which element do you control?"

"Air."

"So your major power is controlling how air moves?"

"More or less, yes."

"Do you have minor powers?"

"Some of us can heal to a small extent, but it takes a lot out of us."

"Maybe you can help me clear up something that I've been a bit confused about."

"Sure, what is it?"

"At the party there was a group of witches and warlocks like you. But since then, I've also learned that the alfar have magic abilities, too. What's the difference between your type of magic and the magic of the alfar?"

"You would have to ask one of them for the details," Gage shrugs. "They keep to themselves for the most part, but from what I've been able to observe, their powers seem to center on mind control and manipulating matter. I once saw an alfar child transform a stuffed dog into a real one right in front of my eyes. I don't think he was supposed to let me see him do it, but it was the most incredible work of magic I've ever witnessed."

I'm sure Gage would be even more amazed if he could see Viktor the cat change into Viktor the human. The topic of our conversation must have interested my feline friend because he saunters out of the French doors and onto the patio, lying down beside my chair.

"Everyone is talking about the cat picking you to be its next guardian," Gage comments. "None of us have known him to choose anyone but alfar royalty."

"I guess he just likes me." It isn't a lie, but it isn't the whole truth either. I don't think Gage needs to know the real reason behind Viktor's decision.

We eat our meal and make chit chat about how unseasonably cool the weather that evening is and how we think the New Orleans Saints will do this season. I like football. I'm not an avid fan, but I like it enough to watch a few Saints games every once in a while on TV.

When we finish our meal Gage sits back in his chair, toying with the cup of coffee in front of him.

"So, tell me, what is your relationship with Julian?"

"I don't quite understand the question. We're bonded, but you know that. What is it that you really want to know?"

"Some people at the party thought you might be lovers the way he kept his eyes on you the whole evening."

"No," I reply with a small shake of my head, "we are most definitely not lovers."

"Do you mind me asking if you're dating anyone?"

"Not in the conventional sense." I then explain the plan Julian and I have set into motion to make my family and friends think we are dating so his presence in my life appears natural.

"That certainly makes sense considering the fact you're still learning about our world. How do you like what you've learned so far? Having any trouble coping with it all at once?"

"Oddly enough, most things haven't shocked me too much. I guess understanding the bond between Julian and me was the most difficult thing to comprehend. When someone tells you they're a vampire, the first thing a sane person does is look for the straitjacket."

Gage laughs. "I can't blame you there. It is pretty out there if you haven't been raised to believe in it all your life."

He falls silent for a moment as he seems to contemplate what he wants to say next.

"Would you mind it if I came over again to see you? I would really like to get to know you better, Sarah."

Just like with Daniel, I know if I hadn't already given my heart to Julian I would have taken Gage up on his offer of a date almost immediately. He's handsome, nice, well-spoken. I would have to be crazy not to give a guy like him a chance.

I'm about to say no when an idea blossoms inside my mind. It could have been me just wanting to see if it would hurt Julian, but the idea of letting Gage get to know me better seems like the perfect opportunity to test my stubborn vampire. Would he even care? After all, he's the one who set up this romantic interlude. He's obviously trying his best to force me into another man's arms. Would Gage's presence in the house make Julian jealous at all? There was only one way to find out.

"I would like that," I say. "When can you come back?"

"How about Saturday? I have to work tomorrow and Friday, but I'm free this weekend."

"That sounds good. I'm not sure what we'll do yet, but I'm sure I can think of something."

"Great," Gage stands from his chair. "I should probably be getting back home. I have to be in early to work tomorrow."

I stand and lead Gage to the front door.

"Thank you for a wonderful time this evening." He leans in and gives me a light kiss on the cheek. "I'll see you Saturday."

After he leaves, I concentrate on my connection with Julian to pinpoint his precise location.

I walk back out onto the patio and take my shoes off to make it easier to walk across the back lawn to the edge of the woods. I find Julian sitting on a fallen tree trunk, waiting for me.

"Did you have a good time?" he asks as I approach.

I'm not sure what comes over me. I'm usually not a violent person, but the moment I see Julian an intense rage takes possession of my body. I slap him as hard as I can across the face. I must have tapped into my super-strength because I hit him so hard he has to catch himself with a hand on the tree trunk to prevent himself from falling off.

"What the hell was that supposed to be, Julian?" I demand hotly. "Your subtle way of telling me you don't care about me? I don't need you to be my pimp! Or were you hoping Gage could make me forget that I love you?"

Julian lifts his hand to his jaw, testing to make sure it still works.

"You need to let go of your foolish romantic fantasies about me, Sarah. We can't have that sort of relationship. I thought I made myself clear on that point last night."

"Crystal," I say, unable to hide my irritation. "You know, I don't see how someone who has lived for four hundred years can be such a coward."

"I am not a coward." Julian's dark tone tells me I've hit a nerve, and I'm not about to let up on it. In fact, I'm about to yank it until it hurts.

"Yes, you are! You're a coward because you can't face the fact you have feelings for me. What kind of man sets up the person he wants with another man?"

"I am not a coward, Sarah." He rises from the trunk, now standing only a few inches away from me. "What I did for you tonight was one of the hardest things I've ever done!"

I can barely make out Julian's expression in the moonlight, but I can hear the pain in his voice clear enough.

"Then why did you do it?" I demand, my anger slowly draining out of me. "I don't want him. I don't want anyone but you."

Julian closes his eyes. "Why are you making this so difficult? I'm trying to make sure you have a chance at something of a normal life. I want you to experience the joys of motherhood and what it feels like to be a part of a family of your own. I can't give that to you, Sarah. I can't father your children. I'm not someone who can grow old with you. I'm trying to do what's best for you. Can't you see that?"

I stretch out my hand and place it over his heart. "I know what's best for me. I just wish you knew it, too."

Julian opens his eyes and looks down at me.

I take a chance and slowly grab a fist full of his shirt with the hand I have on his chest. He doesn't try to fight me as I bring his head down to mine. When our lips touch, the floodgate Julian is using to hold back his emotions for me bursts wide open. He kisses me like a man no longer listening to what his mind is telling him but giving into where his heart is leading him.

I feel his hands travel down my back and come to rest on my hips. He lifts me up into the air until his hands are underneath each thigh. I do what comes naturally and wrap my legs around his waist. I feel him sit back down on the tree trunk, running his hands up the back of my dress. His fingers seem to be searching for something, and I realize he's trying to find the zipper.

I don't want to break the contact between our lips to tell him how to take the dress off. I'm afraid if I do, he'll have too much time to rethink what we're doing. So I let go of his shirt and let the zipper at the side down myself, slipping the dress off the one shoulder holding it on.

Julian's hands find their way to the three hook-n-eyes holding my strapless bra on and makes quick work of unhooking them to slip the thin piece of lingerie off, tossing it onto the forest floor somewhere. I feel his hands glide across the naked skin of my back as they slowly make their way across to cup each of my breasts in a warm caress.

"Sarah! Sarah!"

Helen's urgent call seems to act like a bucket of ice water on Julian. He immediately drops his hands away from my breasts and breaks the contact of our lips.

"Sarah! Kaylee's in the hospital asking for you! Are you out here, dear?"

I quickly scramble off Julian's lap, slipping my dress back onto my shoulder and hastily zipping it back up, sans bra. I don't even wait to see if he's following behind me. I run as quickly as I can to Helen, who is standing by the back door on the patio with a worried look on her face.

"What's wrong? Why is she at the hospital? She isn't due for another couple of months," I say in a rush of panic.

"I don't know, dear. Her mother just asked that you come to the hospital as soon as possible." I see Helen's eyes dart to Julian walking up behind me.

I pick up the shoes I left by the door and slip them back on my feet.

"I'll drive you to the hospital." Julian offers, laying a comforting hand on the small of my back.

I nod my head, unable to think about anything except getting to Kaylee.

CHAPTER 17.

On the way to the hospital, I try to call Susan, Pete, and Ben, but either their phones are shut off or they aren't getting good reception in the hospital because I keep being sent directly to their voicemails.

"No luck?" Julian asks when he sees me drop my phone back into my purse with a disappointed sigh.

"No. I can't get in touch with any of them." I lean my head back on the headrest, trying to steady my nerves and calm my frustration.

"Everything will be fine, Sarah. Don't worry."

I shake my head. "You just don't understand. Kaylee's my sister. I can't lose her, or Em."

"Em?"

"Emma Louise Whitaker is the name of Kaylee's daughter. We've already nicknamed her Em."

"I see."

I close my eyes, trying my best to hold back the tears I feel coming on. Julian places a comforting hand on my thigh and squeezes it reassuringly.

"They'll be fine, Sarah. Don't think the worst."

I try to believe in what he says, but I know I won't feel better until I see Kaylee with my own eyes.

When we get to the hospital, the receptionist gives us directions to Kaylee's room. She isn't in the maternity ward, so I know she isn't delivering Em that night. I find Susan and Pete sitting on one of those foldout couches in Kaylee's room, watching the news on TV when we get there. Kaylee is sitting up in her bed, talking to Ben who is seated on the edge of her mattress holding her hand.

"What's wrong?" I immediately ask when I enter the room.

Susan stands up and walks over to me, giving me a brief hug in greeting.

"Kaylee fainted," she tells me. "Her doctor says her blood pressure got too high."

"It was so weird," Kaylee says as Ben leaves her side so I can take his place. "I was washing some dishes and started seeing these little black dots floating everywhere. Then I got really hot and passed out. Ben found me and called the ambulance."

"So what does the doctor think is wrong?" I ask.

"He's doing some tests to see if it's eclampsia. If it is, he said we might need to deliver Em tonight."

"When will they know?"

"Shouldn't be too much longer. They just needed to run a few tests on my blood and urine." Kaylee's gaze falls to the dress I'm wearing. "I hope I didn't interrupt anything important?" she says with a hopeful tilt to her voice. How can she be thinking about my sex life at a time like this?

However, I can't prevent the rush of blood her question brings to my face.

"Don't worry about it," I tell her, hoping she'll take the hint and not ask for details in front of everyone.

"Well, you look gorgeous," she sighs. "While I look like a beached whale," she half-heartedly laughs.

"You're the most beautiful woman I know, sweetie." Ben leans down and kisses his wife on the cheek.

That's the one thing I like most about Ben. He loves Kaylee almost as much as I do.

The doctor walks into the room a few minutes later with good news. He says Kaylee's condition isn't as serious as he first feared, but that she does have hypertension. So, he wants to see her twice a week for the rest of her pregnancy to keep an eye on her condition.

"If things look like they're getting worse, we can induce labor if we have to," he tells us. "But right now, I see no reason why she can't go home in the morning. Just make sure she doesn't overexert herself in any way and that she rests as much as possible."

Julian and I stay for a little while longer until the nurse comes in to tell us visiting hours are over. I tell Kaylee I will come by her house the next day to make sure she's following the doctor's orders while Ben is at work.

When we get back into the car and are on our way home, I let out a relieved sigh.

"Are you all right?" Julian asks me.

"I'm fine."

Now that my worry over Kaylee is over, being alone in the car with Julian is making me a bit uncomfortable. What is he thinking about? Is he regretting what almost happened in the woods between us, or is he regretting the interruption? I'm not sure which side of the fence he's on, and I don't have the strength to ask. My heart has been through enough for one evening. All I want to do now is curl up in my bed and go to sleep.

Julian seems to be locked in his own little world on the drive home. I want a peek inside his head in that moment to see what tangled paths his thoughts are leading him down.

When we pull up to his house, he brings the car to a stop on the driveway in front of the front door.

"Why don't you go in and go to bed? I can sense how tired you are."

"You didn't get any blood last night," I point out to him. "Don't you need to feed tonight?"

"It can wait," he says. "You need your rest more. I'll be fine. After I park the car in the garage, I'll come inside."

When I reach the second floor, I see Helen just about to walk into her room. I quickly tell her what happened to Kaylee.

"That poor thing," Helen says with a small shake of her head. "Let me know if there's anything I can do for her."

"I think she'll be ok," I reassure her. "If I know her husband, Kaylee won't be lifting a finger much less doing anything that will make her faint again."

Unintentionally I yawn, and try to stifle it with a hand.

"Go get some rest, dear," Helen urges. "I'll see you in the morning."

All I can do is nod and turn to walk into my room. I don't even bother to change into my pajamas. I just slip my shoes off and crawl underneath the covers. I feel Viktor jump up on my bed and curl up against my feet, but I'm so exhausted I don't even open my eyes to look at him. Sleep takes me in its arms, dragging me down into a peaceful slumber.

When I wake up the next morning, Viktor's soft lean body is snuggled against the top of my head again. I reach up and begin to rub his warm belly, receiving a pleased purr of pleasure in return. The dregs of sleep are still clinging to my mind when I realize something is very wrong.

I sit up with a start as I realize Julian isn't in the house. He's not even close to its vicinity. Oddly enough, I don't feel the all-consuming loneliness I have on other occasions when Julian was physically far away. I still feel an ache in my chest and a need to be with him, but my separation anxiety is bearable. At least I don't feel like staying huddled in my bed and sobbing my grief out into my pillow until he returns.

I get out of bed and prepare myself to go over to Kaylee's house. She should be returning to her home this morning, and I am determined to make sure she takes her doctor's advice and does as little as possible until little Em is born.

By the time I venture downstairs, I can smell the sweet aromas of pancakes and bacon wafting from the direction of the kitchen. Helen is standing by the stove, flipping a pancake over with an expert wrist, humming a happy tune to herself.

"Where's Julian this morning?" I ask her when I enter the kitchen.

"He said he needed to meet Petru somewhere." She pulls out a sealed white envelope from her apron pocket. "He asked me to give this to you."

Inside the envelope is a hand-written letter.

Dear Sarah,

Petru called me this morning to let me know Dorka's relative is ready to speak with us. I will be back home in a few days. In the meantime, perhaps you should consider spending some more time with either Daniel or Gage. I'm sure either of them would be happy to entertain you during my absence.

Best Regards,
Julian

I read the letter a second time to make sure I'm reading it correctly. Is he actually suggesting that I spend time with other men after what we almost did last night? I want to crush the letter and throw it in the trash because that's exactly what I think of his suggestion, but I don't. I simply fold it up and tuck it into the back pocket of my jeans.

"Did he happen to mention to you when he would be back?" I ask Helen.

"No, dear, I'm afraid he didn't," she says, sliding the pancake she just made from the skillet and onto a platter of at least twenty others.

Apparently I don't hide my disappointment very well, because Helen says, "I'm sure he'll return as soon as he can. He understands how much his absence affects you."

"It's not as bad this morning," I confess as I take the platter of pancakes to the kitchen table and sit down. "At least I don't feel like crying. That's a definite improvement."

"Oh, that's wonderful to hear, dear," Helen says with a smile. "I suppose it is about time for your connection to one another to transition into a more normal rhythm."

"I'm grateful it has," I confess. "Feeling like my heart was being ripped out of my chest every time he left wasn't working for me at all."

After I finish eating my breakfast, I tell Helen not to worry about making me lunch or dinner because I plan to spend the day with Kaylee and then stay the night at my apartment. I decide to take Viktor with me. Kaylee has always liked cats, but she can't have one in the house since Ben is allergic to them. Actually, I'm normally allergic to cats, too, but since Viktor isn't just a cat he must not exude the same allergens. I just hope I'm right in assuming Ben will be at work all day since it's Friday.

By the time I reach her house, it's a little after nine o'clock and the Durango is missing from the driveway. With its absence I know Ben is gone, since he uses it to travel back and forth to work.

I soon realize a day with Kaylee is exactly what I needed. We play board games like we used to when we were kids, and Kaylee gets a kick out of having Viktor visit.

"Now, who did you say gave you the cat?"

"Just a woman at Julian's sister's party." I shrug one shoulder like it's not a big deal, trying my best to make it sound like nothing important.

"Why would she give you her cat?" Kaylee asks, still confused.

"She said Viktor wanted to be with me."

"How would she even know that? What is she, the cat whisperer?" she asks jokingly.

If only she knew…

"Hey, it's almost lunch time." When in doubt on how to answer a question, change the subject. "What do you have in the kitchen to cook?"

We rummage through Kaylee's fridge and cabinets, quickly discovering that Kaylee has absolutely nothing edible in the house. It's Friday and she and Ben usually do their grocery shopping on Saturday mornings. Since I'm starving, I order us some pizzas from the local pizzeria.

While we're waiting for the delivery guy to show up, Kaylee finally asks me the question she's been yearning to all morning long. I knew she was waiting for me to be the first to mention Julian, but a conversation about him wasn't something I had planned to initiate with her.

"So… what did my little emergency interrupt last night between you and Julian? And don't try to fool me, Sarah Marcel; I saw that blush on your cheeks last night, so don't you dare say nothing happened. I need details, woman!"

I smile at Kaylee's enthusiasm over my love life, but roll my eyes at her nonetheless.

"We made out, but that's as far as it went." I don't think telling Kaylee she's the reason things didn't go any further is a wise decision, not in her condition.

"Was there at least some heavy petting?" she inquires with a playful lifting of her eyebrows.

I have no idea how to respond to that, but apparently my shocked expression and silence is enough of an answer for her.

"I knew it," she says smugly. "I miss the days when Ben and I would spend a whole day in bed together just touching and…"

"Please," I interrupt, placing my hands over my ears "for the sake of all things holy, don't finish that thought. You're giving me information overload here."

"*Pfft*," Kaylee says, waving a hand in my direction like I'm the one being silly. "There's nothing wrong with two people who love each other making love all day long. It's one of life's little pleasures.

I'll bet Julian will be an attentive lover. He just gives off that 'I am man. I will take care of you' kind of vibe."

"I wouldn't know," I reply, desperately wracking my brain for a way to quickly change the subject. Thankfully the pizza deliveryman knocks on the door, promptly solving my dilemma.

I limited myself to only ordering three pizzas. In actuality I probably could have eaten at least six by myself, but I knew Kaylee would start to ask too many questions, and I hated lying to her. Perhaps one day soon I'll be able to share what's going on in my life with her, but now is not the time.

I don't leave Kaylee's house until Ben comes home from work at five. I decide not to stick around so the two of them can have some alone time together. I go directly to my apartment afterwards.

Once we're inside, Viktor transforms into his human form.

He stands in the middle of my apartment, stark naked, looking around the small living room.

"I completely agree with the vampire. This apartment is far too small for you, especially considering who you are," he says, peering at my lovely little apartment as if it's a hovel.

"I like it," I defend, walking to the hall closet to find Viktor a sheet to wear. I definitely need to go buy him some clothes soon.

I hand him the sheet, keeping my eyes averted until he has it draped over his long frame.

"So I take it the vampire will be gone for a little while?" Viktor sits down on the cream-colored sofa in the middle of the room and props his feet up on the espresso- stained coffee table. I don't have the heart to admonish him for his bad manners since I'm prone to do the same thing while watching TV.

"That's what the note said," I tell him, flopping down beside him on the couch.

"From your reaction this morning, that isn't the only thing the note said. What else did the boor write?"

S.J. WEST

"He suggested that I think about spending more time with either Gage or Daniel."

"He suggested *what?*" Viktor is furious. He quickly stands up from the couch, and starts to pace back and forth along the small open space between my coffee table and TV stand.

"I cannot *believe* he's trying to pawn you off onto a human warlock and another vampire's companion. Has he lost his mind? Doesn't he realize there are bloodlines to consider? You're the future Queen of the Alfar. You can't simply have a child with just *anyone.*"

My heart sinks even deeper inside my chest. I thought I would at least have Viktor on my side, but all he seems to be concerned about is an heir, too. It makes me not even want to have a child. What sort of life will I be bringing her or him into? Julian will want my child as a companion, and the alfar will want it as their future king or queen. It makes the decision my parents made for me even more poignant and understandable.

My mother wanted me to have a normal life while I could, but she knew the bond between companion and vampire was too strong to ignore and could never be erased without death being involved. My father completely abandoned his people to be with my mom and me, knowing his decision would leave the alfar without an heir. It must have been why my mother never let Julian or my grandfather meet my dad. They would have known who he was and understood the alfar would want me to lead their people if they ever discovered I existed. Without knowing my father's identity, Julian inadvertently revealed my existence to Queen Shael by taking me to Mira's party.

"Isn't there someone else who can assume the throne?" I ask. "I don't want it."

Viktor immediately stops pacing, and stares at me like I just hit him across the head with a baseball bat a few times.

"Don't want it? It's not a matter of what you *want*, Sarah. It's who you *are*. You are the last descendant of a noble bloodline who can still give birth to an heir. You have to carry on the tradition of your family, which is why you'll be expected to marry someone of alfar blood."

"*What?*" This time it's my turn to be furious. I stand from the couch and place my fists on my hips. "I can't even choose my own husband?"

"Well, of course you can." Viktor finally seems to realize that he's upset me and is now going to attempt to mollify my ire. "He just has to be an alfar."

"But why?"

"Your father was supposed to marry an alfar woman, but he disappeared with your mother to have you. The bloodline of the alfar has been so diluted over the years, a pureblooded one barely exists anymore. Shael is one of the last pureblooded royals left. As it is, there are only a handful who can claim pureblood status. Since she can't have any children, you are the next purest member of House Moonshade. If you dilute the bloodline any more than it already is, your children might as well just call themselves human."

Viktor said 'human' like it was a dirty word. I understand his reasons for wanting to keep the royal alfar bloodline as pure as possible, but logic doesn't stop the heart from yearning to find true love and the happily ever after ending everyone dreams of having in their life.

"Would I necessarily have to marry an alfar? Could I just be artificially inseminated with an alfar donor's sperm?" It was how I had intended to have an heir for Julian anyway. What did it matter if it was human or alfar sperm that I used?

"That's not the proper way to conceive a child," Viktor says rather adamantly. I know he's disappointed by my proposal, but he doesn't say it can't be done my way.

"But there's no alfar law that says I can't do it that way, correct?" I push.

He sighs heavily with disapproval. "If that's what you want to do, I suppose it can be done in such a barbaric manner. But don't your children deserve a father?"

"They'll have one, but he'll be one of my own choosing. I won't be dictated to on who I can and cannot marry! I've already been forced to give up enough. I won't give up my freedom to choose a husband, too."

The corner of Viktor's mouth lifts in a sardonic grin. "You are most definitely your father's daughter. He was just as stubborn as you are."

"Well, I'm glad he was. Otherwise, I wouldn't exist."

"Quite true, Sarah. Quite true."

I become increasingly uncomfortable with the way Viktor begins to look at me. I know he's sexually aroused for some reason, and I attempt to think of a way to stop it.

"You know, Sarah," Viktor saunters over to me with his eyelids slightly lowered and an intimate tone in his voice. "If you don't want to look for a male companion to help you raise your children, I would be more than willing to stay in my human form for as long as you need me. I could be a good father. I know a great deal about alfar life, and I know I could be a satisfying lover to you. All you have to do is tell me what you want and I'll do it."

For me, Viktor's offer comes off sounding like he's applying for a job.

"Thank you for the kind offer, but I don't think that will be necessary."

Viktor smiles. "That doesn't sound like a firm no."

"It's not. I have no idea what's in store for me in the future. You may end up being my last resort."

He places his hands over his heart like I've wounded him. "So, I am to be your last option. I can't pretend that doesn't smart just a bit, Sarah."

"I'm sorry. That's not the way I meant for you to take it. I just don't like closing doors until I know what's in each room. I want to spend my life with someone who loves me and who I can love in return. I won't give up on finding true happiness that easily."

"I understand. You just want me to be your friend for the moment. I just wanted to make sure you knew what I had to offer to help with your dilemma."

"I'll keep your proposition in mind. Thank you for making it."

Viktor places his hands down by his sides. "Did you happen to bring along any of that scrumptious cat food in a can? I'm famished."

Viktor changes back into his cat form. I feed him two cans of Fancy Feast and half a bowl of milk. After he eats, he promptly crawls up onto my lap and watches TV with me. It isn't the most exciting night of my life but at least I get to spend it in my own home, surrounded by my own things.

All day I tried to keep the words of Julian's letter out of my mind. Sitting alone in the darkness of my living room with only the light of the TV shining on my face, I begin to feel the tears I've been holding back burst through the dam of my resolve to protect myself from Julian's cold indifference. Viktor changes form and takes me into his arms, not saying a word, just providing me with what I need most in that moment… comfort. He lets me cry my heartache and confusion out until I fall asleep in his embrace.

CHAPTER 18.

The next morning I get up bright and early. My feelings about Julian are still a jumbled mess, but I decide to push all of that to the back of my mind and heart for now. All I want is a day or two spent somewhere else besides the place where my problems dwell. This need blossoms into a brilliant plan to do just that.

Thankfully, Gage and I exchanged cell phone numbers before he left Julian's house the other night. I call him, praying he answers before I lose my nerve to go through with my genius idea. I sigh in relief when I hear him pick up on the third ring.

"Sarah?" he says, his voice filled with surprise.

"Hey," I chirp, doing my best to sound casual and cool. "How are you doing this morning?"

"I'm doing fine," he says hesitantly. "Are you calling to cancel our plans for today? I was just about to jump in my car and drive up there."

"Actually, I thought I would come down to you instead if that's all right. I could really use a day away from things around here."

"That sounds great! There are a lot of things we can do here on the coast. In fact, why don't you bring an overnight bag?" he suggests. "I'm not sure how late we'll be out, and I would rather you didn't drive home alone in the dark. I make a solemn oath, as a former Eagle Scout, that I will be a perfect gentleman while you're my guest. So don't worry about me taking advantage of the situation. I promise you I won't."

"Ok, I'll plan to stay the night," I say. Even though I'm not physically close enough to read his true intentions, I can hear the sincerity in his voice clear enough. "Can you suggest a hotel close to your house so I can make a reservation?"

"Why don't you just stay at my place? I have a guesthouse out by the pool you can use tonight. It's unnecessary for you to waste your money on a hotel room when I have so much space here. I promise I don't bite."

I'm not sure if his pun is intentional or not but it makes me laugh anyway.

"Ok, sounds good. Text me your address, and I'll be there in a couple of hours."

When I get off the phone with Gage, I feel happy and excited. I decide then and there that I will concentrate on having fun with him that day, and not give a certain vampire, who shall not be named, a second thought. Am I completely deluding myself? Perhaps, but a girl's gotta dream sometimes just to keep her sanity.

Since I wasn't sure what all Gage might have planned for us to do that day, I pack a one-piece swimsuit, a nice dress, and a couple of pairs of jeans, shorts, and T-shirts, plus my toiletries and a pair of pajamas.

"I don't like the idea of you spending the night with a stranger," Viktor tells me, lounging on my bed dressed in his sheet while I pack my overnight bag.

"I plan to take you with me so you can be our chaperone," I inform him as I try to decide whether I need to bring a bathrobe or not. I decide against it. It would just take up too much space in a bag that is already running out of room.

"Well at least you're being sensible. Human warlocks are cagey creatures. Are you positive you can trust him?"

"Yes, I'm sure."

"How can you be so confident in your assessment of this man? You've only met him a couple of times."

I stop packing and look at Viktor. Should I tell him about my empathic abilities? If I do, he will be only one of three people in the world with whom I've shared my secret. Will he be all right with me knowing everything he feels all the time? I suppose there's only one way to find out.

"I'm an empath, Viktor. Trust me. Gage can't hide his true nature from me."

Viktor sits up straighter. "We haven't had an empath in the family for a long time!" I can feel his growing excitement at my revelation.

"Gage mentioned that alfar magic relies on mental abilities. Is my being an empath because I'm half-alfar?"

"Yes," Viktor says resoundingly without even needing to pause to consider his answer. "I would be interested in knowing if you have any other skills. Have you ever done something out of the ordinary that you couldn't explain?"

"No, not that I can think of."

Viktor shrugs. "It could be that you simply haven't had the need to call on the magic within you for anything else. I really wish you had told me about this sooner, Sarah."

"Why?"

"Because if you have the ability to manipulate things with your mind, like I suspect you can, it can be a dangerous power to wield if you don't know what you're doing."

"I doubt I can do something like that…"

"I wouldn't be so quick to dismiss the possibility. The last empath in the royal family made me."

"Really?" That changes things completely. Do I have the ability to manipulate matter with my mind? The possibility is kind of cool and scary at the same time.

"Well, like I said, I've never been able to do anything but read people's feelings. If I can do any other type of magic, it hasn't presented itself."

"Still, we may need to get you a tutor to see just how powerful you are."

Viktor leans back on the headboard of my bed and smiles, feeling somewhat smug about something.

"You know," he says, "I had a feeling there was something special about you the moment I saw you, but I never could have imagined that the next alfar heir would possess magic *and* the powers gained by being a vampire companion. You're quite extraordinary, Sarah."

"Thanks." What else was I supposed to say to that? It didn't make me view myself any differently. The only thing that's extraordinary about me right now is my hunger.

I make myself some breakfast before I hop into my Camry to make the hour-trip over to Gulfport. I hope Gage remembers my eating habits as a vampire companion and has the fridge in his guesthouse fully stocked. If not, that may end up being one of the errands he and I get to run this afternoon.

At around eleven o'clock, Viktor and I arrive at Gage's house. It's located just off Beach Drive. Considering the fact that almost everyone I've met so far in Julian's world lives in a mansion, I begin to understand why he and Viktor think my apartment is too small. The front gate to the property is open. I assume Gage left it that way in anticipation of my arrival. The cobblestone circular drive loops in front of the house, around a grouping of four palm trees surrounding a large three-tier water fountain. The home itself is gorgeous. It's a two-story mansion with pale yellow stucco and white trim. Two white columns mark the entryway and anchor the small front porch. Gage must have been keeping an eye out for my arrival because he walks out of one of the wood and cut- glass front doors just as I put my car in park. When I step out, Viktor meows and jumps into my arms as if to ensure I don't leave him behind.

"Hey, glad to see you made it safely," Gage says as he comes to stand beside us. "Where's your bag?"

"Right there in the backseat," I tell him.

"Is it ok if I get it for you?" he asks, looking at Viktor. "It looks like your hands are a little full right now."

"I would appreciate that. Thanks."

Gage pulls the car door open and picks up my black overnight bag from the back seat.

I can tell he's genuinely happy to see me. I have to say it's a nice, uncluttered feeling.

"Well, let's put your bag in the house and grab the basket of food I have for us so we can head on out to our first destination."

"Where are we going?" I ask as I follow Gage into his house.

"I thought we might take the ferry boat that goes out to Ship Island. Have you ever been there before?"

"No, I always meant to go but never seemed to find the time."

I know a little about Ship Island. Kaylee and I had planned a senior class trip there but never made it. Ship Island is one of the five barrier islands located about 11 miles off the coast of Mississippi. The water on the south side of the island isn't the normal murky brown water you see along the Mississippi Gulf Coast, but a pristine blue, more like the water along the panhandle of Florida.

"Did you happen to bring a swimsuit?" he asks.

"Yes, I brought one just in case."

"Great! Then we're all set."

When we reach the front door of his house, he lets me precede him inside. His house has a definite Southern charm about it. There are glossy walnut-colored floors running throughout the house. A carpeted staircase leads from the foyer to the second floor.

Gage leaves my bag next to the wall by the front doors.

"Come on, let me show you the rest of the place before we head out."

Gage's home seems a bit big for one person. There are seven bedrooms, eight full baths, a living room, dining room, large kitchen with a breakfast nook, and a granite swimming pool in the middle of the back patio. An outdoor stone fireplace is located on one side of the pool, while a deck with a large built in barbecue is located on the opposite side.

Once Gage shows me all there is to see in the main house, he retrieves my bag from near the front door and escorts me to the guesthouse by the pool that I'll be spending the night in. The guesthouse is immaculately decorated and bigger than my apartment. It has a large living room area with a fireplace, kitchen, bedroom, and full-size bathroom.

"I stocked the kitchen in here with some food just in case you happened to get hungry this evening. I'm not quite sure how much companions eat, and I didn't want you to go hungry."

"That was very thoughtful. Thank you."

"Well, I just want you to feel at home while you're here. Maybe if this visit goes well, you'll be more likely to visit again sometime soon."

He smiles at me hopefully, but doesn't seem to expect me to reply.

"Listen, why don't you go ahead and put your swimsuit on underneath your clothes while I finish packing up our lunch? The boat leaves the dock at noon. We'll need to go as soon as you're ready if we're going to make it."

Gage goes back into the main house while I change. I set out food and water bowls for Viktor in the kitchen before I leave to find Gage.

"I'll be back soon," I tell Viktor. "Don't worry about me while I'm gone."

Viktor meows softly and hops onto the bed in the bedroom, curling up to take a nap. Cats sure do seem to sleep a lot.

I find Gage packing up a large bamboo picnic basket in the kitchen. The room is outfitted with custom-built cherry wood cabinetry and black silver-speckled marble countertops. A long kitchen island stands in the middle of the room with a bar and four white cushioned swivel stools.

"Is there anything I can do to help?" I ask, coming to stand next to him. All I see are a bunch of Tupperware bowls.

"No, I think I have everything packed. Do you like to drink wine?"

I shake my head. "I'm not much of an alcohol drinker to be honest. Sorry."

"No problem. I have a backup." He walks around me and pulls out a bottle of sparkling apple cider from the stainless steel fridge.

After he has everything he wants to take packed, we get into his red Porsche Cayenne SUV and head down to the docks to catch the ferryboat. By the time we get our tickets and board the boat, it's twelve o'clock.

"It takes an hour to get there and an hour to get back," Gage informs me after we take a couple of seats inside the ferry by the windows.

I nod and look out at a group of seagulls begging for food from some of the passengers standing out by the side rails.

"So, was Julian ok with you coming over here and spending the night?" he asks me, drawing my attention back to him.

"He doesn't know I'm here," I say, feeling zero guilt about the fact. "He had to go out of town unexpectedly. He said he wouldn't be back for a few days."

"Really?" Gage says in surprise. "I didn't think the two of you could be away from each other for that long. I was always told there was some pain involved if you weren't physically close to one another."

"There is. It was horrible when we first bonded, but now I just feel a dull ache in my chest that won't go away."

"Doesn't he need to feed daily?"

"He can go a while without needing to do that."

I'm not sure if I'm revealing too much or not. Obviously, Gage hasn't been told about the intricacies involved in being a vampire's companion. Am I not supposed to tell him certain things?

It isn't as if I was given a handbook on human companion protocol. As far as I know, there isn't an etiquette class available to teach me right from wrong when talking with an outsider about my new station in life.

Just to stay on the safe side, though, I decide to change the subject and start asking him questions about his hobbies. I learn that we have at least one thing in common. We both love to watch movies. He confesses to love the Godfather movies. So typically male. And I confess I totally geek out for anything supernatural.

Gage confesses to me that he's a terrible cook and never does it unless there's absolutely no other recourse. He has mastered the art of making a respectable grilled cheese sandwich but that's about it.

"Who made all that food in the picnic basket?" I ask.

"I picked most of it up at a little deli not far from my house. I wasn't about to scare you away on our first date with my cooking," he laughs.

I didn't consider this outing a date and wonder if I should correct his assumption. It seems rude to do such a thing, but I definitely don't want him to get the wrong idea about where our acquaintance is heading.

Before I can say anything about it, the boat pulls alongside the dock on the island and we get in line to disembark.

The pier leads up to the old Fort of Massachusetts that's still on the island. I assume Gage must have been there before because he quickly stakes out one of the few trees on the beach in a secluded spot for us.

He unfolds the blue blanket that is strapped to the outside of the picnic basket and motions for me to sit down on it. He then proceeds to open the basket and starts setting out at least ten medium-sized Tupperware bowls in front of me.

"I wasn't sure what you would like so I got a little bit of everything," he tells me.

The fare is what you might expect to get from a deli: cubed cheeses, slices of meat, chicken salad, tuna salad, crackers, chips, finger sandwiches, freshly cut vegetables with a side of ranch dipping sauce, pecan tarts, and chocolate chip cookies.

"Wow, you shouldn't have spent so much money on just lunch."

"Not too worried about it. I plan to go cheap on dinner. We're going to the Beau Rivage's all-you-can-eat buffet. They usually serve crab legs and shrimp on the weekend. I thought you might like it."

I feel an endearing warmth fill my heart because of Gage's thoughtfulness. Unfortunately, it isn't quite strong enough to overpower the ache I feel from Julian's absence, both physically and emotionally. If Julian wasn't in my life, I could easily see myself giving Gage a real chance, but as things stand now, I'm afraid that's just an impossibility.

As we bask in the heat of a southern sun, Gage tells me more about himself. I learn he's a real estate agent, just like Kaylee's parents.

"I should probably put my own home on the market," he says. "It's way too big for me, unless I can find someone who wants to have a half-dozen kids."

I smile as a vision of Gage chasing down six children in his house forms in my mind. "Why did you buy something so large?"

"I didn't. It used to belong to my parents, but they gave it to me when they decided to retire in Florida. It's hard to give it up. It's the only home I've ever known."

"Do you have any brothers and sisters?"

"Two of each. They're scattered all over the world, though. I'm the only one who didn't want to leave home."

"There's nothing wrong with wanting to stay in the town you grew up in. That's what I did."

Gage reaches out, grabs a pecan tart from one of the Tupperware bowls, and deftly pops it out of its miniature aluminum pie dish.

I follow his lead, but stop just before picking one of the sweet treats up.

I feel a sharp sense of foreboding fall over me like a shadow, and I immediately know something's wrong with Julian. It's a sixth sense, just like I had in New Orleans when he was injured.

"We need to go," I say, quickly standing up as my heart begins to race with worry. "I need to find Julian."

Gage looks up at me in surprise. "Is something wrong?"

"Yes."

"How do you know?" he asks, looking confused by my certainty.

"I just do!" I snap impatiently. "We need to go!"

Gage stands up and begins to pack up what's left of our lunch.

"It's going to be a while before the ferry boat returns to the island," he tells me. "It should be back here in about an hour, but then we'll have to wait another thirty minutes for people to board before it heads into port."

"We can't leave here until 2:30?" I ask in disbelief, desperate to return to the mainland.

"I'm sorry," Gage says apologetically, "but that's the ferry's schedule."

If we don't leave until 2:30, that means we won't get back to shore until 3:30, at the earliest.

"Is there any other way we can get back earlier?" I ask anxiously.

"Not that I know of. Even if we could," Gage asks cautiously, "where are you going to go? I thought you told me you don't know where Julian is this weekend."

"I don't," I say, fretting over the situation I find myself having to deal with. I pull out my phone from my back pocket, but of course we're too far away from civilization for me to get a signal. "Damn it!" I say in frustration, tapping the top edge of my phone against my forehead as I try to think of a way out of my predicament. As far as I can tell, there isn't one.

"Can you always sense if he's in trouble?" Gage asks, sounding interested in my companion ability. "I didn't know you could do that."

"I guess I can," I say. "I didn't really think to ask anyone about it the first time it happened. I was too upset to think about anything but getting to Julian then, and after he was all right it didn't seem important to ask anymore. Are you sure there isn't another way off this island?"

"I'm sorry," Gage says sympathetically, "there isn't. But, let's go wait on the dock so we can get on the boat as soon as it gets here. Maybe we can put our heads together to figure out a way to find Julian once we get back on shore."

As Gage and I wait for the ferry's arrival, we discuss various alternatives to find Julian. I don't tell him what it is my vampire companion is trying to discover speaking to Dorka's descendant. It seems like information I should keep to myself for now. The only other person who might be able to help me is Helen. She knows Julian's world better than anyone else. If anyone can help me, she can.

By the time the boat arrives, I'm a nervous wreck. My insides are tied in a knot so tight all I can feel is an anxiousness that I fear will never go away completely. It was stupid of me to come here today with Gage. I thought it would be good and provide me with the distraction I needed, but all it's done is cause me more turmoil. It's almost as if my life will never truly be my own again.

Gage and I are the first ones on the boat and the first ones off when we make it back to Gulfport. As we're walking down the pier back to Gage's car I call Julian's cell phone first, but it goes directly to his voicemail. I suspected as much, but I had to try. If he's in trouble, he either can't reach his phone or whoever is harming him has taken it away from him. Helen is the next person I call.

"Oh dear," she says worriedly after I tell her what I'm feeling. "I have no idea how to find him, Sarah. He didn't tell me where he was going."

I sigh disappointedly. "I know what city he's in but Destin is huge. There's no way I'll be able to find him there on my own."

"Wait a moment," Helen says, sounding like she has an idea, "Julian was supposed to be meeting Petru, right?"

"Yes. Do you have Petru's phone number? Maybe he knows what's going on."

"I have both Petru and his companion's numbers on my phone. Let me text them to you so you can call them directly. Please let me know what you find out, and if you need my help in any way."

"Ok. I will," I promise. "Right now, it's probably better if you stay there at the house in case Julian tries to return home. If my gut feeling is right, he won't be in good shape."

"Find him, Sarah," Helen entreats me. I can hear the strain in her voice as she holds back tears. "He's as stubborn as the days are long, but he's my oldest and dearest friend. I can't imagine life without him or you."

Her subtle reminder that my life is connected to Julian's isn't lost on me.

"I'll find him," I pledge. "And I'll bring him home."

When I get off the phone with Helen I call Petru's number first, but I'm sent directly to his voicemail, too. I quickly end the call and dial Nathaniel's number.

After the first ring, I hear his youthful voice on the other end of the line.

"Thank God!" Nathaniel says, his voice filled with relief. "I had no idea how to get in touch with you, Sarah. Do you feel it, too?"

It's then that I know both Julian and Petru are in mortal danger.

"Do you know where they went?" I ask Nathaniel, assuming if he were with Petru he would have said so.

"Petru didn't want me to know where he was going," he tells me, making my heart sink deeper inside my chest with despair. "But I snuck a peek at the address he was going to meet Julian at."

"Please tell me you remember it," I say, feeling my heart surge with hope.

"I have a memory like a steel trap," Nathaniel declares proudly.

"Where are you now?" I ask hurriedly.

"I'm still in Waveland."

"Come to Gulfport." I briefly tell him how to get to Gage's house so he can meet up with us. I want to grab Viktor just in case he can be of any help. "We'll all go to Destin together," I say, looking up at Gage to confirm that he's willing to go with us.

Gage nods. It can't hurt to take a level-ten warlock, right? I figure the more firepower we have on hand the better.

I don't know what kind of trouble Julian is in, but I am certain of one thing.

I'm going to get my man, and if I find out someone is responsible for the distress he's in, God's the only power in the universe who might be able to keep me from killing them.

CHAPTER 19.

As soon as we return to Gage's home, I run into the guesthouse to get Viktor. I'm still explaining the situation to my cat when I go inside the main house to wait with Gage for Nathaniel's arrival. I notice the odd look on my host's face as I continue to describe what I'm feeling to Viktor. If times were different I might worry that Gage thinks I've completely lost my mind, but Viktor needs to fully understand what's going on. I'm not sure if he can help us or not, but if he can I need to know.

I debate on whether I should mention that Julian and Petru were going to talk to a descendant of Dorka, Bathory's witch friend. If Viktor and I were alone I wouldn't hesitate in telling him, but telling Gage is a completely different matter. I feel as though I would be betraying Julian's confidence if I let him in on the secret.

On the other hand, if this woman is a witch, like her ancestor, she's probably a powerful one, and I should probably warn Gage that we might be walking into a trap. Yet, what if the situation isn't what I fear at all, and I end up divulging information to him that I don't need to? I'm not even sure Julian told Helen what he was doing since she has yet to mention the specifics of his quest to me.

"I have a question about your magic," I say to Gage. "Do you need a wand or potions to use it?"

Gage's eyebrows lower and I can tell he's trying to figure out the reasoning behind my question. "No. I don't need anything but myself. Why do you ask?"

"I just wanted to make sure you don't need to take any supplies, you know, just in case we need your magic," I say vaguely.

A series of rapid knocks and a couple of urgent presses of the doorbell signal Nathaniel's arrival. Viktor leaps from my arms and onto the floor. I run out of the living room and into the foyer to yank open the front door.

"Are you ready?" Nathaniel asks straightaway in lieu of a greeting. The urgency plastered on his face is probably a mirror of my own. We both know our companions are in dire straits and time is running out.

"I'm ready to go if the two of you are," Gage says, walking up behind me with the keys to his SUV in his hand.

We all get into Gage's vehicle and head towards Destin. As soon as we get on I-10, I know it will take at least another three hours for us to reach our destination. Even with Gage driving well over the speed limit, it'll still take us a good two and a half hours to arrive at the address Nathaniel surreptitiously got from Petru.

While we're driving, I decide to use my phone to look at a satellite image of the home in question. It's a four-story mansion built directly on the beach in Destin. It's flanked by two similar homes with barely enough room to walk in between them, so the location isn't an isolated one.

"What should we do when we get there?" I ask the guys. "Just go up to the front door and demand to see Julian and Petru?"

"I have an idea," Viktor says unexpectedly from his spot in the back seat beside Nathaniel.

"What the…" Gage says in shock, having to jerk the steering wheel back into place before we veer off the interstate. Apparently, the surprise of Viktor's sudden transformation caused him to let go of it for a second or two. He glances in his rearview mirror to look at Viktor's smiling face.

"Oh, come now," Viktor says to Gage. "You know how powerful alfar magic can be. Is it really that big of a surprise that I can transform into a human?"

Gage thinks about this for a moment before admitting, "No. It isn't. You just caught me off guard is all."

"Well, it wasn't as if I could warn you beforehand," Viktor says before looking over at a startled Nathaniel. "Are you all right, boy?"

"I…you're…what…" Nathaniel stutters, his eyes grow huge as he continues to stare at Viktor in all his naked glory. It's amusingly obvious that he's at a complete loss for words since he's having trouble piecing a simple sentence together. "I…"

Viktor holds up a hand, palm forward to stop Nathaniel from saying another word.

"Please," Viktor begs, "I'm fully aware that my magnificence has befuddled your little human brain, but maybe it would be better if you just remained silent for a moment while Sarah and I discuss things."

Nathaniel snaps his gaping mouth shut, seemingly not offended by Viktor's suggestion.

"Now," Viktor says, returning his attention to me, "I have an idea."

"Which is?" I prompt.

"Let me call Shael and have her send in a tactical squad," he proposes. "The alfar guard can infiltrate the house and secure it for you."

It sounds like a good plan to me. "How long would it take them to do that?"

"As far as I know, the closest unit is still in New Orleans."

"You can call and arrange for them to meet us there," I say, "but I'm not going to wait for them to arrive. If we can't handle things on our own, then at least we'll have back-up on the way."

"I strongly advise that you let the alfar deal with the situation," Viktor says crossly, sounding exasperated by my stubbornness. "They're trained to fight against not only physical but also magical combat. You are not, Sarah. You're totally ill-equipped to manage either effectively. Now, if you had been raised the way you should…"

"Stop it!" I interrupt heatedly. "I am *sick* and *tired* of people pointing out the fact that my parents didn't 'raise' me the way they were supposed to. My mother didn't *tell me* about Julian and the bond I would end up sharing with him. My father didn't *tell me* I would one day inherit a throne…"

"Throne?" Gage and Nathaniel ask at the same time, both sounding equally surprised.

"I'll explain it later," I tell them off-handedly. I was trying to make a point to Viktor. "I am totally aware that my parents didn't prepare me for this world of yours, but I understand the motivation behind what they did. All they wanted was for me to have a happy life for as long as I could. I ended up having that despite their deaths. I was raised by loving people and was able to experience life without many worries before now. Everyone needs to understand that I'm doing the best I can with the situations I keep finding myself embroiled in. All I ask in return is that you support me and any decisions I make. I am your future queen," I tell Viktor with an authoritative quality to my voice that I didn't know I possessed until that moment. "You will do what I say and not question me about it. Is that understood?"

A slow, gratified smile spreads Viktor's lips. "There she is," he says, lifting his chin slightly higher as a look of pride glistens in his eyes. "There's the leader of the House Moonshade I've been waiting to see. I knew it would surface eventually, but you're exceeding my expectations, Sarah Marcel. I'm very pleased."

A part of me feels a sense of joy in Viktor's praise, and a part of me feels aggravated that he's wasting time.

"I need you to help me come up with a plan that will work, Viktor," I say, letting a little bit of my aggravation show. "Now, how are we going to get into the house?"

"Give me your phone first so I can call Shael," he tells me, holding out his hand. "Then we can discuss matters."

Viktor makes his call. It doesn't last very long. The person on the other end of the line barely seems to ask any questions. Viktor simply tells them that I need help and where to meet us.

"The princess is an impatient creature," he complains to the person he's talking to, "so I suggest you not dilly dally, and come straight away. I'll do what I can to protect her, but she may be too stubborn to listen to reason when it comes to her vampire companion's life." Viktor grunts in agreement at something the person he's talking to says. "Yes. I'll do my best. Just hurry."

After he ends the call, Viktor hands the phone back to me. "Now, let's see how we can get you inside the house without it looking suspicious."

The drive to Destin feels like the longest road trip of my life. It isn't, of course. The longest road trip was one I took with Kaylee and her parents to see the Grand Canyon. It took us two days and a total of 24 hours of driving to reach the gigantic hole in the ground, but it was well worth it. However, the trip I'm on now won't be as much fun. In fact, if I simply make it out alive I'll be fortunate.

When we finally reach our destination, Gage pulls off the road and parks next to the sidewalk two blocks down from the house we need to get into. I see both Julian's Vanquish and Petru's Mercedes parked on the street next to the home's gated entrance. Even without the presence of his car, I would know Julian is inside the house. I can feel him in there. I look at Nathaniel in the back seat, and he nods his head at me.

"I feel Petru in there," he tells me, confirming what I already suspected.

Thankfully the iron front gate is wide open, which will allow Viktor access to do his part in our plan. He quickly transforms back into a cat and prances his way down the sidewalk towards the house. I watch as he turns the corner to head directly towards the mansion. I lower the window on my side of Gage's vehicle and listen for Viktor's meowing. He said he could be loud, but I had no idea he would sound so distressed. His caterwauling is so pitiful you would think he was being tortured unmercifully. Eventually his cries subside, and I know he's been taken inside the house. Well, either that or killed, but I'm trying to remain optimistic.

As suggested, we wait a full fifteen minutes to give Viktor some time to search the interior for Julian and Petru's whereabouts.

I turn to look at Nathaniel in the back seat.

"Stay here," I order him. "You're no good to Petru if you're dead."

"Same could be said for you, Sarah," Nathaniel says, disgruntled by the fact that he's being left behind.

"I know," I cajole, "but one of us needs to keep a look out. Gage and I can pass for a married couple. If I go up to the door with you by my side, I'll look like I'm robbing the cradle. It's just easier if you're the one who stays behind. You understand that, right?"

Nathaniel sighs in disappointment but also in resignation.

"I'll call your phone if I see anything suspicious out here," he begrudgingly answers, agreeing to play his role in our plan.

I look over at Gage. "Are you ready?"

He nods confidently. "Let's go."

Gage and I walk up to the mansion and knock on the solid wood front door. I try to appear calm, but I'm sure my anxiousness is written all over my face. I just hope it works to my advantage in this instance.

The door opens, and standing just inside the house is a dark-haired woman of exceptional beauty. She looks Eastern European with her petite frame, pale skin, hazel eyes, and ruby-red lips.

"Hello, can I help you?" she asks, her voice tinged with a slight accent I can't quite place. She glances at Gage and me, waiting for one of us to answer. She appears to be quite calm. I don't sense that she's a threat to us, which makes me question if Nathaniel got the address correct. Yet I know Julian is inside this house. I can feel him.

"I'm so sorry to bother you," I say, "but our cat is missing. We're going door to door to see if anyone has seen him."

"Perhaps," she says, eyeing us suspiciously. "Can you describe him to me?"

"He's an Oriental Blue Point Siamese cat," I tell her. "He has white fur, pointy ears, and a black ringed tail."

The woman smiles. "Then, yes, I have seen your cat. He was mewling out in my courtyard, so I brought him inside to calm him down."

"Oh, thank goodness," I say, feigning relief. "We thought we had lost him."

"Please," the woman says, opening the door wider, "come in. I fear as soon as I brought him inside he jumped out of my arms and decided to explore my home."

"Well, that sounds like him," Gage laughs easily, taking my hand as we walk into the house together. I don't view Gage's desire to hold my hand as a romantic overture. He's feeling very protective of me right now, and I think he just wants to make sure I remain by his side while we're inside the house.

As we walk through the entryway, the first thing I see is the spiral staircase that winds around to all four floors of the home.

"Wow," I say in genuine awe as I look up and see the ceiling of the fourth floor, "that stairwell is amazing."

"Thank you," the woman says, closing the door behind us. "I had the staircase especially built to get just that type of reaction from my guests."

"This house is huge," Gage comments, briefly casting a glance to the few rooms we can see from the front door. "You must have a large family."

"I'm afraid you'll need to help me search for your cat," she tells us, deftly ignoring Gage's comment. "I'm not quite sure where he got off to."

"Meow," Viktor says. I look up the stairwell, and see him poking his head out between two of the iron rails there. "Meow."

It's then that my suspicions are confirmed. The woman is not as banal as she appears. Our plan was to have Viktor scout out the

S.J. WEST

interior before we came in. If he was able to locate Julian and Petru, he was supposed to find a way to lead us to their position. Apparently he's found them on the fourth floor, since he isn't budging from his perch.

"Oh no," I say in mock dismay, "he hates heights. Poor thing is probably scared to death up there."

"Feel free to go get him," the woman urges me with a friendliness I know is fake now. I've never met someone who is so adept at hiding her true nature from me. It makes me wonder how many people I've misread during my life.

"Thank you," I say gratefully. "We won't be but a ..."

"*Respiratio!*" Gage says, casting his spell as he directs his gaze at the woman. With that single word the woman faints dead away, and falls to the wood floor like every bone in her body has melted. I feel absolutely no guilt as I watch her head hit the tile.

"I know you told me that you could take all of the air out of her lungs to make her black out," I say to Gage, "but I didn't think it would be so instantaneous. How long will she be unconscious?"

Gage grabs her underneath her arms and drags her body to the coat closet near the door.

"She'll wake up in a few minutes," he replies, "so we need to hurry."

After we deposit her into the closet, Gage finds a chair and props the back of it underneath the knob to keep her locked inside. We quickly make our way up the staircase to the fourth floor.

"Hurry up, you two," Viktor says, standing by the railing stark naked as he watches our progress up the staircase. "I can't tell how much blood these vampires have left in them. It doesn't look like much, if you ask me."

I take a deep breath and practically run up the next two flights of stairs. When we reach the fourth floor, I see what Viktor was talking about.

The fourth floor is almost completely empty of furnishings. It's an open space with floor-to-ceiling windows looking out towards

276

the blue-green ocean. Both Julian and Petru are lying unconscious on stainless steel tables, like ones I've seen on TV shows in police morgues. Each of them has a bundle of three one-inch tubes protruding from of their chests. The tubes run down to machines that seem to be pumping out their blood and collecting it into three large plastic jugs.

"I wasn't sure if I should pull the tubes out or if that would do more harm than good," Viktor explains as he stands beside Gage and me.

"The only way they can die is if they lose more blood than their bodies can regenerate," I say, remembering what I had to do after Julian was injured at Mira's party. "Viktor, go down to the car and get Nathaniel. Petru will need to feed as soon as we pull the tubes out of his heart."

Viktor transforms back into a cat and makes a mad dash down the stairs.

Gage and I go to Julian. If I didn't know any better, I would say he's already dead. His skin is the pallor of chalk, and his body is almost completely motionless. I stare down at his face, searching for any signs of life, but I don't even notice his eyeballs twitch underneath their lids. Only the shallow rise and fall of his chest as he continues to breathe gives me hope that he can still be saved.

"After I remove the tubes and Julian starts to feed, I need you to make sure he doesn't kill me," I tell Gage, not trusting Julian to be able to stop drinking my blood once he starts.

"Does he lack that much self-control?" Gage asks in surprise and slight disgust.

"Only when he's near death," I reply. I look down at the tubes jutting out of Julian's chest and grimace. After they were inserted, the skin around them healed. There's no way to remove the tubes without also ripping out a large amount of flesh.

I know the task of removing them lies squarely on my shoulders. Being Julian's companion means that I'm probably a lot stronger than Gage. The tubes will need to be yanked out in one swift motion to ensure their removal does the least amount of damage.

I wrap my fingers around the tubes and tighten my hold. Just as I'm about to pull them out Julian's right hand shoots up from the table and roughly seizes my wrist, preventing me from extracting the tubes. When I look up at his face, I see that his eyes are now open but they're unblinking as he stares directly at the ceiling.

"Leave this body alone. He deserves to die." Even though I saw Julian's mouth move and heard the strange detached voice order me to leave him alone, my mind is having a hard time accepting what I just witnessed. It wasn't Julian's deep voice that spoke to me. Instead, it was the high-pitched voice of a young girl that came out of his mouth.

My heart begins to beat so fast I fear I might pass out from the rush of blood. I look over at Gage, wondering if I'm the only one who heard the voice. When I see his shocked expression, I know I didn't imagine it.

I look back at Julian's face and ask, "Who are you?"

"Who I am is none of your concern. Leave now and let this man face his fate."

"I can't leave," I say. "If Julian dies, I die."

"Then you die," the voice says without a shred of mercy or pity.

"Tell me who you are," I beg. "Tell me what you are."

"A victim of unfortunate circumstance," the voice answers.

A victim?

"Are you a ghost?" I have to ask.

"Yes, she is." This time it isn't the ghost who answers.

I look away from Julian's face and see the woman we locked in the closet on the first floor now standing at the head of the stairs. Viktor is in her arms. She has one hand wound around his thin fragile neck in a threatening manner. I'm not sure why he doesn't just transform into his human form to negate her threat on his life. All I can assume is that she's preventing him from doing it somehow.

I fear she might break Viktor's neck before Gage can get a spell off to incapacitate her. My warlock friend seems to be of the same mind since he remains silent beside me.

In an effort to keep her calm and talking, I ask, "Why is she speaking through Julian? Is she one of your victims?"

The woman's haunting laughter fills the air. "Oh no. Not one of mine. One of his."

"How is she one of his victims?" I immediately ask, assuming the woman is a liar.

"When a person dies violently," she starts to explain, "sometimes their soul becomes restless, like the one you just heard speak. When this vampire and the others were made, some of the souls lingering within Cachtice Castle were able to inhabit the bodies of those they held most responsible for their deaths."

It takes me a few seconds to fully comprehend what she's saying, but I eventually catch on.

"Are you telling me that Julian is possessed?" I ask.

"I suppose that's the easiest way to view it," the woman agrees with a small shrug. "When the curse was cast, the souls found new homes inside those who were chosen to suffer for Bathory's disgrace. I brought these two here to find out which souls each of them possesses."

"Why?" I have to ask.

"I'm searching for one soul in particular," she tells me. "One very important soul, and the only way I could communicate with the spirits trapped inside them was to bring them to the brink of death."

"Who's inside Julian?" I ask the woman, but gain the answer from a different source.

"No one of importance," the voice tells me. "I was only one of many serving girls in the countess' household."

"What do you want?" I ask the spirit. "Why have you remained inside Julian all this time?"

"I want retribution," the spirit tells me angrily. "I want him to suffer just like I did."

"Hasn't he suffered enough?" I ask.

"No."

I don't know what to do or what else to say to the soul trapped inside Julian. It's obvious she holds him directly responsible for her death, but how do you appease a malevolent spirit?

I look back at the woman and ask, "Whose soul are you trying to find?"

"That's none of your concern," she replies snidely. "I really don't like it when someone doesn't understand their place, and you, my dear, don't seem to realize just how dispensable you and those you care about are to me. I think it might be time you learned that very important lesson."

Before I can take another breath, I watch in horror as the woman tightens her hold around Viktor's neck and snaps it.

CHAPTER 20.

My whole body goes completely numb, and I feel like I'm trapped inside a never-ending nightmare. As Viktor's body goes limp with death, everything looks like it's happening in slow motion. When the woman holds what remains of my friend's body over the rail of the staircase, she smiles at me just before she loosens her grasp. Two seconds later, I hear a faint thud as Viktor's body unceremoniously hits the first floor.

"*Urgeo!*" I hear Gage yell, flexing his arm out and pointing a finger directly at the woman.

I hear a whoosh of air as a strong gust of wind pushes the woman backwards. Instead of causing her to tumble down the stairs, her body simply levitates in the air as she laughs at us.

"Is that all you've got, young warlock?" she taunts. "A parlor trick that any child of air magic can do? What a waste of your talents. I sense you could be great if only you gave into true magic."

"What you practice isn't magic," Gage states, almost sounding like he pities her. "You're destroying yourself by delving into the hate that resides in this world. Stop it before it's too late."

"It's already too late," the woman claims proudly. "You're just jealous because you don't have the gumption to do what I have. Too bad you'll have to die because of your cowardice." The woman holds her arms up and chants, "Souls of those who guard and protect, hear my voice and come to collect."

After the utterance of her words, ten cloudy black figures rise up through the floor and surround us. They look like shadows, but their forms are more pronounced than that. I know if I reach out and touch one of them, I'll feel something solid against my hand.

I look just beyond them to find the woman again, but she's gone. It's like she disappeared into thin air.

"Whatever you do, don't let them touch you," Gage warns me as he watches the progress of the dark figures.

"Why? What are they?"

"We call them shades," he replies ominously. "They're malicious spirits that roam the earth. Most of the time they're harmless and stay hidden in the shadows. These are looking for vengeance for a wrong that was done to them while they were alive. I'm not sure how that woman was able to call them to her. I've never seen anyone do that before."

"Can you fight them with your magic?" I ask, noticing that the shades are slowly tightening their circle around us as they float closer.

"I can try to scatter them, but that will only buy us a little bit of time. I don't see a way out of this, Sarah. I'm sorry."

I look over at Julian and silently tell him I'm sorry, too. Maybe I should have waited for the alfar to come to our aid, because it looks like my stubbornness has led us all to our deaths.

As the shades approach, Gage uses his magic to push them away, but that only seems to double their efforts to reach us. I look around for a weapon, subconsciously knowing it's a futile act but needing to do something without feeling so helpless. I grab a nearby stainless steel folding chair and hold it out in front of me like a shield.

As one of the shades reaches out to grab me, I swipe at it with the chair to no avail. The shade grabs me by the arm, causing me to cry out in pain as I feel its touch scorch my skin. I smell the stench of burning flesh, but that's not all I smell. The air around me suddenly becomes charged with the scent of ozone. The shade holding my arm suddenly starts to take on a human form, but maintains its transparency. All I can do is assume it's the form this spirit inhabited during life.

As the shade begins to look more human, I hear myself take a deep breath in surprise as the world I thought I knew gets turned upside down.

"Mom?" I ask as I stare at the shade, the restless spirit of my own mother.

She stares at me for a moment as if trying to figure out who I am. Her eyes grow wide with confusion and fright as she seems to realize who I am. It's almost as if she's seeing me for the very first time, and fully understands what it is she's doing. The ghost of my mother releases her hold on my arm and quickly backs away.

"No!" I scream. "Mom, wait!"

The further back she goes the darker her shape turns, until she's a shade once more. Her spirit melts into the floor, completely disappearing from my sight.

The other shades begin to back away and follow my mother's lead as they fade from my view.

"That was your mother?" Gage asks in awe, looking down at my arm where she touched me. "How did you make her transform like that? I've never seen a shade take on its human form before."

I look down at my arm and see the glowing handprint where my mother grabbed me. Slowly, it begins to fade and my skin returns to normal.

"I'm not sure," I say, confused by what just happened and finding it hard to take a steady breath. "I don't think I did anything special, but why would my mother be a shade and why would she be here of all places?"

"Shades can haunt specific areas or..." Gage pauses like he's concerned how I will take what he says next, "people."

"So, my mother is haunting me?" I ask in bewilderment. "But why? Why would she do that?"

"I heard that your parents died in a house fire," Gage says. "Are you sure it was an accidental one?"

"Of course it was an accident," I say, but even as I say the words I begin to doubt what I have believed for the past thirteen years. "Are you telling me that it wasn't?"

"Spirits only become shades when they believe their deaths were caused maliciously. Your mother must believe, or she knows, that it wasn't an accident."

"But why is she haunting *me*?"

"She might be trying to protect you or tell you something," Gage suggests. "Those are the only reasons I can think of anyway."

Without warning one of the panels of glass behind us shatters inward, effectively ending my conversation with Gage. I let out a small yelp in surprise as shards of glass spray all over us. In quick succession, four people dressed in black battle gear leap out of the open side of a helicopter and duck and roll into the room. They spring to their feet and quickly pull out pistols from the holsters at their hips. The first one of them who jumped through the window does a quick scan of the area before settling her eyes on me.

She's tall, with long dark brown hair and a beautiful but stern face.

"Where did the shades go?" she demands to know.

"They left," I tell her, trying my best to push the image of my mother to the back of my mind. I have people in the here and now who need my help.

"What do you mean they left?" she says, sounding confused by my answer. "Why would they leave?"

"I don't know and I really don't care," I say, walking over to Julian. I have a feeling I know who these intruders are. "Are you the alfar Shael sent to help me?"

"Yes," the woman replies, holstering her weapon and telling the other three with her to stand guard. "She assigned us to be your personal detail."

"Then you have to do what I say, right?"

"Only if you're being reasonable when it comes to your safety," she informs me. "Otherwise, you're supposed to listen to my advice on what's best for you."

"Then take my friend Gage downstairs so he can bring back that vampire's companion," I say, nodding at Petru.

I see the woman snap her fingers at one of her people and point to Gage.

"And someone needs to go down and take care of Viktor," I say, holding back my tears over his loss. Mourning his death won't do me or anyone else any good right now.

"The cat?" the woman questions, making my request sound odd. "Why? He's sitting right over there."

I follow her gaze and see Viktor sitting by the top of the stairs, looking at me as he curls his tail around his body.

"Viktor?" I say uncertainly. Was I really looking at my friend or was he just an illusion? When he stands and walks over to me, I bend down on one knee and pick him up in my arms. "How are you still alive?" I ask. "Do you have nine lives or something?"

Viktor meows as if to confirm what I've said, and then proceeds to lick me underneath my chin.

I suddenly realize I don't care why he's alive. I have my friend back and that's all that matters. I kiss Viktor on top of his head before setting him back on the floor.

I then return my attention to Julian. Without wasting any more time, I grab hold of the tubes in his chest with one hand and yank them out as quickly as I can. The gaping hole left behind doesn't close, and I know he's lost too much blood for his natural regeneration to kick in. When I look at his face, I see that he's still unconscious. If he's not at least partially awake, he can't feed. How am I going to get my blood into his system?

"Do you have a knife?" I quickly ask my new bodyguard.

"Yes," she says warily, reaching around to the small of her back. I hear the metallic scrape of the knife as she pulls it out of its sheath. She walks over and hands it to me. I reach out to take it from her, but she pulls it back just before I can.

"What do you intend to do with it?" she asks.

"Cut one of my wrists," I tell her impatiently.

She lifts a questioning eyebrow at me. "As the head of your security detail, I must inform you that your plan doesn't sound very wise."

"It's the only way to get my blood into him," I tell her, quickly losing my patience. "Now give me the knife before he dies! I can assure you that will kill me a lot faster than a cut on the wrist will."

Reluctantly, probably because she knows I'm speaking the truth, my new guardian hands me her knife.

Before I can chicken out, I make a quick slit across my left wrist and hold it over Julian's mouth. I lean down until my lips are touching his ear and whisper for him to, "Drink."

He doesn't move. He doesn't do anything to reassure me that he heard my words.

"Julian," I whisper again, knowing that I have to do anything I can to wake him up, "if you can hear me, I need for you to drink. If you die, I die, and I don't want to die today. I have too much to live for. I have a niece on the way, and a sister who needs me. I have Viktor to look after now, and Helen would never forgive me if she lost both of us on the same day. Most of all, I have you. I know you think you can't give me the life I deserve, but you're the only one who can. We might not have the idyllic life that Kaylee and Ben or Susan and Pete Hughes have, but we can make a new kind of life with each other. Being together is what matters most. We can make our own rules when it comes to building a family we can be proud of. I love you, and even though you haven't said it in so many words I know you love me, too. We can be the authors of our own fate. Don't leave me now when everything I've ever wanted is right at my fingertips. Live for us. Fight for us. Drink."

Finally, I feel Julian's lips move against my wrist. Slowly he regains enough strength to start sucking with more force, but I know he isn't getting my blood fast enough because the hole in his chest isn't closing.

"Oh, my God," I hear Nathaniel say. I look over and see him standing at the top of the stairs, in total shock as he takes in the scene. When he looks at Petru, I can see his eyes well with tears.

"Snap out of it, Nathaniel," I say harshly to bring him back to reality. I quickly tell him what he needs to do to help Petru before I lower my neck to Julian's mouth. I position my throat until his teeth are in the sweet spot that he most prefers when he drinks from me.

"Bite down, Julian," I order tersely.

He does as I ask, but his bite isn't as fast as it normally is. Instead of making a clean, almost painless puncture wound, I feel his teeth drag through my skin and muscles, causing me more discomfort than usual. I whimper slightly.

"Sting a little?" the alfar woman asks.

All I can do is nod and keep my head down so she doesn't see my tears of pain. I have a feeling showing weakness in front of her wouldn't earn me any brownie points, only derision.

"If it's any consolation, I think it's working," I hear her say to me. "His wound is starting to heal."

Just as I become light-headed from the loss of blood, Julian lets go of me. I don't stand up straight right away. I give myself a few seconds to recover first, so Julian doesn't see me grimace in pain. When I am able to stand and look at him again, I involuntarily cringe anyway at the sight he makes. The lower half of his face is covered in my blood like a grotesque beard.

"Here," the alfar guard says, handing me a handkerchief she pulls out from her vest.

"Thank you," I say. As I take it from her, I ask, "What's your name?"

"Nadia, Your Highness," she answers, bowing her head to me slightly.

"Just call me Sarah," I tell her, even though it ends up sounding more like an order than a suggestion. "And don't bow to me. I'm not as special as you think."

"You are undeniably as special as I think," she argues. "You're the next heir in line to inherit the throne of House Moonshade. I understand that you weren't raised to know or even respect your place among us, but you are to be our next queen. Generations of my family have died to defend your house's bloodline, so I would appreciate it if you kept your contempt about your station to yourself."

"I didn't mean any disrespect," I'm quick to tell her, seeing that I've struck a rather sensitive nerve. "But, as you said, I wasn't raised in the alfar way. You're going to have to cut me some slack when it comes to having people bow and call me 'Your Highness'. I'm not used to it. I'm not sure I'll ever become used it."

"Sarah…" Julian whispers weakly, effectively ending any attention I was paying to Nadia.

I look down at him again, and this time I see that his eyes are open and completely focused on me. I begin to use the handkerchief Nadia gave me to wipe my blood off his face.

"Are you feeling better?" I ask, chancing a glance at his chest and seeing that the last layer of his skin is slowly regenerating.

"Looking at you makes me feel better," he replies with a weak smile.

I shake my head at him in exasperation and continue to wipe my blood off his face. "Only you would flirt at a time like this."

"How is Petru?" he asks, turning his head to look over at his best friend.

Nathaniel is still letting Petru feed from his neck, and Gage is watching over the proceedings to make sure he doesn't inadvertently take too much in his thirst.

"I think he'll be fine," I say, turning my attention back to Julian. "What happened? How did that woman get the upper hand on the two of you?"

"I honestly don't know," Julian tells me. "The last thing I remember is standing on her doorstep. Everything between then and now is like missing time. I don't know what she did or why she did it."

I want to talk to Julian about what the woman said, and about seeing the ghost of my mother. How could he be possessed by the spirit of one of Bathory's victims all these years and not know it? Why is the spirit of my mother a shade and following me around?

But I don't dare bring it up in front of the four alfar in the room. I have no idea what their reactions would be to such concepts. If I'm being honest with myself, I'm not even sure I can properly wrap my mind around everything that happened. The implications are far-reaching, and I don't fully understand what it all means yet.

"We should get out of here as soon as you and Petru feel up to it," I suggest, removing my hand from his face and tossing the bloody handkerchief into a small trashcan by the table.

"Our blood," Julian says hoarsely. "We can't leave it here. It needs to be destroyed, Sarah."

"All right," I tell him, knowing that if Julian or Petru's blood makes it into the wrong hands that more humans could be granted an unnaturally long life like Helen. I don't completely understand all that goes into making someone like her, but I do know we don't need thousands of people being given the ability to live that long. New ideas come from each generation, and the Earth as it is today doesn't have the resources to support a legion of near-immortals. It would lead the world down a path of catastrophe and chaos.

"My people can handle that for you," Nadia tells me.

I look at Julian. "Can we trust the alfar to know what to do with your blood?"

"What?" Nadia snaps, like I've said the most ridiculous thing she's ever heard in her life. "Why are you asking a vampire if you can trust your own people?"

I look her straight in the eyes and say, "I don't know you, and I don't trust you yet. Julian I trust with my life, so back off, Nadia." I look back down at Julian and await his answer.

"Yes," he tells me, looking amused at my handling of my temperamental alfar protector. "You can trust them."

I look back at Nadia. "Then I charge you with the duty of disposing of the blood properly."

Nadia's eyes narrow just a hair as she looks at me. It doesn't take a genius to know that she and I will be butting heads quite often. At least until we're finally able to come to an understanding with one another about her place in my life.

I ask the alfar to search the home from top to bottom for anything the woman who caused this mess might have left behind. It quickly becomes apparent that she didn't live in the house. After a few phone calls, Gage is able to find out from some of his realtor friends that the property is a rental. He does discover what name the woman used to rent the mansion, but it's of no use. Princess Buttercup is obviously an alias to hide her true identity.

After both Julian and Petru are fully healed, we leave the alfar to clean up. Nadia attempts to follow Julian and me out to his car, but I stop her at the door to the mansion.

"We're going back to Julian's home in Pecan Acres," I tell her. "I'll be perfectly safe on the way there."

"That may be the case," she says, crossing her arms in front of her and spreading her legs to make a defensive stance, "or it may not. I've been assigned as your protector and that's precisely what I intend to do: protect you at any cost."

"For how long?" I ask, finding the notion ridiculous.

"Uh, until either you're dead or I am," she states, as if the answer should have been an obvious one.

Viktor leaps at me, expecting me to catch him. I do but just barely.

He begins to lick my face and meows as if trying to tell me to accept Nadia's protection, at least for now.

"Well, you'll need to find your own way to Pecan Acres," I inform her. "Julian's car only has room for two people."

"That's fine," she replies, not viewing this as a deterrent. "I'll be in the helicopter that brought us here. I can watch over your progress home from the air."

I sigh in resignation. The first chance I get I plan to call Queen Shael and ask her to bring Nadia and her team home. All I need is a bodyguard hanging around me all the time.

We arrange for Gage, Petru, and Nathaniel to come to Julian's house the next day. There is a lot that we all need to discuss, but right now isn't the time.

Julian tries to get into the driver's seat of his car, but when I hold out my hand to take the keys from him he doesn't put up much of a fight. Vampire or not, he just went through a traumatic experience. Add in the fact that he's apparently possessed by a vengeful ghost and you have an accident just waiting to happen, literally.

Julian remains quiet on the drive back home. He seems to be ruminating about his experience, trying to decipher what it all means. I can only imagine what's going through his mind. He lost time out of his life that he had no control over. Just the notion of it scares me. I can't imagine having it happen.

About thirty minutes out of Destin, I make a unilateral decision that a detour is in order. I turn off Hwy 98 and merge onto 399 South towards Navarre Beach. It's well after ten at night, and there are no cars in the eastern-most parking lot along the beach.

"Come on," I tell Julian, opening the car door. "Let's go talk."

He doesn't argue. He doesn't say anything. He just opens his door and gets out of the car. I reach back inside to pick Viktor up. He automatically squirms to be let down. I let him jump from my arms, and he runs off over the sand dunes. I don't worry about him too much. I'm sure he'll find me before we're ready to leave.

I meet Julian in front of the car and take his hand with mine. I lead him down the wooden pier towards the shoreline. The sound of the ocean waves helps calm my frayed nerves, and I hope they are having the same effect on Julian.

When we reach the end of the pier, I take a seat on one of the steps that leads down to the beach area. Wordlessly, Julian sits down beside me.

"I need to tell you some things," I begin hesitantly. "But you have to promise me you won't freak out."

Julian looks at me questioningly. "Go on."

I take a deep breath and tell him about the ghost that spoke to me through him, and the fact that my mother is now a shade.

"Considering the fact that this woman was able to call shades in to fight for her, even my mother," I say, "I suspect it was the ghost inside you that she was able to take control of. It would explain why you can't remember anything during your lost time."

Julian stands and walks down the last two steps to the sand. He begins to pace back and forth as he thinks about the bombshells I just threw at him. I don't know what else I can do except sit there and wait until he has time to come to terms with this new information.

"It explains a lot," he finally says, coming to a standstill in front of me. "It explains why we all sought out the person we loved most to become our first companion."

"What do you mean?" I ask.

"If these spirits we contain are seeking retribution, what better way to make us suffer than to turn our loved ones into our food?"

"Is there some sort of magic that we can use to get them out of you?" I ask. "Do we need to call an exorcist?"

"Exorcisms only work for demons. These are lost souls seeking vengeance. I'm not sure what to do about them actually."

"Maybe they want something else," I suggest. "The soul inside you said she wanted retribution for what was done to her.

What if there's something you can do to finally bring her soul the peace she never got? If we can find a way to do that, maybe she'll move on. It might be enough to break the curse and let you live a normal life again."

"But what would she want?" Julian asks. "She's dead. There's nothing else I can do for her."

"Maybe if you did something for her descendants?" I say as a suggestion and a question.

"But I don't even know which one of the countess' victims she is," Julian points out.

"Right…" I say, pondering this obstacle. "The woman at the house told us that neither of the ghosts you and Petru have are the one she's looking for, so obviously she was able to get more information out of them than what your ghost said to me. What kind of magic gives someone the power to control ghosts?"

"Dark magic," Julian says, not sounding happy about it at all. "I've always tried to stay away from those who practice it. It's volatile and can cause havoc in unexperienced hands."

"So you don't know anyone who practices it?"

"I know people," Julian replies reluctantly. "I just don't trust them."

"Well, you're going to have to figure out which one you trust the most," I state. "I don't see any other way to get the information we need from your ghost. Maybe Gage can help us find a fairly dependable one."

"So the warlock knows all of this?"

"Yes. He was there when the ghost spoke to me and when my mother began to materialize."

"And why was he there?"

I stare at Julian for a moment, but there's no question that I need to tell him the truth.

"We were spending the day together," I say. "Your note did tell me that I should spend more time with either him or Daniel."

"I suppose it did," he replies reservedly.

Julian continues to look at me for a while, and I can tell by the pained expression on his face that he knows how much his indifference in the letter hurt me.

"All I want," he says slowly, "is what's best for you, Sarah."

I stand from my seat on the step and walk down until I'm standing directly in front of him.

"And all I want," I reply, "is for you to finally understand that you're who's best for me. Not Daniel. Not Gage. No one else. Stop trying to push me away, Julian. It's not going to work."

Julian's expression doesn't change, but I know it's not my feelings that his face is mirroring now but his own.

"It's been a long time since I allowed myself to hope for a better life," he tells me. "But every time you look at me like you're looking at me right now, I feel a fire ignite deep down inside my soul, yearning to be given more oxygen so it can flare brighter."

"Then let it burn," I plead, placing a hand over his heart. "Let yourself have hope, because sometimes that's all you need to make your dreams come true."

Julian places his right hand on top of mine.

"Did you mean what you said?" he asks me.

"I've said a lot of things lately," I tell him with a smile. "You're going to have to be a little bit more specific than that."

"You said that we can be the authors of our own fate," he gently reminds me. "And that we can make our own kind of family. Did you mean that?"

"I don't say anything that I don't mean," I reply. "I also meant it when I said I love you. I know it's something that's hard for you to accept, but I hope in time you will."

"And if I accept your love," he says, twining our fingers together over his heart, "does that mean you can accept love from a creature like me?"

"You're not a creature," I protest, hating the fact that Julian sees himself that way. "You're a man who got caught up in something that you had no control over."

"But I could have left the countess' household after I discovered what she was doing. I could have saved myself centuries of guilt and pain if I had just done that one simple thing."

"And I'm selfishly glad that you didn't," I confess. "If you weren't who you are today, we never would have met and I never would have found someone to love."

"Yes, you would have." Julian brings up his other hand and gently slides the back of his fingers down the side of my face. "You would have found a man who could give you everything you've ever wanted."

"I have found that man," I tell him without an ounce of doubt. "He's standing right in front of me. You just need to stop projecting what you think I want onto me. I know what I want. I want you. The only question is, do you want me, too?"

"With everything that I am," he answers without hesitation or doubt.

"Then show me," I challenge, hoping he accepts.

Julian glides his hand around my neck, burying his fingers in my hair and tugging on the strands until my head is tilted back slightly. As his face lowers to mine I expect a kiss, but Julian tilts his head to the side until his mouth is so close to my ear I can feel the warm caress of his breath as he speaks.

"I love you, Sarah Marcel," he whispers. "My heart is yours to nourish or to break. For as long as I live I will love no one else, because no matter what happens my life is now forever connected to yours. You are my last companion because death is preferable to life without you in it."

Before I can ask him what his last statement means, Julian lifts his head and promptly covers my mouth with his lips. The kiss is by no means gentle, and to be honest I don't want gentle right now. I need to feel how much the man I love wants me. I need to know that I'm the only person in the world he feels this passionately about, and that I'm the only woman who can satisfy his desires.

Just as I'm about to suggest we find a more private place to continue what Julian has started, I hear the hissing of an angry cat.

Julian obviously hears it, too, because he automatically breaks our kiss to look up towards the pier. He drops his hands away from my neck when I turn to look behind me.

Standing on the wooden rail is Viktor. His back is arched and he hisses at us once more.

I get the message.

"I love him," I tell Viktor. "And I don't care about your stupid alfar bloodlines. My life won't be dictated by your need for an alfar heir, so either support us or leave me."

Viktor closes his mouth and lowers his back. He stares at me in disbelief, and I know I'll end up hearing a lecture about my duty to the alfar sometime later. Right now, I don't care. Right now, all I want to do is continue kissing Julian and worry about the consequences later.

Unexpectedly, a loud roar fills the air around us.

Julian looks down at me and asks, "When was the last time you ate, Sarah?"

The mention of food makes my stomach roar again from being neglected for so long.

"Lunch," I confess, suddenly feeling a sharp pang in my midgut as if my stomach pinched me as a rude reminder that it needs to be fed.

"We should get you some food," Julian declares, taking hold of my shoulders and pointing me in the direction of the steps of the pier. "Move it," he orders, playfully slapping me on the bottom to get me going.

"Hmm," I say, standing my ground as I turn my head to look at Julian over my shoulder, "that wasn't much of a spank. If you want to make me do what you say, I'm afraid it needs to be a lot harder than that."

Julian smiles and quickly complies with my request.

"That's better," I say, taking a few satisfied steps forward.

I hear him chuckle softly behind me as I reach for Viktor and pick him up in my arms.

"I see you're going to be a handful," Julian remarks as he walks up behind me and places an arm across my shoulders.

"A couple at least," I tell him truthfully. "Do you think you can handle that?"

"I think with you in my life, I can do almost anything."

I smile up at Julian and receive a kiss in return.

As we walk down the pier back towards the car, I feel tiny tendrils of pure joy wrap around my heart, encasing it in a protective shell to keep it safe from outside forces.

I know my life won't be easy. It will never be normal, but it will also never be boring. I have a chance to forge my destiny into whatever I want it to become and help the man I love finally find peace and possibly salvation. My life will never be as perfect as my mother wanted it to be, and perhaps that is part of the reason she's still earthbound. I simply don't know, but I intend to find out. I hope she's at least proud of me for following my heart and trusting myself to know what's best.

In the end that's all anyone can do, because none of us knows what the future will bring. All we can do is live strong and love fiercely in the little time we're given on Earth, and I intend to live my life with as little fear as possible and love the man beside me with everything that I am or will ever become.

I may not live a perfect life, but I will live a life filled with love, honor, and absolutely no regrets.

The End

AUTHOR'S NOTE

Thank you so much for reading *Moonshade*, the first book in *The Vampire Conclave Series*.

If you have enjoyed this book please take a moment to leave a review. To leave a review please visit:

Moonshade http://bit.ly/Moonshade1-US

Thank you in advance for leaving a review for the book.
Sincerely,
S.J. West.

THE NEXT IN THE
VAMPIRE CONCLAVE SERIES

Get the second book in the series, and continue Sara & Julian's story.

Sentinel,
Book 2 of *The Vampire Conclave Series.*

http://bit.ly/Sentinel-2US

MORE FROM S.J. WEST
THE WATCHERS TRILOGY

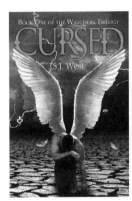  

Discover a world where everything you thought normal is redefined. Where Angels live among humans and your destiny is much greater than you ever imagined. Studying for your next test is out, and saving the world is in...

Since she was eight-years-old, Lilly Rayne Nightingale felt like fate was trying to wipe away her existence through a series of odd, near fatal incidences. Luckily, her best friend Will was always one-step ahead of fate preventing her from being at the wrong place at the wrong time. Will was her knight in shining armor until he broke her heart after their one and only kiss.

On Lilly's first day of college, she meets Brand Cole. Intrigued by Brand, Lilly must decide whether she can give up her adolescent fantasy of being reunited with Will and allow Brand the opportunity to conquer her heart.

Not only do Will and Brand both love Lilly, they share a dark secret neither wants Lilly to discover. Lilly thinks fate is after her once again when a new series of attempts on her life start to take place, but she soon learns someone of flesh and blood is trying to kill her this time.

Exclusively on Amazon, Free on KU!
http://bit.ly/CursedWatchers1

ABOUT THE AUTHOR

Once upon a time, a little girl was born on a cold winter morning in the heart of Seoul, Korea. She was brought to America by her parents and raised in the Deep South where the words ma'am and y'all became an integrated part of her lexicon. She wrote her first novel at the age of eight and continued writing on and off during her teenage years. In college she studied biology and chemistry and finally combined the two by earning a master's degree in biochemistry.

After that she moved to Yankee land where she lived for four years working in a laboratory at Cornell University. Homesickness and snow aversion forced her back South where she lives in the land, which spawned Jim Henson, Elvis Presley, Oprah Winfrey, John Grisham and B.B. King.

After finding her Prince Charming, she gave birth to a wondrous baby girl and they all lived happily ever after.

As always, you can learn about the progress on my books, get news about new releases, new projects and participate on amazing giveaways by following me:

FB Book Page: @ReadTheWatchersTrilogy
FB Author Page:
https://www.facebook.com/sandra.west.585112
Website: www.sjwest.com

Amazon: http://bit.ly/SJWest-Amazon
Newsletter Sign-up: http://bit.ly/SJWest-NewsletterSignUp
Instagram: @authorsjwest
Twitter: @SJWest2013

If you'd like to contact the author, you can email her to:
sandrawest481@gmail.com

VAMPIRE CONCLAVE

The Vampire Conclave Series

Printed in Great Britain
by Amazon